QUAKE

ANDY REMIC

orbit

www.orbitbooks.co.uk

An *Orbit* Book

First published in Great Britain by Orbit 2004
Copyright © 2004 by Andy Remic

The moral right of the author has been asserted.

The author gratefully acknowledges permission
to quote from the following:

Blind Curve
Lyrics by Derek W. Dick (Fish)
Copyright © Charisma Music/EMI Music Publishing Ltd.
All Rights Reserved.

Chord of Souls
Lyrics by C. McCoy
Published by Momentum music/Nephilim Music
Copyright © Momentum music/Nephilim Music, 1988
All Rights Reserved.

Tank Park Salute
Written by Billy Bragg
Copyright © Billy Bragg
BMG Music Publishing
All Rights Reserved.

A CIP catalogue record for this book
is available from the British Library

ISBN 1 84149 204 3

Typeset in Plantin by M Rules
Printed and bound in Great Britain
by Clays Ltd, St Ives plc

Orbit
An imprint of
Time Warner Book Group UK
Brettenham House
Lancaster Place
London WC2E 7EN

DEDICATION

This book is dedicated to my brother Nick – for showing me how to clean spark plugs many years ago and instilling in me a love of all things mechanical, for his invaluable and humorous help when I destroyed my first car and for being the best brother a man could have.

ACKNOWLEDGEMENTS

Thank you to Sonia and Joe, for giving me glittering diamonds of light through some very hard times.

Thanks must also go to my test readers, my agent Dorothy and especially to Tim Holman – for his faith.

And finally thanks to my mum, for endless Sunday morning bike breakfasts and her very special homemade soup.

CONTENTS

PART TWO
LITTLE FLAME

QUAKE

PROLOGUE

INTERNAL COMBUSTION

The Tennagore Valley

Chile, South America

Carter's head snapped violently left, eyes narrowing as Kade's honey-treacle voice whispered a warning. There came a *zip* and something brushed Carter's ear. He flipped himself to the right, hitting the ground hard and smashing into a low concrete wall with a grunt. His hand came up, feeling warm slick blood smearing the lobe of his ear, and his teeth clenched tight in a sick parody of a grin – one that had little to do with humour.

'*It's a fucking sniper . . .*' It was the voice of Kade again. Carter frowned, closing his eyes for a moment, pain stabbing through his brain.

'Leave . . . me . . . alone!' he snarled.

A battle-scarred 9mm Browning HiPower appeared in Carter's fist and, his heart pounding, he checked its magazine. A sniper: that meant he had been spotted . . . At last a guard with more than a single brain cell! But no

3

alarms had sounded audibly . . . which meant he had almost been taken by surprise.

Almost: a razor-fine boundary between breathing the cold mountain air and lying sprawled in a blood-pooled hollow with no face and an empty skull, entry and exit wounds bone-ringed.

Carter slammed the mag back into the sturdy weapon and crawled to his knees, wind buffeting from the moon-lit cratered mountainside above. Shadows swirled in twisting black veils, plummeting and falling down from the high mountain passes and dancing delicately across the massive expanse of the dam.

Carter moved stealthily along the narrow concrete walkway and halted, shielded by a low, rough-rendered wall and glancing down at the shadowed KTM LC7 757cc motorbike, a special custom-built Spiral Stealth Edition packing 289 b.h.p. and a torque rating of 174 lb-ft. It squatted, camouflaged in the darkness and shadows, concealed behind huge steel drums and taunting Carter not just with its proximity but with the knowledge that to reach it he would have to pass once more in front of the cross-hairs of the infinitely patient sniper's scope.

He could see his escape route.

Compromised.

'*It's not going to be easy,*' Kade growled at the back of Carter's mind.

'You don't fucking say,' muttered Carter. His eyes scanned the layout before him, heart-rate increasing slightly at the prospect of the coming fight.

The dam sat high in the mountains, spanning the narrow rock-walled Tennagore Valley. Its highly advanced and masterfully engineered structure had been built at great expense by the Seckito Syndicate in collaboration with a corrupt section of the SNI – the Chilean secret

4

police – in order to irrigate plantations of coca plants, the basic source of cocaine. This refined product was in turn smuggled to the few countries that still prohibited hard drugs, where it commanded prices that were used to finance illegal heavy-duty military arms purchases by the Seckito Syndicate – who then handed the weapons out like candy to the eager grasping paws of the terrorist organisation JWKA and Spirits of Blood, located on opposite sides of the globe but ultimately having the same aim: civilian soft targets and high-profile media coverage.

Spiral had decided that it was time to smash the Seckito Syndicate with a blunt hammer. Seven operations were in progress. Carter's mission was to blow the dam, destroying the coca crop and pushing the Seckito Syndicate into an already-brewing private war against its untrustworthy arms suppliers. This would coincide with the assassination of several key figures, the destruction of three terrorist and corrupt SNI-protected drug factories and strikes by ZZ-guided long-range cruise missiles from HMS *Thunder*, moored over a hundred miles away in the Pacific Ocean.

Accuracy was essential.

The shit had to hit the fan – with perfect feculent timing.

Carter pulled free his ECube; the tiny black-alloy device vibrated softly in his hand and he thumbed a delicate sequence across its surface panel. Digits flickered at him, ghostly blue in the darkness. Three minutes, four-teen seconds until detonation ... And Carter had initiated the Anti-Intrusion Filter on the bomb. Which basically meant that the explosion and subsequent destruction was unstoppable ... the dam doomed within the next few minutes ... the drug crop lost ... the Seckito Syndicate smashed—

'But I'd rather get out alive,' he muttered.

Think!

Sniper: location?

Carter whirled, eyes scanning, calculating the angles and velocities involved; if he could climb down to the bike and fire the engine on remote using the ECube, then—

'Hey, *Mestizo*, what is this stinking bike doing here? It not look like one of ours . . .'

'I have no idea, *hombre*.'

The two guards were standing loose, one scratching his lank-ponytailed head, the other's face illuminated in a circle of orange from a home-rolled cigarette pluming lazy grey spirals of smoke into the cold mountain air.

The alarms sounded, shrill bitch screams, and both men sprung into immediate action, cocking Kalashnikov JK49s and glancing around with urgency and vigilance . . . ready for action and blood.

'There must be a *gringo* here . . .'

Carter heard more guards leap from their restful watches, fired into alertness by this sudden screech of intruder alarms.

'Shit.'

'*Do something*,' growled Kade.

Below Carter lay a spread-out collection of painted concrete buildings; and away from their scatter stretched the dam itself, its summit a metre-wide length of smooth gleaming concrete veering away in a slight curve for over half a kilometre. To the left, the choppy waters of the reservoir lapped, reflecting the shadowy peaks of the snow-capped mountains rearing above. To the right the dam fell away almost vertically, several wide channels gushing with white foam and dropping into the colossal open valley below.

Carter's eyes narrowed as he focused on the exit at the

far end of the dam's ridge. His stealth bike had cruised in unseen. And now there was only one – nastily compromised – way out . . .

He took a deep breath and leapt from the parapet, landing in front of the two startled guards whose eyes went wide, cigarettes tumbling from lips moist with fear spittle. Their JK49s twitched but Carter's Browning boomed in his fist once, twice, and both guards were kicked from their feet, brain slop and shards of bone splattering against the steel drums.

The bodies folded to the ground but Carter was already moving; a bullet zipped past his face, then another past his knee. He leapt, rolling and skidding to the opposite side of the steel drums and their unavoidably thin-walled protection—

'There! The fucking *gringo*!'

Machine guns opened fire and bullets howled around Carter. His Browning came up over the drums, thumping against his hand as he emptied a full magazine across the stretch of concrete and kicking another two guards from their feet in mushrooms of blood-mist. One fell into the reservoir with a splash, and was immediately lost.

Carter slammed his back against the drums and changed mags.

'*I told you so*,' said Kade smugly.

'What?'

'*I told you this was a bad idea. I personally would have used a series of automated rocket launchers. But no, you had to do your fucking James Bond bit and sneak in here like a throbbing gold-speckled peacock on heat . . .*'

'Kade,' growled Carter in the depths of his subconscious, 'we haven't fucking *got* automated rocket launchers – and this was supposed to be a low-key covert mission . . .'

'Well, you've fucked that up then, haven't you? Every man and his bitch is out to shoot you now . . .'

Carter turned, sharp eyes spotting the sniper's position high up in a shadowed bunker on the mountainside. Bastard, he mouthed. He hated snipers. Fucking hated them.

Carter suddenly stood, sighted along the top of the barrel of the Browning HiPower held uncannily steady in both hands, and fired a full thirteen rounds at the tiny firing slot barely visible in the face of the deep-set bunker. He saw spurts of stone-dust leap from the edges, and waited . . . No return fire came. He changed magazines again, then leapt across to the KTM LC7, firing the bike into life and scanning ahead. His ears picked out the sounds of guards approaching . . . He checked the ECube. Two minutes.

'It's going to be tight,' mused Kade darkly.

Tight? I'd love to get my hands tight around your throat . . .

Carter holstered the Browning, stamped the bike into first gear and flicked free the stealth exhaust mods; the bike could run silently, but silence leeched power. Now Carter needed the power more than he needed to remain undiscovered . . .

He screwed the throttle all the way round. The front wheel jerked into the air and the KTM screamed, LVA exhausts spewing from high-level pipes as the back wheel spun, leaving melted tread across the concrete. The bike shot like a needle bullet into the night from its suddenly hazardous hiding place.

Carter gritted his teeth, holding on tight and clamping himself to the broad tank as the front wheel touched down and the cold mountain air tried to smash him from the saddle. The KTM LC7 hammered through the night, a tiny black bullet skimming across the dam's metre-wide walkway; Carter could smell the fresh water to his left, could sense more than see the fearsome drop to his right.

Carter focused. On the narrow ridge of the dam.

On his road to freedom.

Water was gushing, roaring all around him. He accelerated, speedometer needle bouncing against the redline, the bike howling as it hit 220 m.p.h. The world flashed around Carter in a series of stuttering, splashing bright images.

'*Guards,*' hissed Kade in warning.

Carter palmed the Browning and blew the three guards from their feet before they even lifted their weapons. Two hit the ground, and one fell and toppled down the front of the dam, bouncing and flailing like a tumbling rag doll until he was smashed into a battered purple pulp-drenched carcass in the darkness far below.

Carter dipped the clutch and the KTM's front wheel kicked into the air again, the rear wheel ploughing through one of the corpses, losing traction for a moment in a supple compress of flesh and kicking the bike violently sideways. Carter felt, for a terrifying moment, his loss of control as the massive drop to the right tore his eyes from their target and fear rammed its fist down his throat. Then the KTM's front wheel touched down and the bike stabilised. Carter piled on the speed once more.

'*We've done it!*' crowed Kade. '*We're there . . .*'

Carter frowned. His eyes narrowed and he touched the brake, shaving speed out of instinct more than anything he could actually see or hear, his mouth opened, tongue darting against dry wind-chapped lips, and he realised that—

Hell, he thought.

It's a fucking *tank*.

ar machine squatted at the end of Carter's per-
away. Even as realisation hit, guards swarmed
ind the tank's protective armoured flanks and
opened up with machine guns. 7.62mm rounds screamed
like tiny tortured insects buzzing around Carter's face as
he squeezed the brakes and left metres of tyre smeared
against the dull white concrete. He kicked the bike
around, wheel-spinning in a cloud of stinking burning
rubber, then wheelied back the way he had come, ducking
low over the tank as bullets howled past. Several slapped
against the bike's exhaust pipes. It was a miracle no metal
raped his flesh.

'*You've got one minute, Carter.*' Kade's voice was no
longer filled with humour, or arrogance, or mockery.
There was tension there. An edge of fear that chilled
Carter to his very core.

'I – fucking – know . . .' hissed Carter through gritted
teeth.

Up ahead, more guards had gathered.

Suddenly, he grabbed the brakes and twisted the KTM
left; it shuddered to a halt, front wheel hanging over the
terrible descent. Carter glanced down and Natasha's
words came back to him.

You'll come back to me, won't you?

It's not that dangerous, he had lied.

I don't want to be left a widow.

But we're not married! he'd protested.

*All right, then . . . I don't want you to leave your new child
without a father . . .*

But we haven't got a—

*Actually – Natasha'd smiled weakly – I've got something to
tell you . . .*

Oh.

Their lovemaking had been gentle, teasing and soft – a

merging of flesh and sex – and in the warm afterglow, bathed in the iridescent flickering light of the candles, Nats had tickled her tongue down his neck and whispered in his ear, 'You make sure you come back to me, you reckless fucker . . . You make sure you come back to *us* . . .'

Now, Carter gazed at the vertical drop; 7.62mm rounds screamed around him and the world had descended into a blood-red insanity. His lips compressed in a grim line. Kade was screaming at him to turn back and he was counting, internally, the seconds left until the heavy HighJ detonation and subsequent shock waves cracked the dam, allowing the hugely titanic pressure of the reservoir to force its way violently and unstoppably to freedom—

He revved the KTM.

Revved it real hard, popped the clutch and allowed the bike to dip and fall over the edge—

Darkness and the world rushed towards him, gulleys of foaming white smashing to either side in an insanity of bubbling, roaring noise. The bullets were gone, fallen far behind . . . the bike was an insane bucking metallic bitch straining and heaving beneath him, trying its utmost to launch him from the saddle—

The tachometer's needle danced, bouncing against the redline, and Carter's teeth ground against each other as he grabbed the front brake and left a trail of rubber hissing down the concrete face of the dam . . . Then a string of detonations began to go off deep within the bowels of the dam . . . Carter felt them smashing through the wheels and suspension of the bike and he focused his eyes on the distant curve at the dam's base and the dense trees beyond – as the bike's speed peaked at just over 250 m.p.h.

Kade screamed in Carter's head, words of anger and words of insanity: pure hot curses of hatred—

—With a terrifying monstrous lurch the concrete dam moved . . .

—It heaved—

And, with a violent animal moan, exploded.

ADVERTISING FEATURE

The TV sparkled into life with a digital buzz of electro-hum, diamond-sharp images spinning and morphing into the jewelled-liquid logo of Leviathan Fuels.

Do you despair of the filth of low-grade fuel? Do you tear out your hair over the pollution, over the high cost, over the degradation of your children's futures and the destruction of the whole planet? YOU can stop this . . . YOU can change the world, YOU can make a whole big difference . . .

Scene pans: slowly, from belching thundering oil-slick diesel engines and black fumes suffocating the smog-heavy cancer-riddled twisted population of some tar-smeared contemporary dying city . . .

Scene morphs: into a crystalline metropolis, glittering skyscrapers, happy shining faces, definitive cleanliness . . . hospitals closed because there is no scum of dust and depravity and need . . . gleaming cars purring silently along free-flowing highways . . . healthy children of all cultures and religions and ethnic minorities playing together with an inflatable beach ball and laughing as they skip across dazzling white sand and crushed pink seashells . . .

Leviathan Fuels proudly present Premium Grade LVA, four hundred miles to the gallon, pollution-free with absolute guarantees. Go on, make the switch, because you know your children deserve a better future . . .

SCENE DISSOLVES TO BLACK

PART ONE

THE BOOK OF REVELATION

i see priests, politicians?
heroes in black plastic body-bags
under nations' flags

i see children pleading with outstretched
    hands
drenched in napalm, this is no Vietnam

i can't take any more, should we say
    goodbye?
how can you justify?

Blind Curve (Part v. Threshold)
Fish/Marillion

CHAPTER 1

GAME ON

Austria: 11:48 p.m. [GMT]

Durell's dark clawed hands clasped the small and ornately carved silver box tightly, almost reverently, to his chest: as if he carried the container which bore the ashes of God.

He moved, ghostlike and robed completely in black, down the long, damp stone corridors. He turned at intervals, picking passages through the labyrinth until he came to a small, ice-cold chamber. Despite its simplicity and bareness, there was something special about this place.

Something almost holy.

Durell's boots crunched on sparkling crystals. His breath plumed from the hidden folds of his hood.

Two men waited patiently. The first was tall and massively thickset, his hair greying and neatly cropped around a heavy skull. He was hulkingly muscled but his brown-eyed stare was serious and stern, fixed impassively on Durell; and he was as strong as steel.

In contrast, the second man was considerably slimmer, although he was wide across the shoulders in the manner of an athlete; his eyes were blood red and set in a face that carried heavy, vicious-looking scars. The red eyes themselves were criss-crossed with angry, minute marble-veined lesions – a legacy of an old accident involving alkaline chemical agents and a gang of Colombian drug-purifiers. The man's vision had been saved by the miracle of nascent nanotechnology and the Avelach. His eyes were now fixed in a permanent and terrible expression of pain – and they throbbed with a burning hot-acid intensity in their sockets. He, too, exuded power but in a different, more subtle, even more terrifying way – and both men nodded as Durell entered, the small intricately fashioned silver box clutched within the cage of his fingers.

'Is it ready?'

The red-eyed man nodded curtly. Durell stepped forward, and there came a glitter of brightness from within the heavy folds of his clothing. He slid past the two men towards a narrow, tiny corridor. Stooping, he moved into its circular confines.

They journeyed along the winding passage. It led down.

And down . . .

After many minutes Durell finally stepped out onto a ledge, his breath catching in his throat with a sibilant hiss. It was terribly cold, at least minus fifty degrees centigrade, and he slipped slightly on the slick wide expanse of perfectly smooth rock. In front of his eyes opened a giant chamber, mammoth in its naturally carved proportions. Behind him his keen hearing detected the footfalls of the other two men.

The chamber spread out, dimly lit, the rocky walls frost-spattered and glinting, leading out into witch light and going on seemingly for ever. Within the chamber stood men and women – suited in black and grey, masks covering their faces, gloved hands clasping ice-rimed automatic weapons. They stood immobile, insect-like in their poise, waiting.

Durell exhaled a plume of breath-smoke and smiled.

'Does it please?' asked the red-eyed man.

'Yes, they are perfect.'

'We have worked hard since you left us,' said the athletic soldier. His gaze surveyed the masked army and he smiled to himself, the smile playing gently across his iron-hard face. 'And our forces are still growing at an incredible rate.'

Durell passed the red-eyed man the small silver box. 'With the new nano-alterations to the Avelach machine, you should continue your work with more speed.'

Durell turned to the large bearded man. 'And you, my oldest comrade. Are you impressed with the scale of your invention? What it has achieved? What it can *do*?'

'*Our* invention, surely.'

'Yes,' purred Durell. '*Our* discovery. Our invention. From so many years ago, when the world seemed so much more – simple.' He let the word hang against the ice breeze, and then led the way down to the metal steps that spiralled down to the vast chamber itself. The two men followed, cursing as they left strips of skin against the freezing alloy of the staircase's guard rail.

Reaching the smooth rock floor, Durell walked among his soldiers, among the Nex, looking up into copper eyes and smiling with a deformed pride from within the hidden folds of the dark robes.

'Have you heard the news regarding our enemies?' came the voice of the older, grey-bearded man, his words rich and discordant in this place of cold inactivity.

'Yes,' soothed Durell. He gazed into the distance, past

hundreds of Nex. 'Spiral are fools. They think they have us crushed; they destroyed the QIII processor and thought that they had won the war . . . when in fact all they did was delay the battle. So naive of them to think that we had only the QIII to rely on – when in reality the processor was just a tiny slice of the cake. Their arrogance is a crime against all humanity.'

'And Carter? And Jam? And the other DemolSquads?'

Durell sighed. 'Thorns in my side,' he whispered. 'Carter has disappeared, but I have scouts searching for him. Jam has been targeted.'

'And the other squads? Spiral have been rebuilding their strength hard and fast since our . . . assassinations.'

Durell merely chuckled, breath-wraiths emanating eerily from within his dark hood.

'Do not underestimate Spiral,' muttered the bearded man in warning.

'Of course I will not underestimate them. But then, in a beautiful and ironic twist of fate, they have misjudged our strength and our aspirations – *they* are underestimating *us*. They have misread our intentions and they are arrogant enough to think that they have nearly destroyed the Nex with their pathetic search-and-destroy teams. The fools. Just look around you – look at our superiority!'

The two men glanced up, at the fifty thousand Nex who were grouped in battalions within the chamber. Their stares met – for the briefest of instants – and something unsaid passed between them. Hurriedly their gazes returned to the dark husk of Durell.

'We are stronger than we have ever been. Yes, they destroyed our mobile station and the QIII processor – but the development files still exist. The schematics still exist. It has merely cost us time . . . and in that time we have developed another weapon which should level the playing field somewhat.'

'May I ask you about the ScorpNex?'

'The ScorpNex,' said Durell softly, his voice low and menacing, 'was an accident. We have attempted to replicate the procedures that led to its creation and distortion, but each time the subject dies on the slab. If we could find the correct sequence and inhibitors we could build a superior Nex – but that is a problem for another day. Let me show you what the ScorpNex can achieve . . . Kattenheim?'

'Sir?'

'Our new companion needs a demonstration.'

They moved amongst the ranks of silent Nex – scouts, warriors and the elite assassin Nex5 – until they came to a small clearing among them. All around Durell and his two companions silent, immobile copper eyes watched without a flicker of emotion; the only indications of life were tiny trails of breath drifting from chilled lips.

Durell turned to Kattenheim and smiled. The lithe man with the scarred face and blood-red eyes nodded once and shouted in a language unknown to the older grey-bearded man.

Movement from the massive chamber made the large man look up, and he watched in horror as a huge figure lumbered into view. Its skin was jet black, chitinous and threaded with strands of raw pink; disjointed jaws drooled thick saliva from a face that was twisted in eternal pain.

'The ScorpNex,' said Kattenheim softly. 'Our new and . . . *accidental* breed.' He laughed softly. 'Let us say he is one of a kind.'

'Watch,' hissed Durell softly.

Kattenheim gave another call and into the circle came three Nex warriors, their movements perfect and smooth, their copper-eyed stares fixed on the huge ScorpNex and then turning questioningly to Durell and Kattenheim. Kattenheim smiled at the Nex, and gestured towards the massive deformed figure of the ScorpNex.

'Kill it,' he said.

The Nex rolled, spreading out with perfect timing and unnatural fluidity.

The ScorpNex turned, folding its arms, talons slicing its own skin and allowing soft droplets of blood to fall sparkling through the icy air . . .

The Nex circled warily, then attacked as a single unit from three different directions, leaping forward with slim black knives extended. The ScorpNex swayed, smashed blows left and right, then backed away a step as a blade whistled past, a single millimetre from its face. Its taloned fist punched out, skewering a Nex and dragging free a squirming blood-gleaming spinal column. The Nex hit the ground screaming a shrill high-pitched scream as the ScorpNex tensed and attacked, blows raining thick and fast. Within five seconds all three Nex were dead, torn and shredded on the smooth rock floor, blood running into kill channels carved three thousands years ago into the ancient rock.

The ScorpNex folded its thick muscled arms and waited once more, covered in gore and gleaming under the soft light.

'Superb,' sighed Durell.

Blood was trickling, pooling into the stone channels.

'The ScorpNex is much improved,' said Kattenheim.

'Improved?' asked the grey-bearded man, kicking free a lump of meat from his boot in distaste. He stared at the huge figure as it twisted and hissed in front of him. 'This thing is *improved*?'

'It is fast, and it is deadly,' said Kattenheim. 'But the

coding is still far from perfect and needs an increase in conversion timings. And, of course, we need to master the sequence . . .'

'Another problem for another day,' said Durell. 'What matters now are the QEngines, the Foundation Stones . . . and the QHub – and their ultimate integration into the world as we know it.'

The large man with the grey beard frowned. 'QEngine? . . . I don't understand,' he said softly, bewildered by what he had just seen.

Durell's thin black clawed arm reached out and touched the man, almost tenderly. 'You have been asleep for a long time,' said Durell softly. 'You have much to catch up on, much to learn. And then I will show you the QHub and the things it can achieve . . . it will be like the old days, my friend: we will be masters and Spiral will be destroyed. The chaos of the Old God must reign fire from Heaven – before we can turn this world into the Eden we desire! Into the New World. Into Paradise!'

'Yes,' said Gol, nodding softly, rubbing at his greying beard. 'I have been gone for far too long; there is much still for me to learn.'

Northern Siberia: 05:10 a.m. [GMT]

One Week Later

The dawn wind howled and cavorted, kicking up flurries of snow and tearing across the harsh icy landscape, flowing and whirling towards the low darkened brow of the tree line that sported tangled webs of branches and glinting daggers of sculpted snow.

The derrick stood, ominous in its framing obsidian,

rigid and stonelike, a golem sentinel staring forlornly over the snow fields. This mighty behemoth guarded the precious drill string, the casings and collar, and the immensely strong titanium-carbide-VII drill bit.

Movement stirred within a lattice of timber, and a figure wrapped in thick furs moved slowly in heavy creaking oil-stained boots across the high wooden balcony built into the derrick. He lifted dDi binoculars to cold grey eyes that peered out above an ice-speckled bushy beard. A freezing wind blew, cutting through his clothing and biting at his skin with diamond teeth. He shivered, and longed for a large mug of hot coffee spiced with brandy.

A black Range Rover was moving, slicing the landscape in two with its distinctive 4X4 trail, exhausts pluming, engine a distant low growl as snow chains tore the ice. Lights glittered like jewels through the gloom. Gradually it drew closer, and the fur-clad guard reached out to hit a small digital buzzer that sounded muffled down below, off towards the trees where snow-encumbered huts and cabins lay under a smothering of snow.

The guard watched figures stirring, and his eyes flickered, darting from the cabins where the workforce was waking from sex-filled dreams and involuntary erections to the large and richly adorned HQ constructed from hardwood and flown to this prospective LVA site by Chinook. He reached down, picked up a Barrett IV sniper rifle with a digital sight, and settled into position against the rough timber railing. The Range Rover looked delectable in the digitally enhancing sights, a soft doe ready for violent slaughter. So easy, thought the guard in idleness. Bang! Dead. He smiled and unscrewed the cap on his vodka canteen.

Below, the door to the HQ opened and a broad-shouldered man stepped through, clad in a long black leather coat, stamping his boots against the snow and looking up towards the rapidly approaching vehicle. He wore his blond hair shaved to the scalp, a style which only emphasised his heavily scarred face and head.

Kattenheim's gaze was wide as he stamped his boots, shrugging off the ice-chill that tore at his skin, ignoring the ever-present pain in his eyes – as he always did and would always have to. He walked forward, his hands deep in his pockets, and stood, legs apart, his stance arrogant, eyes fixed.

The Range Rover came to a halt and the engine died. Plumes of exhaust smoke dwindled as doors opened, and five men with experience-lined brows and aged faces climbed down, slamming doors and approaching the man with the red eyes.

'You Kattenheim?'

The man in the leather coat nodded, slowly.

'We are the LVA Fuel Inspectors, TF Division, and we are currently responsible for Siberia and neighbouring states. I am sure that you have heard of us? Here are our papers . . .' A sheaf was presented, tattered and coffee-stained, curled at the corners. 'We have permission and directives from Director-General Oppenhauer, Commissioner for the Fuel Inspectorate of Eastern Europe, to inspect this facility and work out sequential plans for the eventuality of LVA discovery. My name is Petrinsky.'

Kattenheim reached out and took the papers, but he did not look at them, instead meeting Petrinsky's gaze. 'Oppenhauer exceeds himself with his timing, for only yesterday we were fortunate enough to hit a lode of LVA which would seem very promising. We are just determining its environmental boundaries, and currently await instructions from our science lab on the best methods for

25

extraction, and for the return of our exterior seismic trucks. Anyway, gentlemen, I am being somewhat rude. It is uncouth to speak like this in the snow. Please, follow me.'

Kattenheim's voice was curiously soft, a gentle low-level growl, and turning on the heel of one boot he led the group of Inspectors to the low steps of the raised hardwood cabin, up the steps and into the luxury of ice oasis within.

Out of the cold, Kattenheim removed his gloves and looked the men over, especially the one who had presented himself as Petrinsky. They were veterans, he could see that immediately, and probably as adept with machine guns as with diplomacy. They carried themselves well – ex-military of some sort drafted in to do what was an increasingly unpopular job – and Kattenheim searched the nuances of the leader's name and accent for hint of his origins; Russian, he finally confirmed, probably St Petersburg, but laced with a myriad of other inflections which suggested a lifetime of travel . . . either travel, or covert operations, around the globe. And now? Why employ ex-military men as Inspectors? Was the Fuel Inspectorate suspicious? Was the job *that* fucking dangerous?

'I will allow you a little time to compose yourselves, and then I will guide you around the complex myself. Please, make yourselves at home. There is vodka and brandy in the silver cabinet over there.'

'As you wish.'

Their gazes met, and Kattenheim smiled again, a slow feline smile without humour. 'Please excuse me.' He gave a brief bow and left the cabin, stepping once more back into the snow, his glance taking in the snipers at the tree line. He gave them a nod, and watched as they melted into the early-morning gloom.

★

Bright winter sunshine illuminated the scene, but was soon obscured behind threatening dark clouds. The LVA explorers had gone to work, and the titanium-carbide-VII drill was spinning slowly, searching the depths of the lode rock via its vanguard of diamond drill casings. The distant diesel engines rumbled, their power translated through the turntable at the base of the derrick, and large groups of engineers stood in and around the turntable near the blow-out preventer. The generators hummed through the gloom.

'What depth is this newly discovered LVA lode?'

'Eight kilometres.'

Petrinsky whistled softly, and turned to the other men; they scribbled on DigitalPads. Kattenheim's eyes narrowed, and he glanced left, past the huge spinning bulk of the titanium-VII drill to where the glistening black pumps waited for the removal of the derrick and their subsequent integration into the LVA extraction process.

The drill ceased; steam hissed from pipes as core samples were extracted and gas sensors were lowered down the carrier stem into the heart of this new breach in the Earth.

'We will have to carry out digital stability checks,' Kattenheim heard one of the men say over the noise. 'There must be some fucking pressure in that drill – I mean, look at the size of it! It must be ten times the size of a conventional oil drill . . . I suggest we close down the machines and reconvene in two weeks' time with the council, then decide upon . . .'

The other Inspectors were nodding.

Snow started to fall from the heavy broiling clouds.

Kattenheim sighed. As if in a dream, he lifted his left hand, gloved in the softest doeskin leather, and gave a small discreet signal.

The man who was speaking was struck suddenly and savagely between the eyes by a heavy-calibre round . . . a coin-sized circle of red appeared, there was a *smack* of suddenly struck flesh and his brains and skull erupted from the back of his head, showering his shocked comrades.

There was a moment of stunned silence, then Petrinsky screamed something incomprehensible as the Fuel Inspectors separated with military precision – Petrinsky whirled low, came back up with the accuracy of a boxer and hammered a right hook to Kattenheim's jaw. Kattenheim was rocked, but he rolled, absorbing the punch with a grunt before spitting out blood and a chip of tooth, his stare fixed on the fleeing men who were sprinting for the Range Rover.

Kattenheim lifted his clenched fist into the air; more shots rang out, and another two of the Inspectors fell. Petrinsky reached the Range Rover, yanked open the door and leapt in as bullets slammed steel slaps against the panels. The engine roared into life as the remaining Inspector reached the rear door of the Range Rover and was shot in the back. Strips of his lung tissue splattered against the black panels as his face thumped against the glass. And then he sprawled in the cold snow and his eyes stared fish-dead at the rear tyre.

Kattenheim looked down at the first man to be killed – his half-closed purple-lidded eyes, the V of blood down the bridge of his nose, his shattered head lying in the puddle of melted snow littered with tiny shards of bone.

The engine screamed, chains tore at the ice.

The Range Rover managed ten metres before the engine stuttered and died.

Kattenheim strolled towards the stranded vehicle, rubbing thoughtfully at his jaw. His gaze met Petrinsky's as he watched the Russian draw a large heavy seventeen-round-clip Smith & Wesson and point it as if in slow motion towards him.

Petrinsky, his face speckled with blood, his hair matted with gore and bone splinters, screamed harshly as he squeezed the trigger—

Kattenheim's weapon came up, smooth, precise, and there echoed a single shot that smashed Petrinsky's bullet from the air. Ricochets sang a brief song of metal. Kattenheim fired again, the bullet entering Petrinsky's shoulder, exiting from his back and drilling into the Range Rover's dashboard. The Fuel Inspector screamed in agony, and was forced to drop his heavy gun from fingers that no longer worked.

'Quite a right hook, Mr Petrinsky.'

Kattenheim held his Glock loosely, as if discussing the time of day. Petrinsky stared into those scarred red eyes, seeing the wide expression distorted by heavy scars, and realised that the emotion deep within that well of controlled pain was not surprise, hatred, loathing, or even a clinical determination to get the job done. The look merely held a sliver of deep insanity . . . trapped and fighting to be free.

And then he noticed something . . . something glittering behind the scars, behind the haemorrhage of finely woven tissue; it was a gleam, a bright gleam . . . the gleam of copper.

'Why, Kattenheim?' he asked. 'Why have you killed them?'

Kattenheim shrugged. 'I simply cannot allow the time deficit.'

Petrinsky frowned.

Kattenheim lifted the Glock and put a bullet into Petrinsky's face, smashing the man's teeth through the back of his head to bone-clatter from the glass of the Range Rover's windscreen. Petrinsky slumped back, a torn marionette. Kattenheim turned, and strolled off into the gently falling snow.

The bodies had been dragged to the edge of the mighty derrick; the titanium-carbide-VII drill was silent. The five corpses were perched on the edge of the Mud Pits, a huge crater of waste from the drilling process – dirt, rock, and any impurities that the drill had torn from the ground. Kattenheim watched the industrial Grade IV Element drop into the crater with a crash and sudden hiss; steam screamed from the pit as the frozen mud and rock and ice was loosened, and started to liquefy as the temperature rapidly rose above freezing.

And still the snow fell.

Kattenheim lifted a small black cube in front of his face and looked into the eyes of another man a thousand miles away.

'Are they dead?' asked Durell.

Kattenheim watched the corpses slither into the mud. The gaping cavity in Petrinsky's destroyed face – the now much larger hole where his mouth had been – filled with grey liquid shale and mud that then flooded his eye sockets until he disappeared from sight. Bubbles rose and died. The Range Rover was pushed to the edge of the giant pit and rolled into the rock swamp; steam rising around its metal flanks, it sank like a dying dinosaur. The industrial Grade IV Element was withdrawn; within minutes the Mud Pits would be frozen solid once more, a silent grey graveyard, a sinister hiding place for the murdered – the slain.

'Dead and buried,' said Kattenheim softly. 'Dead and fucking buried.'

CLASSIFIED SADt/8764/SPECIAL INVESTIGATIONS UNIT

Data Request 777#12300

QIII

The QuanTech Edition 3 [QIII] Military Cubic Processor

The QIII was the first ever cellular processor – the prototype of a true electronic mind – semi-organic, silicon-based and with a mixture of synthetic substances at its core. Via design modes and mechs, the QIII processor was a totally independent piece of hardware.

Working around a digital model of WorldCode Data, the QuanTech Edition 3 was digitally capable of almost anything. A successor to the all-powerful QuanTech Edition 2 [QII] processor which runs at the heart of various Spiral mainframes across the globe, the QIII was capable and fully compliant with any and all global operating systems – from UNIX to Windows it could decode way beyond current 64- and 128-bit architectures. The QIII was so powerful that it could decode and re-encode DNA in millionths of a second when it would take a conventional computer many hours. The QIII was at least 50,000 times faster than any current processor in

31

development. It was destined to have groundbreaking effects on all aspects of computing, from military applications to world economics.

The pinnacle of the QuanTech 3's development was the ability to use WorldCode Data combined with probability math – equations allowing it to successfully predict the future in the simulation of any given probable event. This feature was nearly 100% successful and required only occasional calibration.

The QIII was destroyed when a rogue Spiral operative named Durell abused the military processor (and its sub-systems) and attempted to use this all-powerful machine to take over global military systems, financial institutions and satellites, including the highly destructive Russian PredatorSAT modules.

The QIII was destroyed by Spiral operative Cartervb512. All schematics were lost/destroyed. Further development of this kind of mind were subsequently abandoned.

Keyword SEARCH>> QIII, NEX, SAD, SPIRAL_sadt, DURELL, FEUCHTER, Spiral_Q, Spiral_R, SVDENSKA, PAGAN

CHAPTER 2

BODY AND SOUL

Natasha leant on her elbow, staring out at the freshly falling snow. Mountains reared in front of her, grey and jagged rock scattered with ice and forests sprawling across the lower slopes, all viewed through a reality snow-globe that had been freshly shaken. She smiled, her pretty brow creasing slightly, gaze fixing on the dominant pyramidal peak of the Matterhorn and hand moving protectively to her slightly swollen belly where her baby nestled within.

'I wish you could see the snow and mountains, bubba.'

'Who are you talking to?'

A hand rested on her shoulder, and Nats turned, smiling up at Carter, who grinned. He was bearing a small silver tray on which were two squat glasses of Lagavulin.

'Baby.'

'Ahh,' nodded Carter with mock understanding cascading across his – some would say brutal – features. 'Of course – "baby". How is baby? Is he well?'

'He?'

'Just a wild stab in the dark.'

'Yeah, *she* is well.'

There came a long and comfortable pause. Natasha reached out daintily, took the proffered glass, sipped at the distilled warmth. 'I love this.'

'The whisky?'

'No, this place, the atmosphere. Snow falling gently outside with the Alps nestling in the background; the logs burning on the open fire and filling the room with real heat. The thick carpet between my toes, the glow of candle-light across the perfectly still surface of the whisky . . . and you, here by my side, the father of my growing child. Picturesque, eh, Carter?'

'Hm. How sweet. You've been reading that book by bloody Gillian Brewster again, haven't you? Tsch! Look, did I tell you about the new mod I've got for the Browning HiPower 9mm? It's brilliant, I got it from Simmo down in SP1 stores – a needle clip which slots on the top of the gun and . . . and . . .' He saw Natasha's dark frown.

'Carter.' Her voice was low and dangerous.

'What?'

Her eyes became more focused, her frown more intense.

'*What?*'

'My love, you are *so* romantic. Here we are, holidaying in Switzerland, our very own log cabin within the winter gardens of a five-star hotel overlooking the Zermatter Valley – a honeymoon of sorts for the unmarried . . . and you have to talk about your *large weapon.*'

'It's always worked for me before.' Carter grinned, knocking back the Lagavulin and allowing a look of ecstasy to pass across his battered boxer's features. Carter: ex-military, Spiral operative of the first order; his face had been used too many times to cushion the impact of large

34

men's fists. But still, thought Natasha as she watched him through the crystal sparkling of Scotland's finest malt, he *was* handsome – ruggedly handsome . . . yes, battered and ruggedly handsome . . . yes, beat up, rugged, battered smashed and very definitely ruggedly handsome.

'Are you *flirting* with me, Mr Carter?'

Carter carefully placed the empty crystal glass down on the marble table top and gave her a fearsome scowl – the scowl that had impaled assassins, the scowl that had felled Nex warriors, the scowl that had detonated entire armies into piles of pulp . . . Natasha giggled as he swept her from the low couch with its fur throw-over and lifted her lithe supple form high in the air. He cradled her to him, to his chest, nuzzling her neck, inhaling her scent, prickling his stubble against her short spiked black hair. He could feel her agile limbs beneath the silk kimono, felt the robe writhe across her flesh in an incredibly erotic manner. This sensuous fabric standing between their coupling was far, far more erotic than simple nakedness. Carter's breathing deepened and he looked into Nat's mischievous sparkling eyes.

'You going to come snowboarding with me tomorrow, pixie?' he whispered, and kissed her full red lips. They were too good to abuse by leaving alone, and both of them enjoyed a languorous kiss that spun from long seconds to minutes . . .

Natasha finally pulled away with a pout. 'You *know* I can't do anything vigorous; not in my condition. The doctor ordered!'

Carter glanced down at her belly.

'Nothing vigorous? What a shame.' He sulked. 'I had so many fine games planned for you.' He trod carefully across the plush thick-pile carpet, towards the bedroom and the glow of candles within.

'Games?' Natasha seemed to consider this.

'You remember that DPM commando outfit I bought you?'

'You mean the peephole one?'

'Mm.'

There came a long pause.

'Well . . . if I must,' she murmured huskily as Carter's size ten military boot kicked the door closed and shut off the candles from the sight of anyone out there in the thickly falling snow.

The happy couple had failed to observe a broad-shouldered figure outside, arms folded across his black-clad chest, his balaclava-masked gaze fixed through the tumbling flakes on the window of the room where seconds earlier Natasha had reclined.

Snow fell.

And in the blink of an eye, the figure was gone.

Carter lay, dozing on the bed, Natasha's perfect long naked legs languishing beside his sleepy gaze. He moved close, nuzzling her sweet-smelling skin, and she murmured in sleep, rolling away from him and pitilessly stealing the heavy duvet. The room was dark, illuminated only by the glow of candles around the low bed. Carter rolled to his back, then sat up, stomach grumbling from a lifetime of whisky abuse. He popped a tablet, rubbed at his eyes, then picked up the small alloy ECube from the low carved pine table beside the bed.

An ECube was an electronic communications device issued by Spiral – the current model ran a V4.5 ICARUS operating system, sported a 24GHz RISC processor and 512 gigabytes of static RAM. The tiny alloy machine which doubled not only as a GPS but as a link to the massive Spiral CDb (Criminal Database) was completely solid-state, and had many tiny tricks up its little alloy sleeve. Communications, information, weapons system – the ECube was *the* invaluable asset for any Spiral field operative.

Carter grinned, tossing the ECube in his hand like a softball. He squeezed, and the surface came alive with soft blue digits. Reclining, Carter skimmed through recent reports – global activity, criminal, political, social. He yawned, and dropping the ECube beside the bed once more moved to the living quarters of the cabin, running himself a glass of water and standing, naked, staring out at the softly falling snow in the darkness.

It'll be dawn soon, he realised.

'*Exercise is what you really need,*' taunted Kade at the back of his mind. '*Burn off that puppy fat . . . show us you're the real man you pretend to be, fucker.*'

'Yeah, yeah – drop dead.'

'*You wish.*'

Carter poured himself a second glass of water, then moved to the low pine table and sat, staring at the small flexible GridMap entrusted to him by Jam. 'Keep that safe for me, fucker,' Jam had said, grinning over a pint of Guinness.

'What is it?'

'A map.'

'Of what?'

Jam had tapped his nose conspiratorially, giving his cheeky trade-mark grin. 'Trust me Carter, you do *not* fucking want to know. Just keep it safe. I'll be back for it soon.'

Carter stared at the GridMap now. On it were markings, coordinates, and tiny tags reading 'AnComm Post'. Carter had heard a rumour about AnComms, a back-up form of an analogue communication network Spiral were

– supposedly – in the process of installing in the event of ECube failure in the future. Of course, Spiral was admitting none of it. The official line was that the ECube was infallible. And if their digital wonder-toy was flawless, then why integrate a back-up system?

Still, Carter toyed with the tiny flexible digital GridMap. What was Jam up to?

Pushing the item to one side, he looked down at his paper notes – notes for his speech which he had been diligently working on. His discarded pencil accused him, and the sheets looked far too blank for his liking.

'Shit.'

He sipped the water and, taking the pencil, chewed the end thoughtfully as he remembered Natasha's words – *it's a huge responsibility, you mustn't fuck it up for Jam and Nicky . . . they have placed their utmost faith in you . . .*

'Yeah, right. I wish the bastard had asked Slater instead. I can do without entertaining a bunch of drunken friends and family . . . I would die for Jam, but perform his best-man speech?' Carter realised that he was grumbling to himself, and he forced his mouth to shut. He stared hard at the page, chewing splinters, but inspiration was denied him. He knew that this leisurely atmosphere, this heady relaxation in the mountains should be highly conducive to work and creativity: but the words just would not flow.

He read what he had already written in his untidy pencil scrawl:

The Marriage of Nicky and Jam: Alexander the Great, ruler of the Greek Empire between 336 BC and 323 BC and the only man to ever conquer the exotic continent of Persia, quantified his Royal relationship with the Proletariat as this:

'It is better to rule by fear than to rule by love. If you rule by love, the people can give it - but they can take it away. If you rule by fear, then you can enforce the fear and nobody can take that away from you.'

Jam rules Nicky like Alexander ruled his Empire!

Carter shook his head, dropped his pencil atop the notes which slithered out in a fan, and cursed Jam for the thousandth time. It was one thing performing a dual parachute raid on a terrorist HighJ explosives den, but quite another to stand in front of a group of people – family people – and attempt to fucking entertain them.

Humour.

Carter snorted. He hated the word. Humour was something that happened to other people.

He peeped in on Natasha, breathing deeply in sleep, then on impulse moved to his bag and dug out his Browning 9mm and a few spare clips. He toyed with the familiar bulk of the battered old gun – it nestled in his grip, an old friend.

'You expecting trouble?'

Carter ignored Kade, dressed, and grabbed his snowboard.

'I always expect trouble,' he muttered as he stepped into a landscape of dawn pastel shades that were too good to be true. A living breathing dreamland.

★

Carter stood on the edge of the mountain. Sunlight glittered revealing a virgin dawn, sparkling across the snow like blood wine across a fistful of sprinkled diamonds. He crouched, feeling the flexible solidity of the snowboard beneath him; he twisted his ankles slightly, checking the torque of the quick-release bindings, then kicked himself free.

Silence smashed him in the face. Exhilaration grasped his spine in its adrenalin fist and threw him head first down the mountain. He banked left, breath in a gasp, and a shower of snow hissed behind and to his right. Trees loomed. Carter ducked under branches and kicked gracefully around their grasping fingers. The board . . . sang. Carter grinned harshly behind the black neoprene face mask and ski goggles, breathed out slowly, and fixed his gaze on the vertical drop flashing past on either side in mad waves of liquid snow, white mercury . . .

Peace.

The wave descended across Carter like a white shroud. He was at one with himself; the horror of the past year was gone in a single rush of white injection. Gone, Feuchter and his twisted development of the military QIII processor; gone, the Nex assassins and their hunting and murdering; gone, the images of death and betrayal which had haunted Carter and forced Kade to the forefront of his violent mind . . . gone, the attempt by the rogue Spiral operatives to take over the world from a floating warship in the Arctic seas . . .

. . . And all were as inconsequential as a single snowflake.

Snow hissed by, and below him Carter could feel the board; it was a part of him – they had become one. Carter felt his speed increase and the wind howled past his goggles. He crouched lower, and as the ice trail descended through wind-swaying pines the world suddenly opened up to Carter's right. The mountains fell away into a vast open canyon where far, far below icy waters crashed through narrow rocky pools. Carter veered right, hit a low hump of snow and kicked himself into the air with the board raised in the vertical. Again, everything was silent, but this time with the whole world of ice and snow opening before him, there came a panoramic explosion of blinding white and blasting air . . .

The snowboard slid along the edge of the precipice and a devastating crevasse opened up in front of Carter's eyes. There came scraping sounds, rocks slicing the underside of the board at high speed and leaving deep grooves. But Carter was oblivious to this. Sunlight glinted from the ice and snow and distant peaks and he did not glance down at the far distant sharp serrated rocks or landlocked lakes. The board veered left, hissing away from the edge of the sheer drop in a shower of snow and Carter allowed himself to breathe once more.

The faster he went, the more peace settled over him.

Adrenalin brought him serenity.

But then— He felt something: a splinter in his soul, a hot needle drilling through his mind. The bulk of the Browning pressed against him reassuringly beneath his jacket but the other feeling, uncomfortable and real and nestling in his stomach like a cancer, made his head twitch as it came up, his eyes scanning his surroundings in a sudden panic born of experience and a life spent in deadly situations. It was almost a vibration, deep, subsonic, beyond normal hearing and it made him feel suddenly sick to his very core.

Carter licked at his dry lips behind the mask.

And then the feeling was gone . . . as quickly as it had come.

41

The board and its rider flashed beneath more conifers, adrenalin pumping Carter to even greater speed. Left and right he zigzagged down the insanely steep incline – more treacherous than any black run that a slope designer could dream up – until, finally, it levelled out and Carter's racing raging heart started to calm as the board straightened and he sped left, away from the cliffs and lethal terminal drops.

'*You're still a pussy,*' whispered Kade.

Carter smiled grimly, his face darkly demonic behind the mask.

'I must get it from you,' he muttered.

Reaching the outskirts of the hotel grounds, he snapped free of the snowboard and clipped a strap to the carrying D-ring; the hotel, the Coeur des Alpes, loomed ahead of him, an example of fine Swiss architecture constructed from smooth stone and beech, huge beams fronting finely sculpted gardens. Beyond, down snow-laden paths and cable-car tracks, sat the distant town of Zermatt, huddling under a winter shawl of cloud with curls of smoke reaching like grey fingers into the sky.

Carter walked slowly down the winding path, boots crunching fresh fallen snow, between decorative trees and a variety of winter flowers, splashes of colour from edelweiss, lilies and anemones. He stopped before he reached the entrance; a small group of people had arrived in a horse-drawn sleigh and were excitedly disembarking, carrying skis and sporting loud colourful jackets and louder voices. Zermatt was the 'village without cars' and Carter found some of the alternative modes of transport almost magical . . . another time, another world.

He slung his board over his shoulder and pulled free a cigarette, staring dolefully down at the crumpled weed.

'Last one?' He laughed, a gravelly bitter laugh battered

by a thousand battles and too many wars. Placing the cigarette between his lips, he grimaced as he lit the old friend and blew a plume of smoke into the soothing cool air.

Sitting, Carter watched the world go by, turning occasionally to stare up the slopes; he could make out the holiday slopes, just starting to bustle at this early hour of the morning. But he looked – no, he searched – beyond this façade, this mask, this replication of normality . . . searched for something – else.

'*You're imagining things,*' snapped Kade.

Carter snorted. 'Like your fucking voice, perhaps?' He turned and smiled up gently at a face blocked out by the dazzling sun.

'You OK?'

'Yeah,' sighed Carter. 'Just relaxing.'

'I was starting to get worried.'

Carter winked. 'Just, y'know, enjoying a secret cigarette. The wife thinks I've given up and I thought I'd try and sneak one in while she's back languishing at the cabin, doing all the cleaning and ironing. She's a bit of a dumb ass, thinks she can get her man – secure her victory like Alexander the Great – and then seek to change him by stopping his bad habits.'

Natasha sat down beside him, huddling close and linking arms. Sunlight bathed her beautiful, finely chiselled features, and her dark eyes surveyed Carter with casual violence as her hand curled around his steel bicep. 'So, this dumb-ass wife, what would she do if she caught you smoking out here?'

Carter shrugged, reached across, and gently pecked Natasha on the cheek. 'Probably beat me senseless,' he sighed, rolling his eyes.

'And you would let her abuse your body in this way?'

43

Carter grinned. 'Yeah, I've always loved the violent abuse of a woman.'

They kissed, lips moist and warm as a cool Swiss breeze blew from the mountains, and they drew closer until Natasha's bump pressed against him. Carter pulled away, met her gaze for a moment, then glanced down. 'You're definitely getting bigger. Turning into a right little porker.'

She ignored his jibe. 'I wonder, do you think he'll look like you? A mad little Carter running around, hair stuck up in all directions, cut-off combat shorts and podgy little face all screwed up as he searches for his plastic Browning 9mm?'

Carter's laugh burst free, a sudden explosion of sound. His hand moved over Natasha's belly, gently, protectively. 'I'm sure he'll be a little bastard, just like his father.'

'I can guarantee it,' snapped Natasha. 'Now, are you coming back to bed to warm the covers for me, or what?'

Carter scowled. 'What do I get in return?'

Natasha reached forward, dark eyes fixed on his, and flicked the end of his nose mischievously. 'We'll just have to see what I can come up with,' she crooned huskily.

Carter lay naked on the bed, still covered by a fine sheen of sweat from their sex, and listened to Natasha singing in the shower. He smiled, but the smile was laced with a distant agony and he remembered the bad times . . .

Sleep surprised him, and when his sticky eyes opened it was to see Natasha twirling in her new black dress in front of the mirror, her short dark hair spiked, deep brown eyes beneath well-groomed brows staring disapprovingly at him.

She tutted.

'What?' he croaked.

'Is the father of my child really such a dirty drunkard?'

''Twas only a nip, to keep the winter chill at bay.'

'You say that in the damn *summer*, Carter.'

He grinned, and scratched his belly. 'You finished in the bathroom, then?'

'I have . . . no, wait, let me get my make-up before you lock yourself in with a magazine.'

Carter sighed, and rolled grumpily out of bed.

The meal had been a particularly fine one, the following wine – and sex – almost too much for Carter to bear.

When he awoke, in the darkness, he was struck by momentary confusion. Sex-sweat had left him chilled, and he tried to work out how long he had been asleep. He frowned – why was he awake? He didn't need a piss, or a drink. That usually meant something bad and he rolled swiftly out of bed, palmed the silenced Browning 9mm and pulled on his trousers. If I'm going to fight, he thought, I ain't going to do it naked . . .

Carter hadn't lived as long as he had without being careful.

And clothed.

He moved towards the door, silent across the thick carpet, senses screaming at him that something was out of place; he could hear nothing, smell nothing but scented oil from Natasha's burners and candles, and yet something was wrong. He peered around the door and froze, waiting for his eyes to adjust. Like any hunter he knew that it was movement, mainly movement, that would give away a position – no matter how good the camouflage.

There was a large dark-clad figure, moving with extreme care.

Carter's eyes narrowed.

The man – or woman – was searching through the

45

cabin; Carter watched as hands rifled through drawers, then through Natasha's handbag. Carter stepped silently into the room – but, almost impossibly, he was heard. The figure's head, masked in a neat black balaclava, snapped around, eyes gleaming – then it whirled, dropping to a crouch and leaping with lightning speed at Carter who squeezed the trigger and the Browning spat, a bullet hissing free and smashing into the dark bulk of the figure before it crashed against Carter and sent them both flying back against the wall. Carter bounced to the floor, grunting.

The Browning was knocked free, a fist found Carter's jaw and he felt a tooth crack, blood flooding his mouth as stars danced in front of his eyes for a second. He lashed out with both fists, striking again and again at flesh beneath the mask and he carried on punching as he was picked from the floor and hurled across the room where he hit the wall again. A picture smashed this time, glass slicing strips of flesh from his back and he hit the floor once more, hard . . .

Boots stomped down but Carter rolled with lightning speed, coming up in a crouch and smashing an overhead straight punch into the attacker's groin – once, twice. Then, gaining his feet, he lashed out and gripped the attacker's windpipe. The large masked attacker pulled free Carter's hand with the ease of incredible strength and reached swiftly forward, fingers of both hands curling around Carter's throat before he could step beyond reach and lifting him from the ground with crushing force, dangling him breathless and kicking, eyes wide as the figure rose to his full height. Carter stared into dark slitted glittering eyes.

Carter choked, his hands gripping at the huge muscles in the arms which held him suspended. His eyes narrowed as he realised this huge fucker was much, much stronger than he, and he kicked out once, twice, three times but the grip would not release and Carter was choking, spinning white stars dancing patterns before his eyes and choking, choking and falling, he was shaken like a rag doll and he realised that he was suffocating . . .

Carter's hands dropped swiftly to the waist of his combats and with agony hammering through him and pain burning his brain with hot acid he slid free the thread of MercG that was sheathed there – hidden – as he heard the confused voice of Natasha calling from the bedroom. Carter sensed more than saw the attacker's change of stance, head turning to this new potential threat . . .

He had to act – and act fast.

His feet lashed out ineffectually against the attacker's groin and belly. Carter spun the mercury garrotte, a processor-controlled liquid metal thread activated by mind augmentations, so thin that it could be undetectably concealed and so astonishingly deadly that it could cut through steel, and with a flick of his wrist sliced through one of the attacker's arms. A burning hiss of slashed flesh and bone was barely audible.

The attacker screamed, a high shrill sound, releasing Carter who landed in a crouch beside the severed blood-pumping arm, limp-fingered and twitching and spilling gore across the carpet. The attacker spun, fleeing into the darkness without any further sound as Carter rubbed at his bruised windpipe and focused on regaining his breath and his vision. With his sight returned, he deactivated the MercG, located his Browning and crawled to the cabin door, peering out into the snow. But the attacker had vanished.

'What is that fucking smell?'

Natasha, bleary-eyed and naked, hair tousled, nose

47

wrinkled, stood in the doorway to the bedroom, looking confused.

'Yeah, thanks for your help,' croaked Carter, reaching up to flick on the light. An ambient cosy warm radiance contrasted with the stark images and thoughts that crashed through Carter's brain.

Natasha frowned, then stared down. 'Carter, there's a fucking *arm* on the carpet.'

'Really? You don't say. I wonder how that got there – could it have been something to do with the noise that roused you from your wine-induced slumber?'

'What was he after?' Natasha pulled a blanket around her shoulders and moved to him, crouching. 'Are you all right?'

Carter laughed, sliding the MercG back into its tiny hidden sheath at his waist and rising to lock the door of the cabin. 'Nice to see my health is third on your list of priorities.'

'Did he take anything?'

Carter prodded the severed arm with the toe of his boot. 'I don't know; I disturbed him before he found whatever he was looking for. Maybe he wanted Jam's GridMap.' Carter rubbed at his bruised throat again, noting Jam's map which had been covered by Carter's scattered wedding notes. The simplest hiding place was sometimes no hiding place at all!

'Can you get me a glass of water? The bastard nearly crushed my windpipe.'

'Hence the arm on the floor.'

'Yeah. And get onto Spiral, comm a genetic sample, see if the CDb can find us a match.' He coughed painfully as Natasha passed him some water. He checked first the door, then the carpet, then his Browning. 'The fucker took a bullet.'

'It didn't wake me.'

'That's because the gun was silenced and you were drunk. I never knew I'd curse the damn thing! I could have done with some help, even from somebody who was pissed.'

'You're bleeding . . . God, Carter, you've really been in the wars.'

'Yeah, you'll have fun picking the glass out of my flesh later.'

'Was this guy strong? A Nex?'

Carter stared with a frown at Natasha. 'Too strong,' he croaked, prodding at his windpipe. 'So much for the Utopia I dreamed about. Had to be a fucking Nex – and a big one at that. I was hoping the SAD teams had wiped them all out by now . . .'

'They'll never kill them all.' Natasha stroked Carter's cheek. 'And it looks like they still want you dead, my lover.'

'Yeah,' he grimaced, 'I'm a regular fucking hunted man.'

Music thundered, as if the Gates of Hell had been thrown wide open. Carter frowned, perched at the bottom of the stairs, smoke stinging his eyes, gazing out from this slight vantage point at the hundreds of people filling the hotel function room. After the previous night he was a touch on edge despite Spiral's reassurances that there was no Nex activity in the area. The results of the gene-coding sample had been returned negative: the attacker had not been a Nex. Just a real tough human son of a bitch.

Carter grinned nastily and searched the crowd for a large one-armed man. The Browning in his belt would sort things out if Carter happened across the intruder again . . . and the next time he wouldn't take just an arm as a trophy.

Natasha, behind him, gave him a little push.

'Come *on*, Carter, we're late.'

Carter grumbled and muttered something: something about it being too smoky, too crowded and too loud. And how he had recently been attacked and so should really be at home in bed with a hot whisky and lemon, three sugars.

'How old are you, you moaning old goat? Jesus, Carter, it's not like we go to *many* parties! Make a bloody effort or I'll break your spine.'

'Someone already tried that,' he grumbled, feeling the medical staples that Natasha had applied pull tight in the flesh of his back.

Carter watched Natasha's low-cut black dress disappear into the throng, and he followed, more sedately – like a dog on a leash, growling.

Carter blinked, then stared hard at the flamboyant and very well-presented breasts which had just bumped rudely into his chest. 'Excuse me,' came a voice slurred by High German and beer.

Carter's eyes flickered up from the impressive cleavage to a beautiful young face regarding him with positive appraisal. He shook his head, took a deep smoke-filled breath, and fought his way to the bar where he ordered a litre of Schwarz-Bier and sunk his face into its cold welcoming depths. The liquid nectar soothed his throat, soothed his brain and soothed his temper. Parties were not exactly Carter's scene; it wasn't the party *per se*, more the horde of bustling party people all with their own little agendas. Carter wasn't exactly the human race's greatest fan, and he had the word *cynicism* branded – hardwired – into his brain.

'There you are!'

Natasha twirled into view, giggling, a man on each arm. Carter, with a Schwarz-Bier moustache, frowned at her. His field-staples were hurting – he could feel the tiny pins piercing his skin and muscle – and the bruises on his throat were a testament to his recent attacker's formidable strength.

'Dancing! You coming dancing? This is Hans . . . and, and, and—'

'Mm!' grunted Carter, which translated through intonation to something considerably more rude.

Natasha took the hint, and disappeared, bump first.

Carter ordered another beer. He changed his mind, and ordered two. Then he thought: fuck it, and ordered a third, with a triple-whisky chaser. It's going to be a long night, he thought as the lights dimmed and more lasers kicked spirals of colour across the walls and beams – and the music's volume increased painfully.

'*You happy?*' came the taunting voice of Kade. Carter ignored him, ignored the tone of arrogance and deceit. '*Come on, Carter, talk to me! This is a fine place, full of fine woman flesh – look there! You see her hips? Fine child-bearing hips . . .*'

'Leave me alone,' said Carter softly.

'*But . . . Carter, I can't leave you alone, dickhead. We are brothers. And I feel I should warn you that things here are not as they seem.*'

'In what way?'

'*Ahh, that would be telling.*'

'Kade, you fuckwit, what's on your mind?'

Carter dismissed Kade with a mental surge of anger and, calming himself, leant back against the bar – good solid wood protecting his back – and watched the people around him, a tankard in his fist and a gun in his belt. Fuck Kade, he thought sourly. He was just a bad demon who'd got out of bed on the wrong side and fancied a little bit of shit-stirring as his starter.

51

Men and women gyrated in parodies of dance, as some Swiss musician massacred a song about the mountains and added GBH boot first to the tune with a happy accordion melody. Carter watched the people and the people ignored him – it was as if he wasn't there, an invisible player beyond the boundaries of these strangest of rules, this most esoteric of games. It always amused Carter: stay sober (or sober in comparison to those around you) and you could neatly sidestep the alcohol bubble; withdraw from the party sphere and allow yourself time to watch and study and fundamentally *learn* the mechanics of humankind.

The young German woman with the proud chest sidled along the bar towards him. Carter grabbed his Schwarz-Bier and was about to make a dash, but was too slow in his haste to salvage his drinks. Her talons curled around his bicep and she held him, trapped by manners, imprisoned by etiquette.

'Yes, love?'

'Ahh, English. You here to ski, yes?'

Carter looked into her eyes, saw the gleam of alcohol on her lips, eyed the painted decorative nails around his arm and swallowed hard. She was out for the kill.

'Yes, yes . . . well, snowboarding, actually.'

'Ah, the snowboarding man. Athletic! Can I buy you a drink?'

Carter eyed the three tankards and the huge glass of whisky – the kill-switch in his brain refused to trip. 'Yes, sure, don't mind if I do.' He mentally kicked himself, then caught Natasha staring at him from the dance floor and frowned at her. She gave him a broad wink and he stuck out his tongue.

Carter spent the next fifteen minutes stumbling through a broken conversation – broken because he refused to acknowledge his fluency in German, and thus allowed the poor girl to struggle with her distinctly bad English.

It was when her hand started brushing against his thigh that he made a lame excuse and, finishing his beer, headed across the dance floor and into No Man's Land.

'I'm getting a headache.'

Natasha tutted, boogying with Hans and twirling in a pirouette in front of Carter. 'Do you find me sexually pleasing to the eye, future husband and father of my child?'

'Yes, yes, but I've had enough of this. It's not my scene. I'm going out for a smoke.'

'Bad Carter.'

'Yeah, so shoot me. Every other fucker tries.'

Carter bounced from body to body and finally made the exit. Cold air hit him – crisp and fresh and exhilarating. The sky was partially clouded, but between the puffs of moonlit cotton twinkled stars brighter than crushed diamond. Carter breathed deeply, eyes closed for a moment of ultimate simple pleasure; then he pulled out a cigarette, lit the battered specimen and filled his lungs with a pleasant impurity.

He could hear the thump of the music and a cold wind blew across him, chilling his body after the sweating, heaving, dancing crowd. He enjoyed the cigarette, the beauty of the simple night air around him and the crisp stars above. Enjoyment, he decided, was something without action; without adrenalin; without the defying of death. But then – there was always an intense gratification after shooting a bad man in the face.

Slowly, teasingly, there arose a deep, distant, subsonic rumble.

Carter froze, smoke pluming around his slightly wind-chilled face, eyes narrowed.

The rumble came again, heavier, gravelly and deeply bass. Carter felt a tremor beneath his boots and his hand shot out to steady himself; and then he watched in horror as the hotel in front of him *moved*, shaking to the tune of suddenly screaming voices, and the whole world seemed to fill with a trembling roaring song as the structure thrashed backwards and forwards. The ground was shifting and flexing beneath him and Carter whirled, forgotten cigarette extinguished in the snow as he sprinted for the entrance to the party . . . which spat forth a machine-gun stream of screaming people, faces contorted in horror and fear. With a deep, climactic surge of noise the hotel buckled near its centre and part of the roof disappeared, slipping into darkness. Some of the lights went out in a domino swathe . . .

'Fuck . . .'

Carter fought his way violently through the throng of escaping, stampeding people, 'Nats!' he screamed as the rumbling continued, some Earth-giant coming awake beneath their very feet. The world was a confusion, a shaking, rumbling, heaving insanity and Carter plunged past flailing, screaming people who struggled against him, kicking and pushing, but he was fighting not to get out but to get *in* . . .

Natasha was dancing with Hans, slapping away his cheeky hands as the first tremor warned her through the soles of her boots. The smile fell from her face as somebody cried out. The ground suddenly roared beneath them, walls shaking, glass smashing from the bar and dropping from people's quake-slippery fingers. Beer washed across the floor amid broken glass and overturned furniture. As one,

54

the population of the party turned and ran, scrambling and pushing for the exit as—

Natasha blinked.

The floor opened and a jagged metre-wide scar tore towards her. With a yelp, she dragged free a concealed knife and leapt upwards, embedding the knife in a wide beech beam. It held her suspended as Hans hissed in surprise and disappeared into the gaping black cavity—

Warm air drifted up from the yawning crevasse.

Natasha blinked, licking her lips slowly, nervously.

Hans was gone.

Natasha watched, hands sweating in the sudden blast of heat, as a woman slipped, fingers clawing at the flagstone floor, and disappeared into a deep-seeming infinity of darkness. Warm air stinking of sulphur and other chemicals washed upwards over Natasha and she gagged, bile rising from her stomach, and still the rumbling moaned, then started to increase in tempo again as the crevasse – its movement halted briefly for a suspended moment in time – snaked across the ground once more in a bass-screeching zigzag of tearing stone, towards the terrified bar staff who froze like rabbis in the headlight beams of a fast-moving juggernaut . . .

'Run!' screamed Natasha, swinging her legs and leaping to the apparent safety of one crumbling uneven side of this sudden rift. The fracture crashed across the floor and the whole room seemed to tilt, to upend as the massive bar was torn, its woodwork screaming and spitting splinters like spears, whirled around in a vortex of unstoppable Earth energy and then dropped into the chasm, where it wedged tight at an angle.

The rumbling died.

People were still screaming, but this faded as the crowd fled from the chamber. The huge timber bar, stuck at an angle like a toothpick in a giant's maw, creaked in its undignified entrapment. Below it, in the darkness, Natasha could hear more screaming, one voice hysterical, another sobbing.

'Nats!'

'Carter, over here.'

Then Carter was there, his eyes wide at the jagged angular rift across the floor of the chamber, a tear in the fabric of the rock and leading – how deep? He frowned, glancing over the edge. His boots felt slippery against the loose stones.

'Nats, let's get the fuck out of here.'

More rumblings came from below the earth; the walls began to shake and the muffled sobbing increased in volume. Then the hysterical screaming suddenly cut short as the noise of impacting flesh bounced from walls of rock.

'No! Help them!' Her eyes were wide, pleading.

'Natasha! Get out of here . . .' But Carter knew that it was no use. She was too good a person to put her own safety first . . . her stubbornness was legendary and had led to a million fights. Carter grinned a bad grin: he knew a fucking lousy gig when he saw one, and the crevasse beneath him was definitely a gig to avoid . . .

Carter leapt to the edge of the precipice and kicked at the wide timber of the wedged bar; it was stuck, a ten-metre splinter length caught against a jagged fall of rock. Below, about fifteen feet into the chasm and caught on a narrow strip of rocky ledge, he could see two women clinging on for dear life, eyes streaming with tears, their revealing party dresses torn and ragged.

'Yeah, just like a fucking snowboard,' he growled, and to the cacophony of rising rumbles, the tearing of rock all around, the shaking walls and the vibrating of roof timbers Carter leapt onto the bar and slid down towards the two desperate women – descending into the darkness with its warm sulphur air currents and bad metal-rock stink.

The women's tears were flowing freely as he grabbed a hand, slippery with blood, sweat and saliva. His fingers closed around it in an iron grip and he hauled, lifted the woman in his arms and with all his strength threw her towards the top of the ragged vent . . . She was caught by Natasha's searching hands and pushed to freedom as another roar shook the room, more glasses smashed, and one of the huge ceiling beams split with a deafening crack, showering down jagged lengths of timber – and then collapsed with a tremendous scream, filling the chamber with clouds of debris and crushed stone, sending a shower of sharp rocks flying against Natasha and blocking out the light . . .

Dust engulfed Carter and he choked, balanced within the fissure of rock as everything shook around him, making him feel suddenly nauseous. With eyes streaming he steadied himself, traced the sobbing and choking noises and, reaching down, found the second woman's hand. He lifted her to him and she clung, limpet to rock, face buried in his neck, breasts heaving with panic against his chest. Holding her tight, Carter turned his face away from the dust and closed his ears to the rumbling roar of the world around him. He could feel the bar, perched treacherously and moving as if in rhythm with the shaking earth – he felt it sliding and with a sudden surge of adrenalin and an insane burst of speed and power he sprinted up the incline, boots pushing against the torn handles of beer pumps to propel himself upwards and onwards, somehow miraculously launching himself from the summit to roll, still clasping the woman, to the stone- and -glass-scattered floor. The shards bit into his hands and arms and legs, slicing him open in a dozen places.

'It's fucking collapsing!' screamed Natasha.

Carter watched the bar slide into infinity. He wiped rock dust from his eyes and felt blood flow over his hands and arms. He looked up; the shaking had increased, the whole world was shifting and moving and bucking around them as if in the throes of inebriation, of sex, and he felt pure fear. 'Get the fuck out – now,' he said calmly.

They could die in this place.

Hauling himself to his feet, and dragging the hysterical woman along with them, they sprinted for the exit and the steps leading out into the fresh air. Another beam collapsed behind them, a mushroom of dust billowing around the two Spiral operatives and smashing them with stone buckshot from this natural shotgun. Up the steps they raced and burst out gasping into the cold crisp night air—

People were screaming, sobbing, searching for friends who were missing in the huge crowd. A couple of small groups had moved away from the hotel and were staring with wide eyes, dumbstruck at this incredible disaster. A few were trying to help others, less fortunate than themselves, who had been cut by broken glass or battered by heavy falling stones.

Carter could hear helicopters and distant sirens.

He prised the woman's fingers from their grip on his body, oblivious to her whimpers of thanks. His head turned to one side and he looked up. The screams were muffled by the continuing rumbles and vibrations. The whole hotel was tilted, partly collapsed, a deformed nightmare – and then Natasha was in front of him, her stare locked with his, her face almost unrecognisable through the dust and the grime.

'You can hear it as well.'

Carter gritted his teeth, stone dust grinding between them. 'I hear nothing.'

'You can hear her screaming . . . go and help her.'

Carter took hold of Natasha's face, looked deep into her beautiful eyes. 'No, Nats – I'm here for you. And our baby . . . I'm not part of International fucking Rescue.'

'She is fucking screaming in there . . . she will die. And it will haunt your conscience for ever.'

'Damn you, Natasha, I have our family to think about now . . .'

'Go,' pleaded Natasha, 'I will be OK here . . . go and help her.'

Cursing, and rubbing hard at his eyes, Carter looked up at the collapsing hotel. Then he was running, around the side of the swaying building, staring up at smashed windows and tilted sections of stonework, heading towards the buckled main doors. They were wedged in place by off-camber walls that showered pulped masonry from torn stone arteries. Carter's snow-crusted boot persuaded the doors to open.

The lights – and the hotel power – died.

The hotel was plunged into darkness.

The rumblings of the earthquake had died down a little, and Carter paused. He could still hear the screaming, but it sounded weary now, exhausted, a wail without hope. This fired him on and he ran into the reception area where fallen beams littered his path. He glanced up, could see a little moonlight far above and suddenly a snowflake hit him in the face. More fell through this smashed hole in the centre of the hotel and Carter headed for the stairs. They were twisted like a horribly deformed limb; Carter sprinted up them, boots slipping and outstretched hands groping his way forward. As he reached the landing, there was a terrible groan and the whole mammoth staircase toppled behind him, leaving nothing but a timber-spiked black expanse filled with rising clouds of dust and twisted fists of iron.

The noise subsided slowly.

'Fucking *wonderful.*'

'*Are we having fun yet?*' whispered Kade nastily at the back of his mind.

Carter grinned, a malicious lopsided grin, and wondered if he had made the right choice . . . hmm, a tough one. Standing in the safety of the snow, or rushing headlong into a collapsing hotel?

He glanced around; without the help of the hotel lights the whole place was a maze of shadows. Carter groped his way along one wall, using the fireman's trick of pressing the back of his hand against it instead of the palm – if he met a live cable, the shock would jerk his hand away; but if he searched with his palm open then the shock would cause his fingers to spasm and grip the cable, ensuring death by electrocution.

He paused, listening, the cuts on his hands and arms stinging with that glass-grated, flesh-peeled feeling he so detested. 'Hello?' he bellowed, and tracked the sobbing by sound.

The rumbling began once more.

Carter cursed vividly.

Gentle at first, the rumbling rose as Carter sprinted along a plush carpeted corridor and towards a door from behind which the sounds had come. The walls were shaking, and Carter's teeth rattled as he tried the handle – the door was locked. He raised his boot, but the whole hotel seemed to tilt suddenly and he was sent spinning backwards, smashing against the wall and hitting the floor hard, grunting as the staples in his back pulled tight and tore through living flesh. He felt a warm rush of blood flow down his spine as he heaved himself to his feet, blinking dust from his eyes and struggling to stand upright – and he knew . . .

Knew that he did not have long.

'*The floor isn't the right way up,*' advised Kade.

'I can fucking see that, moron.'

There came a distant, frightening, nauseating crackle. Carter's nostrils twitched as they detected smoke. The earthquake's rumbling continued to increase in intensity.

He kicked down the door and waded into the darkness. But then he stopped, confused by the sight that met his gaze. A man lay atop a woman in a broad bed; she was sobbing but he was gyrating in an act of wanton sex. Carter could see the gleam of his broad back and he took in the stockings on the man's legs and his PVC outfit. Carter's head tilted to one side as dust trickled down from the destroyed ceiling above. The woman was weeping and struggling ineffectually.

'*High-class whore,*' came Kade's unwanted intrusion.

'You think I'm fucking blind?' came Carter's vitriolic reply. Then, out loud, 'I think you two need to get out of here right now.' The woman still sobbed, but the man's hand clamped over her mouth and his wild drunken stare focused on Carter.

'Fuck off. I get what I pay for.'

Carter palmed his Browning and placed a bullet in the man's calf, merging pulped muscle and shattered shin with the bed sheets. The man screamed, rolling free and bouncing to the carpet, grabbing at the gush of blood. He stared up through drug-fuelled eyes, his hands stained with his own life. 'You shot me!'

Carter's boot hammered the man's face, and he picked up the limp, moaning woman from the bed. She was naked except for knee-high boots, and she cradled herself to him as the room shook. Carter moved to the window and

61

stared down onto the decorative flagstones. Too high to jump. He moved back, into the corridor. The smell of fire was much stronger now, and without the staircase he would have to find another means of escape. Carter started to jog, near-naked woman in his arms, struggling to keep his footing on the sloping twisted floor. He could hear cries for help from the wounded man behind, bleeding in the room. 'Find your own fucking way out,' he thought simply. He reached the end of the corridor and stood staring through a huge bay window made up from lots of small panes but with only a few panels of actual glass remaining.

The rumbling ceased.

'Thank God,' Carter whispered in relief.

Rock tore and screamed, and from the window he watched the snaking crevasse appear, sucking snow from the slope directly before him and zigzagging crazily across the gardens towards the hotel. Time should have slowed but it did not, and Carter felt a sense of panic well up madly in his chest. He fought it down.

His mouth was still dry with sudden fear as the world cracked open in front of him, though.

The moaning woman shivered, cold in Carter's arms, as the mountain breeze stroked her skin. He looked down into her beautiful mascara- and tear-smeared face – her eyes opened slowly, confused, and she stared up at him, her full red lips parted slightly. Carter saw there a reflection of his own fear and a bewilderment about what was happening . . .

The sound of screaming, tearing rock filled his ears and the hotel began to sway, throwing Carter off balance. He kicked his way through the frame of the bay window, stomping its wood to match-tinder, and with a disbelieving prayer he leapt towards the snake of rapidly splitting ground.

The buzz of Air Zermatt rescue helicopters filled the air and the song of sirens rose from the valley below. They buzzed, muffled and distant, a dream.

Cold air howled past Carter, whipped at him as he fell helplessly towards the widening, speeding, zigzagging crevasse.

He closed his eyes against the horror . . .

Spiral Mainframe
Data log #12874

<u>CLASSIFIED SADt/6778/SPECIAL INVESTIGATIONS UNIT</u>
Data Request 324#12874

NEX

The Nex Project Nx5

Nicknamed 'Necros' or 'Nex', the Nx5 Project was pioneered in the 1950s as a response to the Cold War games of the USA and Russia.

The Design Brief was simple: create a creature that was a blend of insect and human, capable of withstanding chemical, biological and nuclear toxins. Using an ancient machine originally developed by the Nazis, Skein Blending allowed genetic strands to be spiralled together – woven into an artificial or enhanced creature. When the human element was kept dominant the resulting hybrid had many of the powerful characteristics of an insect. A much increased strength, agility and speed. An increased pain threshold. A resistance to chemical, biological and radioactive poisons with an incredibly enhanced immune system. Increased speed of thought processes. Some grew external and internal armour to protect organs and bones, and all became incredibly lethal killing machines without remorse. The perfect soldier, with an ability to repair themselves.

One downside was a change to the subject's mind-state. Many subjects lost all emotions, lost the ability to love, to nurture, to care. The mind became like that of an insect – sterile and completely focused on tasks.

Spiral withdrew funding following bad media coverage, several laboratory catastrophes and a growing concern over the moral standpoint.

Keyword SEARCH>> NEX, SAD, SPIRAL_sadt, DURELL, FEUCHTER, QIII, Spiral_NX

CHAPTER 3

SEARCH AND DESTROY

Jam and Mongrel stood outside the wide H2 military-green metal-studded door, their faces long, sulking like naughty schoolboys waiting outside the headmaster's office. They exchanged glances, and Jam wrapped his long leather coat more tightly around his shoulders as if this thick black skin was armour; a temporary protective exoskeleton.

'You ask him.'

Mongrel frowned, his naturally brooding Slavic features positively hangdog now. 'I ain't asking him.'

'It's your fucking turn.'

'But you *know* what that big dumb bastard said!'

'Yeah, he said he wouldn't give us any more ammo, and if we came back to ask for more he might just shove it up our arses. *That*'s what the bastard said. I just don't know if he was joking or not – you know, playing around in a friendly sort of fashion, or meaning it in an evil-bastardy sort of fashion. You know Simmo!' Jam scowled, seemingly unsure of himself.

'*Da*, I know him – and I know he fucking unpredictable.'

They both stared at the wide metal door. The plastic plaque screwed into the steel read: SGT SIMMO – STORES. Such a simple epithet, and yet one which had repercussions throughout the whole of Spiral_H, including the different H2, H3 and H4 divisions. In the same way that a secretary could run a school, the guard on a front gate could run a whole electronics corporation, or an air-traffic controller could coordinate an entire airport – so the nasty shaven-headed squaddie in charge of the stores could run the whole of Spiral.

Sort of.

Sgt Simmo was in charge of weapons, ammunition, gadgets, motorbikes, trucks, tanks and helicopters. If you needed something, you had to see Sgt Simmo. If you needed something in an emergency, you still had to see Sgt Simmo. And always, always, always . . . you had to sign for it in triplicate.

'Just follow my lead, pussy,' said Jam, and pushed the door open with a gentleness uncommon for the large killer.

Mongrel, muttering insults, followed Jam into the gloomy office which fronted the huge maze of warehouse stores containing a billion items of equipment. The office shouldn't have been gloomy – it was painted a bright military green, and had plenty of lighting. But something sinister nevertheless created an ominous murky half-light which one could only attribute to the personification of fear in the very air itself, lurking like the bad after-smell of a poisoned curry.

'He's not here,' said Jam, breathing a sigh of relief. 'Fucking horny old goat probably shagging Mrs Spud.'

Sgt Simmo rose from behind the counter, like a glacier sliding ominously into view. He was a mammoth hulk, a man-mountain with a shaved head, black goatee beard, fearsome bushy eyebrows, and the terrible narrowed eyes of a killer. He weighed in at around twenty-four stone and his barrel chest was just that. He insisted on wearing urban combats, even in desert or jungle combat situations. When asked why, he always replied, 'Wouldn't want to fucking blend in, would I?' even thought that, apparently, was the point. His arms, hands, neck and any other bare visible skin was heavily tattooed with lists and military script, and he grinned a nasty missing-toothed grin that told of a life of brawling in pubs.

Mongrel, who was a huge man himself, seemed dwarfed as Simmo reared up from behind that counter.

'What wrong with Mrs Spud?' rumbled Simmo.

'Nothing, nothing,' murmured Mongrel, reading the list of men that Simmo had killed that was tattooed on his throat with ticks against each name. Mongrel always read that list. It went: McGibbon, Dike, Hando, Pilchard, Begbie, Twat-57, Fat Bob Smith . . . and then trailed off into drunken tattoo smush which Simmo would never explain. Not that Mongrel asked, but he knew that if he *was* to ask then an explanation would be forthcoming – in a violent wide-fisted sort of way.

'Mrs Spud is fine lady friend of The Sergeant,' growled Simmo, frowning like an eyebrow avalanche, 'Mrs Spud, as well as cooking fine fish and chips in canteen and always giving The Sergeant his daily feed for free, also gives damn fine good blow job at no extra cost. There no feeling on this world that her false teeth not conjure, so don't you fucking be disrespecting Mrs Spud or The Sergeant be very angry man!' His voice had risen to a roar.

Mongrel was looking down, kicking his size thirteen polished boots against the bottom of the counter, guiltily. 'Sorry, Sarge,' he muttered. 'Really, really – sorry.'

Simmo deflated a little as Jam pushed Mongrel out of the way with a tut and slapped his hand on the counter. He beamed up at Sgt Simmo with the sort of insane wide-faced innocence that had deceived many enemies and sent them to their graves.

'Hi there, Simmo old buddy,' said Jam. 'Listen.' He leaned in close, much to the obvious distaste of Simmo. 'This – um – Mrs Spud . . .'

'Yes?'

'You and her – you a bit of an item then, or what?'

Simmo stared at Jam with eyes that had watched one thousand, four hundred and seventy-two men scream at the point of death.

'Yes,' he rumbled. 'That a problem for you?'

'No no no!' Jam beamed. 'Listen, hey man, it's your choice, she has a fine set of, um, cheeks, I'm sure, and those muscles in her square jaw surely must mean that she does what you said earlier, give a man a good BJ, and I'm sure that when she sits on your fucking face and pisses it gives you a happy warm glow inside – but hey, I need some fucking ammo and our Comanche leaves in five fucking minutes. So be a good lad, and open the fucking gate.'

Jam grinned up at Simmo.

Simmo's fists had clenched. Then he relaxed, deflating once more, and leered at Jam with teeth that had stripped the flesh from a dead comrade's thighs to keep a battle-weary Simmo from starving in the field. He laughed then, an explosion of rattling sound like bones in a tin can, which only confirmed in Jam's mind that The Sergeant was not used to laughing.

Simmo hit the buzzer, there was – predictably – a buzz and the huge iron gate behind him unlocked.

'Thank you,' said Jam, checking his watch.

'I know you only fuck with The Sergeant.' The huge soldier grinned and as Jam strode past a hand the size of a shovel slapped him on the back, nearly sending his face through the iron gate.

Jam coughed, and forced a laugh.

'Yeah, just fucking with you.'

Sgt Simmo frowned. 'You have three minutes. Get what you need and return here for the paperwork.'

'Will do.'

Mongrel followed Jam through the gate and into a wide strip-lit corridor that led on for as far as the eye could see. Doors and gates opened off this central corridor, feeding into hangars and testing stations, into firing ranges and mock terrorist positions; into stores filled with everything from 9mm clips to torpedoes and tank shells.

They headed for the ammunition warehouse, but on the way Jam suddenly stopped at an unmarked door. 'Hey, Mongrel, come take a look at this.' Jam pointed at the unmarked military-green door, which looked just like so many of the other military-green doors.

'I do not think we should,' said Mongrel uneasily.

'Come on, don't be a pussy!'

'Simmo might be watching,' whispered Mongrel.

'Fuck him!'

'Shh! He might hear!'

'Ahh, fuck him. Come on, you need to see this . . .' And Jam was already pushing open the green portal leading into a monumental underground chamber with a dirty stone floor and bare rocky walls stretching off into the distance. The lights were dim, and Mongrel squinted in the gloom as the door slammed shut behind him. A heavy boom echoed through the chamber, making Mongrel jump.

'What is it?'

'Over here,' said Jam, heading off across the dust. Mongrel followed, frowning. He could see nothing and such a huge chamber would not normally be wasted on empty space. Spiral never wasted space. He followed Jam's footprints in the dirt.

'I thought you only had five minutes?'

'Nah, Slater is still in bed and TT is getting our food supplies – funnily enough, from Mrs Spud. TT has a way with Spud. What about you – when do you leave?'

'About an hour.'

Jam nodded, chewing his lip thoughtfully. 'You off to Africa again?'

'Yeah. Nigeria.'

'We're paying a trip to Slovenia; we have a lead there. A hot lead, should see us shave a few more pounds from the Nex. Fry the fuckers and kill the pig, that's what I say. Always did have a thing for bacon.'

Jam halted in front of something covered with a huge green tarpaulin, grabbed a corner, and heaved. The tarpaulin rolled free, revealing the huge bulk of a tank, gleaming dully under a coat of fresh black paint and looking very big, very menacing, and very deadly.

'A tank,' said Mongrel, wholly unimpressed. 'Jam, I have lot of work to do before I head for Africa, I really think . . .'

'Look *closely*,' whispered Jam, placing a hand almost reverently against the flank of the mammoth metal beast. Jam was dwarfed beside the tracks, which rose to the height of his head.

Mongrel frowned, and was about to say something when he noticed the tracks. They looked somehow – wrong. That would never work, Mongrel thought. Then it clicked.

'An HTank?'

'Prototype,' breathed Jam, eyes gleaming. 'Beautiful, ain't she?'

The HTank was a tank so advanced that it made the most modern military models look no better than the French Char d'Assaut Schneider, the early prototype that had failed in the muddy battlefields of the First World War.

It was an HTank, a Hover Tank – with the ability to hover over obstacles, using the most advanced turbo-track matrix-fission engine and track displacements. If the HTank reached a near-vertical wall? The huge beast would tilt its nose to the sky and climb almost vertically with the aid of its colossally powerful engines. And it had a few other tricks up its sleeve . . .

Jam patted the machine, gazing up at it almost adoringly. 'You wondering why it's black?' He waggled his eyebrows in that cocky, cheeky way only Jam could manage, grinning at Mongrel's obvious frown.

'Go on, Jam, why it black?'

'It's not.'

'Da, it is. *Look*,' said Mongrel.

'No, it's not,' said Jam, grinning more widely.

'How that, then?'

'It's a CamCloak.' Jam paused, for effect more than anything, and Mongrel's frown deepened as he shifted from one boot to the other, obviously nervous at the prospect of getting caught by the humourless psycho who was Simmo.

'Jam, we not supposed to be in here!'

'Don't be a bean.'

'Jam!'

'Go on.'

'Go on what?'

'Ask me.'

'Ask you what?'

Jam tutted, running a hand through his short but growing black hair, which had been pampered and nurtured and had broken many a lady's heart. Often he would get grief from the other Spiral operatives – along the philosophical lines of 'Jam, you poof' and 'You look like a fucking girl, get a haircut.' But Jam always put forward the argument that his current locks got him laid, and for that fact alone they deserved respect.

'About the CamCloak, you dumb-spud monkey.'

'Go on, then, but make it quick. I got suspicion Sgt Simmo will be looking for us and waiting for us, and he will not be happy that we go snooping into classified military equipment . . .'

'Instead of just painting the tank, the CamCloak will replicate any environment at the press of a button; you want advanced blending, you got it. The HTank can operate in hostile terrain almost invisibly. And its weapons systems! Fuck, don't get me started on the weapons systems! They—'

'Jam, I going for ammo. Simmo will be really pissed off.'

'Aw, fuck 'im!'

Mongrel retreated, and with a final longing glance at the HTank prototype Jam followed Mongrel across the dusty floor, their boots leaving imprints. A hundred security cameras tracked their slow departure.

Laden with canvas sacks of ammunition in a variety of calibres, Jam and Mongrel made their way along the long straight corridor and paused at the iron gate. They waited, and then Jam peered through between the bars to where Sgt Simmo was seated at the high desk, a sheaf of papers in front of him, his finger poised delicately above something that had captured his attention.

Jam coughed.

There was no response.

Jam coughed again, this time louder.

Slowly, Sgt Simmo turned his huge bullet head on his thick bull neck, which spilled over the collar of his urban-combat jacket, and glared at the two men. Then, casually and without obvious hurry, he reached over and hit the release, which buzzed in an annoying fashion.

Jam and Mongrel stepped through this magic portal, their bags of bullets clanking as they paused in front of the desk and Simmo's raised bushy eyebrows. He grinned at them. It was a particularly nasty grin.

'We need to sign?' asked Jam softly.

'Oh yes,' crooned Simmo. 'In triplicate, on the correct military forms.' He pushed forward the thick pad and Jam stared with distaste at the stains. He took the pen on its industrial-grade chain and leaned forward.

'What the fuck is that?' snapped Jam, pointing.

'Chocolate.'

'You sure?'

'I very sure,' growled Simmo.

'And that? There! What the fuck is that?'

'That is blood,' said Simmo quietly, his rumble like the distant detonation of a nuclear device.

Jam met the large sergeant's eyes. 'How did you manage to get *blood* on your triplicate signing-out book?'

'Man refused to sign,' growled Simmo. 'Called me pedantic triplicate-signing paper-pushing motherfucker. So I stabbed him through hand with pen. Look, there is nick in wood where pen got stuck. It very messy. Got one of tendons wrapped around the nib.'

'Ahh, nice.'

Jam reached forward to sign. He signed.

'In triplicate,' said Simmo.

'Yeah, yeah.' Jam signed twice more.

'And him,' said Simmo, nodding at Mongrel.

Mongrel sighed. 'What you do if there was nuclear war and we had to urgently get whole battalion's ammunition in few short seconds because HQ about to be overrun?'

'You would have to sign in triplicate on the correct military forms. For every item.'

'But you have nuclear bombs blasting overhead, room shaking, lights flickering, nuclear fire screaming across landscape . . .'

Simmo stared hard at Mongrel. 'You would have to sign in triplicate on the correct military forms,' he said without any sign of emotion on his face, without any indication of humour, without any suggestion of anything other than consummate military professionalism.

'Come on.' Jam grinned, patting Mongrel on the back. 'You can see me off at the hangar.'

Mongrel nodded, and they trooped towards the door. Just as Jam reached for the handle, Simmo's low growl echoed across to the two men and made them freeze.

'Just one question, soldiers.'

Jam and Mongrel exchanged glances. 'Told you so!' hissed Mongrel, and turned with an unaccustomed beaming smile across his battered wide face. Jam turned, dropping the canvas sacks and placing his hands on his hips.

'Sarge?'

'You enjoy looking at my little toy?'

'You mean the HTank?' Jam nodded, and pulled out a cigarette, lighting it and inhaling deeply. Through a plume of smoke he said, 'Yeah, nice little piece of kit. Impressive CamCloak, and fucking thick armour, hey?'

'Nice machine,' rumbled Simmo, eyes gleaming.

'What you mean, "your" little toy?' said Mongrel.

74

'Is mine.'

'I . . . I thought it belong to Spiral.' Mongrel smiled carefully.

Simmo shook his bullet head. 'No. 'S mine.'

'You mean it's your HTank,' laughed Jam. 'As in, ownership documentation is stamped in *your* name, you have full financial possession, the HTank does in fact *belong* to you.'

'No. But it still mine.'

'OK, OK. Look, Sarge, it's a very nice tank. We were very impressed. Is it operational yet?'

'Only on The Sergeant's say-so,' rumbled Simmo.

'Whatever you say, buddy.' Jam grinned, placing the cigarette between his lips, squinting through the smoke, picking up his ammo and leading Mongrel to the door. As he was stepping through the portal, he turned. 'One last thing – if I ever need back-up, I'll be sure not to give you a fucking call.'

Simmo scowled, but Jam and Mongrel had gone.

Spiral Mainframe
Data log #12522

CLASSIFIED SADt/6345/SPECIAL INVESTIGATIONS UNIT
Data Request 324#12522

SAD

Search and Destroy Missions

When Durell and Feuchter's warship, currently tagged as Spiral_mobile, was destroyed, hundreds of genetically enhanced Nex soldiers were also destroyed. However,

even without the guidance of their masters –
the true enemies of Spiral – the Nex had a
network of systems in place across the globe
which enabled them to continue operations
and pose a minimal threat to Spiral agencies
worldwide.

SAD missions were instigated: teams of
DemolSquads whose mission objectives for the
past year had been to search out and
completely destroy Nex nests and relevant
minor military outposts.

The SAD missions have been extremely
successful in minimising current threat from
the Nex. Although all the Nex soldiers have
not been destroyed, intelligence shows that
they have almost been terminated. They are
currently running at a 4% strength when
compared to infestation numbers this time
last year.

Most recent find:
Brazil, 18km east of Humaita
Team:
Jam, Slater, TT [Demol12]
Nex destroyed:
40 genetically altered soldiers

Current SAD team leader: Jam [Demol_H]

Keyword SEARCH>> NEX, SAD, SPIRAL_sadt,
DURELL, FEUCHTER

*

The Hangar was huge, housing perhaps a hundred helicopters of different configurations and eight SX7 Harrier
Jump Jets. Jam, Slater and TT stood, staring out at the
rain beyond the corrugated walls and waiting for the
Comanche pilot to arrive. They all carried huge canvas
sacks – clothing, provisions for their operation in the
former Yugoslavia, guns and, of course, ammunition.
Slater had already overseen the loading of three KTM
800Vi motorcycles, which had been strapped unceremoniously beneath the Comanche in lieu of missiles, and all
the group needed now was a pilot.

Jam smoked, watching the rain and listening to Slater
and TT's idle banter. Slater was a huge man whom Jam
had fought with on many occasions and who reminded
him a little of Mongrel – both were tufty-haired and
sported missing teeth from too many NAAFI brawls, and
both took shit from no man. But whereas Mongrel was
pure animal, very much in the mould of Sgt Simmo,
Slater had more of a philosophical air, although it took a
lot to get to know that side of him, and in truth it only
rarely appeared after seventeen pints of lager.

TT, on the other hand, was a complete contrast. She
was ex-Sniper squad and had moved sideways to the
Demolition Teams, or DemolSquads as they were affectionately known. Tall, lithe and muscular, she was
extremely reserved and aloof, rarely speaking unless it
had to do with work. She had high cheekbones and short
blood-red hair, pale blue eyes, and full lips hiding neat
little teeth. She was oblivious to Jam's charms – much to
his consternation – but had proved herself on many occasions with her skill with a rifle and telescopic sight.

'You OK, Jam?'

'Mmm,' he said, flicking his cigarette butt out into the
rain and watching the heavy downpour destroy the filter.

Jam turned, gave Slater a small grin, then said, 'You check the SAD records? I have – just for my own personal amusement, you understand.'

Slater nodded. 'Current statistics show Nex strength running at just four per cent of this time last year when . . . well, when you blew their warship to Kingdom Come.'

'Ahh, the old bomb in the bag,' said Jam, his eyes hard. 'Makes you come over all warm and gooey inside. What the fuck does four per cent represent, anyway?'

'Statistics,' mumbled Slater. 'There are no current numbers . . .'

'Fucking suits and their fucking statistics,' snarled Jam. 'Real figures would had been more use – not four fucking per cent! What's four per cent of an unspecified amount? Jesus! Now, this is our chance to take out a few more unfortunates . . . drop it to two per cent of whatever, eh, mate?'

'Jam . . . better be careful we don't become complacent.'

Jam winked. 'Hah! We eat the fuckers for breakfast nowadays.'

Acting on tip-offs and local military intelligence, Jam, Slater and TT were due to investigate claims of a relatively small Nex 'nest' in Slovenia, close to a village named Trebija. The Brazil6 SAD mission had been the most recent large 'find', and SAD missions were becoming more and more infrequent and thus required fewer and fewer resources from Spiral. A large nest would entail complex military missions with interlocking paths from anything from three to twenty DemolSquads; but for a small gig like this? Jam was happy to do it on his own.

'Probably be nothing. Rice or something on their scanners,' growled Slater.

'You're so pessimistic,' said Jam, lighting another cigarette and cursing himself. He was trying – very
unsuccessfully and at the request of Nicky, his wife-to-
be – to quit. He inhaled the deep blue smoke and slapped
Slater on the back, having to stand on tiptoe to do it
despite his own six feet of height. 'Anyway, you haven't
told me yet if you're coming to my wedding!'

'I have to check my diary,' said Slater.

'You still sulking because I asked Carter to be my best
man?'

'No,' said Slater sulkily.

'Come on, buddy, you know I've been friends with
Carter since fucking kindergarten. We've done some shit
together, fought some fucking battles, been through some
real hard times. And I know you and me are friends, but
you have to accept my decision like a real man, not sulk
like an arse . . .'

'It's just . . .'

'What?'

TT sidled closer, a smile across her full pouting lips.

'It's just . . .'

'Spit it out, man,' snapped Jam.

'He thinks if he's the best man it'll help him pull one of
the bridesmaids, get him a bit of pussy for a drunken
night of debauchery with fruit, or whatever it is that rubs
Slater up the right way.'

'Thanks, TT,' spat Slater, reddening.

'Don't worry.' Jam winked, slapping the huge soldier
on the back again. 'If it is a bit of pussy you're wanting,
then Jam is the man to . . . to . . .' He stared hard at TT.
'What? What's that look?'

TT ran a hand through her cropped hair, then
smoothed her eyebrows which were immaculately
plucked. 'Do you realise that I went to prep school with

79

Nicky?' she said softly. 'We shared a dorm, were very good friends, in fact.'

Jam stared hard at her.

'We used to have midnight feasts, sneak out into the village and meet the boys, got up to all sorts of mischief – me and your soon-to-be wife.' She smiled sweetly at Jam.

'You're fucking with me, right?'

'Not at all.'

'Stop it, because you *are* fucking with me.'

'Why would I lie? You know I'm friends with Nicky, you've seen me talking to her enough times. We joined up together.'

'She never told me that.'

'Why would she? Do you know *everything* about your woman?' She gave a very dark smile. 'Because I doubt it very much, Mr Jam. But the things she has told me about you!'

The pilot chose that moment to arrive. He was a slim man, with bright eager eyes and the disposition of a puppy: always eager to please. He wore his hair long and generously curled like a middle-aged pop star or footballer, and it lapped around his shoulders, buoyed on a current of air, hairspray and expensive Italian conditioners. To Fenny, Hair Was Life. Which was why it had been with great irony that God had made this man bald at the crown – this Deity of Hair, this ultimately vain and narcissistic male of the species. And Jam secretly knew that if Fenny had decided to shun his flamboyant locks, to cast aside his self-love and hair-lacquer abuse, then God would have shown forgiveness and allowed him the mane of a lion.

God punishes those who punish themselves, he mused.

'Hiya, Fenny,' grinned Jam, slapping the pilot on the

back and watching with obvious amusement as his tresses bobbed – as if he were auditioning for a TV advert for the ultimate prodigal pelt.

Fenny carried his HIDSS helmet under one arm and surveyed the group with a convivial and easygoing gaze. This and other friendly characteristics had earned him many friends among Spiral, despite his love of getting drunk and pouring his pint into soldiers' laps.

'Your team going to Slovenia, Jam, you womanising old scoundrel?'

'Yeah,' drawled Jam.

'I think you'll find that there's lots of suspected Nex activity in the city of Ljubljana.'

'Possibly.' Jam grinned, his arm still draped around Fenny's shoulders. 'But I think you will find that it isn't enemy territory until we turn it into enemy fucking territory. Now, I have a question for you, my old friend.'

'Yeah?'

'Well, I don't want you to become tetchy, but every time I see you I always ask myself the question: why don't you shave off your curls? Get a good Number One, sorted.' Jam puffed at his cigarette.

Fenny looked a little confused.

'Why would I do that? Why would I want a . . . ugh . . . a *shaved* head?'

Jam spluttered. 'Well, mate, it's just your curls . . .'

'Yeah?'

'And, and . . . the curls bobbing, and the hairspray . . . it makes you . . . makes your curls . . . like . . . with their bobbing . . .'

'Yes?' Fenny was grinning broadly but with an iron twinkle in his eyes.

'If he had a pint, I'd choose this moment to take a step back,' rumbled Slater. He had walked home from the

NAAFI on too many evenings with a wet beer-stinking crotch and a strand of stray curl caught between his knuckles where Fenny had been too swift and elusive to suffer Slater's left hook.

'Well,' continued the politically inept Jam, 'I just thought you looked a bit, y'know, like a mad clown.'

'Leave him be,' said TT, sidling over. She pushed Jam aside and planted a large kiss on Fenny's lips, making the pilot grin even more broadly. 'I like the curls. Reminds me of—'

'A poodle?' suggested Jam.

'No, a real rock star,' crooned TT. And she slapped Fenny's behind. 'Now, are we mounting up and shipping out into the rain, or are we going to stand here all day and exchange pleasantries?'

'Always the spoilsport,' sighed Jam.

Fenny climbed into the cockpit and engaged the engines. Jam and Slater grinned at each other, as TT muttered, 'You guys are just so savage – you gang up on people and try to tear them apart . . .'

'Me?' squawked Slater.

'Ha,' said Jam. 'That's just fucking life.'

They followed Fenny and climbed into the Comanche's modified cockpit. As a war machine, the originally specced USA Comanche could only carry two pilots, whilst the Spiral Comanche VQ7s had a host of modifications to bring them in line with the requirements of anti-terrorism operations.

Once its occupants were settled, the Comanche leapt into the air, slicing up through the rain with the satisfying roar of twin LHTec engines, leaping into the darkened iron bruise of clouds and heading south, away from the nearby city of London and towards the dark churning mass of the English Channel. Fenny's curls bobbed from the exposed rim of the HIDSS helmet in time with the howling engines.

Southern Europe was still warm at this time of year, the sun beating down from a cloudless late-autumn sky. The Comanche landed in a remote mountain location, trees whipping and bowing under the onslaught of the war machine's rotors.

Jam, Slater and TT climbed free, stretching wearily after the insane strike across the English Channel, France, Germany and Italy. They walked through long grass, ducking beneath the idling rotors, dragging their kit and piling it beneath a large cherry tree. Slater moved off to release the KTM 800Vi motorcycles from beneath the Comanche as Jam lit a cigarette, checked the magazine on his SA1000 and walked out beyond their LZ, a hand shading his eyes. He propped his SA1000 against his thigh as he peered off into the hazy distance. He was sweating within seconds of landing under his heavy clothing, and his gaze took in the steep slopes leading to woodland and distant villages of white buildings with red-tiled roofs – a mountainous landscape of jagged grey peaks filled with a fluid beauty of deep green and the distant glimmers of a winding river.

Jam coughed on his cigarette smoke, his mind settling into a businesslike mode now that he was here on the ground, ready for work and ready for the killing to begin. His lips tightened as he thought of all the friends he had lost at the hands of the Nex; many good men and women, cut in half with machine-gun bullets, throats slit, limbs strewn around after massive terrible detonations. The war had become personal, and so Jam's hatred was personal – he would hunt the Nex to the ends of the earth and slaughter them in their sleep.

Slater approached. 'We're rocking.'

Turning, they watched the Comanche roar and leap into the air, huge rotors glinting in the sun, camouflaged flanks gleaming dully as the huge machine hovered for a moment, banked, and disappeared with a high-powered engine whine. The trees settled, the late-summer scents of the woods and the cherry trees drifting across to the small DemolSquad. The grass hissed in the breeze as Jam cocked his SA1000.

'Time for business,' he said.

Darkness was falling as Jam slowed the KTM on the winding unmetalled stone-littered road which sliced between woodland trails. Tyres crunched, skidding a little on the loose stone, and TT and Slater pulled up close behind him. The three bikes burbled quietly, their 800cc engines ticking over, stealth exhausts electronically stealing any sounds the machines might make and so rendering them, to all intents and purposes, silent.

'Everything OK?'

Jam said nothing. He sat, eyes surveying the incline ahead of him. Heavy woodland, conifers, beech and spruce sloped away to either side, their bases covered with the detritus of a hundred years of fallen branches and leaves. The Spiral operatives watched a deer, brown with soft white spots, wander aimlessly and pause, its head coming up to gaze at them with large oval brown eyes before it sprinted off between the trees, disappearing like a drifting ghost.

Jam gave the military hand signal for silence.

They waited, Jam watching the trail, eyes slowly scanning the tree line ahead and to either side where thick boles were scattered. Perfect ambush territory, his brain was telling him. Perfect . . .

84

With the unclenching of his fist they moved off, slower now, more warily. Something had spooked Jam, and Slater had known his friend long enough to trust the man's instincts. A drinking hedonistic womaniser he might be, but there were two things he was certainly good at: killing and, more importantly, keeping his men – and women – alive. It was an unspoken talent. A gift.

They cruised, moving higher into the mountain pass, the roads becoming more and more pronounced as Vs of worn stone shrapnel, the slopes steeper and more rugged, the trails more and more disused. As darkness fell Jam pulled to the side of the trail where a footpath or deer trail of some kind crossed the rough stone road. Jam pulled his bike onto the trail and, ducking branches which whipped against their faces and heavy canvas combat jackets, they rode through the woods until they came to a huge natural outcropping of massive boulders, some larger than a house and balanced precariously on one another to form a natural wall. Jam pulled his bike up underneath an overhang of rock, beneath a boulder so big that it would crush the three Spiral operatives like insects if it fell. Jam killed his engine, and Slater and TT followed suit. They dismounted, warily, and unslung their weapons, Jam his SA1000, Slater his trusty double-barrelled shotgun with machine-gun modifications, and TT her Barrett IV sniper rifle with digital sights.

They made a cold camp, seating themselves on a huge log which Slater dragged laboriously into the small clearing, and Jam spun his ECube into life. Dropping it in front of him it halted, spinning a few inches above the ground on a cold cushion of matrix. Tiny sections opened from the alloy chassis and a projection spread like liquid across the ground – a contoured map of their surroundings optically linked to the advanced AGPS signals that the ECube was intercepting.

Jam picked up a stick and poked at the green and blue image. 'We're here.' He lit a cigarette.

Slater, who had opened a huge tin of B&S and was shovelling the fodder into his maw cold, nodded in agreement and pointed with his fork. 'The white blobs signify intelligence sightings?'

'Aye. If we cross-section them it gives us quite a narrow field of operations – if you consider the contours of the terrain. If, for example, we give them the benefit of the doubt and assume that they are using bikes like us – then there are only limited paths open to them. Even less so if they are using larger, heavier vehicles.'

'You want to go in on foot?' asked TT.

Jam nodded. 'We'll take it more carefully from here on in.'

They moved with the precision and care of hunters. Slowly, deliberately, examining all the data available to them. Through the darkness the trio moved, in a wide tri-angular formation where they could provide one another with covering arcs of fire if necessary, but not so close that a single grenade or burst of machine-gun fire could take the whole team out.

They climbed the steep woodland incline, Jam at the apex of the triangle, leading the way forward, ECube set to max and scanning the environment for electronic trip mechanisms or mines or any of a hundred other devices that would give away their position.

Jam halted, dropping to one knee.

Somewhere in the distance, an animal rustled in the woods. Jam wiped a sheen of sweat from his forehead – his combats were heavy and the still woodland air was humid in comparison to the UK at this time of year. This, combined with the mountain inclines, was really making Jam and the rest of the DemolSquad work for their money.

The ECube flashed a warning – not with lights, for lights could be detected by the enemy, but with a high-frequency laser designed so that only Jam's eye could match the frequency and see anything there at all . . . Slater and TT, highly tuned to Jam's lead, dropped to one knee also and scanned their surroundings. Jam turned, giving the signal for optical tripwires – very advanced, and regular tactical favourites of the Nex. Slater and TT focused their own ECubes and they stepped silently over the traps.

Closing in, Jam thought grimly, and slipped free the safety on his SA1000.

They moved through the dark woods. More inclines passed beneath their boots, until finally the land began to level out before dipping away through sparse trees towards a small wooden hut built from rough-hewn logs and with an old moss-corroded red-tile roof The windows were blacked out and Jam could detect no sounds, even with the ECube's aural enhancers – but that did not mean that the hut was empty. Switching to thermal scanning, the ECube detected four bodies within the hut – and one seated just outside.

Jam squinted.

Motherfucker, he thought as he finally clocked the guard – a sniper – perched in a tiny hide of leaves and twigs, completely concealed from view. Jam, moving with extreme care, signalled to TT and she crawled forward on her belly and gently released the bipod, resting her silenced Barrett against the soft loamy ground.

Leaves and twigs sprang into view, and she zoomed in on the potential threat. She spotted him easily, for he was a Nex and had copper eyes. Always a give-away, she thought grimly. He was bearing a sniper rifle but did not have it trained on the surroundings.

'Lazy,' she muttered to herself as she squeezed the Barrett's trigger. There came the tiniest of hisses, then a rustle of dry leaves as the Nex guard was taken through the throat – and vocal cords – and sent rolling to one side, blood leaking to feed the tree roots, mouth working in a silent scream of pain, fingers scrabbling at the bullet wound. The second bullet smashed through the Nex's forehead, killing him instantly.

Jam gave the thumbs-up and they closed warily on the cabin. Jam's plan was simple – an MNK, or MindNuke, turned up on full and launched through the window. It would explode silently, and with no flash – and would scramble the brains of anybody within a twenty-five-metre radius. The MNK had different settings and could be used to take out harmless targets with what was affectionately called a 'fry-up'; the DemolSquads had found that on full power the MindNukes were particularly deadly against Nex, whose insect-blending made them almost impervious to bullet wounds unless an accurate head-shot was secured. As DemolSquad members had found the hard way, Nex were very, very tough in one-on-one combat; they felt little or no pain. MNKs evened the odds a little . . .

They halted, and Jam readied the weapon, twisting the two halves of the small silver globe. Having set it, he signalled to his companions and, his SA1000 gripped in one hand, crept through the meagre woodland towards the darkened cabin.

They're asleep, he thought.

Too easy?

Never look a gift horse in the mouth . . .

He reached the wall, his gloved hand resting lightly

against the rough bark of the timbers. He glanced back through the darkness and could just make out TT and Slater, scanning arcs, checking for enemies with ECubes primed and eyesight set to maximum overdrive. Jam eased himself up the wall and peered through the glass. He saw nothing but a small storeroom – but that was perfectly adequate for his needs. He placed the ECube against the glass and there was the tiniest of tinkling noises as a small rectangle of glass was sucked free. Then he pushed the MNK through the hole – and ran for it . . .

Skidding to a halt in the branches, he glanced back.

The DemolSquad sensed rather than heard the MNK detonate; a ripple seemed to pulse through the woods and they all shivered, aware of the damage that these silent and devastating weapons could cause. Then, standing and checking ECubes once more for enemy activity, they strode towards the cabin. Jam kicked the door down and moved forward with his SA1000 primed. The four Nex were dead in their beds, faces twisted in agony, dark copper eyes weeping blood onto their pillows. Jam poked one in the face with the SA1000's barrel and turned to Slater, his mouth opening to congratulate the large warrior on a job well done, a nest destroyed without casualty or even conflict—

A gunshot rang out.

TT was picked up and flung against Slater, her chest exploding to splatter strips of ragged flesh against the huge man, her eyes wide and her mouth spewing blood. Jam leapt forward as a second shot rang out, slapping into the back of TT's lolling head even as her weight carried Slater to the ground. He grunted as he hit the earth of the cabin floor, face to face with his companion, his friend, a woman who had saved his life on several occasions . . . Her eyes were wide, her gaze confused, blood pouring from her mouth to wash over Slater and sting his eyes and drench his hair and jacket.

Her hands were clawed, grasping Slater's combat jacket, but the fingers slowly went slack and Jam stepped over the two sprawled figures with a look of anger and hatred and disgust on his face. He opened up on full automatic, the SA1000's bullets strafing across the woodland in front of him, steel slivers screaming and howling between the trees, kicking sparks from the distance, splintering timber from boles and sending a dark figure suddenly sprinting for cover—

'Slater!' he bellowed.

'I'm with you,' grunted Slater, rolling TT to one side and grasping his shotgun in blood-slippery hands. He paused for a moment, looking down at her partially destroyed face and the pulp of mashed skull. He sighed, deep inside, and spat out her blood – which stained his teeth and run down his throat – onto the dusty floor.

Jam and Slater sprinted through the darkened woods, grim now, faces drawn with bitterness and need. A need to kill. They flicked their ECubes to *pursuit shell* – audible warnings would inform them of an attack from any direction, or other threats such as mortars, mines or approaching tanks.

And the two men put all their efforts into a hot pursuit through the woods . . .

The gunman was fast – incredibly fast.

Jam paused, Slater almost cannoning into his back, and they caught their breaths, their eyes scanning the steep decline ahead of them, leading down through a stand of trees to what appeared to be a narrow stream bed filled with leaves and old broken branches.

They heard the gunman crunch his way free, scrambling up the opposite bank.

Both men opened fire, bullets whining down the hill and embedding in the earth with dull impact sounds. Slater's shotgun barked out devastating shells that tore bark from trees, and the SA1000 hammered savagely. They paused, sweat rolling down their faces in the humid night.

A muffled engine growl sounded as a bike kicked into life. Jam cursed.

They set off, sprinting once more, down the steep slope and then up the other side; the engine noise was loud, but stuttering, an off-road bike of some kind. Jam reached the top of the slope first, launched himself forward on his belly across the branches and leaves and took aim. The bike was weaving between trees and bouncing off unseen obstacles in the gloom. Jam squeezed off a three-round burst. Then another. Then another—

The bike's engine suddenly screamed, its rubber tyres exploded and the whole machine flipped into the air, cannoning into a tree and depositing the gunman dazed on the ground with the smashed bike on top of him. The engine died and the wheels spun, clicking. Jam leapt up and with Slater close behind him sprinted towards the stricken rider who heaved the fallen bike and turned a sub-machine gun on his pursuers—

All hell broke loose as bullets ripped through the woodland. Jam and Slater slammed into trees, and Jam's SA1000 sent a stream of bullets into the darkness. The return fire ceased and the Nex – they had glimpsed his thin grey body-hugging suit and his balaclava that revealed only gleaming copper eyes – sprinted away, dodging athletically between the trees.

'The bastard just won't go down,' snapped Jam. The two large men set off at a sprint once more, arms and legs pumping, lungs heaving, too used to the good life, and they heaved themselves up another slope, boots ploughing through woodland debris until they reached the top—

The Nex was running hard, head down, powering along at an incredible rate. Jam lifted his gun and the Nex, ducking left and right, glanced over its shoulder as the SA1000 fired a single bullet. The Nex was picked up, sent spinning end over end and deposited in an untidy heap beside a small cairn of rocks. Beyond, Jam and Slater could see a drop of some kind, a rocky edge falling away into a dark, shadow-haunted valley.

Warily, the two men, their chests still heaving, moved forward down this uneven rocky slope. Closing on the Nex, both levelled weapons at the still body. Circling, eyes on the surrounding landscape, Jam pulled out a silenced Beretta XI pistol and placed three bullets in the Nex's head.

They stood, panting, covered in grime and TT's blood, faces grim as realisation and horror sank in. Their friend was dead – and the ECubes had given them no warning.

'I have a fucking bad feeling,' rumbled Slater slowly.

'It's like when the QIII processor hacked the ECubes. You get that same sinking feeling? Like you're naked? Vulnerable?'

Slater nodded in the gloom, staring down at the crumpled grey-clad figure. 'What's over there?'

'Well, he was sure running *somewhere* fast.'

'You think there are more Nex?'

'Maybe,' said Jam grimly.

They moved closer to the valley, dropping to their bellies as they neared the gash in the ground. 'I can't see anything,' muttered Jam, and they crawled up to the edge to peer down into the deep narrow V, scattered with dark trees and large piles of rocks, below them.

There was a distant log cabin, and Slater nudged Jam,

pointing with his gun. In the gloom Jam could just make out a narrow bridge of thick wooden sleepers connecting both sides of the valley. Large rocks were clustered around the opposite bank: a perfect defensive location.

Jam set his ECube to scan.

He turned to Slater, confusion in his eyes. 'The cabin and the bridge are not there,' he said softly. 'The ECube can't see anything. It's blind. What the fuck is going on?'

Slater muttered something evil, and Jam turned back, staring down at the valley where nothing moved.

'I'll go back, check the Nex,' said Slater.

'Yeah. You do that.'

Jam stared hard, trying to work out why the ECube couldn't scan these simplest of objects before him. Was there some kind of natural screening? Some source of strange radiation or IR that was interfering with the complex electronic mechanics of Spiral's premier agent device?

A noise interrupted his thoughts – a low, metallic sound – and Jam whirled, eyes squinting into the darkness. He came up onto his knees, his SA1000 presented for action.

'Slater?' he hissed.

Nothing. He could see nothing . . .

Climbing up to his feet, he crept forward towards the crumpled Nex. Then his adjusting eyes picked out the fallen figure of Slater and he dropped to a crouch, instantly freezing, scanning the surroundings. Fuck, screamed his brain as he checked his ECube.

The tiny alloy machine was completely dead.

Jam's face tightened into a grimace.

The SA1000 swung left, then right, as Jam's sharp eyes scanned for enemies. Was Slater alive? Dead? A sniper's silenced bullet? Jam dropped to his belly, and very slowly, using trees for cover, worked his way gradually towards his fallen friend.

As he reached Slater, he hissed, 'What the fuck are you doing?'

There was no response.

Jam crept closer, and to his horror he saw that Slater's throat had been cut. The big man's neck sported a gaping crimson mouth. Blood had pooled in the leaves beneath his head and Jam felt his own heart rate kick up a gear with bursts of injected adrenalin as his fingers reached out and took Slater's shotgun.

'Somebody is going to fucking die,' he growled, rising beside a wide tree for cover, his eyes glaring off into the gloom. He turned – and a huge black shape reared up in front of him, an incredibly sudden movement faster than a striking cobra—

Jam gasped as something huge and hard slammed into his face.

He remembered the rich scent of the soil, and the leaves.

And then nothing.

CHAPTER 4

SEVERANCE

The snow fell heavily. Carter could feel it whipping coldly against his face as his body curled, cradling the woman as they slammed into the flower beds. Carter rolled, bouncing roughly, the woman's scream suddenly halted as air was punched from her naked bruised frame . . .

Carter's eyes shot open as the crevasse loomed before him – a huge frightening maw smashing towards him. His boots kicked out violently against the narrow trunk of a pine tree and heaved them both away, rolling with grunts to the paved path . . . the crevasse roared past, rock grinding rock and spewing splinters, consuming the pine and disappearing beneath the swaying hotel – which buckled like a melted toy, folding around the dancing flames from the boiler room, debris exploding outwards as the earthquake's tremors eventually subsided.

Dust billowed, followed closely by fire. Sirens were still wailing, and helicopter searchlights swept the landscape.

Behind Carter another section of the hotel collapsed with an inferno roar. He could hear the stampeding of boots.

He looked down into the woman's eyes and released a pent-up breath. 'Thank you,' she said softly and reached up to kiss his cheek. Carter gazed once more into the darkness that had so very nearly claimed them.

'A close call,' he muttered—

And then felt it. A presence, behind him. Carter rolled free of the naked woman's embrace and stared up at Natasha's face. Her gaze was unreadable, skin glowing on one side from the hotel fires, eyes gleaming as a helicopter searchlight swept over them.

Natasha helped the woman to her feet and draped a blanket around her shoulders, talking softly to her as she shivered, fear deep in her eyes.

Carter shuffled away from the rip in the earth as stones trickled free at the edges and disappeared into deep blackness.

'This day just gets better and better,' he muttered, finger touching a tiny cut on his face and coming away stained with blood. 'Fuck me,' he hissed, gaze transferring from his finger to the abnormal crack in the world's mantle. A deep sigh escaped his lips and he calmed his raging mind.

They took the rescued woman to a red and white ambulance that had paramedics swarming round it, helped her into the back, then surveyed the full destruction caused by the earthquake. Rescue and emergency services were stretched to their physical capabilities by this sudden disaster.

Carter and Natasha watched sadly as brave Swiss firefighters battled the flames. They held one another tightly under the falling snow. A policeman tried to usher them into an ambulance, but Carter waved him away. 'I need a whisky, not the fucking hospital,' he drawled.

They moved away from the throng of emergency services

and the darkness started to close in around them away from the lights and the fire. Natasha lifted her ECube into her hand and her gaze met Carter's. 'It would seem we have a message.'

'What wonderful timing.'

Natasha activated the tiny screen, chewed on her lip and then smiled up at Carter. 'Some shit is going down; we are summoned to an urgent meeting in London, at the new Spiral_H buildings.'

'So, then,' he pondered. 'Our plan of action is that we find another hotel, get cleaned up, get some food . . . then flag ourselves down some transport and—'

'Now, Carter. They're coming for us *now* . . .'

'Bastards,' said Carter with feeling. 'They fucking *know* we're on holiday. I knew we should have left the ECube at home. Fucking work. Do they know about the earthquake? We're not in a fit state! We need some R&R!'

'It's important,' said Natasha softly.

'Not as important as my down time. Come on, we might be able to salvage something from the cabin – if the bastard is still standing.'

'The police are cordoning off the area – we'll be lucky to get in. They've set up a temporary shelter for the quake victims, further down the mountain pass.'

Natasha met Carter's gaze, looking at his steely eyes, the cuts on his face, his dust- and blood-stained clothes.

'Believe me, we'll get in,' he said, and taking her hand, led her towards the darkness of the hotel cabins and the yellow police tape.

As they walked through the snow, a roar echoed from the valley below. They stopped, turning, glancing past the flames and horror of the smashed hotel, and beyond to the glittering town of Zermatt . . . The roaring increased, rumbling from below and above, the sounds bouncing from the mountains and hillsides, reverberating and increasing until they became so loud as to drown out conversation—

'No,' whispered Natasha, eyes wide, lips gleaming.

The earthquake tore through the town with a single mammoth, clubbing sweep, smashing buildings into pulverised dust like toys stamped under a giant's boot, spitting chunks of shattered concrete, stone and timber up into the air in cascading arcs with shrieks of tearing and cracking; ripping the civilised world apart with appalling ease. Devastating trenches chewed through the rock, opening up to swallow whole buildings, bucking horses, spinning carriages, screaming pulverised people and in a final giant concussive boom like the ending of worlds the haze of lights that illuminated Zermatt was swept away beneath a tidal wave of evil and darkness . . .

In the aftermath, the only sounds were people moaning and the thumping of Air Zermatt's rescue helicopters fluttering uselessly above the terrible devastation.

Leviathan Fuels: Premium Grade LVA
– go on, make the switch, because you know your children deserve a better future . . .

The man wearing the fur coat and glossy yellow shoes stood on the runway staring up at the decommissioned Chinese MIG87 fighter and the small black DigiOpticDV4 camera attached to the nose cone just above the Chinese writing that read 'Death to All Non-Believers.'

'Is it attached?'

'Yes, sir.'

'Will it fucking *stay* attached?'

The technician reddened. His boss, the Big Man, Sir

Ronald Xavier IX and Corporate MD of Film & Film© Incorporated, makers of Film and Supreme Advertisements©, currently contracted to make one new high-tech advert per week for Leviathan Fuels – their biggest and biggest paying customer ever – was seriously fucking pissed off.

More than pissed off. He was *losing money*. And to him that was a crime worse than multiple sodomy.

'Yes, sir – I'm sure it's not going to fall off again.'

'It better fucking not,' hissed Sir Ronald Xavier IX with passion. 'We've lost a day's filming, and that's cost me US$38.7 million. I'd hate to deduct *that* from your pitiful wages.'

The technician paled. He staggered back as if struck by a pickaxe handle, wondering how long it would take him to pay the money back if the unthinkable happened.

Xavier waved him away with contempt, and with a 'Fuckwit' thrown into the employee-abuse list for good measure. He turned his attention to the pilot, who waved in the sort of happy fashion associated with a knowledge of one's own non-expendability. Xavier frowned.

'You know the run?' he shouted.

The pilot nodded, his features insect-like behind his helmet. 'Like the back o' ma hand, man,' he drawled.

'Well, *go on*, then!'

The MIG87 taxied along a short length of runway and then leapt into the air. A sonic boom followed soon after as the jet reached altitude. For the pilot, the world became a huge expanse of blue scattered with marshmallow wisps of cloud. The sun blazed from an infinite heaven and he swung the MIG87, banking sharply left with a scream of engines, then right, before settling into a straight and even flight path.

'Have you patched me through yet?' came the annoyed

voice of Xavier, followed by a low 'Tut.' 'Well, fucking patch me through, you *moron*! What? He can hear me? Jesus Christ Superstar, you just can't get the fucking staff these days . . .'

The MIG87 howled around in a wide arc, plummeted back down in a steep dive and passed low over Xavier's head, making his strands of white hair, so carefully placed over his bald pate, wave wildly.

'Idiot!' screamed Xavier. There was a period of forced calm as he regulated his breathing – and his pacemaker, using external controls linked to his PDA. 'If you kill me, none of you get paid, you morons! Now, head for the first Zone.'

'Roger that.'

That MIG87 slowed, engines decelerating with a heavy whine, and headed for the first Zone. The desert opened up, a sea of undulating sand, towering dunes – a world of harsh and natural emptiness.

'Rolling Camera 3.'

'Roger.'

The MIG87 dropped low, skimming over the sand, huge clouds of it billowing up behind the fighter. The scream of jet engines sliced through the air as the warplane approached a massive rise of rocks – mountainous teeth of the desert, brown igneous rocks from an earlier age of the world, rising to reveal a valley dropping away into a sweeping expanse of sand and sparse spiked vegetation . . .

These mountain teeth were still distant to the camera.

The MIG87 hit its boosters, and the rocks suddenly appeared in the blink of an eye under massive acceleration – and then as suddenly jarred to a halt, rolling as the pilot slammed the machine into hover mode. Then he cruised easily down between two walls of jagged brown rock and on into the oasis within . . .

'Approaching Zone 2, over.'

'Keep it real slow for this bit,' said Xavier. 'Is Camera 5 still on standby? Good.'

From the desert reared a temple, a huge edifice of stone faced in the most wonderful brown- and golden-veined marble. Miraculously, it had not suffered the type of thefts that had robbed the Egyptian pyramids of the same era, and it remained a wonder of ancient architecture, protected by its natural environment, hidden by these towering walls of shrouding rock.

The MIG87 passed over with a throbbing drone. Behind the temple stood five mammoth derricks supporting gleaming black pumps, huge steel arms working to extract precious LVA from beneath the sand and rock. The jet banked, rising above the desert teeth, and then came around in a tight arc, dropping almost to ground level and zipping between the five huge pumps and the tiny specks of people working among the engines before climbing up once more towards the massive inverted ocean of blue sky . . .

'Wonderful!' came the crow of triumph from Xavier. 'A beautiful shot, truly spectacular. Now head for Zone 3 . . .'

Again, the MIG soared and banked, zooming across desert sand and then levelling out to take in the scene from far above: the mountains, their precious treasure of the temple within, and the squat pumps close behind, extracting LVA from below the desert dunes.

'I can see the text now,' said Xavier, voice heavy with treacly emotion. 'Leviathan Fuels – in harmony with our heritage, our ecology, our planet!' He chuckled to himself as the MIG87 soared, cameras still rolling, images still being frantically written to precious disk. The fighter plane passed over the huge slurry pits filled with rock and mud, the excrement of the earth dumped only 500 metres from this most precious landmark, scarring the beauty of the desert . . . it passed over the tiny scummy village that had sprung up close by to house the workers – labourers, engineers, drillers – and their servicing whores: the thick swathe of black bin-liners spilling jelly-shit refuse, the stinking open-air toilet facilities, the barking, snapping dogs . . . and finally past the rear of the temple where a group of humorous youths had scrawled fluorescent green garage-music graffiti over marble that had been hand-carved millennia ago . . .

'Shit. What's he doing? What are you fucking doing? Idiot! Jesus Christ Superstar . . . can we edit that out later? Right . . . is the audio off? Good. Fuck me . . . hey, yeah? Oh, hiya, hey, hi, Lindi, you're looking luscious for a sixteen-year-old, and I can't *believe* the size of your breasts! I was so impressed by the agency shots that I . . . What? Come and get a glass of brandy, love, you very shortly *will* have earned it . . . ooh, yes, that feels real good, yes, yes! Just ease it down and pull it out, yes, yes! Uh, keep doing that – a little bit faster now . . .'
Audio cut.

Due to the impact of the twin quakes, Natasha's ECube received an almost immediate update: new coordinates for a pick-up 160 klicks further east into the mountains, towards Strahlhorn and away from the scene of this colossal natural disaster and the subsequent heavy presence of the world's TV and press media.

Carter stood outside their cabin, yellow police tape wrapped in one fist like a boxer's bandages, a rucksack gripped in the other. They had skipped the cordons – the police had plenty of other priorities out in the darkness, and many screams could still be heard. Carter's gaze swept the grounds in the darkness and he sighed, a deep sad sigh. A heavy weariness and depression descended on two Spiral ops.

'What are those coordinates?'

Natasha repeated the list of numbers.

Carter cursed quietly and hoisted the rucksack. 'We'll need transport. I ain't fucking walking sixty klicks through snow-filled woodland and over mountain trails. I've hurt my back.'

'Could we steal one of the hotel's Snowcats? They're kept away from the main building, in the sheds over there.' She pointed through the gloom to where a rough-timber structure loomed through the falling flakes.

Carter shook his head, eyes hard after witnessing the devastation of Zermatt and listening to the distant echoing cries for help of hundreds of people.

'I was thinking of something a little *faster*,' he said.

Natasha, one hand on the rough-hewn timber of the shed doors, stared hard in the gloom lit only by Carter's Mag-Lite. 'Oh,' she said. 'I see what you mean. You've been snooping here before?'

'I snoop everywhere. It goes with the job . . . Come on.'

'We'll freeze!'

'Yeah, but it's fast. A Snowcat would take us hours! This is a Yamaha RX-16 Snowmobile, with an in-line 40-valve 2399cc Genesis-Extreme V engine, Pro-Action mountain suspension, titanium-fibre Deltabox chassis, Nail-skid resistance and a Camoplast Challenger track. This is the new promotional model – it has a 3D name badge and silver decals. Look, just above the tracks there. And it's been converted to run on the new Leviathan fuel, LVA, so we get real good mileage into the bargain.'

'Carter, you're a fucking geek.'

'But a geek who knows his vehicles. We'll be at the meet a damn sight faster on this than in a fucking Snowcat. Just get some warm clothing on and have a look for your ski goggles.'

Looking around to see if they'd been spotted, he straddled the machine and, using his ECube, within thirty seconds bypassed the digital immobiliser. The engine roared into life, and he flicked the switch for silencers, which slid into place. Carter revved the Yamaha snowmobile's engine and dipped the clutch, feeling the incredible torque just waiting to be unleashed as he watched Natasha pulling on two more jumpers, her Berghaus fleece jacket, ski goggles and thick Gore-Tex7 gloves.

'I hope you know what you're doing,' she muttered, climbing onto the machine behind Carter and pulling her rucksack onto her back – stuff that they had salvaged from the cabin which they considered valuable enough to drag to this emergency Spiral pick-up. Equipment and clothing designed to keep them alive.

Carter pulled his own goggles in place, blipped the throttle, then eased the clutch. The RX-16's 2399cc engine boomed quietly, straining at the leash to be free; the tracks dug in and the snowmobile eased to the shed doors, poked its nose out, then roared free in a shower of snow, banking left, its suspension dipping and tracks clawing the snow as Carter accelerated away from the hotel, away from the police, away from emergency services. And away from the quake zone.

They hammered up the mountain, the engine taking the huge ascent in its stride, snow spraying out behind them as the tracks dug deep and Carter eased the powerful machine between scatters of conifer. The broad sweep of the bright headlights cut slices from the chaotic darkness of the mountain night and tumbling snow, and Natasha looked behind her then, glancing back down the mountain, over the clumps of trees to the glow of the hotel embers and the steady sweep of police searchlights. Snow was still falling, blurring her view, and Zermatt and its horror was gone now. She turned back and hugged close to Carter, allowing him to buffer the wind-chill on this uphill flight to the Spiral rendezvous.

'Something is deeply wrong,' she muttered gently.

But Carter could not hear her.

They stopped for a breather, and Carter killed the RX-16's engine and lights. Darkness swept in like a huge velvet cloak. Snow fell all around, quickly covering their trail with a veil of white and stifling any sounds of movement. Natasha checked her ECube, then tossed it to Carter who scanned the blue digits and glanced up ahead.

There was no real trail to follow, just a newly improvised path – using the ECube to scope land contours, valleys and sudden crevasses. Carter lit a cigarette and the tip glowed in the darkness, illuminating his face through the falling snow.

'We're making good time,' he said.

'I thought you'd quit smoking. Or at least were trying to.'

'That was before the fucking Earth tried to eat me. Twice. And before that huge bastard broke into our cabin and tried to crush my windpipe.'

'That still makes me uneasy,' said Natasha, reaching for the proffered cigarette and enjoying a heavy drag. Blue smoke enveloped her face and she coughed a little.

'I thought *you* had quit,' smiled Carter gently, retrieving his weed.

'It's been a rough night,' she conceded, smiling, but Carter could read the exhaustion and horror in her eyes.

'Which bit makes you uneasy?'

'The intruder. Something doesn't quite fit – about him not being Nex.'

'I'm not the hardest man in the world,' said Carter softly. 'There are plenty out there who can take me in a fight; that's why I use Mr Browning.' He grinned nastily. 'But yeah, I know what you mean. A bullet and a fucking severed arm . . . I wonder what he was looking for? He certainly left empty-handed, if you'll excuse the pun.'

'Maybe he was a scout for the Nex?' mused Nats.

Carter shook his head. 'I don't think so. Those bastards are fairly thin on the ground now – the SAD teams have pretty much wiped that fucked-up genetic mess from the face of the planet.' He shivered, adding mentally that he was also glad that Feuchter, and Durell – his old and bitter enemies – were dead: dead and buried under the sea with the remains of their battleship and improvised war station.

Natasha nodded, and shivered. 'It's getting colder.' She glanced up. 'We could do with somewhere to stop.'

'I think the rendezvous is near a hut or cabin of some sort. We'll have plenty of time to rest when we get there . . .'

The Yamaha cruised through the falling snow, and soon the dawn arrived, its pink tendrils pushing between the snowflakes and turning the sky a cool grey. The falling snow eased until it was nothing more than a scattering of flakes, and the RX-16 found a narrow winding trail through the conifer forests. They cruised for a while, the snowmobile's engine buzzing quietly as it prowled along. Carter's gaze was focused and alert, sweeping the trail from left to right and back.

He halted.

The engine rumbled, spitting exhaust into the cold snow.

'What is it?'

Carter licked his lips, and lifted his goggles, rubbing at his eyes.

The land rumbled, and snow shook from the trees to either side of the trail. The rumbling continued for perhaps a minute, and then subsided. Silence filled the world once more.

'A gentle reminder,' said Carter bitterly.

'The sooner we get out of here the better,' said Natasha.

'I didn't realise that Switzerland was prone to earthquakes.'

'Neither did the Swiss.'

They cruised through the snow for another two hours, then left the trail and again headed cross-country through the forests. At one point the world fell away to the left, a massive vertical drop down into a huge canyon filled with snow and the occasional scattering of black, shining rocks. Carter stopped for another cigarette and Natasha stood, shielding her eyes with her gloved hands and gazing down in awe as the wind whipped at her. Snow began to fall again, scattering patterns down into the valley below, and both of them felt privileged to witness such a display of Nature's awesome power.

'We're so small,' said Natasha. 'So insignificant. It's like, one minute we're dancing at the party, the next the whole fucking hotel is swallowed by the Earth. We think we are so strong, so in control. And yet Nature – she could smash us in an instant.'

'Yeah, you hold on to that thought,' said Carter, flicking the butt of his cigarette away into the gulf of the vast valley. It spun, carried on eddies of snow and wind, and disappeared into the immeasurable expanse of bleak dawn wilderness.

It took them another hour to reach the cabin, located by the ECube's coordinate navigation. It was a small building set against a picturesque location and standing among huddled conifers. It had only a single room, and the outside log walls were piled high with snow. Still, the cabin seemed extremely inviting after the cold of the journey and the bleakness of the long stretches of mountain trail. The snow-heavy undergrowth surrounding the structure was dense and eerily quiet.

They killed the Yamaha's engine and Carter had to dig a path to the front door, which lolled open on broken leather hinges. Working together, they cleared the spill of snow and filled the fireplace with wood from a narrow protected log store out back. It took a good ten minutes to get a fire going because the firewood was damp, but as the small flames finally took hold warmth began to flood out. Wedging shut the door with a heavy, rough-hewn table, they pulled off their wet clothing and boots and set them steaming on the earth floor before the fire, and warmed their numbing hands and feet before the flames.

'The snow has got heavy again. Will the Comanche be able to fly through this?' asked Natasha.

'Our modified Comanches can fly through anything,' said Carter softly. 'They might not be able to land here, but they can winch us up; a real *chilling* experience.'

'How long to the rendezvous?'

'One hour.'

'I'll make us something warm to eat.'

Carter grinned. 'I thought you'd never offer. My stomach is like a Nazi's soul – empty.'

Carter stared at the bowl.

'I can't believe it.'

'What?'

'Of all the foodstuffs you could have brought with us from the cabin, all you brought was B&S.'

'What's wrong with B&S?' Natasha smiled encouragingly.

'Nothing, but . . . well, B&S is just standard military fodder. It's got a fair amount of roughage in it and . . . it's about as bland as bland can be, Nats. Couldn't you have brought something else?'

'Carter, we're only an hour from a pick-up. I wasn't going to go shopping for T-bone steaks!'

'Yeah, but . . .'

He stirred the red gruel. It seemed to be staring back at him.

As he ate, Natasha reclined and skipped through recent files on the ECube. 'You mentioned before that the snow-mobile ran on LVA?'

'Mm.' Carter nodded.

'Seems like Leviathan Fuels are stirring up some interest. NATO's Fuel Commission are talking about investigations. The oil companies of the world are kicking up a right stink . . .'

'So they will.' Carter gesticulated with his spoon. 'Imagine, a new fuel springs seemingly from nowhere – best-kept energy secret ever: it's much cheaper than what's currently on offer, needs only a minor engine modification costing a few hundred dollars, and fuck me if it doesn't do eight times more miles to the gallon as well. The oil companies are fucking green with envy!'

'Apparently it's started a price war.'

'Yeah, and that'll get worse as the competition hots up. But hey, who am I to give a flying fuck about fat-cat billionaire oil industrialists with wads of banknotes falling out of their tax-free Swiss bank accounts? It's a free market ... But let's be honest, if the petroleum moguls had clocked Leviathan Fuel researchers digging LVA out of the rock, then how long would those researchers' life expectancies have been? Nice man with a sniper rifle, anybody?'

'God, you're cynical,' said Natasha.

'I'm just the way the world made me.' Carter smiled sardonically. 'Anything else of interest on our little alloy friend?'

'Jam's still heading up the SAD teams; reports are favourable about the Nex extermination. I'd have thought they would have been wiped out by now, but every time Spiral think they've cracked it and the world goes a bit quiet, another bunch spring up.'

'Yeah, like a bad penny. I bet Jam's tearing his hair out. We're just lucky the Nex bastards haven't got Durell any more.'

'He was one insane motherfucker.'

'Tut tut, Nats, language like that from such a pretty face is most unbecoming in a lady.' He reached over and rapped her knuckles with his spoon.

'Carter! You'll get B&S juice all over me!'

'Don't be so soft. Look at me, fucking wrestling with a crevasse a few hours ago and you're bloody complaining about a little tomato on your dungarees!'

'Wrestling with ... ? Ahhh, that was her name, was it? Nice pair of long legs Miss Crevasse had to her credit. And the way you saved her by mauling her naked breasts with your face was a true miracle to behold. Proper hero stuff, worthy of Hollywood.'

Carter grinned sheepishly. 'Hey, can I be blamed if the woman I rescue is naked except for a pair of knee-high boots? Sometimes,' he muttered, a grim look on his face, 'you just have to take the rough with the smooth.'

Natasha moved towards him, on her knees, and grinned up into his face. 'You're a bad man, Mr Carter.'

'You'd better believe it.'

Thirty minutes later Carter and Natasha were packed and ready to move out. Nats had killed the fire, they had prepped both ECubes with SAR signals and now awaited their emergency holiday-destroying transport with some trepidation. Something big was going down, they could sense it; something big and bad and they were going to be a part of it. The tension within the two Spiral operatives was beginning to increase: emergency Spiral meetings on this scale were not called every day – nor even every year.

Snow was still falling, and Carter and Natasha stepped out to stand beside the Yamaha snowmobile; Carter checked his watch. 'They're one minute late.' He smiled, but even as the last syllable left his lips the sound of a helicopter echoed through the snow above the vast mountainside expanses of sweeping forest, the thump of armoured rotors reverberating through the falling snow.

Carter tutted. Natasha shook her head, staring at him.

'There's no excuse for sloppiness,' said Carter smugly.

'One minute!' laughed Natasha.

'One minute is one fucking minute. It can mean the difference between life and—'

Sudden fire illuminated the sky in smoking trails that converged from three directions. There was a scream of engines and a heavy bass boom; screeching rotor sounds destroyed the peace of the forest and a fireball blasted outwards suddenly in a flare of purple HighJ energy . . . The Comanche was plucked from the snow-filled heavens by three rockets that ignited it and sent it heaving skywards to hang for long timeless moments. Then it fell, trailing black smoke and spitting showers of superheated metal in all directions. It clattered through the trees, its rotors slicing branches and trunks and whining in screaming deceleration, and then crashed into the ground, crackling in the embrace of a sudden raging blue-white fire.

'—Death,' said Carter coldly.

'Three rockets,' snapped Natasha, her Glock in her hand and her gaze sweeping the trees. Carter pulled free his heavy battle-scarred Browning HiPower. His eyes were very cold. 'That should have been impossible,' he said.

'I know,' replied Natasha quietly, eyes scanning the forest with unease. 'The Comanche is supposedly one hundred per cent protected against SAMs. Whatever weapons they used, they were fucking advanced – and fucking invisible. Start the Yamaha.'

The two Spiral operatives backed towards the RX-16, automatically covering one another's arcs of fire as they searched for trouble. They were immediately a team, expecting an offensive; they immediately became as one.

Distant sounds of screaming echoed. The sounds of agony. The sounds of a man on fire . . .

'Fuck,' snapped Carter, firing up the Yamaha. He revved the vehicle and looked back at Natasha. 'You know we've got to check it out . . .'

'It's a trap,' said Natasha.

'*Damn fucking right it's a trap*,' hissed Kade in the dark recesses of Carter's brain. '*Go on, check it out, get a bullet in the brain and end up eating soil and you will be worm food, my brother . . . go on, do it, let's see what balls you really have, you dumb-arse fuck-brain . . .*'

Carter pushed Kade's comments from his raging mind. Anger threatened to consume him, but he controlled it. Out there in the snow one of his Spiral comrades was suffering, screaming and dying, and he could not leave him to cook, or to be shot by – who? The Nex?

Carter grinned a grin that had nothing to do with humour.

'You bastards,' he snarled as he opened the throttle. In a shower of cold snow-ice, he sped off between the trees.

Carter knelt warily beneath the tree line. The Comanche had gone down hard, rotors chewing wood and bark, body shell aflame, and now it lay buckled and twisted in a smoking, blazing mess. Carter's stare swept the opposite side of the small clearing and the trees that had been pulped by the plummeting war machine. Too nasty, he thought. And too fucking open . . .

Crouching, he crept forward.

And saw the body, smouldering in the snow. The pilot had managed to crawl a short distance from the Comanche's still-burning wreckage but his HIDSS helmet had been flame-fried to his face, melded to burning skin, blended with charbroiled flesh and muscle and hair. Carter wrinkled his nostrils, almost gagging as he moved closer. That man must be dead, came the unbidden thought. He must be dead . . . because to live—

It did not even bear thinking about.

Carter paused, gaze scanning the trees once more. Something was wrong, his senses screamed at him. Still he moved forward, and crouched beside the nightmarishly burnt pilot. He forced himself to look down at the scorched blackened face, and only then did the vomit truly force its way into his mouth as he saw eyes watching him from beneath a melted, caked brow and blackened crusted crispy skin . . .

A hand grasped his, a sudden movement that took him by surprise. Looking down, Carter saw that there was no

113

real skin, only an oily, tarry mess of muscle and blood and crisped hide. The stench filled his nostrils and he vomited to one side and heaved until his stomach contracted and spasmed in a fist of horror. He met the pilot's gaze. The man was beyond screaming and his twitching eyes made only one entreaty and that was 'Please . . .'

Carter's Browning lifted and a single shot rang out across the small forest clearing.

Carter's eyes narrowed.

Three figures stepped out of the tree-haunted shadows.

Nex.

Carter stumbled back towards Natasha as the Nex attacked.

Bullets spat from JK49s and Carter leapt swiftly into the forest, rolling behind a fallen conifer where Natasha crouched. The Nex sprinted towards the destroyed Comanche, kneeling beside the fallen pilot. Their grey-balaclava-clad heads turned as their stares fixed on Carter. They rose to their feet and began to run towards the Spiral agents.

Carter's Browning boomed in his fist. One of the Nex was sent slamming to the ground with its blended insect-human brain spreading in a bone-scattered pool of pink snow-mush.

'One down,' muttered Natasha, taking aim—

The other two continued their charge.

They moved fast – inhumanly fast . . .

But then, the Nex were not human.

Natasha fired, once, twice, three times. The Nex weaved left and right, keeping low, legs pumping, JK49s stitching a line of bullets in the log behind which the two Spiral operatives crouched, making Natasha yelp and duck. But Carter's Browning fired seven times, the gun heavy in his fist, and the second Nex was sent sprawling in

114

the snow with only a gruesome ring of smashed bone where once the masked face had been.

'*That's my boy!*' cheered Kade.

Carter snarled as the final Nex reached the log and leapt, its sub-machine gun tracking him as the Browning jerked up. Carter could still see the eyes of the dead Spiral pilot, surrounded by melted flesh: the HiPower jolted in his grip and five bullets sent the Nex lurching over him, legs kicking, blood spraying, to sprawl against a tree and fall twisted and dead among its roots.

Carter climbed slowly to his feet, panting, sweat stinging his eyes and the cuts on his face. Natasha leapt up beside him, licking fear-dry lips. 'You killed them,' she said, awed. 'You killed them all!'

Carter nodded emotionlessly. Pride was his enemy. And complacency meant death.

Natasha turned – and saw that ten more Nex had stepped into the clearing.

'Yeah, but here comes the main course,' muttered Carter as the killers opened fire with JK49s and the two Spiral agents fled, skidding on ice, sprinting as best they could for the sanctuary of the RX-16. Leaping aboard, Carter fired up the engine and with Natasha clinging on grimly he twisted the throttle hard round. Snow spat and streamed from the tracks as they raced off between the trees. Bullets hissed past them, gouging into tree trunks and whistling through branches. They weaved madly left and right, hunched low.

The firing finally stopped.

Carter pulled the Yamaha to a halt, spraying snow against a wall of black glistening rock where ice had formed long glittering stalactites. 'We lost them?' panted Nats through frozen lips.

'Listen.'

She concentrated as Carter killed the engine.

'What?'

'Shit.'

'*What?*'

And then she heard it. Engines. Screaming engines.

Carter fired the Yamaha into life once more and urged the machine on hard; snow shot up behind them as compact black snowmobiles with mounted SMGs appeared, weaving through the trees. The machine guns roared, fire flashing from their muzzles, and bullets slapped into trees and snow all around, ricochets striking sparks from the rock wall. Carter ducked and Nats hung on grimly as the snowmobile rocketed through the snow and trees . . .

Carter glanced behind. Through the haze of kicked-up snow he saw at least ten machines pursuing them.

'Fuck. I thought the fucking SAD teams had wiped out the Nex!' he screamed over the roar of the tortured engine.

'So did I,' shouted Natasha, clinging tightly to him.

Carter dragged the RX-16 around, heading up a steep slope, the engine pulling powerfully. The black snowmobiles started to fall behind as the Yamaha sped from the cover of the trees, swaying slightly through banks of snow and then skimming fast over a field of sloping ridged ice. Up they headed, towards another tree line and the sanctuary of the forest. Rocks glittered all around and with some skill Carter dodged through them, setting into a rhythm with the machine, feeling it as a part of him . . .

A few more bullets skimming past reminded him of their impending doom.

Carter powered the machine on, his stare fixed. Glancing back, he lifted his Browning in his right hand, sighted, fired off ten bullets but hit nothing. 'Moving too fast,' he muttered.

'*Or maybe you're just a shite aim,*' observed Kade.

Kade laughed at him, and that made Carter mad. He gritted his teeth, swerved the snowmobile into the line of trees and suddenly slammed on the brakes. They left a long straight line of grooved ice. Carter leapt free as Natasha screamed, 'What the hell are you *doing*?'

Carter was attaching something to his Browning.

'Remember I was telling you about the mod I got from Simmo? A NeedleClip?' There came a snapping sound, metal grinding metal. 'This is it.' He moved to the tree line where he could hear and now see the swathe of black snowmobiles speeding up the incline, their formation a tight V.

'NeedleClip?'

Carter glanced back, where Natasha crouched behind him.

'Fucking needle *bombs*.' He grinned savagely, holding the Browning two-handed and sighting down the bulky barrel. The NeedleClip had its own sight and squatted above the gun, a small black symbiotic metal cube, its sides laser-carved with a cryptic military designation.

He flicked a tiny switch with his thumb. There was a heavy deep hum which belied the weapon's size and Carter pulled the Browning's trigger. There was a soft click and instead of a bullet, a sliver of metal shot from the NeedleClip, glistening like a tiny, glittering dart as it flashed buzzing low over the snow and connected with the lead snowmobile . . .

There was a searing flash and then a massive boom as the snowmobile and the two that were closely following it were kicked up into the air, spinning, before blossoming into unfurling flaming petals. They soared briefly as the snowmobiles still on the ground skidded to a halt in clouds of powder snow. Then the mangled vehicles fell, pluming black smoke and with their screaming Nex riders clawing at shrapnel-filled faces.

Heads looked up towards the tree line.

Carter fired again as eyes went wide and engines howled in hastily revved panic . . .

Another two snowmobiles were smashed skywards, Nex squirming as the exploding metal melted into their flesh. Black smoke blossomed and a crackling like fireworks going off reached Natasha's ears . . .

The other snowmobiles fled.

Carter turned to Natasha, but she was staring at the ECube. 'We have to get out of here, Carter.'

'What is it?'

Her gaze met his. 'There's more of them, up there through the trees. Hundreds of them.'

'Impossible!' he snapped. 'Why didn't the ECube pick it up before?'

'Remember the shields they used, back in Scotland?' A year ago an assassin had infiltrated Carter's house and had somehow managed to sidestep not only his own personal defence systems but the all-ranging scanners of the ECube. In essence, the effectiveness of the ECube – a Spiral operative's major defence mechanism – had been compromised.

'I thought we'd cracked their technology!'

'So did I.'

Carter cursed and glanced back at the black billowing smoke. 'We've just fucking advertised ourselves.'

'Better than getting bullets in the back.'

'Come on.'

They ran back to the RX-16, leapt aboard, and Carter started the engine, setting off in a straight line.

'Where you going?'

'Towards them.'

'Are you fucking crazy? The ECube's registering more than two hundred Nex. We need an airlift!'

'Yeah, and they'll have one.'

'Carter, they'll be sending search parties to check out the smoke! And the others have probably commed ahead and told them we're here.'

'Yes.' Carter smiled. 'Last fucking thing they'll expect us to do is head straight towards them. If the ECube is picking them up, I'm pretty damn sure they know about it. If they have ECube cloaks, then their technology is more advanced than we suspected . . . and there're more of them.'

Turning back, Carter opened the throttle wide and slid the exhaust silencers into place. Stealth came at the expense of power, but the machine was still functional as they cruised almost silently through the trees, weaving gently, Carter's vigilant stare on the lookout for the Nex search parties that he knew would come.

The engine clicked softly as it started to cool. Carter dragged some fallen branches roughly across the RX-16 in a crude version of camouflage, and Natasha and he set off through the snow on foot.

'I don't like leaving it behind,' said Natasha softly.

'Yeah, but we'll need to get close. The branches should hide it from air obs.'

Snow had started falling again, more heavily. The forest was quiet, almost silent, occasional falls of snow from over-laden branches crumping in the distance.

'What are the Nex doing all the way out here?'

'An interesting thought.'

'I bet Jam doesn't know about their existence.'

'I'm pretty sure *nobody* knows about their existence.'

They moved warily, guns out, the metal cold even

119

through their gloves. Natasha looked more closely at the NeedleClip, amazed that something so small could pack such a punch.

The cold was beginning to get to the two Spiral operatives as they weaved warily through the trees. They had to stand stock-still once as snowmobiles thundered off to one side, flashes of black between the distant tree trunks, and then they dropped to a crouch and waited.

Natasha kept a close eye on her ECube's scanners.

Several groups were moving, spreading out.

'They're searching for us,' she whispered.

Carter merely nodded.

They moved stealthily for nearly forty minutes, creeping from tree to tree, the falling snow their ally, the forest their protector. They halted while Carter carefully removed the NeedleClip and screwed the Browning's silencer back in place. As they moved off again through the thick snow Natasha watched the ECube, but was surprised when Carter's hand came up in a 'halt' signal. She met his gaze as he put a finger to his lips and gestured for her to wait and be perfectly still.

She watched him move carefully through the snow and then crouch beside a stunted conifer tree. He was moving with great care, placing each foot with an infinity of consideration. Then he levelled the Browning and aimed. She heard the hiss of a silenced shot and nearly jumped as a mound of snow seemed to collapse – to reveal a camouflaged Nex bearing a sniper's rifle. Carter signalled for Natasha to approach, and she checked the ECube again.

'He wasn't there, on the scanner.'

'I know.'

'How the fuck did you see him?'

Carter's breath steamed, and his eyes were twinkling. 'Let's just call it magic,' he whispered. He moved towards

120

the Nex and lifted the Heckler & Koch SN5 sniper rifle. 'Good weapon,' he said, hoisting it thoughtfully.

'He's dead?'

'*It* is dead,' Carter corrected gently. 'It was the perimeter guard – we must be getting close.'

'I don't understand: they cloak the guards but not the compound where the ECube is showing hundreds?'

'No point having a guard if he can be seen – even by a scanner. Nobody knows that this base – or whatever it is – is here. Why cloak it? What are the chances of somebody stumbling across it up here? Maybe it's arrogance, or maybe you can't cloak such a large group of Nex – we'll have to sneak in and ask them.'

'Very funny.'

'I'm serious.'

'That's what worries me.'

Moving on through the heavy snow they exercised even greater caution until once more Carter signalled for a halt. They had been climbing a steep incline, an embankment peppered with trees, that overlooked a compound of some sort up ahead. Trees ringed the compound on ridges of land and snow, and low buildings of grey concrete blended naturally with the ground, barely visible – especially in this climate of snow and mist and from the air.

'Probably left over from the Bright War,' whispered Carter, gazing down at the buildings. There seemed to be some activity going on in them but very little outside.

'They are all inside,' whispered Natasha.

'Well, they wouldn't be sunbathing.'

'The buildings look like barracks.'

'Maybe. Who fucking knows what they're doing? All I'm thinking about at the moment is one of those.' Carter pointed, his movements cautious, to where a high fence surrounded a small square of cleared concrete on which sat four squat black helicopters.

'Airlift?'

'They look familiar,' growled Carter, remembering the great air battle that had taken place between the Demolition Squads and the Nex over the Arctic seas and the improvised WarCentre created by Durell and Feuchter after they had betrayed Spiral. 'Some bad shit is going down here.'

'A problem for another day,' said Natasha.

'I agree. Come on.'

They circled wide, Carter on the lookout for guards and snipers, his senses screaming at him and Kade making the occasional maddeningly sarcastic comment.

Carter halted, gesturing. A guard was stationed outside the compound, protecting the helicopters with a heavy machine gun. 'We need to get a bit closer.'

They moved carefully, coming in on the guard's blind side. Carter took him out with a single bullet to the back of the head.

The helicopter enclosure was protected by a digitally locked gate; Carter knelt beside the fence and stared at its metallic strands. 'Titanium IX, very advanced,' he said, impressed. He removed his own ECube and a tiny silver beam emerged from it, slicing through the Titanium IX strands, making tiny pings.

'How did you do that?' said Natasha, frowning.

'A new mod.'

'Why doesn't mine do that?'

Carter smiled, cutting the final strand and bending the glowing edges wide. 'Come on.'

They squeezed through the opening and moved warily towards the first black helicopter, which was cloaked with a veil of snow. 'This is too easy,' muttered Natasha.

'I agree, although I'm pretty sure they're not expecting us. You hot-wire this baby and I'll keep watch.'

'You think they know we're here?'

'Maybe. But maybe they're playing a game with us . . .'

Chilled by Carter's words, and with the hairs on the back of her neck standing up, Natasha gently opened the cockpit and climbed in. With ECube in gloved hand, she began the complex process of hot-wiring the helicopter's digital ignition, utilising her pre-Spiral hacking skills. She was illuminated by the curious witch-light of the snow-enclosed cockpit.

Outside, Carter's mouth was a grim line as his eyes scanned relentlessly around. The cold was seeping into his bones now. His head snapped to the right as a fall of snow toppled from the low branches of a wide pine. He realised that the Browning was already aimed and primed, and he lowered the weapon gently.

There was a distant, snow-muffled click and Carter dropped to a crouch, gun ready.

A figure stepped into the snow from one of the concrete buildings. He was athletic, broad-shouldered, and Carter could tell from his stance, the way he moved, that he was a warrior. He had shaved blond hair and a badly scarred head and face, and he was laughing unpleasantly. As he moved forward, a second figure strode out behind him. This individual was huge, towering a full head over the smaller man who was himself six feet tall. The giant wore a heavy black coat across his shoulders and his face was patched with black, as if he had suffered terrible burns that had scorched his skin. His eyes were small and round and copper, the face deformed and twisted to one side.

'I've done it,' whispered Natasha. 'What the fuck is *that*?'

At her hushed words, the deformed head swung round, stretching forward on a strange thick neck, the small eyes focusing on the helicopter, the crouched form of Carter, Natasha's peeping face . . .

'Well done,' snarled Carter.

'It's fucking looking at us!'

The blond-haired man turned and stared at them. Carter growled, 'Get that fucking chopper started – now!' He lifted his Browning as the huge figure shrugged free the black coat to reveal a heavily muscled body, bare from the waist up, skin merging with black panels scattered across his chest and belly, gleaming as snow settled against their chitinous surface.

'What is it?' wondered Carter.

'*Just shoot the fucking thing*,' hissed Kade.

Time seemed to slow as Carter lifted the Browning HiPower and took aim. The creature – or Nex, or whatever it was – lowered its head on bull-neck muscles and charged, heavy boots stamping through the snow, its speed incredible for something so big . . .

The door to the building, which still stood open, spat forth a stream of Nex carrying JK49s and aiming them at Carter and the helicopter. Kade was bellowing, '*Trap, it's a fucking trap*,' the words piercing Carter's mind as his trigger finger squeezed and the Browning kicked back hard against the heel of his hand—

The creature seemed to flinch to one side, and the bullet hissed past, taking a chunk out of the concrete of the building. Carter fired twice more, the third bullet ricocheting off one of the black armour plates but causing no damage . . .

Behind him the helicopter's engines started and the rotors began to turn, slowly at first and then rapidly picking up speed. The man with blond hair was smiling, stare bright and arms folded, but there was something wrong with his eyes. Carter fired another two bullets as the giant creature reached the eighteen-feet-high fence and leapt, long claws extending from thick black fingers, and scrabbled upwards.

'Carter!' screamed Natasha.

Carter fired several more rounds as the huge creature, small copper eyes staring fixedly at him, clambered up the fence and reached the top. The Browning boomed again, bullets slicing through the air and screeching off the armour plates. The final shot punched the creature back off the fence to land in the snow. Carter watched in horror as it rolled easily and climbed to its booted feet. It snarled, drool pooling from crooked teeth as blood poured from two holes in its protected torso.

'*Give him to me,*' snarled Kade. '*I will fuck him bad . . .*'

More Nex were swarming from the low concrete building. Carter's gaze met the red-scarred stare of the man with the shaved blond hair who nodded, almost as if meeting a friend in the street. Carter bared his teeth in a grimace.

'Carter!'

The helicopter's engines screamed and howled under Natasha's rough ministrations. The creature clambered up to the fence once more, claws gouging a path upwards. Carter watched in horror and fascination, as if in a dream – a waking nightmare. It leapt cleanly up and over as Carter's sweat-slippery hands slotted the NeedleClip to the Browning with a precise click – the down draught from the chopper's rotors was beating against his back but his stare was fixed intently on the mammoth creature that landed in the snow in front of him. It was too close for him to use the weapon. To kill it would be to kill himself. It smiled with twisted fangs.

Carter sensed the helicopter lifting free of the snow. He felt the down draughts increase.

'*Let me,*' soothed Kade.

The creature flexed its claws, stained with its own blood, and Carter tightened his grip on the trigger.

To kill is to die, he thought . . .

'Carter, here!' screamed Natasha once more over the howling of the engines and rotors as he saw a massive group of Nex spread out beyond the fence with their weapons aimed and their faces covered by masks of grey and black. There were too many of them. Even if Carter killed this *thing* he would be cut to pieces in a machine-gun instant . . .

Carter bared his teeth in a tight-jawed grimace. 'You ready for me, you big fucker? You're one ugly piece of shit, that's for sure . . . Come on, let's see what you can do – let's fucking dance.'

Spiral Mainframe
Data log #11952

CLASSIFIED SADt/9083/SPECIAL INVESTIGATIONS UNIT
Data Request 324#11952

FEUCHTER

Count Feuchter

Count Feuchter; German professor, born in Schwalenberg, educated in Munich, London and Prague. Great-grandfather killed by the Nazis during World War II after being tortured somewhere on the German/Austrian border. Mother and two sons fled to Italy,

126

then to England for protection after the war was over; Feuchter stemmed from this bloodline.

He was an expert in computing systems, specialising in processor function and artificial intelligence. He helped pioneer the QII and QIII military processors before turning traitor against Spiral with a group of other operatives.

Among other things, Feuchter was also heavily involved in the Nx5 Project and it is now believed that he continued this research illegally after Spiral withdrew funding and the project was killed. All the Nx5 subjects were apparently destroyed. It was unknown at the time that Feuchter had, in fact, experimented on himself and was willing to take his machinations much further.

He was responsible for many civilian deaths, and a Warrant12 was issued by Spiral in 2XXX after various Spiral DemolSquads were assassinated.

Count Feuchter was killed during the Spiral_mobile mission by operative Cartervb12. His body was never recovered.

Keyword SEARCH>>DURELL, QIII [lvlz], NEX [lvlz] SPIRAL_Q, SAD, SP1RAL_R

CHAPTER 5

BLACK PLANET

Jam swam in a world of darkness. Tiny fish-lights glittered and he watched them in fascination as they swam around and around as if in a bowl. But then a slice of red ripped across his vision and with it came a slashing glass shard of pain . . . deep heart-core pain that he could not push away.

His eyelids flickered open.

Darkness. Dry darkness.

And blows. Boots, suddenly crashing into his ribs and back and head. Dark silhouettes stood over him, amorphous shapes that wobbled and wavered, illuminated from behind by the yellow orange flickering of live flames. Jam curled into a tighter ball, his broken teeth gritting together and filling his mouth with blood and pieces of bone.

The blows continued, and a deep voice said, 'He's awake.'

The blows increased in intensity, smashing into Jam, pounding him against an anvil of agony. He felt a rib break with an audible crack but the pain flowed all through him and was everywhere, a dull throbbing interspersed with the thud of heavy steel-capped boots — connecting with his flesh. He felt blood pooling under his face on the dry dusty floor, on the cool stone and he watched it with interest, his vision shaking, vibrating, as the blows continued to rock him and the beating subsided. Gradually.

The dark shapes retreated. Faded like ghosts.

Jam coughed and tried to sit up. But he fell back to the stone floor once more. He closed his swollen eyes, his face pressed down against the warmth of his own blood and his eyes fluttered closed and eventually, after a long time, unconsciousness claimed him.

He dreamed of Slater.

Slater stood in the forest, talking through the gaping smile in his throat in a language that Jam found difficult to understand. 'What's the matter?' asked Slater, the flaps of sliced flesh puckering like lips. 'You don't fucking like what you see, eh? You did this to me, you bastard, you fucking did this to me . . . your fucking complacency led us all to our deaths . . .'

'But I'm not dead!'

Laughter, spraying droplets of blood.

Jam tried to say, 'I'm sorry,' and he tried, tried so hard to force the words from his mouth but it would not work, his tongue and lips would not cooperate and he could not breathe, awesome pain was smashing through his chest and ribs and he could not exhale the air with which to apologise to this man, one of his greatest friends.

Slater moved closer towards him, blood splattering from the wound with each footfall and raining down across the woodland floor. His eyes were filled with pain and sadness.

'You killed me, Jam,' he cried and tears of blood ran down his cheeks. 'You fucking let me die out there . . . and it hurts so much . . .'

And now Jam was spinning – then reality kicked him in the face with a blow of brightness. Flames, flickering orange and yellow and dancing like a demon of fire, washed across his face and he blinked rapidly, pupils dilating, mouth opening to allow a single silent sigh to escape.

'He's awake again.'

Shapes blocked out the flames once more, broad-shouldered figures that converged on Jam. A blow crashed against his shoulder, and he suddenly realised that they were using thick sticks like pickaxe handles. He tried to cry out 'Stop!' but the blows rained down and he tried to crawl away but his arm was broken and it gave way beneath him with a crunch as splintered bone poked and tore through his flesh and he screamed and that seemed to give his attackers a new lease of life as the blows rained heavier and harder and faster and the world was spinning spinning spinning and Jam fell into a deep well of Slater's slopping gore-filled blood and lay there staring at the stars and tasting bitter salt.

'When are you coming home?'

Jam stared at Nicky's face. It glowed with health and serenity. He took her chin in his cupped hand, smiled and, leaning forward, kissed her lips. She responded, and was warm and sweet and soft against him and he felt his love for this woman overwhelming his mind and their tongues danced and he felt at calm, at peace, at one with the world—

He pulled away.

Her mouth opened, and she said, 'You said you'd never

leave me, you'd said you were too good and they would never get you' – and a stream of black maggots spewed from her throat wriggling past her white teeth and they covered him, tiny jaws biting at his flesh and tearing at his eyes and he tried to cover his face but they pushed between his fingers sliding on their own slime and juice and Jam screamed and his eyes flew open—

The length of wood, the same diameter as the heavy end of a pool cue, connected with Jam's forehead with a dull slap. Stars spun across his vision and he rolled, trying to get away from the agony, but the blows rained down on his back and shoulders and neck. Suddenly he turned, snarling and rolling to his knees and lashing out blindly. There came a grunt of surprise as his broken fingers hit one of the attackers' groins and his fingers closed, his own bones crunching together as a heavy blow to the head smashed him down – so he grappled the nearest leg, pulling it close, and his blood-covered teeth closed on the struggling leg and he bit, he bit hard and he bit deep . . . he felt the cloth give way to flesh and the blows were thundering down across his back but he would not let go and the muscle was warm and wet and salted and sliming like an eel in his mouth. Jam bit and bit and he chewed and he ripped the sliming calf muscle from the bone, tore it like tender juicy steak to the accompaniment of a high-pitched shrilling sound – until darkness claimed him in its long dark flexing claws.

Jam came awake curled up in a ball, and for a long time there was no pain. Everything was gloomy, dry, and he stared at the black floor beneath him and the dust there, thick dust in which pools of his own saliva and blood had congealed. His tongue slowly worked around his dry mouth and he gently eased a piece of broken tooth to his desiccated lips, slowly pushed it out of his mouth and watched it fall to the dust. Pain started to come then, in gentle throbbing waves and from every single molecule of his whole being. He realised that his eyes were filled with gunk, gritty and dry. And then he tried to move.

Pain lanced him.

It was as if a million knives stabbed at his flesh.

He suddenly realised that he was naked, but it did not matter. The pain was too great for him to worry about such trivial indignities.

Faces flickered through his mind, their lineaments forming photographs that were models of clarity. Nicky, her sweet smile, her loving eyes. Slater, his broad strong caring face. TT, her sardonic smile and mocking gaze. And Carter – broad and strong and battered, a face that could be trusted and that offered no compromise.

Gradually, the pain faded a little and Jam did not try to move again. Instead, he allowed his gaze to move around. At first he had thought this place was dark, but there was a reasonable light source – a dancing radiance from a flickering tallow torch. Flame-light caressed the walls, which were black and even and smooth, like obsidian or black marble although he could not make out any real details. He could see a bed, low down against the ground, a wide flat slab, again fashioned from obsidian or marble. And the floor, he realised, was not dust, but sand.

Jam coughed, and pain from his ribcage filled him with molten fire.

How many broken ribs?

He suddenly became aware of a figure standing behind him. He could tell by the shadows against the wall up ahead, and he tensed, waiting for the blows to rain down again. But they did not come, and Jam groaned from a dry throat as he rolled himself over and looked up at the slender dark shape in the gloom.

The figure was dressed completely in black, but instead of the trade-mark Nex balaclava, the face was bare and visible and gleaming in the flickering orange glow. It was deformed – only a little, but the evidence was still there. The Nex was not entirely human.

'You are the one known as Jam, Spiral operative on the TSAD Division?'

'Not me, pal,' said Jam slowly, his voice little more than a slurred croak. 'You've got the wrong guy.'

'Indeed, you have been responsible for the deaths of *many* of my colleagues.'

'Sorry, mate.' Jam forced a smile through cracked and bloodstained teeth. 'I was just out walking my fucking poodle when your thugs picked me up.'

'This is yours.'

The Nex produced Jam's ECube and held it up for him to see. Jam said nothing, and the Nex smiled, a gentle upturning at the corners of his slightly disfigured face. And then Jam realised what was wrong – the eyes were not quite right, slightly offset, and the nose a bit too low, and the teeth too . . . pointed.

'My name is Mace.'

'Pleased to meet you,' said Jam, huskily through his pain. 'I'd shake your hand but your men have broken my fingers, so I'll just have to wait until I can put a bullet in the back of your insect skull.'

'Tut, tut,' said the slender Nex. 'Such aggression is unnecessary.'

'Like the aggression your men have shown me?'

'An eye for an eye . . .' The Nex smiled softly. 'Do not think because we have been *altered* that we do not have feelings, do not have friends, do not have loved ones. Your people are responsible for the deaths of many Nex . . . there were a few retributions being sought.'

133

'Yeah, fucking great.' Jam went silent, his mind working. 'What do you want? Why haven't you killed me?'

'Bright, as well, for a non-Nex. As I was saying, my name is Mace and I will be your interrogator, your torturer, and ultimately your *friend*. We will spend many, many long hours together, you and I, Mr Jam. You will tell me everything that you know. *Everything*. And we will *learn* from one another – yes, you and I will learn one another's deepest and most intimate secrets.'

'Fuck you.'

'Now who is showing open aggression?'

'Fuck you.'

'Really, Mr Jam, you should learn more respect for those who dangle you from a thread, those who have the power to crush you like a –' he chuckled with dark humour, '– like an insect. Those who hold the power between your life and – ultimately – your death.'

'Fuck you.'

Mace moved closer, lowering himself to a crouch. Jam realised then that his hands were bound, with serrated titanium wire that dug through his flesh and ground jaggedly against the bones of his wrists.

'I won't tell you anything,' said Jam calmly, his stare fixed on the bright copper orbs of the Nex.

'On the contrary,' said Mace, his voice soft and hypnotic as he pulled free a leather pouch and removed a long, slender hypodermic. The syringe was filled with something silver – like the brightest of mercury.

The needle slid in.

The injection filled Jam's veins and *flowed* with every pulse of his heart.

His eyes went wide, and suddenly he screamed a scream so long and loud that he thought his lungs would bleed. Mace smiled, nodding understandingly as Jam writhed on the floor, knowing that the pain that the Spiral man had felt so far was as a tickle to a child, a brush of feather against skin, a mere inconsequence.

'On the contrary, Mr Jam, you will tell me *every*thing.'

```
Leviathan Fuels: Premium Grade LVA
— Go on, make the switch, because you
know your children deserve a better
future . . .
```

Charlotte smiled her sweetest smile, her all-winning smile, the smile that was guaranteed always to get her exactly what she wanted. She tossed back her dark curls and moved towards Freddy, one hand coming to rest lightly on his shoulder, her gaze meeting his, seeing the longing there, inherently understanding the bright lust lurking like a tiny flame within their amorphous depths. I have you, she thought. I have you eating from the palm of my hand. And you *will* do whatever I desire.

'I think we should make the switch,' she purred with alacrity.

'What?' Freddy's eyes went wide, not quite understanding, confused at Charlotte's sudden change of direction – from lust monster to base domestic conversation.

'The switch. To LVA. It's all the rage – every news report on the TV is bleating on about how wonderful this new fuel is. It's revolutionising the oil industry, you know.'

'Is it?' Freddy pulled away, dropping onto the settee with its floral pattern which he truly hated. The floral pattern was a concession he had made for a night's good hard sex, with a digitalVid showing Charlotte performing all manner of disgusting and perverse acts on his body – with her tongue stud – thrown into the bargain. He sighed at the thought, hating the fucking awful shifting couch, and was dragged back to the present. 'I don't think so,' he mouthed, slowly, uneasily, unable to meet her gaze.

'But LVA *is* all the rage! Everybody's doing it!'

'We're not.' Freddy smiled his false skull smile, transferring his gaze from Charlotte's supple form to the TV beyond. This was what he hated: the constant domestic chit-chat. It tortured his brain. Couldn't she see? All he wanted was peace and quiet! Couldn't she *see*? All he wanted was a few fucking minutes' peace every fucking day to compose his own fucking thoughts without domestic fucking haranguing.

His own space.

His own study! Now, that would work . . . a place he could call his own, a place he could be at one with himself. Shut – and lock – the door. Leave the world, and Charlotte's moaning and braying donkey laughs, behind.

'But everybody at work has switched to LVA.' Her lip came out then. A sulky one. 'Why do we have to be the odd ones out? We'll appear strange! Our friends will look down on us!'

'Keeping up with the Joneses, eh? It's got fuck all to do with your buddies at work, and everything to do with our depleted bank balance. How much was this fucking God-awful settee? Jesus, it's like an advertisement for vomit.'

'But you don't understand, Freddy!' she whined.

'The answer is no.'

Charlotte pouted again, moving towards the kitchen door where she leant against the frame and reached for the settee remote control. She spent a few minutes flicking through the designs and watching the floral patterns shimmer and morph across the surface of the settee while Freddy ground his teeth in total annoyance.

It gave him a headache.

A proper fucking *headache*.

How had she picked a settee with a hundred digital floral designs, with every single bastard one an absolute pile of shit? A pain to the eyeballs too. *And* a pain to the wallet . . . but no, she had to have one, had to have her way, had to maintain that pretence of social superiority and puerile domestication.

'But *everybody* is getting LVA! I know it sounds like a lot of money to get the transfer done, but we'll save in the long run, honest we will.'

'We've just spent six months of our fucking salaries on a world cruise! The damn holiday will take us the next two years to pay off! And now you want this? Now listen – which part of "no" don't you understand?'

'But *you* don't understand, Freddy!' Her voice suddenly changed, from an erotic purr to a schizophrenic snarl in the blink of an eye. Below him, floral patterns flickered and changed and he felt incredibly sick. His stomach *heaved* with the swirling remnants of a fried breakfast. But then, at least his decorative projectile vomit would be a far superior design pattern when compared with the swirling artistic smush squirming beneath his buttocks like dead frogs in a bucket of custard at this inopportune moment in time.

'No, Charlotte, you're fucking doing it again. We don't have a conversation any more! You get an idea in your head, and if I don't agree with it then you hit me with a tirade of "buts" until I wither and die like a rose under Bio-CHEM. I'm fucking sick of it, you hear?'

'Sick of it?' she raged. 'I'm offering you the chance to keep up with everybody else! I'm offering you LVA – it's always on the TV, always on the news, all our friends have got it . . .'

'But *we* haven't fucking got it,' snarled Freddy, rubbing at his moustache in annoyance. He climbed to his feet, grabbed his jacket and stared hard at Charlotte's face. 'You've changed since we met, you've really changed. I don't know you any more.'

He stormed from the house, slamming the front door.

'Please do not slam the front door,' called an automated voice with a comedy robot accent.

Charlotte chewed her lip for a moment. Her eyes flickered to the TV, where yet another ad for LVA ran for the full ten-minute slot. In any hour of TV, only twenty minutes was actually programme content – the rest was made up of ads, although her mother said that it had got worse over the years.

'Leviathan Fuels proudly present Premium Grade LVA,' burbled the ad as a smiling man filled his gleaming car with fuel, and then drove across a desert with his family on the rear seat playing happy family games. 'Four hundred miles to the gallon means you can drive across the Sahara on one tank! And it's pollution-free with absolute guarantees – go on, make the switch, because you know your children deserve a better future . . .'

Charlotte reached for the telephone.

When Freddy returned, it was dark, the wind howling outside like some diseased banshee. The house was quiet, except for a low burble of TV, and Charlotte was standing waiting for him. Freddy clutched a credit card receipt in his fist, and Charlotte's eyes dropped to the slip of paper.

'Ah,' she said.

'Yes, you might well say fucking "ah". I can't believe you went behind my back, Charlotte! I can't believe you've been bought by the marketing, the hype. You'll bankrupt us. We just *haven't got the money!*'

'But you *don't understand* –' Charlotte insisted with urgency.

138

'I understand perfectly,' said Freddy coldly, and reached for the largest gleaming kitchen knife.

'What are you doing?'

'Charlotte.' He took a deep breath, eyes gleaming in the gloom. 'I am making you see sense.'

As he murdered her, and she screamed and gurgled, the TV happily babbled the benefits of buying LVA fuel to a background symphony of slaughter.

Jam could feel movement. He came awake groggy, aware that he was being dragged across rough sandy stone by his ankles. Occasionally his head would bump against hard objects, such as steps, but thankfully most of the corridors were linked by ramps. Jam's groggy eyes came open and he could remember the pain following the injection – like pure burning molten metal had been flushed through his body, through every vein and artery and blood vessel. It had crucified him internally, seeped through every pore, wrought evil magic on every limb, every organ until pain had truly been his master. He had wept – but to weep was only to bring more pain on himself and it had gained him nothing.

And now he knew: every human had a breaking point. For some it was financial destitution. For some emotional rejection. For some, cancer. For some, torture. And they had found his limit, his threshold – for Jam had never felt anything like this internal rampant raging fire. And he knew that if they had asked him questions then, to his very great shame, his unbearable sorrow, he would indeed have told them everything.

But there had been no questions.

Just torture . . . and then they had left him until, after many hours, the pain gradually began to throb, to fade, to subside.

139

This worried Jam even more than a torturer's interrogation would have. As he was now dragged, bound with titanium wire, up and down sand-strewn ramps through narrow dark corridors and past sandstone walls created from mammoth rectangular blocks, his mind ticked over. If they had not asked him questions when he'd been ready to talk, then maybe they already knew the answers. And that thought chilled him more than anything had chilled him before.

What came next?

A welcome death?

Jam's head bumped against the ground and he grunted. The two Nex dragging him halted, looked back, smiled and kicked him several times. He took the kicks without a sound . . . after the injection, they were as nothing.

He was dragged along again, for what seemed an age; but in reality he had no real concept of time. Finally, they entered a chamber. It was large and cool: the floor was paved with white marble, and silver pedestals were set out in symmetrical patterns, each one capped with a shallow bowl containing a liquid which burned on the surface, providing light. At the centre were ten benches, ornately carved from marble and sandstone. As Jam was lifted and placed on one, he noticed curious grooves and channels – and his unease grew. It reminded him of a sacrificial altar.

'What's happening here?' he croaked through smashed lips. One of the Nex swiftly planted a wide fist in his face. Stars exploded in his vision and when he could see again he realised that he was alone.

For long hours he lay, shivering with the biting cold until a figure finally appeared.

It was the slender black-garbed figure of Mace.

'Hello again, Mr Jam.'

'What do you want of me?'

'Of you? Now we require . . . nothing.' He smiled and nodded, like a psychiatrist listening attentively to one of his patients.

'I thought you needed answers to questions. About Spiral.'

'We have cracked your ECube. As we suspected, you are Level One. You are a Prime. We have all the answers we could ever need. We know your identity, and we have your codes.'

'What the fuck is this?'

Mace simply smiled, and more figures moved from the shadows. These were cloaked and masked, and they carried metallic objects with slender silver pipes. Jam looked from one to the other, then Mace pulled out the hypodermic syringe filled with bright mercury and Jam started to struggle against the wires that bound him. They bit through his flesh, bit deep, and blood wept tears across his bruised skin.

'No!' he shouted. 'Get away from me . . .'

'I fear this will sting a little.'

As Mace came close, Jam stared into the twinkling copper depths of the Nex's eyes. 'I *will* fucking kill you for this, you cunt,' he snarled.

'Of course you will,' came the gentle reply. 'As you can see, my patients always do.'

He chuckled. The sound was ice.

The needle slipped into Jam's vein again. Fire screamed through his system and just as vision was failing and pain was consuming him in the flames of a billion infernos, he heard Mace's voice quietly say, 'Take his measurements . . . decide which advanced inhibitors will work . . .'

And then he was falling, falling into a well of desolation and he had always thought he was so strong, so powerful, so in command and in control and these fuckers had reduced him to little more than nothing, a shell, a carcass of rotting flesh.

Jam awoke in his cell. This time he was lying in the sand, staring at the heavy stone door with heavy-set steel bars across a small opening that was an excuse for a window. It was through these slits that the flickering light came, and Jam slowly rolled into a sitting position, thankful at last to be alone.

He breathed deeply, but pain lashed at him from his broken ribs. He slowly rubbed broken fingers across his battered face – everything about him felt tender, loose, shattered. Bones in a tin can. He examined his hands – four fingers were snapped. His hands moved across his naked body: every inch of skin, it seemed, bore a bruise and was tender under his gently probing fingers. One ankle had a torn ligament, and there was some damage to one kneecap. His broken arm had been realigned and tightly strapped with some kind of bandage – blood-stained – but at least it meant they possibly had some further use for him. Besides these wounds, it was only his back that was giving him problems and he hoped to God they hadn't damaged his spine with their heavy blows.

Focus.

Jam settled his mind, using army meditation techniques taught by an old sergeant now dead. His breathing became more deep, more relaxed, and he inspected himself more thoroughly – internally and externally. Apart from the physical injuries, it was more the mental strain that worried him . . . and he felt it, nestling at the back of his mind like a dark maggot feasting on his brain.

Fear.

He acknowledged the word, the feeling, and realised

that it was something he was unused to. The fear was of the hypodermic and the silver fluid – and the incredible pain that would follow. Because he knew; Jam knew that they could do that to him, again and again and again until his will was broken. Until he was nothing more than a spastic shell.

Escape.

The word flared in his mind. Before, while being beaten by the Nex, the only feeling that had flared in his subconscious was a need for survival; but now that he had a moment to think and reflect he knew how great was the danger that he – and the rest of Spiral – were in. For a start, the Nex were far more numerous than he'd realised. Spiral were winding down the SAD anti-Nex teams when they should have been putting more manpower and more *fire*power into them.

These fuckers are far from fucking dead. And they're up to something bad . . .

But who commands them?

Who leads?

And just what are they doing?

He mused over this for a while, until the word sidled back into his tortured mind.

Escape.

The impossible.

How to achieve the impossible?

His stare scanned the walls; solid and slippery and very, very high. The room seemed almost to be carved as one unit, although he could in fact see very fine joins between the building materials. The floor was covered with a fine detritus of sand, which meant that they were probably somewhere hot – a desert region, or at least adjacent to one. Therefore he had been airlifted, carried some considerable distance from Slovenia.

The torturer – Mace – had claimed they did not need to question him due to their cracking of the ECube, but Jam doubted this very much. Yeah, just fucking with me prior to more torture, he thought grimly to himself. But then, if they *had* cracked the ECube, had wormed their way through its security features, then in theory they had access to all the Spiral networks and criminal databases . . . and maybe even staff files, mission specifications – everything was stored *somewhere*. They would know where the new major Spiral HQ was, in the heart of London . . . and the other secondary HQs . . .

He shivered, chilled to his very core.

Focus.

One step at a time.

Escape.

Jam dragged himself to his feet, using the low bed to lever himself into a standing position. Waves of pain throbbed through his injured body, but at least he could stand. He limped around the cell, and spotted a tray near the door with a bronze jug of water and a loaf of fresh bread. At least they didn't intend to starve him to death . . .

He ate the bread slowly, for it hurt some of his broken teeth to chew. The water stung his mouth but he forced himself to drink despite the curious stale taste. If they wanted to kill me, he thought, they wouldn't have to use poison – a single bullet would do the job more neatly.

When he had finished his spartan meal, Jam hobbled to the cell door and quietly peered through the bars. The corridor beyond was fashioned from the same huge sandstone blocks that he had seen when he'd been dragged to the large chamber for his second experience of torture under the needle. He could see two brands burning further down the corridor.

'Hello?' he called.

Nothing. No sound, no reply, no interest.

Returning to his bed, Jam sat and picked up the bronze jug. He drained the last few drops and went to work to see what weapon he could fashion from this primitive piece of metal.

The door opened. Three figures stood silhouetted against the flames of the torches.

Jam groaned, lying on the floor, and the figures moved to stand around him. Slowly, Jam rolled over and pulled himself into a seated position, shading his eyes – for with them his torturers had brought light.

As they halted, Jam noticed that one of the Nex had a limp. He lifted his eyes to connect with the burning copper gaze, and he smiled sweetly. 'Fine piece of meat.' He licked his lips. 'Put a bit of Savlon on that, did you, laddie? To take away the sting?'

The Nex growled.

Jam laughed. 'Come on, fucker, I'll eat your fucking heart.'

'Enough.'

The voice was rich, deep, commanding and Jam transferred his gaze to the speaker, who was shrouded and hooded but still dominated through sheer size. Then he glanced at the third figure, standing slightly back – again wrapped in a cloak but with a deformed face showing patches of black and a mouthful of crooked drooling teeth.

'My, but you're all butt-ugly. Like mescaline-popped whores on a crab-riddled Russian sailor.'

The dark figure made no sound, no movement. 'Let me introduce my companions,' came the rich deep voice. 'This is Yushalo.' He gestured to the Nex with the limp whose gaze burned with hatred. Jam smiled, licking his blood-crusted lips. 'You owe him a great debt for his pain. And this is Xsala, apprentice to a Nex you know well – Mace. He would wish to test his newly found skills on your flesh.'

'Hey, you not brought Mace with you? We could, you know, sit down, maybe party a little. You brought any cider? It would be so much fucking fun.'

Xsala moved forward and looked down at Jam. He towered over the Spiral operative and growled something low and crude. His hands, black and twisted, came from beneath the cloak and long black claws slid free of sockets. 'Little man need know when not to speak with disrespect. We cause much pain.'

'Fuck me, bit of a drool problem you're having there, old fella.' Jam smiled, wiping the slime concerned from his skin. Xsala backed away, giving a heavy bass growl, and Jam transferred his gaze to the shrouded figure. 'You fucking want something, or have you just come to watch a weakened man suffer in pain, you perverse arse-fuck?'

'Perfect,' said the shrouded man softly, and turned with his colleagues, leaving the cell. The door closed and the light retreated as Jam frowned, face twisting with confusion.

'What the fuck does that mean?' he bellowed through the bars, but only a gentle hiss of cool breeze, sending a veil of sand swirling across the floor, replied.

Durell stood in the cold chamber, listening to the hum of the cooling fans. Ice rimed the smooth stone walls and made the polished marble floor treacherous to walk upon. The chamber was huge, the ceiling vaulting far above, the slightly concave walls stretching as far as the eye could see. Low slabs of stone were arranged in order, rough-hewn beds of natural rock, many bearing bodies covered with foil sheets.

Durell sighed, moving between the slabs, the cool air caressing him. He pulled his robes tighter around him, despite enjoying the cool air on his skin. He shivered.

It never used to be like this, he thought.

As he approached a slab, anonymous among all the others, Mace rushed towards him, a sorrowful look on his face which Durell knew had been placed there for his benefit. Nex felt few emotions, and a display was nearly always for effect – a throwback to the times when the Nex had been wholly human; a reminder of origins before the integration with insect kind; an almost unconscious physical echo.

'We can do no more.'

Durell reached out with a clawed, twisted hand and pulled back the foil. There lay a body – the body of a man called Feuchter. His head lay twisted to one side, most of the back of the skull missing and what was left glittering with ice. His body had been laid out: parts of the skin were scorched and while the face was perfect the contents of the brain behind it had been destroyed during the final battle he had fought so many months ago against Carter . . .

'He was like a brother.'

'The brain matrix is too far destroyed; we have tried and tried again to repatch and rebuild and model the organics, but there just isn't enough left. We could bring the body back to life, but not the mind. He would be in a deep vegetative state.'

Durell toyed for a while with the notion of bringing the body back, just so that he could look at his old friend animated again, just so that he could talk to him . . . But then, they would not be able to talk, they could not laugh

147

together, they could not *plot* together . . . Feuchter had been one of the few first Nex who had not been horribly deformed by the process of blending.

However, Durell himself had not been so lucky.

He reached out, one clawed hand resting against Feuchter's cold dead forehead. He closed his eyes deep within the folds of his hood, tears welling, burning his skin as they rolled from eyes that were no longer human. And he felt rage welling from some unknown source within him, burning him like a poisoned blade . . . and he knew that he did not have emotions, that he was cold and calculating but this finality and hatred came from somewhere deep inside him. He would destroy Spiral, he would destroy the DemolitionSquads – and he would kill Carter.

And that just as an aside. As a footnote.

Footsteps echoed across the cold stone, and Durell's head came up. Xsala was there, flanked by Nex guards with JK49 sub-machine guns. 'We have problem,' rumbled the huge warrior.

Durell nodded, tears still burning his skin, and covered Feuchter with the foil sheet one last time.

The door opened quietly and a Nex guard stepped in with a tray containing bread and water. His gun was slung across his shoulder negligently and he bent to retrieve the old tray – but it was gone.

'Surprise.' Jam grinned wildly, slamming the edge of the tray into the Nex's throat. Choking, the Nex dropped to one knee and Jam stepped in close, stabbing his new hand-folded bronze dagger through the Nex's eye. Blood poured out, staining Jam's hands, but he held the crude home-made dagger there tight in his fist as the Nex twitched and fought, kicking feebly. Jam drove the

148

dagger in deeper, one hand cradling the back of the Nex's head until finally the legs ceased their kicking and he gently rolled the cooling corpse to the ground. He dragged the body into the cell and, after pulling his blood-smeared dagger free, he yanked off the Nex's trousers, thin cotton jumper and boots and squeezed into them, pulling them on with choked-back yelps and groans of agony over his broken limbs and his many cuts and bruises. The clothes smelt strange – metallic – but Jam was beyond caring. The boots were incredibly tight and they crushed his broken feet, but he did not care as he lifted the JK49, checked the full magazine, closed the door and stood in the corridor, nose lifted to the scent of a gentle breeze.

He felt empowered.

Jam grinned a crooked, blood-crusted grin.

'I'll show you, fuckers,' he muttered.

He reached down and activated his ThumbNail_Map. The ThumbNail_Map was a device, a tiny scanner which replaced an agent's actual nail; to any security equipment it scanned as organic – human tissue – and yet with the right mental augmentation it would illuminate and scan the surroundings, giving an operative an immediate indication of his or her whereabouts. The ThumbNail_Map was still a prototype, but Jam was thankful for it now as the tiny image spun across his nail and located him in the centre of wherever he was imprisoned – a maze of corridors stretching off all around him as he found true north.

Jam moved stealthily, eyes and ears alert.

It was night, although he'd had no way of knowing this while he'd been in his cell. He moved down a long corridor and came to an intersection. Following the ThumbNail_Map, and climbing up a long sloping ramp at a fast limp, Jam halted, blood drying on his fist and finger poised on the JK49's trigger. He listened carefully, listened past the pounding of the pain in his skull.

He moved swiftly, hiding in the shadows as boots trod the stone and four Nex glided past bearing JK49 sub-machine guns. They seemed alert – too alert, and Jam wondered if his escape had already been discovered. He had to assume that it had.

He limped on at speed, pain jolting through him, navigating, thoughts whirling through his now rapidly functioning brain. Priorities: escape, warn Spiral of possible security breach and apparent Nex hive – and Nex mission – kill a few Nex into the bargain and get the fuck away from whatever shit-hole they had dumped him in . . .

Which desert country? Africa? Iran? Australia?

The ramps flowed past. He could hear more activity, distant but coming closer. He forced himself on to greater efforts, pain pounding him from his broken bones and grinding ribcage. He came to steps and groaned inwardly, body jolting with each step, the agony making him want to howl and vomit at the same time.

'Where do you think you are going?'

Jam halted, JK49 trained on a dark figure up ahead, his broken fingers and constant pain making the gun's barrel waver a little. Light gleamed behind Mace, casting his frame in shadows that stretched down the ramp. Jam blinked, pain his master, and he could feel himself swaying and he wanted to scream, 'No! Not now, don't fucking let me down now!' but he was so weak and had lost too much blood and suffered so much pain that he thought, Fuck it! – and opened fire, bullets striking a spray of sparks from the stone by Mace's head—

Something smashed into Jam's back, forcing him down onto one knee. Bullets flashed across the space in spark

150

showers, and then the shooting stopped. Cordite filled the air and the silence was deafening, reverberating from metal-scarred stone. Again, a heavy blow crashed into the back of Jam's skull and his nose slammed against the stone ramp and broke with a terrible crack. He heard himself whimper in the voice of another man, a weaker man, a destroyed man. Got to reach freedom, he thought. Got to warn Spiral . . . he tried to lift the JK49, to whirl and take out the Nex that had crept up behind him in terrible silence – but his body would not work, his fingers would not obey his mental instructions. His vision was hazy and blood had flooded his eyes, filled his mouth and he gagged, drooling crimson to the stone floor. He tried to focus on Mace but a heavy boot stomped on his hand, and he heard his remaining working fingers snap.

Jam's vision swam.

And Mace was there. He held a hypodermic filled with bright silver.

'No!'

'What a shame you wish to leave behind our hospitality,' drawled Mace. 'I do, of course, humbly apologise in advance for the agony that is to come.'

'No . . . more . . .' said Jam through mangled lips, stare fixed on the hypodermic.

Mace bent and thrust in the needle. Jam arched his back, screaming . . .

A large dark-robed figure moved into view. Burnt hands came up and threw back the hood and Jam was transfixed by the horror within. The slitted copper eyes stared down at him with true malevolence.

'I did not introduce myself before,' came the voice. Shoulders moved with a crackling of twisted flesh and tendon.

Jam, panting, head spinning, tried to push himself

away from the monstrosity looming over him. With a curious movement, the heavy robed figure leapt at him and Jam writhed, trying to get away—

The unearthly eyes came close.

Their faces were mere inches apart.

'Who are you?'

'I am Durell,' hissed cold breath.

'But you're dead.'

The head shook, and with his evil eyes gleaming like metal Durell whispered, 'No. Carter shot me, the ship was destroyed . . . but I was never *killed* . . . oh Jam, our delicate nemesis – you have so much to learn.'

Jam's mind was reeling. The hot mercury screeched through his veins. He was crying tears of blood as his gaze passed from the Nex to Mace and finally back with a shudder to Durell.

'I will show you,' said Durell soothingly, 'I want you to know what it is to be a Nex. I want you to understand, my friend.'

Durell reached slowly, teasingly, towards the broken Spiral agent with the tentative care of a lover . . . reached towards the helpless body of Jam with long, curved, bloodstained claws.

And Jam closed his eyes.

CHAPTER 6

FOUNDATION STONES

The small copper eyes stared at Carter and the creature's twisted fangs drooled a little saliva. One claw dipped to touch its own body and it glanced down at its blood. Then it smiled nastily. 'I think you suffer much pain, little man.'

The wind from the black helicopter increased behind him and realisation suddenly struck Carter. Natasha had lifted the chopper into the air and she was dipping the nose, the rotors tilting to form a vertical wall of flashing blades. Carter dropped to the ground and rolled under the flashing tips of the armoured rotors as Nats guided the machine forward a touch. The blades hissed and skimmed the snow.

The creature tried to leap forward, but was beaten back by the violent wind and the promise of instant flashing titanium death. Carter stared from behind this thrumming wall of lethal blades. Natasha held the helicopter steady with a hum of cold matrix engines, wavering only a little, and Carter smiled at the entity as if from behind a shimmering screen of liquid metal.

'Next time, fucker,' he snarled.

'My name is Dake, and I'll be waiting for all eternity,' snapped the huge creature, blood pumping from the holes in its body – which it ignored.

'Carter, I can't fucking hold it!' came Natasha's panicked scream.

He moved fast, climbing into the chopper as the armoured creature turned and walked leisurely to one side. The Nex opened fire; JK49s thundered across the snow and Natasha urged the helicopter into the air, bullets leaving trails of tracer all around and striking a triple thump across one alloy flank.

'Quick thinking.'

'We're not out of this shit yet.'

They climbed steeply, engines howling and bullets screaming past them as the world of snow opened up like a huge white veil. The sky was a deep cool blue and Carter calmed his breathing, staring straight ahead, ignoring the whiz and hiss of bullets until the chopper finally sped out of range . . .

'*Well done*,' came the corpse-cold voice of Kade.

'Yeah, you want something?'

Carter could feel Kade smile – could sense the smirk as Kade mocked him. '*You should have killed it. I would have killed it. You are showing your weakness, Carter, showing your fucking age . . .*' Kade spat the word like a bullet. '*You're getting old, slow, weak, spineless, and it won't be long now, my friend, before some big Nex fucker cuts you in half and leaves your bleeding twin carcasses twitching on the pavement—*'

'I thought you were here to help,' whispered Carter.

'*Just trying to make you strong, brother. Just trying to warn you against the ravages of age, the natural slowing of the body, the terminal illness of the perpetually decaying mind . . .*'

154

'There's only one decaying mind here, and that's yours,' snapped Carter. He forced Kade away.

Carter realised that his eyes were closed, and he opened them, peering out across the spectacular snow-clad mountains of Switzerland and the villages and towns tucked neatly away in the Earth's folds.

He released a deep, pent-up breath.

'We lose them?'

'They're not taking up the chase.'

'We scared them away?' laughed Carter, an edge of disbelief to his voice.

Natasha looked at Carter and grinned. 'No, I think the dumb bastards shot up the other two helicopters! Jesus, give the Nex soldiers an IQ, somebody.'

'Better we don't make them too intelligent,' said Carter, rubbing at his eyes. Exhaustion hit him with a right hook. The recent quakes, the events at the hotel, witnessing the destruction of Zermatt, the chase through the snow, the destruction of the Comanche and the final escape from the massive deformed and twisted killer they had met in the snow – all combined to bleed him of energy. 'God, I'm fucking tired.'

'Get some sleep,' said Natasha. 'I'm OK with this thing.'

'You only got your pilot's licence recently . . .' He sounded a little worried.

'I'm fine, Carter. Get your head down, and then we'll switch in a couple of hours when we hit the bad weather.'

Carter's hand reached out and touched Natasha's thigh; then he dragged free his heavy quilted jacket and rolled it into a ball, resting it against the cockpit glass. The heavy thrumming of the rotors merged with his thoughts and the vibrations of the machine around him.

He dropped into sleep and fell through darkness. His dreams were like night.

The creature watched as the black helicopter soared high into the blue heavens, small copper eyes focused and intent. 'I know you,' it grated between horribly deformed jaws, and flexed its bloodstained talons. The sounds of gunfire echoed, chasing the fleeing Spiral agents and the being turned, looking at Kattenheim – who stood with arms folded, a slight smile across his brutally scarred face.

'You smile? They escape! You want we pursue?'

'No . . . Carter! He doesn't remember me,' said Kattenheim softly. 'Mr Carter does not remember me – which is a good thing, I think. But I surely remember him . . . although, in all fairness, I was less attractive then.' He laughed softly, fingers gently caressing his disfigured visage.

The ScorpNex chuckled too, a deep rumbling sound and a distorted mimicry of its master. It lifted a claw and made a reverberating cracking noise, like hollow bones snapping, like the cracking open of a human skull. The nearby Nex immediately ceased their machine-gun fire and turned to file back into the low concrete buildings, guns hot in smooth gloved hands, eyes emotionless and fixed on the next task ahead.

'You sure we not chase? We kill good, Kat.'

Kattenheim shook his head, and led the massive creature into one of the buildings. Inside, a soft orange light flowed around them, and there was incredible heat. They moved to a low-ceilinged chamber and seated themselves on the bare earth floor. The light bathed them both, glowing against skin and armour, gleaming from their glistening eyes.

'Kattenheim?' came a deep, rumbling voice.

'Durell. It is good to hear your voice.'

'You have an intruder?'

'A certain Mr Carter, I believe.'

'That fucker . . . an unhealthy coincidence that he found you, I hope – although I doubt it. Did you allow the ScorpNex to taste his blood?'

'Carter . . . escaped,' said Kattenheim, with a wry gentle smile. 'He is a very, very resourceful man. Once he was discovered he did not flee the area. He brought the fight to us.'

'It is extremely unfortunate that you did not secure his death,' said Durell coldly.

'The ScorpNex retained his scent. It got within inches of taking him out . . .'

'And yet, not close enough. Carter is too fucking resourceful.' Durell laughed, a cold, unlovely sound. 'It's almost as if he is one of us.'

'Yes.'

'Now, Carter is heading for London and that on its own may be enough for us to secure his demise. Have the Foundation Stones there been initiated? The QEngine testing complete?'

'The testing was perfect. We had one hundred per cent accuracy rates, and the engineering could not be faulted. The QHub is working smoothly and I will upload the processor links when we finish this dialogue.'

'Good.' Durell's voice was thoughtful. 'Kattenheim, my friend, it would seem that we are nearly ready for the assault. I know we were planning on building . . . but it would seem events are overtaking us . . . we are being pushed, as always, by the enemy that is Spiral.'

'They think themselves all-powerful,' said Kattenheim softly.

Durell laughed, a laugh of genuine humour this time. 'Spiral are fools and they will die like fools,' he said.

As Carter and Natasha flew further west, the weather worsened over Germany and Natasha had to activate the ECube to aid with navigation. Rain lashed down around the small black helicopter as they swept low over the sprawling Black Forest, dark and foreboding under heavy leaden skies. When Carter awoke from his slumber, he dictated a quick sitrep on their position and the ECube blipped an acknowledgement from the Spiral controllers. They already knew of the Comanche's destruction and had sent out automated scouts called PopBots – tiny semi-sentient globes of black alloy about the size of an apple that would analyse and report on the crash site.

The rain smashed against the cockpit and with much awkwardness Carter and Natasha exchanged controls, swapping seats and allowing the more experienced Carter to drop the helicopter even lower until they were flashing above the sweeping forests and banking past the occasional castle that stood on a jagged tier or cliff of rock.

The ECube rattled in Natasha's hands just as she was falling into sleep's welcoming embrace. Groaning softly, she squinted at the machine and read the data flashing across it.

'Shit.'

'What is it?' Carter glanced at her, one eye on the rolling sweep of darkened green below them, one eye on the shocked whiteness of Natasha's face. 'Bad news?'

'Very bad news. It's Jam's latest SAD mission; it has been reported as a failure.'

'A . . . failure?'

Carter stared long and hard at Natasha as the implication sunk into his weary brain. 'What are the CSRs?' The seconds seemed to last an age. He could not bring himself to acknowledge the very real possibility of Jam's death.

'The whole team are missing – Jam, Slater and TT. They were on a mission in Slovenia, up in the mountains researching a possible sighting by a local cattle farmer. PopBots were subsequently dispatched, but nothing has been discovered – no bodies, no vehicles, nothing. They have simply disappeared and all that remains is a coordinate from Jam's ECube's automated PanicBurst, nano-seconds before the ECube deactivated . . . or was forced to deactivate.'

'Not good.'

'They're not dead, Carter.'

'Have you heard yourself? ECubes don't fucking deactivate – they're nearly indestructible! And if his PB initiated, that meant vital signs gave his ECube a severe and violent kick up the arse. No, it's a bad situation . . . has anybody been assigned to an investigation?'

'Not yet,' said Natasha softly, her gaze fixed to her lover's stern jaw, the swathe of stubble across his face making him appear older and rougher. Whatever had happened, Natasha knew then – in that instant – that Carter would find out. Find out and kill like no other man on Earth could kill, if he thought it was necessary . . . and deserved.

'Once we have been briefed at this Spiral meet, then I will go and find them – if they're still alive.'

'But this looks important. Hundreds of Squads are being drafted in . . .'

Carter glanced at her, frowned and said, 'If there are hundreds of Squads being drafted in then they won't

need me so much. I'll put in a showing and then I'm
gone ... find me the coordinates and put in an
Investigation Request. Do it, Natasha, do it now.'

'You don't know yet what Spiral wants ...'

'Spiral can fucking wait. This is Jam. This is my
friend.'

They travelled in silence, rain thundering against the
cockpit. The black helicopter lifted, rising into the
deluge to skim over a series of high and densely forested
hills, then dropped like a black bullet into a valley following the course of a wide river swollen by the storm.
In the distance lightning flickered, illuminating the darkness for an instant in electric blue with a touch of
blinding white.

Carter blasted headlong into the storm.

The gentler terrain of France provided an easier ride for
Carter and Natasha as the rain slowly lessened, and
there appeared several tentative glimpses of watery sunshine. But after the churning slate-grey waters of the
English Channel the weather worsened once again.

Carter could not stop thinking about Jam ...

Dead?

He could not be dead ...

Carter's mouth was a thin grim line as they headed
towards London and the Spiral meet at this most secret
of HQs a couple of miles from the city centre. Disguised
among a scattering of high-rise buildings, bland and
nondescript, it was an architectural nonentity, bleached
concrete with silvered windows. The Spiral HQ was a
wholly unremarkable building above ground – but below
was a warren of the most incredible high-tech activity,
linked by mammoth networks of deep tunnels to other
HQs, the SP1_Stores and several UK military bases.

It was also linked via the newly blossoming Spiral-GRID.

As the black helicopter swept across southern England darkness was falling. The 'copter whined low over rolling fields and damp autumn woodland, over drenched towns and bleak tarmac. Headlights cut swathes below, and Carter lifted the helicopter a little, avoiding urban areas where he could, and as the sprawl of the Home Counties stretched towards him and the population and housing density increased so he lifted the helicopter further and further into the storm until they were buffeted by wild winds.

'Not far now.'

'You'd make a wonderful navigator.' Carter smiled wearily. 'Your accuracy and grasp of details in navigational matters are astounding.'

'Yeah, Carter, and you'd make a superb comedian.'

'I try, I try. After all, life's a fucking joke.'

They were closing on the bleak concrete of the Spiral HQ as a sudden deep rumbling echoed across the world, reverberating and booming through the heavens, an almighty noise that drowned the sounds of the storm . . .

'Bad thunder,' said Natasha softly.

The chopper's rotors spun, glistening under the rain. Carter frowned.

The 'thunder' did not halt. It increased in tempo . . .

'That's not thunder,' said Carter slowly, eyes widening as the distant buildings far below seemed to vibrate, trembling and swaying, and he dropped the helicopter and suddenly, like a deck of cards toppling a whole section of streets collapsed, crushed by some invisible lump hammer. Carter's eyes lifted to the distant glow of London. He powered forward through the rain, the rumbling all around them, sometimes rising in pitch, sometimes dying off to nothing more than a distant grumbling.

The lights of London loomed close, and Carter closed on Spiral HQ's concrete tower. The wail of klaxons was springing up now from all parts of the city – fire engines, police cars, ambulances, their sirens howling through the storm – and Carter saw another building, a magnificent Victorian stone edifice, crumble and spew its contents across the street, whirling bodies tossed like pulp through the air to mash with the crashing stones—

'Fuck,' hissed Natasha.

Carter said nothing.

'What's happening, Carter? What the fuck is going on?'

They swept over the HQ; below swarmed a hundred Spiral operatives, some just recently arrived for the meet, all heavily armed and all glancing up from the wide expanse of roof as the helicopter dropped from the skies . . .

They brought the stolen Nex chopper down to land on the roof and immediately they were swarmed over by heavily armed guards. The earthquake took London in its fist and shook it and crushed it and fucked it hard . . . lightning flickered, illuminating a scene falling dropping *spinning* into Hell as streets compressed into piles of rubble and buildings were uprooted like concrete trees and spewed in a parody of dominoes . . . and below there was screaming, and the flashing of blue lights, the wails of sirens. Police and military helicopters took to the air as the networks were flooded by a million distress calls and all anybody could do was stand there and watch from the rain-soaked parapet as in a few short minutes the earthquake ripped the guts from London and left ugly rancid entrails showing from beneath the battered torn streets.

'I don't believe it,' hissed Natasha, rain soaking her hair and her pale shocked face, dripping from her eyelashes, lightning flashing in her eyes and tears mingling with the rain. 'I just don't fucking believe it.'

Carter stood, silent, eyes wide and absorbing the horror show before him.

The building shook.

'Get back in the chopper,' growled Carter, his hand touching Natasha's back, guiding her towards the vehicle. The rumbling beneath their feet intensified, vibrating through the soles of their boots to a distant backing track of screams. Spiral HQ suddenly lurched, and the men and women present were launched across the ground, some falling, others staggering. There came distant groans of stressed steel like a dinosaur screaming in pain. Carter was dragging Natasha now, towards the helicopter which – disappeared.

The building was torn in half, a huge gash ripping across the ground at their feet. Spiral operatives disappeared in the blink of an eye as the structure was separated, dragged into two halves by convulsions of the bucking ground beneath them. The helicopter fell, plunging through the gaping wound in the concrete, and the entire section of tower block drifted away from the severed other half and then halted, leaving a gap of perhaps three or four metres. The whole building was torn in two – a teetering parody of a skyscraper – and Carter could see offices, carved as if by a huge magic sword, sliced neatly in two. The helicopter crashed down further, smashing through the rooms and equipment and people, twisting and compressing until it became wedged a hundred metres below them.

A cold wind blew.

Carter's head turned swiftly left and right; people

were screaming, some hanging on to the edges of this sudden rift as their comrades rushed to help. The rumbling continued, a roar of concrete unrest. He licked his lips, realised that he was holding on to Natasha with a grip of iron and dragged her back as they moved away from the precipice.

Machine-gun fire rattled from the rubble-strewn streets below.

'We've got to get out of this fucking building,' Carter snarled.

Nats was pale, speechless.

Carter ran back to the parapet and watched the swarm of Nex sprint across the rubble, their submachine guns spouting fire. Several Nex were punched from their feet by return fire from the Spiral building. Below him, he felt the structure shudder – as if wondering whether or not to collapse . . .

'*You only have a few seconds,*' Kade whispered softly.

Being the Spiral HQ, this building which was nondescript to look at nevertheless had a host of innovative design features; one of these was safety chutes from roof to ground. As the people on the roof milled around in horror at the events unfolding beneath them, several activated the chutes which sprung into life, huge tubes jettisoning diagonally to the streets below. Carter tried to warn them but the noise was too loud. He watched helplessly as twenty or so jumped into the chutes and sped to the safety of the street below – and straight into a hail of JK49 fire at the hands of the crouching and merciless black-masked Nex.

Carter's Browning was out. He leaned over the parapet and started firing, a grim look of hatred on his face. Thirteen bullets found thirteen heads and blasted thirteen brains across the rubble. In a smooth movement

Carter released the empty mag from the gun and slotted a fresh one home. More bullets spat from the Browning. Others saw Carter's actions and followed his example – still more bullets rattled down on the Nex. The falling rain was joined by a hailstorm of metal and the Nex turned, retreated to a nearby building and took up defensive positions behind crumbling brick and stone, guns coughing and crackling whenever a member of Spiral tried to escape—

Natasha touched Carter's arm.

'We're fucked that way,' he snapped, whirling around. 'We're going to have to head for the tunnels under the HQ – head for the SpiralGRID . . .'

The earthquake chose that moment to smash and stomp its way across the helpless city of London.

Carter and Natasha and a hundred other Spiral people watched an invisible scythe sweep across buildings containing thousands of people, a wave of energy which crushed the buildings into the ground.

The collapsing edifices pumped dust and stone up into the rain-darkened sky and the screams were terrible to hear.

Natasha dragged Carter around and pointed.

'Look, there are children over there – on the other side of the gap.'

'What? *What?*' Carter's eyes narrowed. 'How fucking bad can it get?' he snarled. He sprinted to the edge of the precipice; the building had moved a little more, was still juddering and vibrating, responding to invisible signals at the heart of the quake. The wrecked helicopter had groaned and screeched its way down another few metres. He glanced hurriedly at Nats. 'What the fuck are children doing on the roof of the Spiral HQ?'

'There's a crèche, you moron.'

'For fuck's sake! A crèche *here*?'

There were five children, milling around the doorway to the roof, their small bodies framed by a rectangle of yellow. They moved slowly, in a daze, directly opposite to where Carter and Nats stood gazing over the chasm in front of them.

More machine-gun fire howled from the streets below as Spiral led an offensive against the Nex. Nex bodies were flipped spinning and spraying gore, until a large detachment of DemolSquads forced the Nex further back, away from the perimeter of the rumbling building, and set up a temporary front line of safety before the shaking Spiral HQ.

As Carter glanced up, Natasha turned, ran and leapt the four-metre-wide chasm between the two sections of the building.

'No!' he snapped – but it was too late.

She landed lightly, boots crunching stones, and glanced around, grinning back at Carter. She sprinted forwards and gathered the children to her, the girls crying into her shoulder, the boys with tear- and grime-smeared cheeks trying to look brave in the face of this nightmare.

She herded them towards the gaping rift, which groaned and grumbled.

The building – or its two separate halves – rocked dangerously, steel and concrete screeching in torture, showers of dust and tiny lumps of concrete raining down.

Carter whirled and grabbed at the nearest man's sleeve. 'We need help.' He met the huge man's stark grey-eyed stare. Carter pointed.

The man, bearded, clad in black and with an SA1000 slung over his shoulder, nodded and followed Carter to the edge of the precipice. 'Hold my back.' Strong fingers grasped him, and Carter edged himself towards the crumbling torn edge.

The quake smashed more waves of destruction across London.

Again, Spiral HQ trembled as the earth beneath it was raped.

Natasha picked up the first child, a blond-haired boy with a red nose and snot covering his upper lip. Her stare met Carter's as she gave a smile of calm and control – and threw the child across the abyss. Carter caught a tight grip on Tigger dungarees, and he turned, depositing the child on the ground. 'Over there!' shouted Carter. 'Go to that woman over there!'

Seeing their plight, more Spiral operatives had come to help. As the earthquake roared around them and they faced certain death, they put aside their own fears and need for escape to offer help—

Natasha threw the second child. Carter caught it.

Stone crumbled from the edge where he stood and he glanced down involuntarily. The stolen Nex helicopter was a crumpled heap now, compressed and crushed between the heaving, buckling stone, brick and steel. Huge strands of reinforcing wire stuck from the concrete like severed rusting arteries. Far below, Carter could see fire and smell burning. Smoke trailed up towards him in lazy black spirals.

The third child flew across the gap, arms flapping, and smashed into Carter's chest. His own arms wrapped tight, securing the little girl, and he passed her back to the human chain that had leapt into existence to aid these stranded children . . .

The fourth child came, screaming, mouth wide. Carter grasped at her as she bounced and slipped, but his strong powerful fingers grabbed her clothing and passed her gently to the ground.

'Mummy!' she whimpered.

The huge man with the beard smiled, and patted her head. 'She'll be on the ground now, luvvie. Go on over to the chutes – it'll be fun and then you'll see her again.'

'Thank you.'

The big man smiled again, then grasped Carter's jacket more tightly.

'One more.'

'One more,' agreed Carter, breathing deeply.

Black smoke billowed up from the unnatural crevasse. His gaze met Natasha's through the smoke and heat as more tremors roared around them. Carter could feel the building moving beneath his boots and he suddenly felt sick to the core of his soul.

What the *fuck* is going on?

Natasha lifted the last child in her dirt-smeared fingers. A little boy, short hair, chubby tear-stained face, but with a look of defiance on it: he dangled precariously from her grasp. She took a step back and Carter could read the exultation of rescue in her face, in her glowing deep brown eyes as she launched the boy across the chasm and through the smoke and Carter's hands grappled blindly, slipping from the boy as the Spiral man behind him reached forward, plucking the child from Carter's fumbling grip and hauling the boy to safety . . .

There came a deafening, screaming roar that went on and on and on and Carter wanted to cover his ears and his eyes were streaming and then he was engulfed by a wave of dust from below which cut into his eyes and mouth and he yelled, saliva drooling from grey lips. The section of the building on which Natasha stood began to sway crazily and she lost her footing and fell to one knee.

Her stare was fixed on Carter through the dust as the building moved, shifted and started to crumble . . .

'*No!*' snapped Kade.

'I can save her,' growled Carter.

He leapt across the chasm, into the dust.

ADVERTISING FEATURE

The TV sparkled into life with a digital buzz of electro-hum, diamond-sharp images spinning and morphing into the jewelled liquid logo of Leviathan Fuels.

You may be wondering who Leviathan Fuels are? After all, we have only been on the scene for a few months, but with this . . . Over-cheerful Japanese scientist holds up a small metal object with a complex series of tubes and dials . . . *you can convert your road vehicle, be it diesel, petrol or gas, to run on LVA for only a few hundred dollars – LVA, a new fuel for the future, the fuel of choice for over two million happily satisfied customers. . .*

Scene dissolves: two cars driving through spotless mountain passes high in the Alps. One car runs out of fuel and an angry man stands by the kerbside, kicking the tyre and pulling his Mr Bad Mr Angry face, whilst the second car . . .
Scene cross-fades: drives on, and on, children [1 × black, 1 × white, 1 × oriental] singing happily on the back seat and playing extremely violent hack-and-slash-'em-ups on their 3D HoloStation . . .

400 hundred miles to the gallon! Go on, make the smart choice . . . choose Leviathan fuels. Your children deserve a better future . . .

Scene/text scroll R→L [Arial black] acr. vid: *And now, we have over 11,000 fuel outlets across the civilised world!!! Be smart! Become a Leviathan! Leviathan Fuels will change your life.*

SCENE DISSOLVES TO RED

CHAPTER 7

BREED

When you're a kid, summer lasts for ever. School finally shuts in a tumult of chaos and high spirits, and the weeks stretch away for an infinity, long days spent running through tall grass, down the park, the Church Fields, through Witch Woods and towards Jacob's Ladder and the Old Nazi Bunker where they imagined a previous litany of war crimes had taken place.

Summer lasts for ever . . .

'*Until you die*,' sneered Kade.

The pain whirled inside Carter's brain: the agony of memories; the poisoned narcotic needle of childhood; the atomic blast of innocence and naivety and the high bright insane fucked-up whirling loss of these delicate treasures . . .

'It could never be the same again,' he muttered.

As the black quake dust filled his mouth.

'*Oh, to be a child again*,' mocked Kade. '*To languish in the mire of mockery, to paddle in the piss-stream of puerile poetry, to reel in the eternal uncertainty of pain and confusion and*

hate . . . it is like a dream to me, a bad dream, a dark
dream . . . the best of dreams, my dark and twisted brother.'

'Remember it?' whispered Kade.
   'Remember it, my friend?
   'Surely you hadn't forgotten?
   'Surely you hadn't forgotten about . . . Crowley? How
poetic. How romantic. So beautiful I could be fucking sick . . .'

It was summer. The days were long. The summer holi-
days had come and school was like a distant mad, bad
dream. The days flowed into one another as the boys
played on Church Fields: one day they were soldiers
engaged in some terrible war against terrorism – just like
their dads – another they were space heroes spat out into
the universe on a terrible mission. On yet another they
were aircraft pilots, killing all the evil and terrible drug
barons in Colombia. They ran through the grass, into the
woods, down to the river. They played in the park, in the
concrete tubes, on the swings and the slide. They paddled
in the shallow fast-flowing river, imagining incredible
depths sporting terrifying monsters. Morris brought his
BMX-i with Alloy-Kick2 to enable high stunt-jumping
and they built a ramp off the top of the steps leading
down the edges of the Church Fields; they dared one other
to jump the two-metre drop and Carter was the first,
flying through the air with a shout of triumph, the BMX-i
landing with a violent wobble and a clang as the back
wheel bottomed out through under-inflated tyres.
   The days were long and good.
   Childhood, it seemed, would never end.

'But you're not thinking, Carter, not thinking straight. Have
you forgotten Crowley? Have you forgotten that bastard? What

he and his friends did? Don't tell me you pushed that out of your mind as well, you spineless worthless cheap whore bastard . . .'

'Get him!' came the roar.

'Run!' hissed Carter.

'Why?' asked Jimmy in innocent fear.

'Run!' Carter cried.

They ran, Carter holding Jimmy's hand, guiding his blind brother down the narrow woodland trail; they stomped through mud, kicked nettles and plants from their path, could hear the distant roar of the river. They suddenly changed direction, trying to lose their pursuers. We can hide by the river, thought Carter, Jimmy's hand sweating with fear in his own. He tugged Jimmy along, guiding the younger lad, his brotherly need to protect intense . . .

'And the rest,' mocked Kade, *'Don't blank it out, Carter; remember it. Remember it all.'*

'We're going to kill you!' came Crowley's hoarse thundering yell.

Evil laughter drifted down through the woods; a comedy accompaniment.

Carter could hear the river growing closer. He increased his speed, dragging Jimmy along behind him. The two boys hurtled down a narrow trail, weeds and nettles whipping at their bare legs.

'I can't run any more,' wept Jimmy.

'Come on, push yourself . . .'

'I can't!' wailed the younger boy.

'Come *on!*' Carter hissed, slapping his brother around the back of the head. 'You'll get us both caught and

175

Crowley will mess us up bad. You remember what he did to Morris? You *remember*? He's still in the hospital!'

With Jimmy wailing they pushed on, the sound of the river coming closer and closer and closer; and then it exploded into view in a burst of colour and noise and movement and Carter dragged Jimmy to a halt. There was a steep drop directly ahead of them, sheer rock falling into the fast wide flow that cascaded violently over pebbles and large water-polished boulders.

'Where are we?' came Jimmy's panicked voice.

Carter's twelve-year-old gaze swept along the river bank. And then he saw it: a huge wide pipe crossing the river. A makeshift bridge whose interior was used to carry sewage. It was bright green and had two high iron-railing fences at each end to protect its precious cargo from the abuse of vandals.

'This way.'

They ran along the top of the river cliff towards the pipe.

The boots of Crowley and his band of followers – Glass, Trigger and Johnny Jones, and a couple of nameless giggling girls in the chase for fun and the cheap thrill of bullying – thundered after the two boys. Rain started to fall from a suddenly dark sky.

The narrow ledge rapidly became muddy, slippery and treacherous. Jimmy clung with one hand to Carter, and with his other to clumps of grass, his mouth gasping at the sudden violent downpour, his lips twitching with fear and surprise at this sudden change in their fortunes . . .

'You're making me wet!' screamed Crowley from behind them, his logic twisted, his hatred a physical entity living like a demon within his big fists.

Carter stopped and turned, his hair plastered to his head. Crowley was grinning at him from the beginnings of

176

the narrow ledge; behind him his worms jostled, vying to see what was happening. Carter heard the giggles of the girls, Mandy and Trish, the stink of their cheap child-whore perfume drifting through the rain.

'Don't come any closer,' said Carter, his voice low and suddenly dangerous.

'Or what?' said Crowley. 'I'll do to you what I fucking did to Morris. And he's still in the fucking hospital.'

'Why don't you just leave us alone?'

Crowley said nothing, just grinned a real nasty grin. His shaved head gleamed under the rain as the smirk fell from his face, leaving a mocking evil in its wake.

'We know you're strong,' said Carter wearily, wiping rain from his own face. 'What have you got to prove?'

'Nothing,' snapped Crowley. 'Nothing at all. I just like hurting people.'

Jimmy shook Carter's arm, his grip tight.

'What, little brother?'

'I'm frightened.'

'Come on, we'll go across the pipe. The girls won't be able to follow – because they're girls. I can see them getting fed up already – they didn't expect to get wet.'

'I don't think I can get across the pipe – we tried before, remember?'

'But you're bigger now,' said Carter soothingly, despair creeping into the edges of his soul. He tugged at Jimmy's hand; obediently, the younger boy followed.

Why wouldn't Crowley give up?

Why didn't he clear off and torture somebody else?

They crept along the muddy ledge over the suddenly raging river. The drop below the two boys was terrifying, at least thirty feet down to rocks and the raging waters beneath. They edged along and, glancing up, Carter gritted his teeth. Crowley, Glass, Johnny Jones and Trigger were following. They had left the whining mud-splattered girls behind.

It became a race.

A slippery, treacherous race.

Sliding in mud, grabbing on to the wet grass for support, they edged along towards the distant green sewerage pipe; the fans of iron at each end – designed to stop people using the wide pipe as a bridge as well as to protect it from vandals – grew slowly closer, gleaming slick in the rain.

'Are they getting any nearer?' gasped Jimmy. He was splashed with mud, his face red with exertion, his hands bleeding from the sharp blades of grass and occasional thorns.

'No,' said Carter.

They raced on. Once Jimmy slipped and Carter grabbed his collar, hauling the younger boy back onto the ledge. After a few minutes the pipe loomed close, gleaming under the rain, a wet, gradually sloping green tube connecting the two banks over the raging torrent—

They reached one end of the pipe, panting for breath, and Carter leapt lightly onto the slick surface and helped Jimmy up. 'You remember? Remember last time how you climbed?'

'I . . . I think so,' said Jimmy.

'You little bastards!' shouted Crowley, still wrestling his way through the mud. He was splashed and coated with it and now his face displayed true fury and a controlled hatred. His black Guinness T-shirt was plastered to his rotund and stocky barrel frame.

Carter hoisted Jimmy up, and the boy grasped the iron rungs; his feet found purchase on the horizontal cross bars and he began to climb. Carter jumped up behind his brother and hand over hand they climbed to the top.

Jimmy tentatively reached across and eased himself over the crooked lip, with Carter close behind, giving him support—

They climbed down and landed lightly on the other side.

Crowley reached the foot of the iron fan. He grasped the vertical bars, pressed his face against them and glared at Carter and Jimmy – only a foot away from him but protected by this barrier.

'Better get used to that look,' said Carter.

'I'm going to kill you, then make you watch as I smash and kick your little shit of a blind brother to fucking death,' said Crowley, illogical as always. He spat through the bars at Carter who backed away, turning to follow his brother tentatively across the slippery pipe—

Crowley, Trigger, Johnny Jones and Glass were all climbing, Crowley in the lead as was his right by physical strength. His boots made short work of the climb. He launched his body over the top and landed in a crouch. His gaze lifted and fastened on the retreating backs of Carter and Jimmy.

'Stop!' he shouted.

Carter and Jimmy turned at the sound.

'You've got nowhere to run,' growled Crowley, his voice husky and filled with the heady emotion of the hunt and its climax: the kill.

The rain pounded; in the distance thunder rumbled, the snarling of the storm. Black cumulonimbus towered over the boys – insignificant insects far below against the tiny glossy green pipe. Beneath the pipe the river raged, its torrent crashing across the stones in a fury of savage, natural power.

Carter moved protectively in front of Jimmy. Jimmy's hand came to rest on Carter's shoulder.

'What's happening?' whispered the younger boy.

Crowley moved closer. Grunting, the other boys landed on the pipe behind him and moved to back Crowley up, slipping and sliding on the wet surface, their faces split into grins.

They had played his game before.

And the outcome was always the same . . .

Pain.

'You want to fight me here?' sneered Carter, peering nervously over the edge of the pipe.

'Why not?' growled Crowley.

And then—

'*Remember it, Carter? Remember the details, the gory details? Don't push it away like a pussy—*'

There came a sudden wail.

An abrupt and shocked cry, filled with desperation . . .

Jimmy slid from the pipe, hands trying feverishly to grasp the slick wet metal. He slid from view, his scream echoing forlornly through the rain—

The slap of the impact sent a shiver through Carter.

But he did not look down.

He stared; stared hard, icily at Johnny Jones, at Trigger, at Glass; and then stared with an infinity of hatred at Crowley. The stances of the boys had changed; they were leaning, peering over the edge, rain pouring down around them.

Crowley was the first to look up, his face ashen, transfixed by Carter's dark stare.

'Shit,' he whispered. 'You see? You see his fucking head?'

'All his brains came out . . .' whispered Trigger.

The boys' faces were locked in masks of shock; their eyes wide, their mouths forming silent Os.

Carter did not look down. He stared, arms hanging

180

limply by his sides, dark eyes drilling into Crowley – and the others . . .

Crowley took a step back.

'Don't fucking stare at me, Carter – it's all *your* fucking fault! You brought him here!'

Carter said nothing.

The storm pounded him with its darkness.

Trigger and Johnny Jones turned, ran down the pipe towards the metal fan; they were closely followed by Glass and the three boys climbed the iron grillework and thudded heavily into the mud on the opposite side, leaving—

Crowley, facing Carter.

They stared at one another. Crowley's face was ashen, sweat- and rain-streaked, his tongue darting out to lick at his lips. Carter's head dipped a little, his eyes hooded, before peering back up at Crowley, his mouth a solid straight line without expression. His was no longer the face of a child and echoes of something dark squirmed across his features.

Carter moved first.

Slowly, he knelt on the pipe. Only then did he glance over at the river below. The torrent had already washed away the brains and the blood, but Jimmy lay twisted on a bank of large oval rocks, water gushing and white foam bubbling over and around him, one hand flopping loosely in the flow.

His head had been cracked open like a macheted coconut.

And he was quite obviously dead.

Carter stood in one fluid movement.

Crowley licked his lips and began to back way, rubber boot soles squealing on the pipe.

'Fight me now,' said Carter softly, his words almost lost under the downpour of rain.

'N – no.'

'Fight me *now*, you fucker.'

Crowley turned, boots slipping and sliding on the pipe; he sprinted, then leapt at the iron fan and scrambled up and over. He jumped from the top, sprawling face down in the mud; he did not stop then, but scrambled to his feet, his dirty face twisted in pain, and limped off into the woods.

The rain lessened.

The storm's pounding finally stopped.

Shafts of sunlight broke through the heavy black clouds, beams slicing vertically from the heavens. They picked out many things: rain-glistening rocks, wet leaves on trees and plants, a boy standing on a pipe with his arms hanging limp by his sides . . . and they gave a sunlight halo to a twisted dead boy amidst a tumult of churning white foam.

There came a steady, slow, rhythmical dripping sound.

Drip, *splash*.

Drip, *splash*.

The drips connected with a square tile, white and gleaming in its hospital sterility – a frame for the small puddle of blood forming on it. Slowly, very slowly, the pool of blood grew – widened – a Rorschach image evoking gore and torture and hell and death.

Carter sat on the blue plastic chair, his head clasped in his hands, staring at the white tiles of the hospital corridor. Occasionally a bustle of trolley and tubes and nurses would rush past him, accompanied by a distant cacophony of sirens and engines and shouting. Carter's hair was matted with dirt and oil and smoke and blood. His face was a blank canvas peppered with cuts and bruises and streaks of grime. His broken nose leaked blood to the tiles. His eyes were vacant pools leading deep into the void.

'Mr Carter?' A soft voice; the voice of somebody used to delivering bad news.

Carter did not respond.

'Mr Carter?' A little louder.

'Yes?' His voice was gravel. His voice was the scraping of tombstones.

'We have stabilised her.'

'You have?'

'Yes . . . but I don't want to give you false hope. It's bad. It's really, really bad.'

'And . . . the child?'

'It's hard to tell at this stage – we need to run more tests . . .'

There was a whirl of violent movement and the doctor blinked, the cold metal of the Browning pushed under his chin tilting his eyes towards the tiles of the suspended ceiling and the bright strip lights. The man swallowed hard and did not move. Did not blink.

'Well, run more fucking tests, then,' snarled Carter.

Slowly, the doctor backed away and Carter could read many signs in his face: panic, fear, anger, hurt. Carter felt bad. He knew that the doctor was doing his best. Doing his best in the insanity that had become every London hospital still standing . . .

Slowly, Carter slouched back to the blue chair.

Tears ran down his cheeks, tracing lines through the concrete dust there. He rubbed them savagely away with the back of his hand, and placed the Browning on the blue plastic beside him.

'*Don't worry about him,*' said Kade. '*All fucking doctors are vermin. They deserve to die horrible deaths, deserve torture and carnage in their souls.*'

'Fuck off.'

'*Don't be like that, Carter . . . I saved you out there, in that fucking chaos.*'

'Fuck off.'

'*Carter—*'

'I said fuck off!' screamed Carter, lurching to his feet. Blood from his nose sprayed out, splattering across a sterile white wall. Three nurses stood stock-still, staring at him with undisguised horror.

Carter slumped down once more, glancing at his own appearance. His clothing was grey and torn. His hands too were grey with dust, scratched and cut and battered and bruised. He could feel dust grinding in his eyes and it filled his mouth and throat and lungs, making him cough and choke.

He knew that he looked bad.

And outside, hundreds of others looked far, far worse . . .

The nurses scuttled away. Carter laughed suddenly, then started to cry again with his head in his hands, his blood dripping to the white tiles on the floor.

Natasha, he thought.

Natasha.

After the jump from the building he remembered little. The sensations of falling, heavy lumps of concrete and masonry smashing into his body from all directions . . . and then dust, filling his vision and his rasping lungs.

He awoke choking, coughing, choking again. Everything was grey and, strangely, there was no pain. And suddenly the noise smashed through his world, an insanity of sound – crashing and smashing, rumbling, screaming, hundreds of people screaming, shouts and wailing sirens, the bark of orders, the distant muffled roar of engines and a throbbing of helicopter rotors . . .

Hands pulled at him, rolling him from the mountain of collapsed rubble. He sat on a buckled pavement surrounded by lumps of rock and stone, staring up at firemen, police, JT8s with sub-machine guns slung over their shoulders. People were carried past on stretchers. A fireman stooped to touch his shoulder with surprising tenderness.

'You OK, mate?'

'Yeah,' he coughed, and spat a ball of grey phlegm onto the cracked pavement.

'Were you in the fucking collapse?'

'Yeah.' Carter nodded, dumbly, and could read the look in the fireman's eyes. A look of awe.

His head was spinning. He could still see the look of fear on Crowley's face from his dream and he rubbed at his eyes, stinging with dust and dirt. Screams invaded his consciousness and Carter pulled himself to his feet, pain pulsing through him in waves. Everything felt weak – battered by concrete, pulverised by the toppling building.

Natasha.

He lurched forward, limping, looking frantically through the people lying on stretchers and waiting for the next wave of emergency vehicles. He moved towards the helpers wading through the rubble and pulling bodies free, some living, some motionless and battered and dead.

People were crying, standing beside the collapsed building and crying.

All around him, London was a living chaos.

Carter started to dig, pulling free a huge section of concrete and rolling it down to the pavement. He worked with other grim-faced men heaving rubble, digging with his hands, pulling at beams and twisted metal. With five other men he heaved free a huge section, which rolled with a thud to the pavement.

They waited for a crane, which did not arrive.

More distant sirens wailed.

The sounds filled the world.

For hours Carter worked.

Until his fingernails snapped.

Until the bloodied skin was worn from his fingers.

Until he sank into a crumpled heap on the pavement and slept, crouching under the black dust.

'Carter?'

He wasn't sure if the tears were tears of gratitude or fear. He took her trembling hands in his.

'I love you, Carter, you hear?' She coughed, her face twisted in pain.

'How is she?'

'We need to get her to the hospital. You can ride with us if you want.'

'Yes. Thank you.'

They had found her crushed under a heavy section of twisted concrete, semi-conscious, mumbling for help. It had taken hydraulic lifting equipment to free her and Carter, acting on impulse, maybe through some twisted sixth sense, had homed in on her as she was carried to the ambulance. He had stumbled forward through the rubble and dust and screaming confused people to drop to his knees by her side.

The ride in the ambulance had been a long, tense experience—

And now?

Now they would play the waiting game.

★

'Mr Carter?'

Carter's head jerked up. The doctor he had threatened with the Browning stood with three other doctors huddled close by. They all stared at him suspiciously.

'How is she?'

'The news is not good.'

His face grim, Carter climbed to his feet, hands hanging limply. He walked slowly forward, and said simply, 'Tell me.'

'Natasha has severe internal injuries. She has a ruptured spleen, heavy internal bleeding – we've managed to stem most of the blood loss but there are still problems, and we may have to remove one of her kidneys. After operating, she failed to regain consciousness and is currently in what we call a state of obtundation, or coma.'

'And the baby?'

'The baby is still alive.'

'Thank God,' whispered Carter.

He seemed to slump then, his whole frame collapsing against itself. He seemed somehow smaller, less menacing, almost . . . weak.

'*Every man has a breaking point,*' whispered Kade. '*Don't let this be yours.*'

'Fuck you.'

Carter moved backwards and sat down tiredly in the seat. The doctors looked at each other, then seemed to shuffle forward a little, gaining confidence in numbers.

'Ahh . . . Mr Carter, this isn't the waiting room. You really should move back through those doors where all the other relatives and friends are waiting—'

Carter's head lifted.

The doctors stared hard at him.

One muttered, 'Well, maybe . . . maybe on this occasion . . .'

'When can I see her?'

'You may come through for a short while now, if you wish . . .'

Carter nodded, pocketed his Browning and followed the doctors. They left him at the door with the words, 'Five minutes only,' and then they dispersed into the corridors and wards of a hospital pushed way beyond its limits.

Carter stepped through the portal.

The lighting was subdued, the background filled with the hum of machines. Natasha was linked to myriad matt-black monitors that glittered with small coloured lights. Tubes snaked from her nose and side, and she was attached to an umbilical cord of IV fluids and drugs.

Carter looked down at her face. Her eyes were closed, her face scratched and heavily bruised. Carter reached out and touched her cheek gently but there was no response. He could feel the warmth of her flesh beneath his battered fingers.

'Don't you die on me, girl,' he whispered.

His hand moved, coming to rest gently on her abdomen. He imagined that he could feel the precious cargo within her womb: beating with life, struggling to grow and survive and to be free.

Carter bit his lip and gritted his teeth so that cords of muscle stood out along his jaw. His gaze returned to Natasha's face and he crouched low, his mouth to her ear. 'Come on, baby, come back to me. Don't leave me on my own. Not now.'

He bowed his head and cried.

The nurse gently prised him away from Natasha, smiled understandingly and helped him from the room to the white-tiled corridor. There was a shout and Carter's red-rimmed eyes failed to focus through the aftermath of tears. He blinked them away, to see Mongrel and Nicky striding towards him.

'Carter, we just heard,' growled Mongrel. 'How is she?'

'Bad, Mongrel, she's in a real bad fucking way.'

'Oh, Carter.' Nicky embraced him, held him, and he buried his head against her neck, smelling musk and sweat and woman; they sank to the seats and Carter suddenly looked up into her eyes.

'Any news of Jam? And Slater and TT?'

'No, nothing . . .'

Carter nodded. He could read her pain. And desperation.

Mongrel spat onto the white tiles. 'Spiral have regrouped, and retreated between HQs 2, 5 and 7.'

After the original bombing of the Spiral headquarters in London a year earlier by the traitors Durell and Feuchter, Spiral had rebuilt itself – but had realigned its structure using the same premise on which the Internet was based. No single hub in complete control – but a myriad of powerful cells, units that could act independently of one another, each containing a core of the whole and strands of the Spiral mainframes . . . so that in times of crisis, no single devastation could make Spiral weak again.

Mongrel continued, 'They work hard to find out just what happened in London yesterday. London not the only city hit – Moscow, Paris, Hong Kong. We need you to come back with us to HQ2 – we need your help, Carter . . .'

Carter glanced up at Mongrel then, frowning suddenly. 'Sorry, mate, I'm staying here.'

'There's nothing you can do, Carter. Natasha is in coma – and they'll let you know when she awakes. We desperately need your help . . .'

Carter stared hard at Mongrel. 'How the fuck do you know that Nats is in a coma? You said you had just heard. What's fucking going on here? What are you not telling me?'

'Tell him,' whispered Nicky as her eyes filled with tears.

Mongrel sighed, glancing around. 'This place not secure.'

'Just fucking tell him,' she snapped, and Carter held her tight, feeling her trembling.

'We have intel on Jam,' said Mongrel. 'He not dead – despite the PB from his ECube. We think he being held hostage, possibly in Slovenia, more details to follow . . . I need your help to get in there and get him out.'

Carter stared hard at Mongrel, who held Carter's gaze without flinching, without weakness, without backing down.

'I love Jam,' growled Carter slowly, carefully, his voice controlled. 'But as you can see, I have my own fucking problems. Or hadn't you noticed?'

'I need you, Carter,' said Mongrel. 'I can't do this alone.'

Carter got to his feet, turned and stared at his two friends. A battle raged within him. 'Look – a few short hours ago you know, you fucking *know* I would have jumped at the chance . . . I would never let Jam suffer and I would give my life for him. But now . . . have you any idea what you're asking me? I am needed here, Natasha needs me . . .'

Mongrel took a deep breath . . .

And Carter caught the connection, the quick glance between Mongrel and Nicky.

'What?' he snarled. 'What the fuck is it?'

'Let us say that doctors have not quite been candid

with you, my friend,' said Mongrel softly. He moved closer, placed a hand on Carter's shoulder.

'What do you mean?'

'Natasha is dying. Slowly, but she *is* dying.'

Carter stared hard.

'And when Natasha dies, your baby will die with her.'

'Fuck you,' whispered Carter.

'It's true,' said Nicky softly.

Carter shook his head. 'No, it's not true . . . it can't be true . . .'

The Browning pressed against Mongrel's chin. The metal was cold and hard and Carter's face was a twisted nightmare of insanity and hatred.

'Be calm,' whispered Nicky.

'I will fucking burn you,' hissed Carter, staring into Mongrel's eyes. 'How can you feed me this shit? How can you fuck with my mind like this?'

'I need your help,' repeated Mongrel, voice strong, gaze unwavering despite the pressure of the Browning. 'Put your gun away, Carter. You won't shoot me. Not here, not like this.'

'Want to take a fucking bet?' he snarled.

'There's more,' said Nicky softly.

'Much more,' said Mongrel. 'Tell him about the Avelach.'

'The SAD teams have been killing the Nex; hunting them down and slaughtering them. But Jam was onto something – a machine, a machine they call the Avelach that is used by Durell and Feuchter to *create* the Nex. The Avelach is old, really old. The Nazis discovered it during World War Two – but for decades it remained unused.'

'So what?'

'This machine that's used to create the Nex – well, its

191

primary function is to heal. It could bring people back from the brink of death, save those who were mortally wounded . . . only Durell and Feuchter found a way to subvert the mechanics of the machine, to twist it and force it to create abominations . . . Blending, they called it.'

'Jam knows where machine is,' said Mongrel softly. 'If we find Jam, we can get machine and we can heal Natasha.'

Carter took a step back, his gaze incredulous. 'I don't believe it,' he hissed. 'You would use Natasha and my unborn child to force me into helping you to bring Jam out alive? In the hope that some fictional fucking machine will save her?'

'It's far from fucking fictional,' rumbled Mongrel.

Carter met his gaze.

'You cunt,' he whispered, his head shaking.

'I never claimed to be anything else,' said Mongrel, his heavy-browed face filled with thunder and power, his iron-strong voice steady, unwavering.

Carter sat down. Slumped. Pocketed his gun. Put his head in his hands.

Mongrel and Nicky exchanged glances. Nicky gave a tiny shake of her head.

They waited . . .

Finally, Carter looked up. His eyes were filled with tears. He licked his battered lips. 'I want proof,' he said softly. 'I want proof that Natasha and the baby are dying . . . and I want proof of the fucking machine's existence.'

'We can show you,' said Nicky gently.

Carter frowned then. 'If you're fucking with me, I guarantee you one thing.'

Mongrel nodded in understanding.

192

'A single bullet in the fucking brain.'

'Let's go – we're wasting time,' said Mongrel, and strode off down the hospital corridor.

Carter sat in the doctor's plush office, toying with his Browning. The main doctor delivering the report, Pat Callaghan, a tall dark dashing stud of a man, was looking nervously from Carter to Mongrel – and then back again.

Carter stared at the medical notes.

'So – she is dying.'

'Yes. Very slowly. It might take a single week, maybe two. But the damage is too great; we could try nano-implants, but in terms of replacing kidneys and liver, they are unproven and we have been getting high failure rates . . . and in the current situation they are not the easiest mod to come across. The biggest problems lie in Natasha's internal structural damage – her body is rejecting her own organs, and we cannot work out why.'

'And the baby?'

'If you look at Scan 5, you can see it is currently healthy and alive. Kicking, shall we say.'

'Can you not deliver the baby? By Caesarean?' Carter's voice was cold, almost uninterested . . . but Mongrel and Nicky knew that he was forcing himself into a state of detachment – working out the best way to get the job done . . . the job being the saving of Natasha and their unborn child.

'We *could* deliver, but the trauma would certainly kill Natasha immediately. Due to the crushing injuries she has sustained, several organs and arteries have been moved – they are in the way. There is no clear path to the child without immediately putting Natasha in, shall we say, a terminal situation. And the other angle is that it's almost as if Natasha's body has caged her baby. The shock of such a long-drawn-out operation could also kill the child. In fact, I would say there was an extremely high probability. It might work . . . but then, we wouldn't do it until there was absolutely no alternative.'

Carter tapped his Browning against the desk.

'Doctor Callaghan, can you leave us for a few minutes?'

'What? But – it's my office . . .'

Carter stared at the man, his battered grime streaked visage a picture of menace. Without a further sound the doctor slipped from the room. Carter stared hard at Mongrel and Nicky.

'Our motives are not completely selfish,' said Nicky softly. She placed a hand on Carter's shoulder. 'We want Natasha back as well – we love her, you know? But Jam needs our help, and he holds a key to a machine that can save Natasha and the child. With no compromise . . .'

'*If* the machine exists, and *if* the machine works like you say it does.'

'Jam was onto it; had been for a long time. Yes, he was heading up the SAD teams, but down in Egypt we stumbled across metal sheets with diagrams, instructions – took them from the dead fist of a Nex scout. The diagrams were on metal sheets carbon-dated to 6800 BC – some of the oldest "documents" ever discovered by man.'

'Who has this machine?' asked Carter tenderly.

'We're not sure. Jam had coordinates that he was going to check out after his mission in Slovenia. But then the shit hit the fan and the team went AWOL. He carried the coordinates in his head.'

'What makes you think Jam is still alive?' asked Carter. 'For his ECube to initiate a PB he must have been on the verge of death. That's the way it works, yeah?'

194

'Yes, he was assumed dead initially. But the Spiral mainframes, piloted by the QII processor, were sending out random signature scans – they picked up a signal from Jam's ThumbNail _Map. It only activated for about three nanoseconds, a distorted burst that the mainframes couldn't pin; but it meant he was using the implanted device. Which meant he had to be alive.'

Carter sighed.

'You can stay here, Carter, while Natasha slowly deteriorates. Watch her die,' said Mongrel, his face grave but showing no weakness. 'Or you can come with me, help me track Jam and find this Avelach machine.'

'The machine used for creating the Nex,' said Carter softly. 'Oh, how ironic. I would use it to save Natasha's life! The machine responsible for so much *taking* of life.'

'They have abused it,' said Nicky.

'Yeah, somebody always does.'

'A gun is just a metal box containing bullets – unless there's a finger to pull the trigger,' she whispered.

Mongrel nodded. 'Nicky will coordinate between HQ2 and here, checking on Natasha; she will study metal sheaves we have, work out how to operate this machine for when we find it and steal it. That way, we signal her to rendezvous – and all we have to do is pull machine out and get here. Before that, all we need to find this Avelach device is Jam and coordinates in his head.'

'I don't like this,' said Carter.

'We've been granted clearance. Grade AA. Straight from top. With full-support WarCover and WarClearance – if we need any help.'

'Our starting point?'

'Where Jam was taken out,' said Mongrel softly. 'We'll pick up his trail. He must have stumbled upon something.'

'I thought it had been scanned by PopBots?'

'It has,' said Mongrel, 'but I believe human eye see more than dumb-ass electronics.'

Carter climbed to his feet, face sombre.

'You need time to get cleaned up? Have a MedScan?' Mongrel was looking him up and down.

'No. I just want five minutes alone with Natasha.'

'We'll wait by hospital entrance.'

Carter nodded and left Mongrel and Nicky behind. He could read their uncertainty, their fear, their *need*. He walked back down corridors, some filled with screaming wailing patients, overflowing from waiting rooms with relatives and friends, and finally reached Natasha's side room. The ward Sister made eye contact with Carter in the corridor and smiled wearily; he let himself in.

The monitors were chattering and bleeping with the subtlety of harmonics.

Carter gazed down at Natasha.

Tears filled his eyes but he pushed them angrily away.

He took Natasha's hand. It trailed tubes.

'I will save you – save you both,' he said, smiling gently.

'*Another of your empty promises*,' snapped Kade, emerging from the depths of Carter's mind. His arrival was a black blossom opening its petals to welcome the radioactive death-light of a black planet.

'Empty promises? No,' said Carter softly, shaking his head. 'I will save her. I *have* to save her.'

'*There are other fucking women.*' Kade chuckled smugly. '*You don't need this one. Ultimately, she's just another dead bitch. Come on, Carter, let's fuck off, find you some fresh slick meat from the nightclub pork-market.*'

'I have to save her,' repeated Carter. 'Because, if Natasha and the baby die . . .' His voice went quiet, its volume dropping to that of an unsettling lullaby. 'If they die, then I will bathe the world in blood. I will seek out and butcher God – and all his children. This I swear.'

Kade did not – for once, could not – reply.

Carter's emotions *burned* him. And, silently, Carter's dark twin departed.

CHAPTER 8

SCORPNEX

In the dream Jam walked down a long dark corridor. There were a thousand black obsidian doors all leading from this central aisle and Jam strode, gaze flicking from one to another, his long black coat flapping around him, heavy leather boots stomping through the cold frost and leaving heavy tread imprints. And then he stopped. He could feel the malevolence beyond.

Slowly he reached out, turned the handle and was flooded with a wash of violet light. Shielding his eyes for a moment he heard the growls creeping from within, and he stepped tentatively forward – could suddenly see the horribly deformed Nex emerging from the violet mist – and he said, 'What is wrong with you?'

'Everything went black,' whispered the deformed ScorpNex through twisted fangs. 'They changed me, they made me into . . . this.' It looked down in horror at the merging of carapace and muscle which still bled between strands of twisted spaghetti flesh.

It moved forward, a bloodstained claw coming up towards Jam.

'Help me,' it said, drooling thick yellow saliva laced with skeins of blood.

'Please God, help me . . .'

Jam's eyes flickered open. He was cold, terribly cold, and his breath flooded out in smoke. He could see a massive vaulted ceiling above him and it was rough-hewn stone, hung with glittering ice stalactites. He groaned long and low, agony throbbing through him like a distant scalpel carving his flesh. He turned his head to the left and saw hundreds of stone-slab tables spreading off into the frosty, gloom-laden half-light. Each supported a body: some were perfectly still, some twitched, some were bent into arched shapes and frozen in a rictus of torment – a stop-motion dance of suffering.

And then Jam saw the wide straps holding the victims in tortured bondage against the thick stone slabs.

He tried to move, then realised that he too was strapped down.

He hissed in pain and frustration.

'Don't move. It won't be long now.'

Jam's head jerked to the right – and there, fore-grounded against a backdrop of human suffering, stood Mace. His face was pale, gaunt, just a little deformed, and smiling softly.

'Where am I?'

'This is where we create the Nex,' said Mace. He removed a small leather case from which he took the syringe. The needle glinted brightly against the gloom. The silver liquid glistened within, holding Jam's gaze in anticipated horror.

Jam licked his lips nervously.

'No, not again, you fucker,' he croaked.

'You will like it this time,' said Mace softly, placing his

hand delicately against Jam's forehead. 'The inhibitor has worked . . . you will feel no pain.'

'No . . .'

The needle slid into his flesh and Jam tensed, tensed so hard that he thought he would burst. There came a burning sensation . . . and then nothing. He floated, gently rolling through a mental landscape of silver blossoms.

Another voice. Drifting lazily in the dream.

'Do it.'

Jam opened his blurry eyes and could see the black robes of Durell, the hint of slitted copper eyes within the hood. He smiled, filled with warmth – and then cold tore through him and he gasped. Mace was holding something that wriggled and Jam blinked, slowly, eyes stuck with honey – three times he blinked, and then focused on the—

Scorpion.

'What . . .'

He was going to ask 'What are you going to do with that?' but his mouth would not work properly. The coldness had flooded him, turned his blood to ice, his saliva to frost, his eyes to glittering insect jewels.

Mace came closer.

The scorpion was struggling, its shell a dark and glistening terrible black – as if oiled and carved from stone. Mace held up a clenched fist and Jam tried to struggle as the need for survival kicked in. Durell produced a small silver box and opened it with a tiny click—

Mace lowered the scorpion into Jam's mouth. He wanted to scream but could not, wanted to struggle but the ice injection had hijacked his limbs and his will. He could feel the scorpion move inside his mouth, its legs pressing against his tongue and gums. He gagged, nearly vomiting, but the cold injection held him in thrall. The

arachnid's claws brushed his teeth, the sting lashed out –
once, twice, three times – but there was no pain even
though Jam could sense the poison entering his system
like bad blood. Mace's fist opened and he held a horde of
squirming scuttling cockroaches, their stench stinging
Jam's nostrils. He poured them into Jam's mouth along-
side the scorpion and all Jam could feel was a hive of
activity in his mouth and then down his throat. All he
could think was, *This is a dream, a nightmare, I will wake
up soon*, but whenever he opened his eyes he was still in
the stone chamber and Mace was still staring down at
him like a scientist conducting an experiment.

Another injection. This time in the throat.

Jam tried to scream, but the insects blocked his mouth
and in panic he realised that he could not even breathe.

Durell handed a black disc to Mace, who stepped forward and smiled down at Jam.

'Soon it will all be over,' he said, copper eyes shining
with—

Kindness?

Fuck you! screamed Jam's brain, but he was too busy
trying to thrash his head from side to side to disgorge the
crawling insects. Mace placed the disc over Jam's mouth
and stepped back—

'You must welcome the Avelach,' he crooned, almost
singing the words.

The disc was terribly cold and then it felt like liquid yet
simultaneously solid metal. Jam felt it move and spread
and change and *expand* as the thick black catabolic sub-
stance spread out from his mouth to his throat and neck
and head. Then it sped across his naked torso and over
his arms and legs until he could feel the tight cold metal
cage clamping his flesh. It covered his skin completely,
this dark liquid metal, spreading across all of him.

201

The Avelach coated him.

It entered him.

It *raped* him.

And for a moment it soothed his pain. The cold spread over his naked skin like a chilled layer of smoothest silks – and then flowed into his eyes, and into his mouth to scorch his lips and tongue and gullet. It burned, and it burned bad.

Jam tried to scream and the cold oil-metal flowed and filled his lungs and merged with the insects in his mouth and throat. He breathed sulphur and insect blood. He drowned in white phosphor. He imbibed napalm.

The pain was eternal.

The agony burned him for a billion years.

And then it was over, and a dry and dusty harmattan blew across his soul. His soft tears ran like silver droplets of molten ice across his scorched skin.

The imago had begun.

Durell sat back against the black leather high-backed chair, the cold all around him, soothing. His hands rested against the freezing leather. His head drooped, his slitted copper eyes gazing down at the stone floor.

As Mace entered, Durell glanced up, hood thrown back, his horrendous disfigurements producing no more than a flicker of momentary interest across Mace's face.

'It is done,' said Mace.

'Has it been successful?'

'As you know, we have changed the coding of the sequence and the make-up of the inhibitors – and we've used a slightly different breed of cockroach. Only time will tell if this will yield another ScorpNex.'

Durell laughed softly. 'The problems of trying to

replicate a mistake! How many specimens have died so far? I have lost count.'

'There have been sixty-eight attempts,' said Mace, his copper-eyed stare fixed on Durell.

'And this is the sixty-ninth? With luck Jam will prove his toughness and his will to survive. That was what made him *Spiral*.' Durell spat the name like a ball of sulphur phlegm.

'Yes. He has thus far shown great resilience – and we have done our utmost to keep the Blending pure.'

'How long?'

'The next few hours will enlighten us.'

'Good. Keep me informed.'

Mace moved forward through the gloom. At this time of the night everything was silent; the Nex attendants were in their nests and Mace was completely alone . . . except for the hundreds on the stone slabs in this cold underground world.

He stopped in front of Jam . . . the Avelach had long since retracted to its former shape and the black metallic disc, the *machine*, had been removed from Jam's face and mouth and placed back in the sanctuary of the silver box that had been fashioned to protect and recharge it.

Mace moved forward. Jam's head was tilted back, his eyes closed, his face a deathly white. His lips were tightly closed and, reaching out, Mace prised open Jam's mouth and clenched teeth. Reaching inside, he pulled out the shell of the scorpion – which was so brittle that it crumbled to dust under his fingers. Carefully, Mace scooped out the remains of the cockroach carapaces and allowed them to fall to the stone floor, across which they drifted softly in response to the cool breeze. Then, slowly, he undid the straps that fastened Jam to the bench and ran his hand down Jam's naked and treacherously cold flesh. It felt glassy, cold, hard – and slightly tainted with oil.

Mace smiled.

'Good,' he said, nodding to himself.

Jam could feel them inside him. He tried to force them away but they would not and could not leave him.

we are together
merged
as one
they have made us one

Pain blended them in fire and flowed like acid through his veins. A metallic copper stink like the stench of old bad blood pervaded his nostrils and tattooed his tongue and it was him, a part of him, injected into his flesh and blood and brain.

Jam fell into a dark pit of despair.

Then awoke.

He lay for a long time on the stone, not really thinking, just mentally searching his body for signs of injury. Everything was cold. Stone was beneath him. The air was crisp and biting against his lips and tongue. He was breathing, his chest rising and falling, and he could feel air entering his lungs and then smoothly leaving again.

Slowly, he opened his sticky eyes.

There was no pain.

That was the first real thought that struck him.

No pain.

He had spent the last few days suffering physical and mental torment so severe that he thought he would break – both mentally and physically. But now the pain had gone and all that remained was the cool and soothing embrace of frost.

He moved his hand, lifted it to his face. His flesh was white, chalk white and he examined his hand, its structure, the tapering of his fingers, the roundness of his nails. He turned his head to one side, realised he was in a cell . . . but not the dry dusty cells of his initial beatings, rather somewhere cold and sterile. There was a single light source, tiny against the damp stone wall; nothing more than an insect glow.

Jam sat up, looking down at his chalk-white nakedness. A bad metal taste was in his mouth and he spat again and again. But it would not leave him.

'Was it just a dream?'

His voice rattled hollowly in the stone cage of his skull.

On a low table there stood a clay pitcher of water and a cup. Slowly, testing himself, Jam stood, bare feet shuffling on stone, and moved to pour himself a cup of water.

Something did not feel right.

Within himself . . .

His body felt . . . somehow *wrong* . . .

He drank the water to quench his terrible raging thirst, and staring down at himself he was deeply confused. He remembered with a shudder the insects in his mouth, but then he also remembered long dreams of corridors and fires and Slater shooting ice bullets into his face.

He rinsed his mouth with water, but still the metal taste would not leave him.

And then a wave of nausea convulsed his body and he dropped to one knee, vomiting the recently imbibed water onto the stone floor. His athletic frame heaved, and heaved again . . . his stomach disgorged bile until there was nothing left. But still the nausea swamped him and he continued to heave until his muscles screamed at him and he thought that his stomach would tear itself physically apart . . .

205

Then it was over.

On his knees, panting, drooling saliva, sweat beading on his forehead, soaking his hair, Jam stared down at his shrivelled penis and flat stomach bathed in a sheen of sweat. He was trembling violently, and cursed his lack of clothing . . .

Is this just another form of fucking torture? raged his mind.

An insane anger filled him.

A true need to *kill* . . .

He stumbled towards the door, raised his hand to knock and sensed rather than heard or saw figures outside – looking in on him, anonymous. He smashed his fist against the door, then recoiled in horror as he felt the bones of his fingers crack and splinter within the padded flesh of his fist. A gasp escaped his cold blue-tinged lips, more shock than the sudden pain that flared from the six broken bones and he whirled . . . but felt his ankle snap and dislocate and compress. He stumbled, fell, felt his left leg shatter within his flesh and lifted his gaze to the ceiling, screaming as he collapsed onto the stone.

Outside, Durell said, 'The pain has begun.'

Mace nodded, deep in thought. 'It will not be long before the imago is complete.'

The room had thick plush carpets and a roaring fire in the hearth. Gol stood in front of the weaving flames, warming himself and staring at the painting above the immense stone fireplace – *The Education of the Virgin* by the Austrian artist Franz Anton Maulbertsch. Gol traced the fine strokes of oil on canvas, his gaze absorbing the flying angels and almost demonic use of blacks and reds above this seemingly pure act of instruction. The fire crackled, an aural background to Gol's calm, and he turned to warm his back as he swirled the brandy in the glass thoughtfully.

He took a gentle sip of the 1794 Hennessy, and the spirit burned his mouth and warmed its way to his belly like liquid fire. Gol sucked in air and surveyed the room.

Small single-pane leaded windows looked out over a heavy rain-filled valley under deep veils of darkness. The walls were panelled ceiling to floor in oak, and lined with many bookshelves sporting dusty old tomes. Furniture was period, in keeping with the fine theme of the room – and of either Austrian or Swiss lineage.

Rain rattled against the windows and a savage night wind howled outside, driving down with animal fury from the mountains.

Gol sipped the brandy again, its mellowness soothing him. He looked up as a huge heavy oak door swung silently inwards and Durell moved forward at a slow pace. He stared at the fire for a while, then turned towards Gol.

'Is everything all right?' Gol asked.

'Yes,' said Durell softly. 'It is too warm in here.'

Gol nodded. 'Thought I'd light a fire . . . is that OK?'

'I do not like the warmth; it makes me itch.'

'I can have it put out . . .'

'No, no.' Durell held up a hand. The cloth fell away to reveal something black, crusted and glistening. Gol swallowed hard, staring into the depths of the hood that hid the slitted and almost feline copper eyes.

'Is it working? With Jam?'

'We think so. But due to such high previous failure rates we are keeping a very close eye on him. He just has the nominal pain and metamorphosis to complete and then –' Durell smiled '– then he will be one of us. No other specimen has reached this far.'

Durell moved to a large table and it seemed to ignite,

to glow, as the surface became digitally alive. Durell and Gol stared down at the glowing map and Durell pointed.

Gol nodded. 'Have the Foundation Stones for Core3 been initiated?'

'Shortly,' said Durell.

'Then we are close?' asked Gol, sipping once more at his brandy.

'Yes. We are close.'

Jam dreamed a hard bad dream. He was falling, through a long dark tunnel that seemed to lead downwards for ever. Wind ruffled his hair and the world was filled with a complete silence. Jam shifted in the slipstream, fear a distant echo, pain a distant dream . . . The walls around him were fashioned from glistening black rock, speckled with frost, glimmering with ice, and suddenly a ledge loomed out of nowhere – a jagged, rocky extrusion with which Jam collided, grunting in pain, spinning off with stars fluttering in his mind to career from the opposite wall of this vertical tunnel—

Down.

He could taste blood – and something else.

And then he saw it. Just as he thought that the fall would be eternal and he could drift lazily in the cold air currents for a blissful eternity, he saw the water spread wide and the tunnel disappeared above him, sucked away into blackness. Jam could make out distant glittering waves. The sea was an oil, a dark obsidian mercury, and he sped down towards its cooling enveloping embrace . . .

He saw it *shift*.

Move.

Squirm . . .

And he realised that it was alive. Crawling and alive.

He flowed towards the sea of insects and fear suddenly

struck him with a cold left hook. He could feel it, panic bubbling in his throat, and then he realised that the feeling was the skittering of tiny legs on his body and tongue and teeth. His mouth was filled with cockroaches frantically squirming to break free of this teeth-barred organic cell.

He could feel their panic.

Their will to survive.

He bit down, crushing some of their bodies, and felt their blood run down his throat, a flood filled with torn legs and tiny pieces of carapace. And then the scorpion moved up his throat and Jam felt vomit heaving within him. The sea rushed towards him, and engulfed him and darkness flooded his world. He smashed through the crust of crawling insects and into an oil which burned his flesh and stung him. He realised with horror that it was a toxin, a thick and swirling poison and he was finally able to scream out a verbal ejaculation of spewing wriggling insects—

Jam sat up, sweat pouring from his brow. He screamed, fingers scrabbling at his mouth, and he looked down in the gloom. He could see something that had crawled up from his ankles and shins, covering his lower legs with a sheen of glistening black, and had then halted around his knees, merging with his pink flesh, twisting between strands of shredded skin and muscle . . .

This cannot be happening to me, he thought.

This cannot be real.

Nicky . . . Nicky . . .

He pictured her sweet face, hair tied back, eyes twinkling—

He pictured her moving towards him, mouth parting slightly, sweet breath tickling his lips, his eyes closing as her kiss taunted him and lust surged through his body like a drug—

He pictured her dying, screaming with insects in her hair like tiny black blossoms, squirming.

'No . . .'

He sat up, hands moving down to the hard skin of his lower legs. What is it? Just what the fuck is it?

Pain welled inside him, and he suddenly noticed a swelling in his groin, to either side of his testicles. The skin there was inflamed, puckered with tiny spikes of black. Jam arched his back as he felt the spikes prick his skin under his questing fingers and he screamed, screamed and screamed and screamed until there was no more breath and no more light. And no more hope.

Jam awoke on his side, curled into a ball. He felt strange. There was no pain.

He rolled onto his hands and knees, and looked down curiously at the backs of his forearms. Merged with his brown skin was a series of thick black marks with tiny spikes poking free. He rocked back onto his heels with a clack of chitinous armour and flexed his forearms. Spikes sprang free, rippling up his arms and glinting eerily in the gloom.

Jam breathed deeply.

His mind settled.

He blinked lazily.

There came a sound at the door and his head jerked left, spikes erecting along his forearms, eyes compressing to narrow copper slits. The door opened, flooding the chamber with light, and Jam recoiled with a hiss, armoured feet clacking across the stone—

Durell stepped in.

'Welcome,' he crooned, throwing back his hood.

Jam rose to his full height, spine crackling softly, and he could feel saliva pool from his twisted jaws. His head swung left, then right, and he could smell the scent of fear.

'Follow me.'

Durell left the cell and Jam stooped, armour scraping the stonework as he followed Durell down a series of long stone corridors. They came to some steps and Jam leapt lithely down them, landing heavily and cracking a stone flag. They travelled on down stone ramps under the dim glow of electric bulbs into the depths of the castle.

Not once during the journey did Durell turn round.

And Jam found himself surveying the dark expanse of Durell's back. His head swayed from one side to the other, eyes fixed on that broad back and strange metallic thoughts flickering through his brain

Kill

Kill

Rip flesh burn and turn and flee

Master

Control . . .

Master

Durell led Jam into a huge stone chamber decorated with tapestries and burning brands in iron brackets. Set in the floor, scooped from the rock was a large sunken pit lined with huge blocks of rectangular stone, measuring maybe ten metres by ten. There were intricate old weathered carvings set roughly in some of the blocks lining the pit; the floor was criss-crossed with grooves and gutters leading to wider channels feeding off around the edges.

Gol stepped into the chamber and Jam's copper eyes locked onto the large grey-bearded man. Jam saw Gol swallow, hard, and walk tentatively around him to reach Durell's side.

'Is he safe?'

'Yes.'

'I fucking hope so . . .'

'I will show you.'

Across the chamber, through a narrow stone arch, came Kattenheim. He held a man by the arm, a man who seemed deflated, beaten, withdrawn. As they walked his head came up and his stare widened in horror as he saw Jam—

'Fuck, no,' he gasped.

Kattenheim heaved the man into the pit, where he landed heavily before scrambling to his feet, pushing his back against the stone of the wall. His gaze roved wildly searching for an avenue of escape. Kattenheim lifted a huge-bladed axe and tossed it into the pit where it clattered with a shower of sparks against the stone. The man scrambled forward, lifting the weapon. He understood the game.

'This is Scarlet, a former captain of the Australian SAS and latterly of Spiral, DemolSquad 142. We captured him and a few others of his ilk in Tibet on a mission that went badly wrong.' Durell reached out, patted Gol's shoulder, smiled a hidden smile. 'Don't worry. Watch.'

'Come on, you fuckers,' Scarlet was screaming, anger firing him into action, brandishing the large-headed axe in both hands and readying himself for battle.

'Kill him,' said Durell softly.

Jam's triangular head tilted, dark copper eyes fixing on Durell. Then, with a hiss, he leapt into the pit and strode towards the man swinging the axe. The axe whirled, then smashed down.

Jam spun, ducking low under the sweep of the heavy blade, and powered a right hook straight against Scarlet's jaw that sent the man spinning to the ground to lie

212

stunned. The axe clattered uselessly against stone. Silence suddenly reigned.

Jam paced up and down, seemingly unsure. Then he leapt into the air, both armoured feet coming down with a heavy crunch on Scarlet's head. The Spiral man's skull cracked open, spilling liquid pulped brains into the kill channels. Jam's face lifted questioningly to Durell.

'Athletic,' said Kattenheim softly, red eyes watching the proceedings with interest. 'Much faster than the other Scorp.'

'Summon the Nex.'

Three Nex warriors were called and they arrived, wearing their tight black suits and thin boots, and carrying Armalite X sub-machine guns. They stood silently, waiting, copper-eyed stares fixed on Durell. Gol forced himself not to take a step back. He set his face in the cold stone mask of the stoic.

'You are unsure?' asked Durell.

'Let us see,' said Gol softly.

'Kill it,' snapped Durell, pointing at Jam.

The three Nex moved swiftly apart, Armalite X guns lifting and opening fire. Dozens of 5.62mm rounds screamed across the chamber, striking sparks from stone. Jam leapt high into the air, bullets spinning and whining beneath him. He twisted in mid-flight, kicked off from one bare stone wall and landed suddenly among the Nex—

The Armalites ceased firing.

Jam punched left, then right – he flexed his arms and spikes rippled upright. He slashed them across the first Nex – ripping its face clean off. It fell, screaming, to one knee, blood pumping between its fingers. More bullets spat from muzzles. Jam whirled low, kicking the legs from under a retreating Nex and then slamming his fist through its back to explode in a slurry of purple from its chest. His free hand plucked the Armalite X from its twitching fingers, and with his fist still embedded in its ribcage and with bullets skimming past his head Jam fired off the magazine's contents into the third Nex's face. He watched emotionlessly as it collapsed into a smoking heap.

Cordite smoke drifted lazily.

Jam withdrew his fist with a slurping noise from the still-twitching Nex and it collapsed, spewing blood that ran down the walls into the kill trough and along the channels designed to carry away the detritus of slaughter.

Jam calmly found a fresh mag from the Nex's ammo belt and moved towards the Nex without a face. It was making a low keening sound and rocking on its knees. Jam filled its head full of scything metal and then allowed the Armalite X to clatter to the stone floor, his eyes lifting to stare at Durell and a snarl flickering across lips that had once been human.

'Well done, my child,' said Durell softly.

'I thought they were supposed to fight *inside* the kill trough?' said Gol, having felt the passing of bullets and looking at the blood on his boots and lower trousers.

'Jam improvised,' said Durell. 'What think you, Kattenheim?'

The German ex-para nodded in appreciation. 'Strength, speed, agility, improvisation, lack of mercy. Ideal. A beautiful weapon to turn against Spiral . . .'

'And the DemolSquads,' said Gol softly.

'One final test.'

'Is that necessary?'

'Oh yes,' said Durell.

Kattenheim disappeared, then returned with a small group of Nex soldiers. Between them they dragged a woman and three children – and without breaking stride they tossed them into the kill trough. Durell watched with amusement as two of the children became hysterical upon seeing streams of blood down the wall and the split-skulled corpse of Scarlet. The woman cradled them to her, covering their faces. She glared up at the small gathering with hatred across her face.

'An innocent family, how sweet. A positive example of what the human race can achieve – pinnacles of organic evolution,' said Durell softly, smiling sardonically. 'Jam – kill them.'

'But . . .' hissed Gol, his head turning—

Jam leapt forward into the pit and, arms glistening with human and Nex blood and gore and brains, moved towards the cowering family. His dark eyes surveyed them, head swaying a little, and tiny spikes sprang up along one heavily muscled and armoured forearm.

'Is this necessary, Durell?'

Durell's slitted eyes gleamed. 'Death is always necessary,' he said, his words forming sombre lyrics to the music of anguished screams and gurgles that followed.

Gol sat in the room which he used for meditation. The castle in which Durell now based his operations was huge. Built of grey stone many hundreds of years previously, and modified by Durell to certain very specific details, it held an ancient feel; the walls were thick and designed to repel invaders, and much of the décor – oil paintings, tapestries, Swiss and Austrian furniture, thick German rugs scattered throughout the many stone corridors and rooms – was original. Huge black iron brackets lined the walls. Windows were edged with lead and rattled in high winds.

Gol was seated on the large bed, naked, legs crossed, eyes closed. Rain howled against the windows, but he was switched off from the current reality; in his meditation he relived his past—

Running, running . . . pursued by the Nex. He could hear the sweep of the Comanche's rotors overhead, hear the whine of its LHTec engines, feel the presence of the Nex and their sub-machine guns close behind his sprinting form – with his arms pumping, fist holding the precious silver disk with the schematics for the QIII processor. He had done the honourable thing, done the only thing he could to protect the information and give Spiral a chance of winning the war—

Sacrifice . . .

He leapt from the clifftop. Into the narrow chasm with the glittering river far below.

A Nex ran over the cliff behind him, not because of any programmed response but through a lack of ability to kill its speed.

Gol fell, wind tearing through his beard and hair—

Tears flowed across his cheeks and were snatched away by the wind of his fall—

Something hit him in the back of the head, and twisting mid-fall Gol saw the Nex trying to lift its sub-machine gun, copper-eyed stare fixed impassively on his face and its single focused intent obvious—

It would not let him live.

It wanted to place a bullet in his face – as extra security in case the impact following the fall didn't kill him.

Free-falling, the glittering river speeding close, Gol lifted back his mighty fist and delivered a thundering left hook. Blood spurted from the Nex's mouth, along with a tooth, and Gol hit it again – and again. Bullets suddenly howled as the Nex pulled the trigger. Gol reached out, grabbing the hot barrel. It scorched his flesh and bullets flashed off over his left shoulder, cutting

216

lines in the stone walls of the flashing, speeding canyon—

They grappled, spinning.

Gol pulled the Nex close, slamming his head into its face once, twice, three times, four times – until it went limp and they were spinning, spinning and falling and the river loomed up suddenly close and frighteningly real and—

They plunged below the waters, the Nex first, Gol wrapped closely in the creature's loose embrace. The force of the impact seemed to knock all life from Gol. Blackness swamped him, and he felt the second impact against the river bottom with a blow of pain pounding through every limb. He felt the Nex's body come apart beneath him, and felt his own frame smashed against the river bed like a corpse flung by the sea at an unforgiving wall of rock—

Blackness poured like dark honey into his mind.

And then . . . nothing.

Gol had awoken on the river bank, both cliffs towering far above. Ten Nex stood around him, their copper eyes staring into his face.

'Is it dead?'

'Not yet.'

Cold laughter rippled.

'Drag it to the truck. Durell might want to question it.'

Gol caught a glimpse of the silver disk, the disk he had given his life to protect, shoved beneath dark grey clothing. He was dragged along the ground and heaved into the back of a truck where pain screamed at him from every part of his battered body. Unconsciousness claimed him.

★

Darkness, as violent jolts hammered through the truck's suspension. Gol kept his eyes tight shut and did an internal diagnostic. He could feel both legs and one arm broken, and something was wrong with his spine. He also thought his jaw was broken. The jolts from the truck did not help. They fed the pain a diet of need and Gol welcomed the darkness when it finally – eventually – came once again.

When he awoke, bright lights were shining into his face.

'This will hurt a little,' said Mace, smiling down as the needle slid into Gol's throat. The burning came over him as a rush and he screamed as Durell approached, copper eyes staring down with a hint of . . . compassion . . .

'Welcome back, my oldest friend.'

'Fuck you, Durell, you are a traitor . . .'

'Ahh . . . we will speak again in a little while. Mace, take the sample for the clone.'

'Yes, sir.'

The pain had consumed Gol as the liquid burned through his veins and the insects filled up his mouth. Then he was eaten and swallowed and raped by the Avelach.

Gol opened his eyes in the present – and breathed calmly. Rain clattered against the windows and the night had fallen as Gol had relived his transformation from human to Nex.

He smiled.

Strange, he mused, how betrayal is all about perspective.

But now he was Nex, now he was part of Durell's army – and now he could see everything clearly.

And still . . .

218

Something was wrong: a splinter in his brain, a tumour in his soul. He knew now that he was fighting for the right side and that becoming a Nex had saved his life and transformed him into a superior life form – even if they had used different experimental inhibitors so that his Nex status was slightly – how would they describe it? – different. They would destroy the evil named Spiral. They would turn it, as Durell had said, into a New Eden. They would rule, and they would be like gods looking down from Olympus . . .

Gol smiled.

His body relaxed.

He felt the slow pulse of blood through his Nex veins.

Gol uncurled from his meditative crouch and leapt to the floor. He padded over and poured himself a brandy, allowing the liquid fire to scorch his throat and warm his belly.

Something disturbed him.

Gol wasn't like the other Nex.

He didn't crave the cold, like the other Nex.

And although his emotions were subdued, he still felt empathy to a greater extent than the cold copper-eyed killers . . .

And his eyes—

Something had happened – or, more importantly, had *not* happened to his eyes. Most Nex had copper orbs, a side-product of the inhibitors used and the Blending process . . . but for some reason, this physical transformation had not affected Gol—

And it set him apart.

He was different.

A mongrel among pure-breed Nex.

Gol moved to the window, staring out at the rain. He sipped his brandy and the face of Natasha popped into his head, surprising him. My long-lost love, he thought with a wry smile. My child, I wonder where you are now? I wonder what you are doing?

Still fighting for Spiral?

These thoughts were idle because he knew that deep down in his soul the emotional link between himself and his daughter was severed. And despite his intelligence telling him that this was a part of being Nex, still something burned deep within him, a tiny candle flame which didn't so much feed his emotions as make him remember what it used to feel like.

'It's better to be alive, yes?'

'Kattenheim, you made me jump.'

Kattenheim padded across the rugs and poured himself a brandy. Then he turned, red eyes surveying Gol with interest – with a sparkle of scarred intelligence that made Gol wary.

'Am I right?'

'Yes, but that's a strange question for you to be asking.' Gol moved and pulled on a thick jumper and a pair of heavy combat trousers. Dressed, he turned to stare out at the rain once more.

'I've seen you . . . and Durell has seen you. We understand – that you are different from the other Nex. This is not a problem.'

'But?' Gol turned, laughing softly in his deep melodic voice. 'There is always a but . . .'

'Durell trusts you implicitly.'

Gol's deep brown-eyed stare met the blood-scarred gaze of Kattenheim and he saw nothing but strength and single-mindedness there. A focus of purpose. The intent of the insane. Gol breathed deeply, then sighed, moved to the window and looked out over the rain-swept forests, hazy in the distance. 'You, however, do not trust me. You see me as a threat. You think Durell is mistaken in his trust because of our old bonds, our old ties. You think he is misguided.'

'Yes.' Kattenheim moved closer and Gol could feel the threat. His body tensed involuntarily, awaiting the first blow as the Nex part of him fired into immediate readiness . . .

Gol turned his back on Kattenheim.

'You couldn't have killed the women and children,' said Kattenheim softly.

'No.'

'Why not?'

'I cannot explain it.'

'I can. You are not fully Nex . . . the Avelach Skein Blending was interrupted; the machine did its work healing you, and the process of merging you with your insect companions had begun . . . but it happened when the war was at its height. Mace was called away during the process – it was left incomplete. You are not fully Nex. You never were.'

Gol shrugged. 'It's of little consequence.'

'No,' said Kattenheim. 'It is of *great* consequence . . . You are a half-breed, Gol, and I think you are the weakest link in the chain to our future. I am watching you – and the Nex are watching you. It was my suggestion that we either finish the process – but apparently this is an impossibility – or . . . kill you.'

Gol turned with a snarl. 'Fuck you, Kattenheim. I believe in what we are fighting for – if you want to fuck with me then we can take it down to the kill trough. Now, if you've nothing constructive to add then I suggest you fuck off and complete your duties – we have a lot of work to do, the QHub can still be refined and I need my sleep.'

Kattenheim turned and left. Gol smiled, releasing a deep breath.

Still got the fucking fire, he thought.

I can still kick some fucking ass—

But Kattenheim?

Gol had seen him fight, and knew deep down that he could not beat the man . . . the *Nex*, he corrected himself. Kattenheim was just too fast. Too deadly. But then, it didn't matter because they were on the same side. Right?

The same side?

Gol stared out at the rain, which fell in vast vertical sheets, driving across the landscape, across the trees and slopes beyond the castle, running in cold rivulets and streams along the crushed-stone road that led from the heavy steel gates down through the dark forests and into the valley below.

I'm not sure which side that is any more.

SIU Transcript

CLASSIFIED SR12/7252/SPECIAL INVESTIGATIONS UNIT
Hacked ECube interception
Date: September 2XXX

California CT15: Sector XH

Seismic Reactor Research Facilities **[SRRF]**

Dr Brian,

In short, we are deeply confused. The recent devastating quakes measuring between 7.2 and 9.6 on the Richter Magnitude scale which have hit Beijing, Salvador, Moscow, London, Zermatt, Bangkok, Berlin, Stockholm, Paris, Budapest, Tokyo, Baghdad and New York do not relate directly to previously understood contours of seismic activity. Quakes have always followed patterns - the contours of geological plates and known fault lines in the world crust. This new breed of quake, however, does not seem confined to such known parameters and areas of historical and recent seismic disturbance.

Here at the SRRF we find this extremely disturbing, and combined with the sudden flurry of seismic activity apparently on a worldwide scale, would go so far as to suggest a moderate state of global emergency. Something seems to be happening to the world which we cannot understand nor link to any physical activity - earthbound or solar. In short, we are stumped. Suggested courses of action are:

- Intercontinental surveys of known faults and suspected recently discovered fault lines

- Satellite-instigated land and sea surveys to be carried out within the next 36 hours

- Undersea exploration subs to digitally scan recently discovered fault lines or expected fault lines

Please advise ASAP.

Dr Jeremiah Sulokov

CHAPTER 9

THE HUNT

The small black helicopter howled through the storm, rain pounding from its insect-like shell as rotors sliced through the downpour and low-lying storm clouds. Below, dark fields rolled into one and occasionally the chopper skirted a town or village, its lights glowing distantly under the storm's onslaught. Mongrel peered down, trying to work out their location.

'You know where we are?'

Carter, cigarette held in one fist, ignored Mongrel's question as smoke curled up past his face and gathered in the tiny cabin of the chopper. Mongrel scowled, and leant forward to Fenny.

'Where we are?'

'Near Merthyr Tydfil.'

'Is that close to the Sp1_plot?'

'Another couple of minutes. Better get the ropes ready.'

'Roger that.' Mongrel smiled his toothless smile.

'You OK, Carter?'

Carter flashed him a weak smile, then allowed it to drop from his battered face. He dropped his cigarette, crushing its glowing tip under his heavy boot. 'Fuck it, come on.'

They moved into position and each readied their coils of rope, one on each side of the fast attack chopper. Suddenly, Fenny slewed the vehicle around and both Carter and Mongrel stared down into black nothingness. The rotors thumped and the wind howled.

'Out, guys.' Fenny grinned, curls bobbing, and flicked the release.

The doors swung open and Carter and Mongrel dropped their ropes into the darkness. Carter tightened his gloves, and watched Mongrel disappear into the rain and the black.

'You're a good lad, Fenny.'

Fenny nodded, still smiling. 'Send me a postcard, eh, Carter?'

'Where I'm going, you wouldn't want to see the sights.'

Then Carter was gone, dropping down the rope which hissed under his leather gloves. Rain and cold struck through him immediately, making him gasp, and he pulled tight just above the ground, bobbing for a second, then jumping free and landing in a crouch. Trees reared around the two Spiral agents and they found themselves buried in the depths of a storm-darkened forest.

The black chopper leapt into the sky, trailing the fast-ropes and reeling them in as it climbed. Within seconds only the sounds of the storm could be heard, howling and grumbling.

'Which way?'

Mongrel pointed, then stowed away the gentle glow of his ECube.

They set off at a steady but fast run up a steep incline and deeper into the woods. The going was tough under the heavy downpour, the woodland floor slippery and treacherous with mud, branches and a layer of leaf detritus. Dressed all in black, the two Spiral agents dropped to a crouch. Both carried M24 carbines that fired 5.46mm bullets and had MicroX2 mags, which could hold sixty 'compressed' bullets each.

'How far?'

'Three klicks.'

They ran, pushing on through the rain. Darkness swallowed them and occasionally they would halt and check their ECubes, scanning for possible enemy activity. After the quake in London and the sudden re-emergence of Nex soldiers cutting Spiral agents in half as they fled the building, Spiral found itself in a high state of emergency.

The enemy, it would seem, were far from dead.

Carter pointed his carbine into the darkness. Below his clothing nestled his trusty old Browning and within his head squatted thoughts of death and revenge.

They moved at an easier pace now, closing on the SP1_plot in an old abandoned farmhouse. Its walls were overgrown with vines and ferns, the roof long ago fallen in, leaving rubble cascading in terracotta waterfalls across blankets of moss. Mongrel's ECube showed no sign of enemy activity.

Mongrel rose to march ahead, a smile on his face, his head turning – but Carter grabbed him, dragged him back down to the ground and placed his finger against his lips. Mongrel nodded, and slowly Carter eased himself forward on his belly, rolling down his balaclava and allowing himself to blend with the darkened trees and the soft floor of the water-soaked forest.

Inch by inch he moved forward, his eyes and ears alert. After every inch he would halt – check around himself in all directions, listen, make sure of his next small step.

For long minutes he lay in the rain, then edged forward. Wait, move. Wait, move. Wait . . . move . . .

And his sharp eyes saw them.

Nex.

Motionless: waiting, watching. One was perched on a low wall against the farmhouse itself, merging chameleon-like against the tangle of ferns in the gloom. The second crouched just inside the farmhouse doorway, and the third – the hardest to spot – was squatting under a bush beside a tall oak tree which spread out its branches to touch the leaning outer wall of the derelict building.

Fuckers, thought Carter.

'*And even more serious,*' whispered Kade, '*is the fact that the Spiral plot has been compromised. Bubbled. They know the location . . . I wonder if they know you're on your way?*'

Slowly, with murderous care, Carter retreated.

Inch by painful inch—

'What is it?'

'Nex,' said Carter.

'Let's take them . . .'

'Wait. Don't go fucking rushing in there – check the ECube again.' They both watched the tiny face of the electronic cube. Carter tutted when it scanned, again and again, showing no sign of Nex intruders – or of any life whatsoever – in the vicinity.

'Come on, Carter,' growled Mongrel. 'We used to fucking eat these bastards on the SAD missions . . . pile in, blow them to fucking Kingdom Come. No problems . . .'

'This is different,' said Carter.

'How?'

'I can't explain it. Something has changed.'

'You're fucking imagining it – come on!' Mongrel moved forward. Cursing, Carter moved off to one side to provide him with cover. The carbine was slippery in his gloved hands and he checked the safety, nudging the mag to make sure that it was firmly in place.

Mongrel moved forward through the trees.

Carter circled off to the right, putting distance between himself and his comrade, positioning them for an attack on two fronts. He crouched, rubbed rain from his face and eyes, and fought to control his breathing.

He eased himself forward and caught sight of the Nex on the wall. He halted, pacing himself, then heard the blast of Mongrel's carbine sound from the woods as it punched bullets through the door frame.

Carter lifted his own M24. The Nex on the ground jerked its head left, copper eyes staring straight at Carter. It seemed somehow different from the Nex on the SAD missions and those he had met out in Switzerland. It moved with such incredible speed that Carter was still rolling as the bullets from its weapon tore a line of smashed twigs and shredded leaves into the air and cut a vertical stripe up a tree. Carter rolled, his carbine bucking in his gloved hands but the Nex was gone between the trees—

A vanished ghost.

Carter could hear Mongrel's gun. And return fire. Bullets zipped through leaves, slammed into tree trunks.

Carter scrambled right, then sprinted down a small slope and around towards the back of the house, trying to catch sight of the Nex. Then he saw it. Their eyes met and those copper orbs drilled him and he smiled a bitter smile and both their guns roared at once, and Carter felt the breeze of bullets ripping past his face as the carbine barked in his hands and the bullets picked the Nex up, flipping it over to crash into a tree, drilled and bleeding and—

228

It crawled to its knees and tried to change mags.

Carter sprinted forward, his boot smashing against its face and sending the Nex rolling against the tree's roots. Carter placed his boot on its chest and its head lifted to look at him coolly.

'Luck,' it hissed, its voice soft and asexual, copper eyes glowing.

Carter grinned. 'There's no such fucking thing,' he said, and drilled the Nex's face full of metal.

'Carter!'

Mongrel's voice was tinged with panic. Carter sprinted up the incline and dropped to his belly. He caught the muzzle flash of guns firing from the edge of the house, and crawled forward until he was beside an old, crumbling outbuilding.

The sounds of automatic fire halted.

Carter calmed his breathing, and wiped a speck of blood from the back of his glove.

'Carter!' came the call again. More sub-machine-gun fire – and Carter realised that both Nex had pinned Mongrel down. He sprinted forward, using trees and ferns for cover, past the farmhouse. Mongrel had to be in the shit—

To call Carter's name?

Out loud?

Carter veered right, ducking under tree branches. His carbine juddered in his grip, cutting one Nex in half. The other whirled, and as Mongrel's bullets tore into its chest with metallic blows Carter lifted his M24 and put ten bullets in its head, hammering it to the soft ground where it lay still, blood weeping from its wounds.

Silence fell.

Cordite smoke was smothered by the rain, which fell softly.

Mongrel sprinted to Carter, a look of deep shock on his face.

Carter checked his weapon, then sighted off among the trees, checking for further signs of enemy movement.

'Thanks,' panted Mongrel, fishing for a new magazine in his belt. 'They nearly fucking nailed me.'

Carter said nothing, merely looking off through the rain.

'They much faster than I remember,' muttered Mongrel sombrely. 'I not fucking hit them! Fired whole magazine at them but nothing, not hit one fucking thing . . .'

'Something's definitely wrong,' said Carter softly. 'I can feel it in my bones. We have become complacent . . . but these Nex, they were not some soft target.'

'I'll listen to your advice next time,' said Mongrel.

'Just don't be so fucking eager to jump in boots first, mate. This ain't a fucking game.'

They moved across to the farmhouse, scouting left and right. Standing in the doorway, Mongrel initiated his ECube. This Sp1_plot was a large armoury – as distinct from some of the more moderate stashes that were located in other parts of the world. This was an Sp1_plot specifically used for AA clearance – WarClearance.

There came a distant mechanical noise, a soft whirring sound and the interior of the farmhouse folded free to reveal a wide metal ramp leading down. Mongrel walked down the ramp, boots echoing hollowly on the rain-slick alloy, and Carter followed, carbine ready for action in case of nasty surprises within.

'I've not been here before,' said Mongrel.

'I have . . . before the TankerRuns; me and Jam had a mission – a big Demolition.' He smiled grimly as he was swallowed by the earth and the clever intersections of

230

alloy ramp folded above him to leave the interior of the ruined farmhouse exactly as the two men had found it.

Tooled up with weapons and supplies, Carter moved through the huge alloy bunker and said, 'Mongrel, grab that end of the sheet.' Mongrel obliged, and they hauled the heavy tarpaulin from the Comanche. They stood lost in wonder for a moment as they stared at the machine's matt-dark roughly camouflaged flanks. Missiles were already in place, and Mongrel wheeled a KTM LC7 stealth bike free of its stand and checked the machine for fuel. 'We taking one or two?'

'Two,' said Carter, lighting a cigarette. 'You never know when we might have to split. Double the firepower. And we can still carry plenty of missiles.'

'You really out for fight this time, aren't you?'

'Stakes are fucking high,' said Carter coldly.

They spent a few more minutes checking out the KTM motorcycles, fired them into life a few times and checked the on-board guns and fuel. Then Mongrel hitched the two machines beneath the Comanche as Carter rolled four missiles across the stone floor with a clattering of steel against stone and stood them in the corner, red nose cones menacing in the gloom of the bunker's emergency lighting.

'Weapons of death,' rumbled Mongrel, staring at the missiles with a strange look on his face – a mixture of distaste and pleasure. Carter merely nodded, cigarette held limply between his lips, squinting as the smoke stung his eyes.

Within minutes they were ready. They had checked their carbine magazines and tooled up with extra-*special* weapons, advanced first-aid kits and many other supplies that they thought they might need. Some they stuffed into packs, other equipment they packed into the Comanche.

Climbing on board, they settled into their positions. Carter flicked a few switches and watched the glow of instruments light up in a glittering array. He pulled free his rolled-up balaclava and settled the insect-like HIDSS over his head.

- Battle data initiated, came a soft smooth female voice in his skull.

- All weapon systems primed.
- Targeting sequences aligned.
- Your Comanche is ready for battle.

'Ready for action?' Carter said.

'Always ready,' rumbled Mongrel.

Carter punched a button and above them the interior of the derelict farmhouse folded into a tunnel of alloy panels that cleared them a vertical path. With engines whining, then increasing in pitch to a dull roar, Carter focused on his displays and eased the Comanche up from the ground, nose lifting slightly higher than the tail. Alloy panels passed his vision, followed by the damp moss-covered bricks of the old farmhouse. Then they were up into the dark and the rain.

Behind, the alloy panels fell neatly and precisely back into place.

'Phew . . .' breathed Mongrel, rubbing at his eyes. 'I hate vertical take-off.'

'That's nothing. Look down there.'

Mongrel glanced down – just as distant automatic fire punched through the darkness and bright tracer-round streaks sped towards them.

'Nex?'

'Hmm,' said Carter, arming the mini-gun. Its mechanism whined as it spun into action. Carter lifted the

Comanche up into the broiling dark clouds, where it hovered for a moment. Then it dived, engines howling, towards the dark mass of woodland below and Carter pulled the trigger. Hundreds of heavy-calibre bullets cut and punched through leaves, branches and Nex – bodies were mashed and pulped into the Welsh soil as the Comanche's nose lifted. The dark war machine banked with a howl and sped off into the night, mini-gun smoking and glittering rain-slick rotors thumping with the rhythmical thrumming of precision engineering.

'How many you hit?'

Carter shrugged. 'Not enough. But it'll give the fuckers something to consider as they plan their next move.'

They sped on in silence, the Comanche vibrating with restrained power. Carter guided it south, and within minutes they hit the Bristol Channel, glass-black under the canopy of night. The Comanche dipped low along the coast, coming up over Exmoor and hugging the ground as it sped on at insane speeds. Carter lifted the chopper high through clouds and rain as they passed over the M5, a solid snake of gridlocked traffic, lights stretching off in skeins of immobile metal.

'What's going on down there?'

'Probably a knock-on effect from the quakes . . . is there any sitrep on them?'

Mongrel pulled free his ECube and scanned for a few moments, battered face lit by a ghostly blue. 'London was the most heavily hit – some coincidence, no? A series of quakes smashed across south coast, from Kent to Devon, and also in Manchester and Glasgow . . . fuck, looks to me like most of United Kingdom has been hit . . .'

'What about the rest of Europe?'

Mongrel nodded. 'Lot of seismic activity – Europe

affected, Africa, Middle East, Russia, China . . . something very fucking wrong here, Carter.'

'Tell me about it,' Carter said bitterly, picturing Natasha's face.

The Comanche powered on low over the English Channel, across France, Germany, and then to Switzerland. Carter found himself gazing down and remembering events from only a couple of days before when life had seemed so good and he had been complaining about his party lifestyle.

'*You fucking fool*,' mocked Kade.

'Yeah, like I need you to remind me.'

'*And look at the big hero now, rushing off to save Jam . . . you'll end up getting us both killed, Carter, you big pussy. This gig is an arse-fuck and you fucking well know it—*'

'Leave me be.'

'*Don't come crying to me when you're dead in a shell hole with your brain full of Nex metal, just like—*'

Carter frowned at the sudden silence. 'What's wrong? What are you not telling me?'

Kade remained silent, brooding, and then Carter felt him depart. It was like a weight lifted from the inside of his brain.

'You all right?'

Carter glanced round at Mongrel, who was staring at him strangely, concern in his dark eyes. Carter nodded, taking a deep breath and calming his battering heart.

'Yeah, never felt better. We'll be passing near the Kamus soon . . .'

'A wonderful sightseeing opportunity,' snapped Mongrel. 'Just great for the kiddies.'

Carter laughed then, a short sharp bark, and took another deep breath. Tiredness was creeping up on him but he pushed it away. Mongrel was no pilot – and so Carter had to keep going on reserves of adrenalin and energy that he had forgotten he had.

'We need to refuel?'

Carter gazed out, down at the distant mountain that lay below, glittering with ice. 'No. We'll get to Slovenia without a problem – and if we're desperate for fuel there are stocks at the Kamus. Spiral keep an S1_plot there now.'

'So I heard. Not happy about that.'

Carter turned again, helmet tilting sideways. 'You there when the troubles kicked off?'

'*Da.*' Mongrel nodded. 'Me and Slater, and a few others – we found some of the bodies.'

'Was it ever explained?'

'Was it fuck,' snorted Mongrel. 'And even if they'd found out what sent them people crazy, blowing each other's fucking heads off with shotguns, do you think they'd tell us humble squaddies about it? Hah. I spit on the Kamus. It bad place. Carter, there some things in this world we don't understand – we claw our way into space but there still a million secrets here on the planet . . . things we will never understand and never explain. And that mountain, where they build the Kamus complex – it bad place, Carter, real bad place.'

They flew on in silence through glittering clear skies.

Carter landed the Comanche under cover of night, thirty kilometres away from Jam's last recorded ECube coordinate. The rotors spun down, making the surrounding trees thrash wildly, and the air was warm and humid with the promise of a brewing storm.

Engines hissed and clicked, the Spiral agents dumped their kit on the ground and jumped free, and Mongrel unlocked one of the KTMs and wheeled the bike across the grass, kicking its stand into place and placing his hands on his hips. He took several deep breaths and smiled a warm smile.

'I love Europe. I love this place! Smells like home!'

Carter frowned. 'Where exactly *is* home for you, Mongrel?'

'Ahh!' He tapped his nose, dark eyes hooded.

'No, really, where do you come from?'

'Eastern part of Europe.'

'Which country? Europe is a big place.'

'I big guy! Ha! I come from lots of places. Well travelled, you might say. Son of a Thousand States.'

Carter lit a cigarette and rubbed at his tired eyes, drawing deeply on the weed and coughing heavily. 'Like that, is it? Right, I'll get a brew on, then get my head down for an hour . . . I can't remember the last time I slept rather than being simply unconscious. You up for stag?'

'*Da*, Carter, you get some shut-eye. I'll guard.'

Mongrel patted the weapon and glared off into the surrounding trees.

They sat, each with a half-pint mug of sweet tea, a small pan of water bubbling between them on a tiny frame heated by a hexi-block. The Comanche squatted behind them, a terrible dark machine, engines still hot. Around them long grass waved in the wind, and the last dying scents of autumn invaded their nostrils, soothing their souls and transporting their minds – at least temporarily – away from the horrors of the recent earthquakes.

'I need you to tell me about the machine,' said Carter softly, after finishing his fourth cigarette and most of his tea. He dropped in another teabag and five spoons of sugar, and gently poured water from the bubbling pan.

Mongrel, who was still staring off into the trees, his

236

M24 carbine ready for action, gave a small sideways glance at Carter.

'What you need to know?'

'Everything.'

'I already tell you.'

'No,' said Carter, cold eyes fixing on Mongrel's face. '*Fucking* everything.'

Mongrel gave a little laugh, and scratched his cheek with dirt-crusted fingernails. 'Ahh, *fucking* everything. That's different, then.' His face became a little more sombre and he stared off, steaming brew in one hand, other nursing his sub-machine gun. 'We were on SAD mission in Nicaragua – one of world's most active earthquake zones. Odd, that, no? We in northern mountains east of town called Ocotal. We were scoping out a silver mine, where several Nex apparently seen trying to break in one night. It was hot, humid, I was relaxing while Jam was on stag . . . next thing I know I fucking staring straight up at Nex. He look surprised to see us, that for sure, in our little bivvy. Jam took bastard out with single bullet between the eyes. Dropped fucker there on spot while I was still having horny dreams about air hostess on the flight over Caribbean.'

Mongrel sipped at his tea, then reached over and added another two sugars, stirring the brew with a plastic spoon. He grinned at Carter, showing his missing teeth, and said, 'I do like a sweet drop.'

'I can fucking see that. Go on, what happened with the Nex?'

'He was carrying metal sheaves – encoded. We tried to descramble codes on spot, but they were too complex; we took them back to Spiral HQ after mission and Jam got some top guys on job. Took them fucking *month*, and we got call when we were on other job in

New Zealand. When we got back, Jam went into meeting with these guys and afterwards gave us restricted briefing. He said it had gone straight to top within Spiral, and sheaves had been very important find. They had detailed a machine, named the Avelach, which was very, very old.'

'How old?'

'About 10,000 years.'

'That's before all modern civilisation.'

Mongrel nodded. 'I know that. That what confuse us all, because machine very, very complex. Too complex to come from such primitive age – unless there been another civilisation hidden from us, or dating techniques not accurate on substances found.'

Carter sipped his brew, staring off into the warm night darkness.

'Go on.'

Mongrel shrugged. 'All I know, Jam did some missions alone, and on his final one he said he thought he'd found out location of machine. I asked where it was, he gave me cheeky Jam grin and then headed out here for what appears to be his last Search and Destroy mission with TT and Slater . . .'

Carter frowned. 'He *thought* he'd found it? So he hadn't *actually* discovered the location?'

Mongrel shook his head, gaze meeting Carter's. 'It's our best shot, old buddy, our best chance. If anybody know where this machine is, it is Jam.'

'It must be at an old Nex base. After I killed Durell and Feuchter, the Nex had no command structure left; it could be fucking anywhere. Would the normal Nex even understand what the machine was if they had it?'

Mongrel shrugged again.

Carter lay back and closed his eyes, mind working.

They sat in silence for a while. Finally, Mongrel said, 'You very down, Carter. Let Mongrel cheer you up.'

'No, no . . . you're OK.'

'No, really, Carter. I have story make you piss pants.'

Carter's eyes fluttered open. Mongrel had yet another half-pint of tea clasped in his mitt and Carter grinned. 'If you drink any more tea then *you*'ll be the one pissing his pants.'

'A man needs tea when he on stag,' said Mongrel seriously. 'Help keep guard awake!'

Carter sighed, and propped himself up on one elbow. He stared at Mongrel, and could feel the malevolence within the huge man: the tension, the violence, the hatred. Mongrel was a psychopath born and bred, a poison-brained fucker of the lowest order, a face-smashing bone-pulping kneecap-breaking spine-tearing dirty low-down son of a bitch. Carter loved him, but also hated him.

'You OK, Carter? You look at me funny.'

'I'll live.' Carter smiled, rubbing at his eyes. Despite his weariness, sleep eluded him.

'That wasn't fucking question,' Mongrel said. 'Listen, I tell you of my wonderful sexual exploits . . .'

'Well, if you really, really, really must,' said Carter uncertainly.

'Har har,' said Mongrel, beaming. He settled back, resting his huge hands on his knees, his eyes dark and yet filled with an inner humour that Carter had rarely seen in this large killer. Carter smiled softly to himself, realising Mongrel's ploy. The psychopath was trying to bring him back down to earth, to cheer him up; to take his mind off the violence to come and the horrors that awaited them . . .

And to sidetrack him from thoughts of Natasha.

'I was stationed in Burma, at Pyinmana. We had great NAAFI, run by some of hottest chicks ever to wear sweaty shorts.'

Carter nodded, hooded eyes half-closed, the weariness of the past days creeping up on him. 'And this is your story of how you bedded all these hot chicks with quirky chat-up lines?' Carter yawned.

'Nah,' chuckled Mongrel heartily. 'It story of how I end up with worst chick in universe. Imagine this, I'm in for quiet drink with Tequila, tall broad-shouldered red-shaved son of bitch, and me and Tequila minding our business, like we always do, not looking for no trouble or nothing like that . . . except for time we threw that man through plate-glass window, yeah, and time Tequila set that woman on fire, but yeah, we minding our own business and Tequila at bar, talking to this fucking hag. I mean, she was *fucking* hag. Bitch-bag of the lowest echelon, har. Tequila comparing tattoos with this bird . . . now, I don't like to labour point, but she was fucking dog, Carter. A fuck-een dog. She was tall, long black hair like rat-diseased barbed wire, big arse like two badly parked Land Rovers. Kara she was called. Hmm . . .' There came a long pause.

Carter rolled his head, easing the tension in his neck. His hand came to rest on his Browning. It was cool and reassuring, battered and yet – perfect. His friend. His comrade in death. His metal lover.

'Yeah, Kara Red,' said Mongrel at last.

Carter propped himself up on one elbow again, momentarily intrigued. 'Red? Strange name?'

'Nickname,' grunted Mongrel, pulling out a packet of cigarettes and offering one to Carter. Carter, with a look of pain, waved the weed away and Mongrel laughed a hearty cruel laugh. He lit up, inhaled deeply and winced

as smoke stung his eyes. Gravely, he croaked, 'Kara Red –
she'll take you to bed, and fucking bleed on you.'

Carter cringed. 'I wish I'd never asked.'

'That's nothing to what you'll soon fucking wish, mate.
Right, so Tequila at the bar, pissed out of his shell, comparing his fucking tattoos with this bitch whose face,
Carter – fuck me, it was that bad, putting your fist in it
would be doing her favour. It was like she was sucking
heifer's arse soaked in vinegar. Like she was being seriously bum-fucked by steroid-pumped Australian donkey.
Tequila comparing tattoos—'

'Is this a long story, Mongrel? I'm pretty tired . . .'

'You'll like it. I promise you.'

Carter sighed. 'Go on, then.' He eyed Mongrel's cigarette hungrily.

'I got eighty spare, mate.'

'I've given up. As from now.'

'Only in body, but not in soul.'

'Just tell your fucking story before I change my fucking
mind and shoot you.'

'Temper, temper. Tequila comparing tattoos with this
death-bitch, they talking about fade and quality of lines
and other drunken arsery. I wander over, staggering,
sloshing beer down my front like real man should – just as
this bitch announce in high-pitched donkey-cackle that
she's got tattoo on her big toe.

'"Let's see it," I say, playing with one of my few
remaining broken teeth. This Kara goes through this
lengthy rigmarole, kicks off her shoes, peels off her blue
and black striped tights – class bird, this – and then peels
off her sweat-soaked sock to reveal red rose laid delicately
across the skin of her large toe, toenail missing, presumed
dead. Me and Tequila, we exchange glances, and it a
fucking miracle we didn't puke our beer back into our

glasses and I peers at her through the old beer goggles and says, "Does it *smell* like rose?"

'This Kara stares back at me, without a hint of humour. "Nah!" she squawks. "It smells like *Stilton*." We reeled at disgust of situation, and as you imagine, outcome was as you expect.'

Carter chuckled. 'You shagged her?'

'*Da*.' Mongrel nodded. 'Nothing wrong with that – when class cheese-bitch offers roll with her Stilton feet, you take it on chin like man and accept it like drunken arse with possibility of no future.'

Carter stared long and hard at Mongrel as the huge ugly ex-squaddie finished his cigarette and immediately lit another, coughing on the blue smoke.

'We live in different worlds, Mongrel.'

'It get worse.'

'How can it fucking possibly get worse?'

Mongrel grinned. Most of his teeth were missing. Carter often wondered how he chewed, but every food-stuff imaginable simply slid into Mongrel's gaping maw and disappeared without any apparent need for mandibles. Steak never caused him a single problem. Bacon was shredded with ease.

'Well, I'm shagging this Kara, right, and she really going for it – sweaty arse high in air, me on my back, her tits wobbling like jellies in dark above my face. She pumping me like fucking milking machine and moaning and screeching like mangling of badly meshed tank gears. I thinking I proper king, despite her smell, but then – and this gross even me out, mate – she farts: proper evil-stinking cloud of poisonous mustard gas that engulf fucking room like fucking nuclear winter.'

'Mongrel, that is *bad*.'

'It get worse,' Mongrel threatened for the second time.

'How . . . no, no, just finish the story and then I can get my head down.'

'Har. Well, this Kara Red, she shit all over me.'

A silence followed.

Carter stared hard at Mongrel.

'*Really?*'

'*Da.*'

'She, like, shit. All over you?'

'*Da.*' Mongrel beamed, and smoked his cigarette.

'Did this bother you?'

'*Kanyechno.* I threw her down stairs.'

'Is that the end of the story?'

'Pretty much.'

'Mongrel, you're a fucking animal – but I concede, Kara Red was, shall we say, a thousand times worse.'

'She change her name to Kara *Brown* after that. After she got casts taken off her legs. But then, at least it gave her opportunity to air her fucking Edam feet.'

'Stilton.'

'Whatever.'

Carter finally managed to catch an hour's sleep. He awoke groggily, Mongrel passed him another cup of tea, and he resigned himself to a smoke.

'You see anything?'

'It's as dead as a croaked beetle out there.'

They packed up their gear and, several hours before dawn, set out on the KTM LC7 bikes with stealth mode engaged. Carter rode one machine, Mongrel the other. The bikes left the fields and woods leading down from the deserted hilltop and joined up with narrow tarmac tributaries, each side dusted with gravel and loose stone and spreading off into moonlit fields. A river flowed to their left and they cruised along in silence without lights,

Mongrel with his M24 gun across his lap and holding onto the KTM with one hand, eyes focused and looking for trouble.

They travelled the dark roads for an hour, only passing a couple of cars – a Mercedes and a Skoda – which they skimmed past in silent dark blurs. Finally, leaving the roads behind, they headed up dirt trails until they finally pulled the bikes off the tracks and rode, standing on foot pegs, over rough ground until they halted the machines on hissing Brembos and killed the hot engines.

They cammed up the KTM stealth machines with ferns and branches. Then Mongrel checked his ECube and they moved off through the gently rustling trees, packs shouldered and M24 sub-machine guns at the ready, proceeding patiently – and with care. As if their lives depended on it.

Which they did.

'There.'

Carter squinted at the distant cabin and allowed his breathing to ease. He pulled out his Browning and checked the mag for the hundredth time, then flicked free the safety on the carbine.

'You sure?'

'Yeah.'

'You cover me . . .'

Carter moved forward, and Mongrel rocked back on his heels, squinting around in the pre-dawn glow. Carter approached the rough-walled cabin warily, weapon ready for action, mind screaming abuse and firing him into a full adrenalin state . . . he reached the doorway and dropped to a crouch, glancing back at Mongrel who was covering arcs of fire.

'*You need at least three men for this,*' chastised Kade.

'You offering your services?'

'*Well, you know what they say: if the going gets tough—*'

'Then Kade gets going?'

'*Fuck you, Carter.*'

'Temper, temper, little man.'

Carter moved warily into the cabin. It was deserted and he moved cautiously through the rooms, but his sharp eyes could see nothing. He was just turning to leave when he saw it – a tiny square of glass missing from the window. An ideal size and position for a—

'*Mindnuke,*' said Kade.

'Hmm.'

Carter touched the edges of the hole; they were perfectly smooth and had obviously been sucked by an ECube ready for MNK insertion. And an MNK meant . . .

Nex.

Carter returned to Mongrel. 'He was here.'

'Fucker, I fucking knew it. They should burn those PopBot scouts. They're a waste of fucking time!'

'The question is, what happened next?'

'No other signs?'

Carter scanned the surrounding countryside, and shook his head. 'No, nothing obvious. Come on, I'm going to have to do some tracking the old-fashioned way . . .'

It took Carter an hour to pick up the trail. The sun was rising steadily in the sky, making both men feel uneasy.

Carter pointed. 'You see it?'

'See what?'

'Look closely.'

'What at?'

Carter sighed. 'Boot imprint – Spiral issue. They were

245

fucking here all right, and running in that direction.'
Carter pointed with the muzzle of his carbine.

'Come on.'

'Wait . . . slowly, Mongrel. These things take time. And
let's not forget the DemolSquad's recent fucking disappearance.'

They moved cautiously through the woodland, from
tree to tree. Stopping, checking distances, checking other
trees and foliage for signs of passing. Occasionally they
risked a scan with the ECube, but knew now not to trust
the device at all . . . it seemed that the Nex were playing
their covert games once again and had access to digital
superiority.

Carter crouched beside a tree with strange markings in
the bark. 'Something big, heavy and metal hit this.'

'Like what?'

Carter shrugged, 'A bike, something like that. I tell
you, Mongrel, some bastard has tried hard to cover this
up – there should be fucking tracks everywhere. And
look – even metal particles have been removed from the
trunk.'

'Could it have been Jam's bike?'

'I'm not sure. But it looks like we're going in the right
direction.'

They squatted in a clump of thick bushes where the valley
dropped off to one side. They watched for several hours
as the sun toiled across the sky. A cooler wind blew from
the south but it did little to relieve them of the sweat
drenching their thick clothing.

Carter had pointed out the bridge leading over the
valley, with rocks clustered at either end. They had spent
a good hour watching the small log cabin down in the
valley bottom, but had seen no activity at either location.

'I think we at dead end,' said Mongrel eventually.

Sweating beneath the bushes, prickled and poked and uncomfortable, Carter pulled free his ECube and activated the tiny black alloy device. Lights flashed in his eyes and audio signals blipped.

'That's . . . strange.'

'What?' Mongrel shuffled closer, smelling of fallen leaves.

'Neither the bridge nor the cabin appear on the ECube. They're invisible to the scanners . . .' Carter shook the alloy device.

'Yeah, that always work for me – four billion dollars' worth of development technology fail to function so give the little fucker shake. Kicks it up its arse good.'

'I don't understand,' muttered Carter. Then he killed the tiny device and glanced out from their shelter.

'You want go look?' asked Mongrel cautiously, staring into the valley, his eyes straining to detect movement.

Carter nodded.

'I think we wait for nightfall,' growled Mongrel. 'I think good idea we sit back, wait, then get closer look without sun bouncing off our guns to give away our position, eh, Carter? *Carter?*'

Mongrel turned.

Carter had gone.

'Fucker!'

Mongrel crawled from beneath the prickling bushes to see Carter gliding towards the rocks shielding the bridge; he dropped down and disappeared. Mongrel eased his own bulk forward, keeping trees and bushes to his right – until he finally stopped in a good spot and glanced all around, nervous now, licking sweat from his lips.

He glanced around for Carter, but could not see the man.

'Mad fucker,' he grumbled. 'Why we not wait for night? You get us both shot!'

And then he saw Carter – underneath the bridge, fastened as if by magnets and moving beneath the thick wooden boards which stretched out between the two horizontal iron H-section supports.

'What he doing?'

And then Mongrel saw the dull glint of a machine-gun nest – just a hint. It lay concealed among the rocks and he caught a fleeting glimpse of black – a barrel sleeve with drilled holes for cooling during firing. It could be nothing else . . . and it was positioned in a brilliant natural defensive location overlooking the only way to cross the valley:

The bridge.

'What you doing, Carter? You get yourself fucking drilled!'

But Carter was committed and, eyeing the bridge, Mongrel knew that he himself had neither the skill to negotiate the structure in the way that Carter was doing nor the strength to sustain his own body weight for such a lengthy climb.

I need to lose bit of weight. If I survive that long, he added to himself.

Sweat rolled into Carter's eyes like acid and he blinked as it stung him. He licked his dry lips and found a fresh handhold, moving over another few inches beneath the thick ancient timbers of the bridge.

The temperature beneath the bridge was high, the air humid, stagnant. And he couldn't reach his water canteen. *Bitch*.

Slowly, Carter advanced, his mind switching between images of Natasha lying supine in the hospital bed with tubes emerging from different parts of her body, pictures of the baby on the scan imager – a tiny white blob against a background of glossy black, barely distinguishable as head, torso, arms and legs but miraculous nevertheless – and then to Jam's smiling, cocky, mischievous face, stubbled, a dangling loose cigarette, and holding the coordinates for the machine that could save both Carter's woman and their child.

The wood above him was bleached by the Slovenian sun; it creaked occasionally and tried continually to spit dust into Carter's upturned face.

He moved on in this inverted crawl, inch by painful inch, boots tucking into crevices, fingers finding holes and gaps, muscles screaming at him.

Don't blow your position, warned his brain.

But another part of him, the shell inhabited by Kade, wanted to rush in with guns blazing and kill everybody, slaughter them like sheep. But then, what did *he* want? He wasn't even sure what he was looking for any more . . . surely anybody who had covered their tracks so well out in the woods wouldn't leave Jam's body or his KTM motorcycle lying casually around?

And then he heard it.

A low engine rumble.

No, he cursed. It can't fucking be!

But it was: a truck, a big eight-tonne vehicle with heavy off-road tyres and a canvas roof. It approached with a steady growl and a meshing – a thrashing – of gears and Carter worked harder, moved faster, but realised—

He could not beat the truck.

'Son of a bitch.'

He heard the vehicle drop two gears, its engine pitch increasing on the slight incline before the bridge – and then twin heavy thumps as the front tyres mounted the span. They clattered across the thick wooden beams, and

Carter was almost knocked from his perch by the initial crashing impact. He gritted his teeth, tightened his muscles, and prayed . . .

The truck's six rear wheels slammed onto the bridge.

The whole structure started to vibrate.

Badly.

Carter felt a shout welling in his throat as the truck's wheels bludgeoned the wood and vibrations pulsated through his arms and legs. Dust and dirt poured down into his face, causing him to cough and choke. Spitting, Carter glanced down at the terrible drop beneath him—

The shaking and battering seemed to last for ever.

It pounded him like a piece of metal between a hammer and an anvil.

It felt like a train rolling over his head.

And then it was gone.

Carter choked back a sneeze and cursed, his eyes slits of anger, and then continued his horizontal climb with fingers and arms burning, his Browning digging into his ribs. He finally reached the side and swung himself onto the tiny narrow ledge underneath the bridge, panting. Then, climbing around the iron struts, he pulled himself up a little, peered around, hoisted himself up onto the rocks and leapt into the tiny protected circle of the machine-gun nest.

It was small and circular, sand scattered on the floor. The large T80 Heckler & Koch heavy machine gun sat on a tripod pointing out across the open expanse of bridge and was manned by a—

A merc?

Human.

Carter grinned at the sudden surprised and horrified look on the man's bearded face. He slammed his fist into the soldier's nose – twice, three times, splattering blood across the sand and pounding the man into unconsciousness. Carter peered out from the back of the machine-gun nest, grinning fiercely as he saw Nex dismounting neatly from the back of the truck that had tried to dislodge him and send him tumbling into the valley. Grunting, he dragged the tripod across the sand, checked the belt of ammunition, and levelled the T80 out of the back of the machine-gun nest. The Nex had assembled in ranks of eight – twenty-four in all – and they stood to attention with weapons by their sides, their copper eyes focused.

Carter waited, his own eyes bright, picturing Natasha . . .

And he remembered the Nex outside the Spiral HQ as the quake pulverised London – murdering the innocent, fleeing Spiral operatives, men and women, without remorse or even a flicker of emotion. To Carter, the situation had looked suspiciously like a trap.

The Nex outside the truck were joined by more of their kind, mixed with a few mercenary soldiers. 'Sorry, boys,' muttered Carter, feeling himself go cold and dead inside. 'You're fighting on the wrong fucking side . . . hope the money tasted good and you spent it well.'

He opened fire.

The T80 roared and bucked beneath his hands as a hail of bullets flew across the narrow stretch of land, mowing down the Nex in a swathe of bloodied flesh.

Some reached for weapons.

Some turned to sprint—

Some leapt.

All were pulped by the onslaught of the heavy machine gun.

Scythed down.

Slaughtered.

Bullets slammed into the rear of the truck, puncturing

251

all six rear tyres in tiny deflating explosions. The vehicle settled slowly down.

Carter released the trigger and his pent-up breath and surveyed the destruction with a cold eye. He heard a moan from the mercenary at his feet, looked down, saw the man struggling with his own SA1000 and palmed his Browning, placing a single shot in the contract soldier's brains. The merc crumpled back, eyes glassy and staring. Carter sighed and shook his head.

He suddenly felt sick of death. Sick of killing. Sick of slaughter.

'*Don't be a pussy*,' said Kade.

'I'm just tired.'

'*Don't be so soft – people trying to slot each other in a fun-filled military scenario is what makes a human* human; *it's what sets us apart from animals . . . it's what makes life so fucking worth living.*'

'Not for me.'

'*Want to bet?*'

Warily, gripping his M24 carbine, Carter stepped away from the machine-gun nest. He could hear the truck's engine, still idling with a low grumble and spitting exhaust fumes. Boots pounded the bridge behind him and he whirled low – to see Mongrel's face looming into view. Carter returned to cover the compound in front of him with his weapon.

'I hear heavy gunfire – what fuck happened?' Mongrel stumbled to a halt. '*Bozhey moy!*' he whispered, surveying the carnage.

Carter lit a cigarette.

'You kill them all?'

'Let's find out.'

Covering opposing arcs of fire, Carter and Mongrel moved warily forward, halting and staring at the

252

compound across which they had stumbled while on Jam's trail. The buildings were all fashioned from wood, some painted in brown, a couple in dull blue. They were raised on low piles and beneath each hut was a dark and gloomy patch of dead ground. There were ten huts, set out in a semicircle in a natural hollow. Rough vegetation grew between the decrepit old buildings, and many walls had been badly patched with crooked joinery.

'A good place to defend,' said Mongrel, his gun pointing from building to building.

Carter nodded, drawing heavily on his cigarette. 'This is an old Second World War barracks or camp,' he said. 'I've seen pictures of this place before . . .'

'Used by?'

'The Nazis.' Carter smiled bitterly. 'How fucking fitting.'

They moved through the camp, clearing the buildings one at a time but each knowing instinctively that they were alone. The Nex were not the sort of enemy to set up camp and hide – in battle they were fearless and would not squat in a building waiting to be discovered. They would attack . . .

Happy that they were finally alone, Carter moved to the truck while Mongrel moved over and nudged one of the Nex corpses with his boot. 'By fuck, they stink . . .'

'You think *they* smell bad? You should have tried the TankerRuns,' said Carter, reaching into the idling truck's cab and killing the engine. Silence settled across the camp and Carter shivered. 'A million rotting diseased bodies . . . now *that* was a fucking smell. Christ, this place is awful – you can feel it in your bones. It has a *bad* history.'

'Yeah. Come on, we need to find out where they took Jam . . .'

'If he's still alive.'

'Yeah, if he's still alive.'

Most of the wooden huts were empty, or had nothing but simple camp beds and the most basic of equipment. One stood out as the obvious HQ and had many locked cabinets and high-tech computer equipment – which appeared out of place against the ancient and rotting surroundings.

They searched the HQ and used Mongrel's ECube as a SecScanner, flicking free digital locks and hijacking the computer systems to allow access to hidden files. After thirty minutes of snooping, Mongrel slumped back in a chair and wiped a fine sheen of sweat from his forehead.

'It's all fucking financial data,' he said at last, confused.

'Yeah, food supplies, stone and cement prices, exchanges of stock for things like diesel and LVA fuel.'

'Have you scanned these?'

Carter shook his head. On the desk were several thin metal sheets, with encoded data pitted in their surfaces. Mongrel idly ran the ECube over them and projected a digital beam onto the nearest wall.

Figures flooded the surface in eerie blue as the ECube decoded: columns and rows of numbers and data.

'More buying and selling,' said Mongrel.

'Wait.'

'What?'

Carter peered through the figures, the beams of the projected blue light cutting neatly through his cigarette smoke. 'Look, the third column details the transfer of titanium-carbide drill bits. And the fifth is cooling oil, used in drilling.'

'So?'

'This looks like equipment for mining – oil or . . . LVA?'

'This irrelevant to us, Carter.'

'No, look at the digital stamp and the signature. Director General Oppenhauer, Commissioner for the Fuel Inspectorate of Eastern Europe. He's the guy who inspects all the new LVA drilling operations that have been opening in Eastern Europe – why would he be authorising sales, purchases and transfers of this equipment? And what the fuck have the Nex got to do with LVA?'

Mongrel shook his head. 'Maybe after Feuchter and Durell were killed the Nex signed on as mercenaries. Maybe they protect places like this and you just machine-gunned a load of innocent merc soldiers.'

'It's still illegal to employ a Nex, ever since Spiral shut down the original operation decades ago. An abomination against God, one politician called it, although in my humble opinion all fucking politicians are fucking abominations against God themselves. Just by their very natures.' He grinned sourly.

'What connection then?'

Carter scratched at his stubble. 'Not sure, Mongrel, not sure . . . what could the Nex possibly want with LVA? It's just a fucking fuel – sure, they could make money out of it but . . . you make money out of lots of things.'

'Maybe they funding another war . . .'

Carter met Mongrel's stare. 'Doesn't even bear thinking about,' he said softly. 'Come on, I don't think we're going to find anything here to do with Jam – we're at a dead end. We should go down and check out that second log cabin – maybe he spotted another nest of Nex there.'

'Yeah, and those dead Nex you kill, they stink.'

'Lead the way.'

'After you, Mr Carter,' said Mongrel, a glint in his dark eyes. 'This looks like your gig now.'

★

It was late evening and Carter halted beside the truck. Mongrel nearly stumbled into the back of him.

'Don't fucking move, and don't make a fucking sound,' said Carter.

'What is it?'

Carter rolled his eyes. 'There's a sniper up on the hill . . .' He eased free his Browning whilst his visible hand dangled free, holding the M24 carbine. His left hand disguised by Mongrel's bulk, he turned his body slightly, an easygoing smile on his face as his head turned and—

The Browning flashed up.

And Carter began firing . . .

The cliffside was steep, rocky, scattered with bushes and a few tiny clinging trees. Bullets whined, spitting dust from rock and thudding into vegetation. A scream echoed, followed by, 'Stop! Stop!'

Carter, dropping his M24 to the hard-packed ground, ejected the Browning's mag and slotted another in its place. Mongrel lifted his carbine and covered the hillside. Carter took the Browning in both hands and sighted down the short barrel.

'Throw out your weapon,' he bellowed.

There came a short pause, and a rifle with a telescopic sight attached sailed through the air and landed on the hard ground with a clatter. Then a woman stood up, waving weakly, one hand to her shoulder where blood was visible, seeping between her fingers.

'You hit her,' said Mongrel.

'Good.'

'But it's a woman . . .'

'Good.'

'But she . . .'

'Yeah? She could still have put a round in the back of

your fucking dumb-skull head. Mongrel, you've always been a dickhead when it came to women – go on, help her down and I'll cover you.'

Mongrel moved forward, warily, as the woman scrambled down the steep cliffside and slipped, rolling and sliding the last twenty feet to hit the ground hard. She sat up, covered in dust, coughing. She had a sweet oval face, perfectly unblemished skin, and thin blonde hair tied back into a ponytail. She wore rugged outdoor clothing with natural colours designed to blend with her surroundings. And blood was pouring from her shoulder.

Casting around, eyes and ears alert, scanning the rest of the hillside, Carter followed even more carefully and watched Mongrel help her to her feet.

'Who are you?'

'Please don't kill me.' Her English was good, but laced with a heavy accent.

'That depends on your answers.'

The woman's gaze moved to the truck, and the pile of Nex. 'Oh,' she said, eyes riveted on the carnage, the strewn limbs, the gaping maws, the strings of flesh.

She peered into Carter's face. 'You kill them all?'

'Yes. Now answer the fucking question or you'll be next on the fucking pile . . .'

'Carter!' snapped Mongrel, frowning.

'My name is Mila. I work for a small unit called the SVLA who seek to kill those . . .' she gestured. 'They have invaded us, our country, they have camps all over the world . . . and they killed my brother . . .'

'So you were going to pick them all off with your little pea-shooter?'

'No, I was just observing, watching them come and go. You have done a job for us all . . . I cannot believe you spotted me.'

Carter ignored her, turned, and moved to the rifle. It was old, polished, well cared for. More like a family heirloom than a working weapon. Carter threw it to Mongrel, who caught it in one huge hand and looked at the scratched stock.

'She survive?'

'I need few minutes to clean wound,' said Mongrel. 'Luckily, your round tore through muscle and not shatter bone. Lucky your fucking aim was out.'

'There was a bush in the way.' Carter grinned. 'Now, come on, we need to move out . . . we need to get away from this place. You can sort her out in the woods.'

'Why are you here?' asked Mila, her features screwed in pain but her teeth clenching as if trying to put on a brave face.

'We're looking for somebody.'

'Mongrel, you dick!'

'What fucking harm, Carter? She might have seen something! She say herself she been sat watching the Nex . . . maybe she see our friends? Yes?' He glanced towards Mila, who was nodding.

'A man? Short dark hair, short beard, travelling with a real big man and a woman?'

Mila looked nervously from Carter to Mongrel, and then back again.

'Yeah.' Carter nodded, eyes suddenly wide. 'You saw them? Here?'

'Here,' said Mila softly, blood running between her fingers.

Carter ignored her obvious pain. 'Had they been captured?'

'The first man had, yes. They beat him – kicked him when he was on the ground. But the others . . .'

'Yes?'

'They loaded their bodies into the back of a truck. Like that one. With dark grey motorcycles.'

'Gotta be them,' breathed Mongrel. 'Fuck . . . that means Slater and TT dead. Fuck. What did they do with man who still alive? One they beat?'

'They took him to the Kataja Quarry. I could show you . . .'

'How do you know this?'

'I followed. I was gathering information, remember? Watching them. But I couldn't go too close, these people – with the copper eyes – they are crawling all over the place. It is far too risky for me to approach the quarry itself.'

'How far is it?'

'About fifty kilometres from here.'

'Come on, let's get back to the bikes – we can sort out her wound and plan our route.' Carter turned and allowed Mongrel to help the woman along the dirt road behind him.

They passed the pile of Nex corpses and Carter did not look down.

They were nothing more than dead meat.

Reaching the bridge they stepped out onto the wide thick timbers. Carter turned, gesturing to Mongrel to check his weapon, when he saw something, a glint – a change – in Mongrel's eyes. His head snapped round to see, at the entrance to the bridge, a *creature* . . . it was a good head over six feet tall, with a huge neck and a face from a nightmare. It had twisted, drooling fangs and small copper eyes – and torched black skin, as if this *thing* had been burnt. The body was heavily muscled and bare from the waist up – but from the lower abdomen black armour merged with flesh and scattered in irregular glinting panels down its groin and legs. Long claws extended from thick black fingers and Carter stared in horror as the figure sighted him—

And seemed to smile.

Like a bad.drug-induced dream his words came back to haunt him. 'Next time, fucker,' he had snarled . . . and suddenly his show of bravado didn't seem like such a good idea.

'*My name is Dake, and I'll be waiting for all eternity.*'

Unfortunately, this particular eternity hadn't actually lasted that long.

It had come around much quicker.

Carter swallowed hard.

'What is it?' yelled Mongrel, his carbine lifting—

And then they realised that the creature carried a weapon.

It opened fire, heavy boots pounding swiftly across the bridge towards them, saliva pooling from the twisted deformed mouth and bullets hammering from the sub-machine gun it carried—

They turned and dived for the protection of the machine-gun nest, rolling into temporary safety. But before they could do anything there came a crunch of boots on rock and the creature was staring down at them, twisted jaws working silently—

'Carter,' it hissed.

Carter's M24 opened fire and the Nex was punched backwards from the rocks under a hail of bullets. The gun yammered in Carter's hands until he released the trigger; the explosions echoed around the valley, fading rapidly, and in the silence that then fell Carter glanced at Mongrel.

'It fucking *knows* you?' Mongrel scowled.

'Long story.'

'I hope you just killed it.'

'Don't fucking bank on it.'

Carter poked his head warily from the confines of the machine-gun nest. Then, followed closely by Mongrel and Mila, he stepped onto the packed earth of the road—

A roar erupted from the opposite side of the rocks.

Carter calmed his breathing.

'Go on, then,' said Mongrel.

Carter glanced back at him and smiled grimly. 'Cheers, mate,' he said. 'Why don't *you* go first?'

'I ain't going first,' mumbled Mongrel. I got fucking wounded woman to look after . . .'

Carter moved forward – and the ScorpNex attacked, slapping Carter's sub-machine gun out of the way with a heavy claw. The gun skittered along the dry road. Carter ducked a heavy blow and whirled low, skipping backwards . . .

'You remember me, little man?'

'I could never forget a face like that,' snapped Carter dryly.

Again it leapt at Carter with awesome speed, and he dodged a blow, swaying to one side and then skipping out of the huge ScorpNex's way. Suddenly it whirled on Mongrel, and with a mighty blow sent him flying backwards to land on his back, blood flooding from his nose. Carter charged as Dake whirled—

He slammed his fist three times into the creature's nightmarish face, heavy smashing right hooks, then ducked low under a double whirling slash of the creature's massive claws. He dodged left and hammered a side-kick to the ScorpNex's chest – but the impact had little effect and the creature grabbed Carter's leg. It launched him through the air to land heavily on the ground where he bounced and rolled to a halt. Carter

261

uncurled, stood smoothly and drew his Browning, snarling.

He started shooting.

The ScorpNex took five bullets – flinching with each impact – by the time it reached Carter, but had managed to sidestep five more. It struck the gun from Carter's grip and blood splashed his face and arms as it grabbed him by the head in both heavy claws and lifted him from the ground. Carter gasped, the pressure pounding through his brain, but he lifted both boots smoothly and with his heels he hammered the ScorpNex's face once, twice, three, four, five, six, seven times until he felt its fangs and then its jaw crack—

It dropped Carter—

Who sprinted towards the bridge. In a second the ScorpNex was after him, bounding along almost on all fours, heavy arms and claws lowered to help drag its twisted frame along the ground. Carter sped out onto the bridge and the ScorpNex was right behind him. He knew then that he could not outrun the creature. It was faster and stronger and infinitely more powerful than a mere human . . .

'*Let me have him . . .*'

'*I will burn him . . .*'

'*I will fuck him* hard . . .'

Carter fumbled in his webbing, pulled free an HPG – a chemical grenade – and dropped it onto the bridge, where it rolled for a moment, awaiting the initiation burst. Dake leapt at Carter who dodged a heavy blow, smashing a fist into Dake's battered face where Carter's boots had already wrought serious damage. Carter evaded another blow, then a third and he was backing away across the bridge's beams as he counted—

And initiated the HPG sequence with a mental impulse from an implanted augmentation.

The HPG exploded and Carter caught the edge of the blast. It picked him up and threw him down the bridge, where he landed tumbling, limbs flailing, and rolled to a confused halt. The ScorpNex was flung, twisting and thrashing, against the heavy iron struts of the bridge, crushing bones and snapping one thick iron beam which sagged, its supporting bolts severed.

A ragged hole appeared in the timbers of the bridge, four metres in diameter, its edges splintered with thick daggers of wood. The valley lay below the hole – a distant expanse of greenery.

Silence seemed to reign for a moment—

'Carter!'

Mongrel was sprinting as Carter rolled to his knees and coughed, spitting and heaving onto the beams beneath him. He took a deep breath, calming himself from the sudden explosion of violence, blood streaming from his nose and ears. Then he climbed shakily to his feet and started to jog back towards the jagged hole and the prostrate figure of the ScorpNex.

Is it dead? he thought.

It just took a fucking HPG blast . . .

It *must* be dead . . .

There came a crackling of chitinous armour.

Slowly, the ScorpNex uncurled and climbed to its feet.

The blast had sliced a layer from the side of its face, arm and torso, and one eye was mangled, hanging against its black armoured cheek. Its claw moved to its side and there was blood and gore there too – from the incredible impact with the bridge's iron strut. But it pulled itself to its full height and a deep-throated chuckle rolled out across the bridge.

Carter faltered but his face set in a grim line. He knew he had to finish this thing and finish it now. He accelerated towards the ScorpNex, blood coating his face in a violent demon mask. The creature suddenly dropped to a crouch and leapt forward powerfully to meet Carter head on.

CHAPTER 10

WORLDSCALE

Jam dreamed.

'You killed them.'

He stared at Nicky's face. Tears flowed down her red-puffed cheeks and he hung his head in shame, staring at his scuffed boots, then rubbed at his face and looked up again.

The accusation in her eyes felled him more easily than any bullet.

'It wasn't me,' he said softly, his own tears flowing.

'You even killed the fucking children,' she snarled. She stepped forward and hit him then, a heavy right uppercut that made him rock. He absorbed the punch, eyes staring down, and tried to explain but everything swirled in his brain and his thoughts were clouded, sluggish, confused.

'You ripped them apart.'

'It wasn't me!'

'You tore off the children's faces, you fucking bastard, I saw it, saw it all . . . and you will rot in hell for what you have done . . .'

Jam's head jerked up. His eyes suddenly narrowed, and

he lashed out, claw slicing through Nicky's neck and ripping her from collarbone to breastbone with a sickening wet crunch of torn flesh and crackles of snapping tendon and gristle. Her body peeled apart in two segments that hit the ground dead, without making a sound. Her blood pooled out and her eyes grew glazed, staring blankly at the wall. Jam's head tilted to one side, staring at her in contemplation and he reached out to nudge her separate halves with his foot.

Jam awoke in the dark. He was crying. The chamber was cool and that pleased him, the chill on his flesh soothing his raging mind. He shifted, awkwardly, joints stiff as he rolled to his feet with clacks of armour. His head tilted and he could feel saliva pooling in his mouth, between jaws that would not close properly—

But then—

That was him, wasn't it? He had always been this way.

He moved to a wide bowl of water and stared down through the gloom at his gently swaying reflection. His small copper eyes took in the patches of black – almost as if it was scorched – armour on his face, twisting and merging with raw pink flesh. His jaws worked continuously, tiny movements almost as if he was chewing, and he could feel his back teeth grinding together.

Remember?

And he remembered the woman from his dream.

She had been crying.

Why? he thought.

The children he'd killed – they'd been nothing more than fresh meat, the meat of the enemy. They would have grown into soldiers and come looking for the Nex with guns and death – it had been a simple extermination process. In the same way that you would step on an insect . . .

266

Jam frowned, his mind spinning.

He could still see the look of pain in the dream-woman's eyes, and it confused him. She knew him; but he could not remember her name and that was strange. It burned him . . .

Her pain.

Jam curled up and sleep claimed him quickly in a black embrace.

Durell stared down at the map, its glow softly illuminating his disfigured face. Colours glittered across this synthetic microcosmic world and Durell nodded to himself, small tongue darting out to lick his dry lips.

He felt . . . nervous.

Things were coming together.

Plans were merging.

And he could feel the shifting of power.

Spiral, he thought.

He felt Gol enter the room behind him and he tensed a little. He laughed softly to himself, revelling in the knowledge that Gol was Nex, a slice of Nex, but not quite a pure-breed.

Not so Jam.

No. Durell smiled. Jam had turned out a thousand times more pure than he could ever have dreamed possible. Jam had proved himself to be beyond reproach . . . a true Nex . . . true *ScorpNex*—

'It failed,' said Gol.

Durell turned, unable to read the emotion in Gol's expression.

'So be it. We were lucky with Jam; the ScorpNex protocol is extremely difficult to replicate and it will take time. However, with Jam's conversion I am pleased that we have yet another general willing to die for our cause.'

'Yes.'

'Gol, I believe you had a little chat with Kattenheim?'

'Yes. He—' Gol smiled. 'He does not quite believe that I am with you. He doubts my loyalty, I think.'

'Ignore him. Kat always did overreact. But he is strong and powerful and fast – don't antagonise him unduly because I need you both with me.'

Gol gave a single nod.

'What are your thoughts on Natasha?'

'It is a very sad day,' said Gol carefully. 'She is my daughter and I love her. But she has chosen her own road in life. She has chosen Spiral and she has chosen to die for Spiral . . . I cannot protect her for ever. She is her own person now.'

'Very philosophical. Now.' Durell's hand came out, resting on Gol's shoulder. Gol looked deep into those slitted copper eyes and sensed that Durell was waiting for a reaction: a glimmer of horror or disgust or revulsion—

Gol forced his face to remain calm, unmoving.

'I have a job for you. A delivery.'

'The Foundation Stones?'

'Yes, four of them. I want you to go with Kattenheim and Jam, make the delivery and check their installations. Then we can work on links to the QHub and initiate the QEngine with its final settings.'

'Is the army mobilised?'

'Nex soldiers are on the move,' said Durell softly. 'The pieces of the jigsaw are slotting neatly into place.'

Gol nodded again. He understood.

The small black chopper piloted by Kattenheim came in low over the desert, swirling a dust storm in its wake, the thudding of its rotors echoing over the vast flat plain. Rocks loomed from the shifting sand dunes and Kat brought the chopper down with swift precise movements. The blades spun down whining as Gol leapt out onto the flat rocks, closely followed by Jam who shielded his eyes with an armoured black forearm.

Grabbing a pack, Kat followed and the three of them stood on the desert sand. They gazed at the twenty Nex who had spilled from low wooden barracks to meet them, sub-machine guns at the ready. One of them came forward and saluted.

Kat returned the salute. 'Are events progressing?'

'They are,' came the sibilant, asexual voice. 'We have been expecting you.'

They walked across the sand-blown rocks under the beating sun. Gol could see a massive pen where perhaps a hundred huge trucks were parked. As they moved past the rocks the true scale of this particular encampment opened up in front of him – there were a thousand hastily constructed wooden barracks containing perhaps thirty thousand Nex in all. The desert camp during this hour of the day was quiet, with only a few Nex scouts running errands – it was at night, during the cooler hours, when it truly came alive.

Entering a wooden cabin, where fans cooled the dry desert air, Kat moved immediately to a table filled with maps. Gol stood, waiting, and looked occasionally at Jam.

This new ScorpNex – a Skein Blending of a man he had once known – had shown no recognition. Years earlier Gol had scripted several missions with Jam – in their younger and wilder days – but this transformation, this blending seemed to have eyes and mind for one thing and one thing only: combat – combat leading to death and destruction.

'What do you think?'

Jam turned, small copper eyes staring at Gol, and Gol resisted the urge to take a step back. Jam's huge shoulders rolled as he moved and turned and stared out over the desert.

'Too hot,' he rumbled.

'No, the scale of the Nex.'

'There are many,' Jam said, drooling long strings to the wooden boards. 'They put up good fight when the time comes – they put up good kill.'

'And that time may be sooner than you think,' said Kat, rejoining them and smiling grimly. 'We got some nosy fucking Americans in an armoured column advancing a few kilometres to the west – I think we need to go and give them a taste of our power.'

'I thought we were under orders to avoid conflict until the time had come?'

'The time is here and now,' said Kattenheim softly, his red eyes alive. 'Durell has given the order. From this point forward we are Active.'

Kat led the way, and Gol and Jam followed, climbing back into the small black helicopter. Within a few seconds the rotors spun into life and the chopper jumped into the air.

'There,' said Kat.

Fifty tanks, engines revving, moved out from a giant compound with thick timber walls and a massive sagging tarpaulin roof; in desert colours they blended in well. Around fifty black helicopters leapt into the air behind Kat and flew past in air support of the heavy section of armoured ground vehicles . . .

'This should be good kill,' said Jam.

'This is just a taster,' replied Kat, and powered forward in the wake of the small army.

The American armoured column had halted, engines rumbling, awaiting the return of their scouts. Infantry and desert-modified Humvees backed up the thirty M1 Abrams tanks in full desert regalia. The units had been detoured due to intelligence provided from an anonymous source. There were perhaps a hundred men in the column, and they were not expecting a fight.

Sergeant Thorpe stood on the tank's turret, digital binoculars held to her eyes and tongue licking at desert-scorched lips. She watched the scout's Humvee bumping back towards them at high speed, a trail of sand whirling in its wake. She tutted in annoyance.

'The dumb bastard will make us stand out for miles!'

She scanned the horizon but could see nothing else of interest. She cursed the desert for making her feel so hot and dry. She watched the Humvee slew to a halt, tyres half-buried in the soft sand, and knew, her heart sinking, that they might be digging the huge bastard out in a few short minutes—

The driver, a squat reliable soldier named Hamill who sported a crew-cut, a good tan and expensive Croc-III shades, leapt out as if on fire and screamed, 'They're coming!'

'Who are coming?'

'The enemy!'

Thorpe frowned from her position on the tank. She felt a shiver course through her despite the heat. 'What fucking enemy?' she growled, her voice husky with a sudden taint of fear.

'Tanks!' screamed Hamill, heading for a truck, boots ploughing sand. 'Lots of fucking tanks!'

Thorpe scanned the horizon once more. All she could see was the slowly settling wake of Hamill's Humvee.

'Cleo, scanners?' she shouted.

'Nothing, sarge.'

'You sure?'

"I'm fucking *sure*, sarge.' Cleo sounded mightily pissed off. 'Hamill must have been on the fucking vodka again, the drunken bastard. I tell you, he puts all our lives at risk . . . what is it?'

'Cleo,' came Thorpe's calm, calculating voice. 'Are you *sure* those scanners show jack-shit?'

'One hundred per cent positive, sarge.'

'Contact!' screamed Thorpe, bringing around her machine gun as the Nex tanks filled the horizon and the black swarm of helicopters leapt into view. Their sounds smashed across the desert and Thorpe watched in horror as sudden explosions echoed across the undulating plain . . .

Everything became a sudden madness. There came a whistling, then a *crump*. Thorpe saw one of the M1s picked up and tossed across the desert, fire blazing around its hull, gun twisted as it described an arc and connected with the ground, ploughing a trough and being ripped apart. Another tank was picked up, then another – and then the helicopters came in as Thorpe hit the dirt hard, rolling, her SA1000 rattling in her hands as the choppers swept overhead—

Bullets flew all around.

Trucks exploded.

Thorpe heard screams.

Something happened, and with her head spinning Sergeant Thorpe was thrown through the air. Something hit her hard in the back of her head, and she remembered staring at the sand and hearing roars and concussive booms all around her, and she wanted to roll over, to fight this sudden unprovoked enemy that had come from nowhere.

'I can't believe it,' she moaned.

She seemed to lie for an eternity where she'd fallen.

She could feel blood running across her hips and belly.

Her throat was dry, parched.

Water, she thought. Just . . . water . . .

Hands rolled her over. Three dark figures stood over her, blocking out the sun, and in her confusion she could have sworn that their eyes glowed like copper, like tiny molten suns.

'Water?' she whispered.

'Be quiet, bitch.'

The sub-machine gun touched her face and blasted her pretty features in a spray of gore across the desert sand.

The BBC London helicopter swept over the Thames, camera panning from the destroyed Houses of Parliament to the leaning, mortally wounded tower of Big Ben.

'The whole of London mourns today for all those killed and maimed in a great tragedy,' came the sombre voice of Mr McSouthern. 'Here we witness the aftermath of the most terrible earthquake ever to hit the United Kingdom.'

Again, the camera swept across the carnage.

It zoomed in on collapsed buildings, cars crushed by massive slabs of concrete, exposed steel wire and sections of fallen brick. Emergency personnel and civilian volunteers picked their way through the devastation and tanks and bulldozers were being used by the military to clear a passage through some of the blocked roads.

The vid_scene switched to the London Underground, where collapsed tunnels spewed crushed Tube trains, full of twisted limbs and bodies, to fill the screen. Blood pools lay still under flickering strip-lights as water gushed from smashed pipes above the subways and silent, stationary escalators, washing dirt, blood and mucus from the rictus death-grins of a thousand crushed commuters caught underground when the quake struck . . .

BBC London's camera viewpoint switched then. It moved to the south coast of England, where a collapsing coastline had swallowed individual houses and whole small villages in a mammoth cave-in, taking them tumbling and sliding into the English Channel.

No part of the country was unaffected; there were sweeping vid_scenes from Inverness, Glasgow, down through Manchester, Birmingham, Nottingham, Oxford, London and onwards to Portsmouth . . . fallen buildings, loss of power on a massive scale, overcrowded hospitals – a nation pushed to the limits of its emergency services in the sudden aftermath of an insane devastation.

'The roads are severely gridlocked up and down the country,' came the voice of Mr McSouthern, 'and are causing endless difficulties for military personnel and vehicles who have been drafted in to help with the country-wide disaster zone . . .'

Within the hot, dry Libyan drilling station, the titanium-carbide VII drill bit rotated at high speed within its protective Plas-7 sheath, the rock and stone detritus sucked up and away by thick alloy-rubber hoses. Ivers stared from behind a mask of mud and rock flecks, eyes searching for defects or any hint that the drill bit was faltering – variations in speed or angle of descent, excess vibration, changes in the extracted rock slurry.

The platform was a huge hardwood structure, set some four kilometres below the earth's surface. It nestled, together with the Sub-3KM control quarters of the drilling rig, in a small hollow of rock. Ivers and his team of LVA-ENG Level-2 engineers worked in shifts and analysed data deep below the earth's surface to make sure that the drilling process went smoothly. As their superiors always stressed: a drill that doesn't drill is a drill that loses money.

'Slow her to twenty-five,' shouted Ivers, back over his shoulder, then returned his gaze to the spinning drill bit. He felt tense, nervous. He hated this job. It had the allure of being extremely highly paid, but it was even more dangerous. If a titanium-carbide VII drill bit snapped at anything over 32 speed, then its operators would all be pulped to blood and liquid flesh.

Ivers chewed his lip, craving a cigarette. Instead, he reached into his overalls and popped a stick of chewing gum into his mouth. He didn't like gum but at least it gave him something to do with his jaws.

Of medium height, with sandy-coloured hair, Ivers was quite stocky, with the trade-mark powerful arms and shoulders of the LVA engineer class: as the saying went, 'To work a rig, a man has to be stronger than a fucking pig'.

A red light flashed, reflecting from the Plas-7 sheath. Ivers turned, frowning, and Kesstelavich gestured that somebody was coming. Ivers cursed, stepped forward to the TBD console and checked the readings. All were OK, tiny needles flickering in the amber. They were on target. The drilling was going according to plan, despite them pushing the machinery hard.

Ivers turned, waiting for whoever it was to arrive and wiping sweat from his brow. Probably another fucking fuel inspector, he thought. I fucking hate inspectors. If a child, teenager or adult shows any inclination of wanting to become educated in the inspectorate, they should be taken behind the bike sheds and fucking shot in the back of the head, he growled to himself through his tough and tangy strawberry chewing gum.

That's how much he hated them: always fucking whining. Always finding some little tweak that supposedly had to be made, some fucking little justification for their hugely disproportionate salaries, and forever covering their own arses with a plethora of pointless paperwork.

Wankers.

Ivers frowned as the two figures came into view. The first was heavily robed, face hidden within the folds of a black cloak and, with a sudden, sinking feeling of dread he realised it had to be—

The top man.

The money behind the LVA phenomenon.

The Big Boss.

Ivers knew of this almost mythical figure through reputation and gossip. He had never met the fellow before, but had spoken to the friends of friends who had been inspected by this dark-robed money man, this suit without a suit. They said that he wore the robes because he had contracted some horrible disease that had eaten his flesh. Ivers shivered, feeling a little sick as he imagined strips of flesh hanging from a green pus-filled face.

And Ivers knew: this man was *strict* – far worse than any snivelling waddling bureaucratic turd of an inspector with a comedy clipboard.

Behind the dark-robed figure stood a large man with greying hair and beard. He had huge hands and a violent look about him, as if he should be wearing desert camouflage gear instead of the dark trousers and loose jacket that he now wore.

Ivers put a false smile on his face as the figures ignored Kesstelavich – who Ivers saw sigh with relief – and headed straight towards him and the TBD console.

'Ivers,' came the cool, intelligent voice from within the folds of the robe.

'Yes, sir. It is a great honour for you to pay us a visit . . . ahh.' He glanced up, but could see nothing but darkness within the folds of the hood, abetted by the natural gloom of the working LVA extraction platform. When nothing else was forthcoming, he blurted, 'I – have not got another inspection scheduled for at least three days. I thought that our work was satisfactory and, and, and—'

'It is,' came the smooth voice. 'Do not panic, Ivers. I am not here to inspect; in fact, your team has provided sterling service while in our employ.' A hand – a *claw* – emerged from the robe and Ivers found himself taking the metal sheaves and staring at the place where the twisted darkened hand had briefly been. Suddenly, realising his rudeness, he glanced up into the darkness of the hood and felt sweat roll down his entire body, sticking overalls to his flesh in a clammy, uncomfortable embrace.

'Release orders. You and your team are relieved of duty for exactly one hour.'

'I . . . but . . .'

'Scan the documents. They are all the authorisation you need.'

Ivers turned, clumsily juggling with the metal sheaves. He scanned them on the console and then turned back, a look of confusion on his face. 'I . . .'

'Drop the speed to five.'

'Five? But it—'

'Do not question me, Ivers. Drop the speed to five – then take your unexpected one-hour break and be thankful that you do not need to hear answers to questions you really should not be asking.'

'Yes, sir.'

Ivers gathered his documents and together with Kesstelavich, Rothwell, Oldroyd and Kenny headed for the pressure lifts. He glanced back once as the figure watched him depart, and saw the large grey-haired man produce a small pack and stare at the engineers until they disappeared into the gloom of the vertical ascent . . .

Durell threw back his hood as Gol passed him the QEngine – the 'Foundation Stone'.

Durell smiled, the smile looking strange against his deformed face.

'Let us show the world what we can do,' he said softly.

The Priest wore a grey robe, wooden rosary beads swung against his massive barrel chest and a small battered leather Bible nestled in his huge palms. He stroked the cover, his gold-flecked brown eyes closed for the moment, mouth silently incanting passages from his Holy Book – the words of his God. Outside the cockpit windows of the Comanche the desert rolled by, and eventually The Priest opened his eyes. His keen gaze focused on the featureless expanse beneath him.

'We shall be there soon,' said Heneghan, her voice soft. Her head was encased within the HIDSS and hid her shoulder-length hair and smiling oval face.

'We will be there when God allows, sister,' came the soothing voice of The Priest as he folded his hands humbly in his lap, at peace with the world.

The Comanche flashed through the clear blue skies, its engines humming.

The sun beat tattoos of light across its dull desert camouflage.

And below, the world rolled by uncaringly.

An hour passed, and The Priest came awake with a start. Getting old, he chided himself sombrely, and yawned, stretching his considerable frame in the confines of the Comanche's cockpit. Getting too old for *this*.

'ETA four minutes.'

'Thank you, Heneghan. May God bless your children.'

'I'm sure he already has,' she said.

'No, no,' said The Priest shaking his head in all seriousness. 'I would know about that sort of thing.'

The HIDSS helmet turned, the blacked-out insect-eye panels staring hard at The Priest. He smiled gently at the pilot and gazed out of the window at the distant mountains past Al Hijaz. Saudi Arabia – the Arabian Peninsula.

Rub al'Khali – the Great Sandy Desert.

Rub al'Khali – three hundred thousand square miles of mostly unexplored desert. Three hundred thousand square miles of sand and rock, a plateau baked under the scorching sun for millennia, a land without any obvious attractions . . . And once the home of Spiral_Q: a high-tech base where the major development of the military QIII Cubic Processor had taken place under the watchful gaze of a man named Count Feuchter.

The Priest watched calmly as the Comanche banked, sunlight gleaming from its fuselage, and soared in a huge arc around the blast zone that marked the erstwhile site of Spiral_Q. A huge crater squatted against the desert – and although the preceding year had allowed much of the area to be reclaimed by the desert sands, the enclosed vertical shaft beneath the surface still remained – along with much half-buried detritus of twisted alloy, steel and shattered glass.

'Take us down,' said The Priest softly.

The Comanche settled gently, its rotors whipping up huge sand eddies. Heneghan slowly shut down the engines but left them primed – in case they needed to lift off in an emergency.

Heneghan had been on missions with The Priest before.

And they were never simple . . .

279

Opening the cockpit, The Priest stuck his nose out into the heat and looked around. He climbed down and jumped, sandals sinking a little and the hot desert sand burning his toes. He breathed deeply, enjoying the fragrance of purity within the Empty Quarter; enjoying the sudden rise in temperature. It reminded him of thick black coffee, lapping blue sea water on luxurious sandy beaches, and snorting camels with thick strings of saliva between their evil teeth.

Smiling softly and ignoring his new-found discomforts, and still holding his Bible, The Priest moved across the sand towards the site of what had once been Spiral_Q.

'It's been a long time, Lord,' he muttered, glancing up into the vast blue vault above him. The sun burned down and the Priest felt a single trickle of sweat roll down his body beneath his grey robes. He smiled, nodding in understanding. 'These things are sent to test us.'

Heneghan had set the Comanche down a good distance from the Spiral_Q blast site; the Comanche's scanners had reported that the ground was extremely unstable – especially for heavy vehicles – and so The Priest toiled across the desert under the sun, occasionally reaching up to touch the string of wooden beads around his throat and muttering words into the sky.

He halted as he came to the first signs of the bomb blast and High-J explosion.

A twisted length of alloy, perhaps eight metres long, lay half buried by sand. Parts of the metal were fused with glass. The Priest found himself shivering involuntarily.

It must have been a huge and devastating explosion, he realised.

A true vision of Hell.

He waded on through the soft wind-blown sand, past more twisted melted struts and a huge ball of fused glass, twisted and deformed and blackened. The Priest gradually worked his way towards the epicentre of the explosion site, reaching the edges where a rim of sand had been superheated into black glass, now sand-blown and weathered in rugged sections. He halted and gripped his Bible tightly as if seeking some strength from above.

'The infidels wreaked much havoc on our world!' he boomed, his voice echoing around the pit in the sand. His eyes went suddenly wide in his broad strong face, and his hair whipped wildly in the desert wind. He grinned then, and sidled towards the edge of the huge crater.

The Priest moved closer, pocketing his Bible in a hidden pouch inside the long grey robe. He dropped to his belly and edged even nearer to the edge. He felt the ground shifting beneath him, gently, in warning, and gritted his teeth as sand blew into his eyes. A warm wind drifted up from the pit.

Pulling free a tiny alloy device, The Priest looked behind him and attached it to a large block of melted metal. Tiny motors whirred and the device – a 'Parasite' Skimmer – ate into the metal and secured itself. The Priest pulled on a pair of gloves and, gripping a length of thin, almost silken thread, turned to lower himself over the edge of the abyss . . .

The world seemed to go suddenly quiet. And dark. Sand drifted down after him, getting into his nose and mouth and making him splutter a little. His sandals scrabbled against the wall and then he swung out, drifting through nothingness. He dropped like a lead weight, rotating slowly into the gloom, which slowly enveloped him.

As he descended, tiny motors droning almost silently above, his eyes began to adjust so that he could scan the walls and the remains of the twisted beams. For a moment he touched down, on an old section of buckled alloy floor. His descent halted, The Priest pulled free his Spiral-issue ECube and set it to scan. Blue digits flickered, illuminating his face with an eldritch glow.

```
> ECube v5.0 ICARUS
> Initiating GTf Scan
> Scanning
> Codecs secured; Δ### ...
> 01001101 01010101 01011111 512enc
> Results ... ... ... 00000
```

The Priest cursed, and spat heavily into the gloom. More sand drifted down from above, spiral eddies which made the huge barrel-chested man want to sneeze.

Sandals slipped treacherously on the old smashed floor. He allowed himself to step free once more into the vastness of this blasted subterranean cavern and, dangling like a fish on a hook, he lowered himself deeper into the enveloping darkness.

He seemed to drift downwards for an age . . .

The Spiral_Q building had been excavated *deep* . . .

His sharp eyes scanned continuously, and three more times he halted to initiate his ECube. Three more times it gave him negative results.

'Why hast thou forsaken me, Lord?'

The Priest rolled his eyes heavenwards – the heavens being a small square hole of light high above him – and then lowered himself deeper into the pit.

He saw more and more detritus that had survived the insane chemical stomping of the original High-J blast. Buckled panels littered with sand, huge sections of mingled glass and alloy twisted into bizarre alien formations and shot like bullets to embed themselves into the walls.

Molten metal had run down the walls and cooled to hang in glittering globular stalactites from girders and battered steel H-sections.

Finally, he reached the bottom.

The Priest's sandals touched down on a surface of merged metal and glass. Most of this hard base was covered with sand, which rose in great piles at either end of the huge blasted site and lay scattered in humps and drifts.

The Priest looked around in the ghostly light.

He shivered.

This is not a place for man, he realised.

Not even a place for God.

Warily, he pulled free his ECube and stopped, his hair ruffled by some cool breeze. Listening, he was now on the alert for intruders as he pulled a Glock 9mm from inside his robes, the gun small in his huge hands. He flicked free the safety catch with his thumb. His tongue licked against the dryness of his mouth.

Are they here?

Nex.

The Priest scanned again, then set his ECube to search for interlopers. His eyes narrowed as the tiny alloy device confirmed that they were alone. But he did not trust it. He was the sort of man who put his faith in his eyes, his ears and The Almighty – not in billions of dollars' worth of computing technology.

The Priest made a short tour of what had been the structural basement of Spiral_Q. Below his sandals, through a four-foot slab of fused glass and metal, lay the original floor of the building – the base's original *base*.

```
> ECube v5.0 ICARUS
> Initiating GTf Scan
> Scanning
```

```
> Codecs secured;  Δ### ...
> 01001101 01010101 01011111 512enc
> Results ... ... ... 11110
```

The Priest moved a few feet in one direction, eyes focused now, the Glock forgotten in his hand. He dropped to one knee and placed the ECube against the once-molten floor.

```
> Scanning
> Results ... ... ... 11111
```

'Bingo!' he called piously.

The Priest climbed back to his feet and shook a little sand from his sandals. Again, something seemed to haunt him and his nostrils twitched. There was a faint metallic scent. He whirled around in a low crouch, Glock in his grip and stare searching—

'Nothing.'

He laughed a hollow laugh and glanced up at the sunlight far above. He felt as though he was at the bottom of a huge coffin, or a deep tomb leading straight down into . . .

Hell.

He traced patterns against the ECube and blue digits glowed for a moment. Then a narrow white beam sliced from the tiny alloy machine and swiftly cut a neat slender shaft of metal and glass from the recently formed false floor. Tiny claws gripped the top of this column and, grunting, the Priest pulled it free and laid it to one side.

The Priest knelt once more and peered down into the space thus exposed. He could make out a small alloy panel at the bottom, dusted with black from the original fires that had raged in the insane inferno . . .

'Ah,' he said.

In the gloom behind The Priest, something uncurled.

'Found you, you bugger.' His gold-flecked eyes shone and a smile spread across his broad face. With the ECube buzzing, and his Glock forgotten on the floor to one side, The Priest shuffled and leaned forward, his gaze fixed, his hand stretching out and his brain spinning at the implications of what he had discovered . . .

A cold breeze blew—

Behind The Priest, talons slid free of their armoured casings, touching softly against the fused glass floor of Spiral_Q as slitted copper eyes opened – and blinked lazily in the gloom.

Spiral Mainframe
Data log #12327

CLASSIFIED SADt/5345/SPECIAL INVESTIGATIONS UNIT
Data Request 324#12327

DURELL

All existing files relating to Durell were destroyed (by the man himself) prior to his betrayal of Spiral.

It is known that he was heavily involved in the Nx5 Project early on in his career. He worked with Gol and Count Feuchter. It is known that he carried on with this work illegally after Spiral withdrew funding and closed down the operations.

It is believed Durell was the instigator in creating the Spiral_mobile, an anti-Spiral warship designed to overthrow world powers and take control of the world's military and financial institutions via the all-powerful QuanTech Edition 3 processor.

Cartervb12 filed a report in December 2XXX relating to the death of Durell at his own hand. No body was ever recovered and there is suspicion that Durell is still at large.

Durell is the most dangerous individual ever encountered by Spiral. His knowledge and lust for power are insatiable. He is considered extremely dangerous and ranks No. 1 on Spiral's terrorist hit list.

Substantial rewards are offered for information leading to his capture and/or extermination.

Keyword SEARCH>> NEX, SAD, SPIRAL_sadt, DURELL, FEUCHTER, SPIRAL_mobile

PART TWO

LITTLE FLAME

and i hate your country
and i hate your world
i hate your god's people
who breed on earth

over to the other side
i'm caught stepping out
i'm gonna recreate a religious experience
to tear my fucking heart out

Chord of Souls
McCoy/Fields of the Nephilim

ADVERTISING FEATURE

The TV sparkled into life with a digital buzz of electro-hum, diamond-sharp images spinning and morphing into the jewelled liquid logo of Leviathan Fuels.

Leviathan Fuels are proud to announce their recent acquisition of important contracts . . . not only are most global emergency services signed up to have vehicles converted to LVA, but 78% of military contracts have been acquired worldwide – this gives LF a dominant share of the world fuel market and they thank you all!

Smiling American soldier puts armoured arm around dishevelled refugee figure and gives him a hug, ignoring the JK49 swinging against the feeble refugee's legs – **Scene dissolves into**→ A disco full of Korean and Norwegian soldiers, drinking together, laughing, soon joined by mechanics with greasy arms and oil-stained fingers who proclaim loudly the benefits of LVA mod upgrades→

Scene folds into cube/spins around a digital representation of the Earth and then fades into→ An entourage of fire engine, police squad car and emergency ambulance, all cruising the tarmac in an unspecified country and sweeping majestically around curves – *be smart, the whole world is converting to LVA and you don't want to get left behind in the dirt . . .*

Scene dissolves into→ Children running along a dirt road under the pounding rain. Behind them stands a small unkempt boy in the road, hair dishevelled, face grubby, eyes red from crying. He is squawking as his ex-friends run away and leave him whining in the road . . .

– Four hundred miles to the gallon! Go on, make the smart choice ... choose Leviathan Fuels, your children deserve a better future ...

Car sweeps past, stops, picks up the little boy – the sun comes out, the world burgeons with greenery and sparkles with flowers, the boy giggles and everything is all right. Car disappears, sporting bumper sticker saying: **LVA, make the RIGHT CHOICE**

Scene/text scroll R→L [Arial black] acr. vid:
(*Be a part of the club, join the fastest-growing user group in the world – check out **www.leviathanfuels.com** for more information on your nearest dealer, stockist and fuel emporium.*)

SCENE DISSOLVES TO BLUE

SIU Transcript

CLASSIFIED SR19/1178/SPECIAL INVESTIGATIONS UNIT
Hacked ECube interception
Date: September 2XXX

Our breaking headline for this evening is the assassination of the President of Leviathan Fuels, Chanya Verisimilov, who was gunned down today at 3pm on the marble steps leading to the Central Leviathan HQ in Prague, Eastern Europe.

Four men wearing balaclavas and bearing

assault JK53s opened fire without warning from a truck, killing Verisimilov and three bodyguards instantly and severely wounding many reporters and paparazzi who were standing nearby taking statements and photographs.

Special Forces were immediately deployed and cut off the truck's escape route. Despite some eyewitness accounts of the men surrendering and holding their hands in the air, all the assassins were accidentally shot in the forehead at point-blank range and have therefore been unable to comment.

Leviathan Fuels have currently been storming the globe with massively expanding fuel sales, an economic alternative to petrol- and gas-powered vehicles that requires nothing more than a simple engine modification. They recently acquired emergency-service and military contracts on an almost global scale, and it is rumoured that they are in the running to supply a new type of LVA which NASA and other space agencies can use to power contemporary developments in space-going propulsion systems. They are also rumoured to be developing a new type of shuttle engine with NASA, the RFFSA and the CPLSA.

Verisimilov's family were unavailable for comment on the brutal, vicious and bloody execution of a beloved husband, father and grandfather – despite constant and repeated questioning from a variety of media.

CHAPTER 11

INFILTRATION

The pain from the HPG blast and the fight fuelled Carter. His teeth gritted as the ScorpNex leapt towards him on the bridge across the valley – but even as the huge creature leapt, the Browning flew from Mongrel's sweating bloodstained fist. Carter caught the weapon, skidded to a halt, lifted the gun and fired—

The first bullet missed.

The next two crashed into Dake's already battered chest . . .

The fourth glanced from an armoured plate on the ScorpNex's face, and its leap faltered. It fell, landing clumsily, a claw coming up to its side in a reflex gesture. A low growl spat from its twisted mashed fangs and Carter sprinted forwards, booted feet connecting with Dake's already smashed face. The ScorpNex teetered – then stepped backwards and toppled through the ragged, splintered hole left by the HPG blast.

It vanished . . .

And everything suddenly fell silent.

Carter and Mongrel met on opposite sides of the hole

and looked down where the ScorpNex tumbled towards the ground far below. There came a deep, echoing crunch.

'What fucking ugly son of bitch,' said Mongrel.

'You looked in the mirror recently?'

'What was it, Carter?'

'Some kind of Nex.'

'You did well them, *compadre*.'

'Thanks for the Browning.'

'A pleasure. Cup of tea?'

Carter grinned wearily through the caked blood on his face. 'I'd fucking love one, mate.'

Darkness was creeping softly over the horizon and insects chirruped in the long grass, calls echoing back and forth from their hidden sanctuaries. Trees wavered gently in a breeze that mercifully dispersed the humidity of the early-autumn evening. Carter dropped to the ground, winced at the pain in his body and limbs, then fished out a cigarette and lit the weed with shaking fingers.

'I thought you were quitting.'

'Yeah, yeah, fuck off and see to your new girlfriend.'

Mongrel reached down and placed a hand against Carter's shoulder, making him wince a little in pain. Carter glanced up into eyes filled with concern. 'You OK, mate? You did well back there – really, really well . . .'

'I'll live.'

'Which is more than I can say for that ugly fucker,' snorted Mongrel. He patted Carter's shoulder and moved to the KTM's packs and the medical kits within.

Carter sat for a while, savouring the cigarette smoke and allowing his body to calm itself after the violent adrenlin rush of the previous few hours. He looked at his hand, which was still shaking, and smiled to himself. A long time since I got the shakes, he mused.

'Yeah, which just shows that you're returning to your mental roots.'

'Meaning?'

'That you're growing soft again. Where's the tough-fuck Carter I know and love? The one that blew the faces from three terrorists in Egypt with a High-J shrapnel bomb and kept their face skins as souvenir masks? Where's the cold-hearted bastard who shot that South African woman in the back of the head, even after she had surrendered? And where's the fucker who murdered them all – the men, the women and the fucking children – on that hot sunny day in Belfast?'

Carter's cigarette smoke plumed blue into the sky. He watched idly as Mongrel helped Mila remove her holed and bloodstained jacket.

'In Egypt, I kept the face of *one* terrorist because that was all that was left of him, and Spiral wanted DNA samples to link him to bombings across four different continents. The South African woman had killed six DemolSquad members with a sniper rifle, one of them a very old friend and I knew she would fucking get off on some international diplomacy clause and continue her reign of slaughter . . . and Belfast?' Carter's voice went terribly cold. 'Why, Kade, Belfast was all *your* doing.'

Mila was lying back, her head resting on Mongrel's jacket. He was laughing and joking with her.

Kade faded, gently, slowly, leaving Carter with a throbbing head. He killed the cigarette and ground the butt into the soil with his boot.

Kade was wrong, he knew.

Kade was wrong about him . . .

Once, a young and newly recruited Spiral operative on Demol18 had said to him, 'Wow, you're Carter . . . the

Butcher . . . the man without fear.' The young man's eyes had glowed with awe and apprehension – and a need to be like Carter.

It had disgusted him.

Made him feel unclean to his very core.

There are no more heroes, he thought.

No more heroes.

They just didn't get it. Killing wasn't something that was good, that was fun, something you could just do and go home, have your tea and put your feet up and watch TV, secure in the knowledge that a good shower would wash away the blood. Killing was just something that Carter had to do because he had to do it. He was good at it, he acknowledged . . . brilliant, even. And he was intelligent enough to understand that the people he killed, the people he murdered, were bad men and women, killers themselves, terrorists with soft civilian targets in mind. He was protecting the innocent. Cleansing the scum from the earth.

And yet he knew that his hands would never, ever be clean . . .

And it burned his soul with darkness; with bad blood.

'Carter!'

He glanced up, lit another cigarette, and was glad to see that his mild case of the shakes had subsided. He stood, groaning at the pain. The HPG had kicked the living fuck from his body and he started to wonder if retirement wouldn't be such a bad idea after all. Yeah, retirement – again.

'Aye?'

'You need to hear this.'

Carter moved closer, looking down at Mila who glanced up at him, a nervous smile on her lips. She looked to Mongrel for reassurance, and he beamed a winning, encouraging smile – the same smile that had bedded him many a drunken lady. Carter shook his head in weary disbelief.

He forced a smile to his face, despite the pain.

'Yes?' he sighed, catching the canteen that Mongrel threw. Standing slightly behind Mila, Mongrel cupped his hands to his chest and winked. Carter shook his head again and took a long drink of warm water.

'Tell him about the quarry.'

Mila smiled again, seeming to relax a little. Mongrel had dressed the wound well and her painkillers were kicking in.

'There are many of these, how you say, Nex there. They always wear masks, they always have those bright copper eyes and they are so fast . . . so fast . . .'

'You say they killed your brother?'

'Yes. He was only thirteen, out with four of his friends. They were children, Mr Carter, they were only little boys. They tried to get away, ran through the woods. One had lagged behind, saw them all shot in the back by these Nex and then dragged off through the trees. They were given no warnings, no mercy.'

Mila was crying now, tears flowing freely down her cheeks, her face looking down at the ground and her mud-crusted boots. Carter felt his chest tighten, his heart going out to this beautiful young woman . . .

'*Careful* . . .' hissed Kade.

Carter ignored him and, reaching out, took her hand. It was lightly tanned with long fingers and rough nails. But it was a pretty hand and Carter looked up to realise that she was looking at him, looking at him strangely.

'You say there are many Nex at this quarry. How many?'

'I have seen maybe one or two hundred.'

'*What?*'

'There are barracks. And there are human workers there as well, men, engineers who work on the machines.'

'What machines?'

'The pumps.'

'Pumping LVA?' asked Carter softly.

'Yes, the new fuel, I think. It is taken in tankers – I have seen all this.'

Carter smiled, squeezing her hand, and said, 'We need to see this place. Are you ready to move?'

'Carter, she's just been fucking shot . . .' said Mongrel.

'Are you ready to move?' he repeated.

'I will show you. Are you going to kill them?'

Carter pulled free his Browning HiPower and checked the thirteen-round magazine before hammering it back with a solid *click*.

'Yeah, we're going to kill them all,' he said coldly.

'*There's my boy,*' sneered Kade. '*Just like the old days . . . Welcome back, Butcher.*'

Darkness flowed over the woods. It flowed over the mountains. It gradually extinguished the light in the sky like a thumb and forefinger snuffing out the glow of a candle flame.

A gentle wind stirred the tall grasses in the valley, and blew the warm scents of a dying summer over the rocks where something moved. Slowly, a dark shape gradually uncurled and turned small copper eyes towards the moon.

The ScorpNex growled softly, claws moving across its body and dipping into the wounds it carried, wounds that went deep into its frame and caused it a burning agony it would never forget.

Pain pulsed.

But, more than this, a need pulsed within its mind.

A need to kill.

Revenge.

A need to kill Carter . . .

The ScorpNex rolled onto its side and lay drooling for a while, and then it heaved its bulk onto its knees and vomited on the ground. A low keening sound came from its broken jaw and it managed to pull free a tiny grey ECube – a copy of the Spiral-issue device. The grey plates spun free and a voice spoke.

'You failed.'

'Yes.'

'How could you fail?'

'Carter . . . he is . . . hard to kill.'

'Can you walk?'

'I . . . think so.' Claws clamped tight shut in pain. Copper eyes glittered.

'Can you hunt?'

'I need help.'

A sigh. 'Stay where you are. We have your location – we'll send in a chopper, bring you out.'

The signal died, the grey ECube copy whirring to itself.

The ScorpNex rolled onto its back and made soft sounds of pain. But in its eyes burned a singularity of purpose and a need for revenge.

The two KTM motorcycles cruised down the dirt trail as darkness finally fell. Much to Mongrel's disappointment Mila had chosen to ride with Carter. As they cruised, tyres crunching, Carter was painfully aware of her delicate hands on his hips, the slim and beautiful woman pressed close behind him, her face against his broad, heavily muscled back.

Focus, he thought.

Flicking on their headlights, they slowed their speed as falling darkness impeded their progress. Mila pointed out the mountain trails they were to traverse.

They travelled through the night, passing down a long winding trail that descended alarmingly along the side of a mountain through dense woodland, switchback bend after unlit switchback bend, hairpins chasing hairpins until it briefly levelled and then began to climb steeply, straightening as they ascended another mountain trail through night scenery of moonlit splendour.

At one point Carter rolled to a halt and Mongrel pulled up beside him.

'What is it?'

Carter pointed. There, ensnared in his headlight beam, was a brown deer, eyes wide, nostrils flared. It suddenly started, galloping off into the darkness. Carter grinned.

'I love this place,' he said.

'Such a shame we have dirty job to do.'

'Yeah, a real shame.'

They travelled warily for perhaps a couple of hours along dangerous roads and trails. Eventually Mila patted Carter's thigh and he pulled over to the side of the road.

'It is best we leave bikes here,' she said, her lips close to his ear. 'You want me climb off?'

'Yeah.'

The two Spiral agents quickly cammed up the bikes and then, allowing Mila to take the lead, they set off through thick forest, once more climbing a huge rugged mountain and fighting their way through the trees.

Occasionally the moon fell behind clouds. Then complete darkness dropped like an obsidian cloak. Mila stayed close to Carter who refused to return her rifle, allowing a disgruntled Mongrel to strap it to his pack instead and hump the excess weight like a pack mule, muttering a string of expletives.

Both men carried their M24 carbines with reloaded magazines. Both felt twitchy, watchful after their realisation that Jam had not been on such a simple SAD mission – but a much more dangerous operation.

Poor Jam, thought Carter sadly.

When had he realised?

Thought he was taking out a few rogue remainders – a few specimens left over from the war of a year ago. When in fact he was stumbling headlong and blind into a whole fucking battalion!

And they had captured him.

Beat him. And . . .

Murdered him?

Carter could think of no other fate that might await his friend. But then, Nicky said that the Spiral mainframes had picked up signals from Jam's ThumbNail_Map – many hours after his disappearance and apparent ECube PB. Which meant that they had not killed him – at least, not straight away – and he had managed somehow to escape . . . for a little while at least. Or maybe he was free now and they were chasing ghosts?

What now?

Carter's mouth was a grim line in the darkness.

If the enemy had him, then Jam's future did not look rosy.

As they walked, Carter's eyes scanning left and right for signs of danger, ears alert for any slight change that could signal the presence of an enemy, he found a part of his mind drifting, wandering. He was focused on his journey, but a part of him fell back to remembering the old days—

Reading in the sun, wearing shorts and T-shirt, and

301

Natasha running outside with a bucket of water to drench him to the bone . . . Carter chasing her, screaming and threatening, with Samson barking around their feet, almost tripping them in the long grass, Carter lifting her in his arms and then dropping her into the dirty green water of the dog's paddling pool amidst the shed dog hairs as she squealed with indignation and disgust . . .

Wandering hand in hand on a distant foreign beach, toes curling in the sand, laying out a rug and unpacking their impromptu and hastily purchased lunch. They had eaten, drunk beer, lain in the sun until the tide had crept in and the waves had splashed their dozing bodies . . .

'Here.'

Carter halted and they dropped to their bellies, peering up the incline to the ridge above them that was scattered with conifers and sycamores. 'You sure there are no look-outs?'

'No.' Mila's face looked bleached in the moonlight. 'This is the place I have always come to watch – and learn. I have been here maybe ten times. I have never been seen.'

'You two wait there,' Carter ordered her and Mongrel.

He dropped his pack to the ground and eased himself forward cautiously up the slope, inch by inch, careful and precise in his movements. At the top the ground levelled off between the trees and Carter waited patiently, allowing his eyes to adjust to the moonlight falling between the branches and leaves. Then he eased forward, M24 carbine held loosely and Browning secure at his hip.

He saw the ghost night-glow of perimeter halogen lamps.

And then the world opened up in front of him . . .

The Kataja Quarry was huge, a mammoth circular depression between high steep red rock walls tumbled with vegetation and rock scree. The rock walls fell away to a massive flat basin, again littered with rocks and scrub bushes, with the odd pine standing forlorn and isolated. To one side squatted six large barracks, each capable of housing perhaps a hundred men – or Nex – and built from rough-sawn timber. They looked relatively new. All the windows were blacked out, but Carter could just about distinguish a few chinks of light round the edges of the blackout curtains. Beside the barracks stood a smaller building, obviously some sort of operational HQ. On the corrugated roof were sophisticated satellite scanners and transmitters. This Op HQ too looked newly built.

Away from the barracks stood a set of buildings, made from corrugated galvanised steel, which were obviously older. These buildings hunkered beside the huge black gleaming LVA pump which even now was quietly thudding and churning, pumping the new fuel into five gigantic container tanks – each at least forty metres in diameter and painted a dull matt black. Near the barracks stood a couple of grey tracked tanks, their engines off, and perhaps fifteen large six-wheeled trucks like those Carter had seen back at the old camp. They were obviously used for troop transport.

Carter scanned the quarry.

'Quite an operation you've got here, fellas,' he muttered, and shuffled himself around to get a better look.

The Kataja Quarry was fed by a single wide road. Four more tanks served as heavy protection, and two tall timber guard towers stood bleak against the night with two snipers posed in each of them. Two more towers were positioned towards the back of the quarry, each tower again sporting two snipers. And then Carter saw them – almost perfectly camouflaged beside the four rough-timber sniper-towers:

SM-7 surface-to-air missiles.

Deployed from Mini-SM7.8 Blocks in III/IV and IVa configurations, the SM-7s were much more compact and discreet SAM weapons than had been used in earlier wars. They employed electronic countermeasures in the form of mono-pulse send/receivers for semi-active III-TR radar terminal guidance and inertial midcourse guidance. Launched from the SM7.8VLS Vertical Launching Systems the SM-7s were perfect for both low- and high-altitude threat interceptions and had almost total success rates even if target aircraft employed electronic counter-measures such as the ECM-6, Lockheed 52s and Sikorsky 2212 ASAMs.

'Shit. There goes a fucking air strike.'

Carter waited patiently, watching, counting, observing.

The ground area was policed by Nex, heavily armed with sub-machine guns and pistols. They patrolled in teams of four, and there were at least eight teams operational – which meant a minimum of thirty-two Nex on the ground, eight operational snipers, and six T76 tanks which Carter had to assume were armed and ready for action. And all that backed up by serious SAM support and God only knew how many Nex in the barracks.

'*A lot of firepower,*' said Kade.

'The game's getting bigger.'

'*You think Jam is in there?*'

'He could be. This is where they took him, and the bodies of Slater and TT. If we don't go in this is where our trail stops. This would be our dead end . . . and the death of Natasha and my child.'

Kade did not reply.

Slowly, Carter eased back and rejoined Mongrel and Mila.

'Big?' Mongrel asked.

'Fucking huge,' said Carter softly. 'Four-man Nex patrols, snipers in watchtowers, and tanks.'

'I hate tanks,' rumbled Mongrel.

'What I don't understand is why so many Nex are there. They suddenly protecting the LVA? Mila, have there always been this many soldiers based here?'

'No. Originally it was quite small camp, when they first start mining. Only in last few weeks have they brought in so many more men . . . these Nex. Now whole area is deserted; they frighten everybody away, and even police keep away.'

'Greasy backhanders,' said Mongrel.

'Maybe.'

'What's your plan?'

Carter smiled, meeting Mongrel's fearsome gaze. 'Quite simple. You and Mila wait here, I go in alone. I'll find out if Jam is being held there.'

'No.'

'What the fuck do you mean, "no"?'

'I brought you in on this, Carter. I go in to see if Jam is there. He's part of my team, I am responsible for him getting caught . . . I should have been there.'

'What?' sneered Carter. 'You think if you'd been present it would have made a difference? Use your brain, man – all it would mean is that I'd be here alone looking for four dead bodies instead of three.'

'Or not here at all,' growled Mongrel.

'Listen, I know how you feel, Mongrel – but look at the facts. You're a demolitions expert – that I'll grant you. If this place needed blowing up, I'd be happy to let you waltz in with your High_J and get the job done. But I'm good at covert; in fact, I am the fucking best. And you know it.'

Their gazes locked.

'You know it, Mongrel. I'll be in and out in one hour.'

'Let me come with you, Carter. It too dangerous.'

Carter shook his head. 'No, no, my friend. You have your new companion to babysit. After all, you can't say we really know her. What if this is a set-up? A trap.' The word tasted bad on his tongue.

'She not one of them, Carter.'

'Prove it.'

'I know it. In here.' The huge man put his fist to his heart.

'You know fuck all, Mongrel. The only way you come with me is if we put a bullet in her skull. Are you willing to do that? Then stop your fucking whining . . . you came to me in the hospital when Natasha was dying because you needed fucking help – and yeah, I've got my own motivations but you came to me for a reason: because I get the fucking job done. Now leave me to do it.'

'What you want me do?'

'Looking at the fucking defences, I'd say an air attack is out of the question. Bastards have learned from past mistakes, eh, Mongrel? Our only option would be heavy tank back-up to take out this Nex *army* – and the other main problem is the single road in and out. It channels an attack . . . but then, that will only be a problem if I bubble it.'

'I think Spiral need to know about this place now. They can form their own conclusions.'

'OK. You send out a WB as I head in. Call in some choppers and tanks in case the game goes a little pear-shaped. I'm going in now while we still have the cover of darkness . . .'

'Why not wait for back-up?'

'I've got a bad feeling about this place . . . and there's no time like the present. Time is running out. I need that machine . . . *Natasha* needs that machine. Or –' Carter's eyes went hard 'I – won't be held responsible for my actions . . .'

Mongrel watched Carter disappear into the night, fading like a ghost in a bad dream. He wore his balaclava once more, and had armed himself with some serious weaponry.

Mongrel sat with his back against a tree, M24 across his lap as he hurriedly composed his digital report for Spiral and sent it on in the form of a WarBurst. Highest priority. Straight to the top.

Mongrel smiled grimly to himself.

'Will he be all right?' said Mila softly, blonde hair blowing in the gentle breeze.

'Yeah, Carter is the best,' said Mongrel.

'Shall we keep watch?'

'We will have to be careful.'

'I've been watching these people for months and I've never been caught. I am careful, and I am invisible.'

'Carter spotted you – up on that slope.'

'Yes.' She nodded. 'He is good. How you say, a killer? A psychopath?'

'I wouldn't go that far,' said Mongrel.

'I would,' said Mila. 'I see it in his eyes. He is a little insane, I think.'

'In this world, *Iyubimya*, I think we all are.'

Carter crouched in the darkness at the edge of the quarry, senses alert and ready for anything. He clipped free his Sp_drag – nicknamed a Skimmer or Parasite Skimmer – and connected it to a rock. Tiny drills ate into the stone and secured the device. Taking a deep breath of humid night air, Carter stepped off the rim and into the Kataja Quarry.

Below, halogen lights glowed.

Trucks were coming and going, engines revving in the floodlit rock arena. The LVA pump worked effortlessly, ceaselessly, and he could imagine the thick pumping of the rich fluid into the huge containers – ready for refinement and distribution around the world . . .

Focus.

Jam . . . location?

The obvious. Op HQ.

Carter's boots trod the almost vertical wall with infinite care; a single loose rock, a single trickle of stone and he could be highlighted, sighted by a sniper – and pop. Dog meat. Carter took his time. He had another three hours of darkness . . . there was no immediate rush.

Squatting on a large protrusion of rock, Carter waited, wire coiled behind him and giving him a life-umbilical to the rocky mother wall. He watched the Nex patrols again, his sharp eyes noting their movements, their efficiency and yet their – complacency? Or was it arrogance?

Carter grinned. He'd given a few arrogant Nex presents that they would never forget.

Moving off once more, he eased his way down the wall and imprinted on his brain a map of the layout of the military installations and buildings and the Nexes' patterns of patrol. As he reached ground level, touching down softly, he flicked a tiny switch and the Sp_drag released from its hold on the rock and wound itself slowly together, allowing Carter to stow the device away in his belt.

He crouched, calming his breathing.

He palmed his Browning and secured the M24 carbine tight across his back. He screwed the Browning's silencer into place and remembered the last time he had used the mod – back in Switzerland when it had almost got him killed. Now he needed its stealth . . .

Carter eased his way through the bushes and rocks and halted, watching the patrolling Nex. They worked well – tight units with heavy firepower.

Carter focused on the Op HQ. The door opened and three men stepped out, moving across the flat hard-packed ground to the group of corrugated rusting buildings beside the LVA pump. He chewed his lip, listening to their conversation . . . but got no clues about whether Jam was present, a prisoner, dead or had been shipped away to some distant location.

Could he risk an ECube scan?

No. The enemy might pick up the electronic tracking pulses. And then he would be fucked.

Carter rested back on his heels, calming his thoughts, forcing images of Natasha and their unborn child from his mind. He could not afford to think of them now.

Carter waited . . . a good half-hour passed and activity seemed to lessen. Five trucks roared off in support of six large LVA tankers; their lights cut through the night and their engines howled, heavy wheels whirling up the dry dust and then leaving a deathly stillness in their wake.

The patrols seemed to lessen.

Carter checked his watch.

3.20 a.m.

Time to move.

Taking a deep breath, and timing himself between Nex patrols, Carter set out from the rocks around the edge of the quarry so that he could zigzag across to the rear of the Op HQ through as many shadows and trees as possible . . .

And hope that the snipers didn't spot him.

Mongrel checked his watch.

3.17 a.m.

'Come on, Carter, what the fuck you doing?'

Mongrel and Mila had watched the quarry for some time, noting the loading of Nex troops into trucks, the filling of LVA tankers, the continuous drone of the LVA pump. Then, when he could see no sign of Carter, he eventually decided that it was too risky to keep popping their heads over the ridge line . . . it could get them shot.

So they retreated down the slope a little and listened, waiting for any sounds of infiltration or discovery – sirens, gunshots, anything.

'You OK?'

Mila nodded. She was tired, pale, and looked very weak. She was trying hard to put on a brave face but Mongrel could sense her weariness.

'I am fine.'

'How old are you?'

'Twenty.'

'That's young.'

She shrugged. 'I am still full woman,' she said, smiling.

'You need to sleep?'

'No!'

'Come here, girl.' Mila moved over to Mongrel and he took her in his arms. She rested her head against his huge chest. Her eyes closed, and Mongrel looked down at the top of her head, the fine silken web of hair. He inhaled her perfume. Lust was not far from his thoughts.

Mongrel's eyes scanned from left to right, then he shifted a little. Mila sighed against him.

He hefted the M24 thoughtfully, wondering idly how Carter planned to get Jam out in the event that the Spiral agent was unable to move under his own steam.

Carter would think of something. He would probably secure Jam in that event and await heavy back-up . . . And soon – with luck – the tanks would arrive.

Mongrel nodded to himself, his tongue chasing a crumb around the cavernous toothless interior of his mouth. Damn crumbs, he thought. Closely followed by, Fucking teeth.

Metal pressed against the back of his head.

It was quite obviously the barrel of a gun.

'Drop the carbine, fucker.'

Mongrel froze – the hairs on the back of his neck prickled.

They emerged from the darkness, drifting like ghosts with sub-machine guns levelled at his face and the sleeping form of Mila. They were Nex. And there were twelve of them . . .

Slowly, Mongrel dropped his M24 and shook Mila awake.

'Oh!' she said, her gaze alighting on the Nex. 'Oh.'

'Well done. You led them straight to us.'

'I . . . I did?'

'We've been watching you for weeks,' said a Nex softly, copper eyes burning into Mila's face. It stepped forward and smashed the butt of the gun against her head, sending her sprawling across the ground to lie still, blood flowing freely from her wound.

'And you . . .'

Mongrel launched himself at the Nex, who neatly sidestepped, its fist lashing out to slam against Mongrel's jaw. He rolled, countered with an uppercut but the Nex dodged and rammed the sub-machine gun into Mongrel's face.

The large Spiral operative hit the ground.

Five heavy kicks sent him spinning into unconsciousness.

They bound the two captives with wire, and dragged them down the slope towards the truck which idled, exhaust fumes spitting grey into the dark humid night.

'Just one more.'

'How perfect.'

The truck disappeared quietly into the night.

Carter dropped to a crouch, a low hiss escaping his lips, the Browning tight in his fist. He rolled into the shadows under a wide pine tree, felt needles prickling through his clothing and waited until the stealthy footfalls of the patrol had passed.

Releasing his breath slowly, he crawled to the edge of the wooden walls of the Op HQ and moved to the nearest window. It had been blacked out but, standing, Carter could see through a chink in the curtain.

The Op HQ was empty . . .

He watched for a while, just to make sure.

Carter, hand touching the wall, slid along the side of the building and glanced up again towards the sniper towers. He could see two Nex, motionless, copper eyes scanning like those of automatons. With a swift movement Carter reached the door and slid inside, closing the heavy wooden slab behind him.

The Op HQ was a large room, perhaps twenty metres square. On one side of the chamber was living accommodation – low single beds, four sets of bunk beds, a wide, rough-hewn oak table with a scattering of chairs – and in the corner a kitchen assembly with cooker, sink, kettle and a disarray of pans and cups. To the right the whole twenty-metre wall was taken up by oak benching littered with all manner of computing equipment, scanners, a satellite-control deck, and other complicated machinery that Carter suspected had something to do with the SAM defences. Lights glittered on small grey alloy consoles – blipping orange and green, then a cascade of purple which seemed to shower across the displays. Beside the high-tech computer equipment were several large wall boards containing maps and documents, and a fixed digital map; it was towards these that Carter gravitated.

'*It's too quiet.*'

'I know.'

'*It could be a trap . . .*'

'But I need to find Jam. It's no use sitting in the woods all night.'

Carter stared up at the maps. They ranged across several continents and seemed to display LVA sites operational and potential – and several that were under investigation by the Fuel Inspectorate. Countries included Egypt, Afghanistan, China, Peru, Russia, Norway and Australia. Carter lifted his ECube and it captured the information with a digital whine.

Moving to the console, he activated it and the digital map buzzed into life. Passwords were requested and Carter rested his ECube against the computer terminal – it clicked softly, and letters and numbers flickered at incredible speed across the display as the ECube hacked the terminal and the digital map spun into focus . . .

Again, LVA sites were displayed . . .

And other markings scattered across the map, highlighted in a bright orange that glittered softly.

Carter's eyes were drawn towards London as—

Glass smashed from all around the room as five windows imploded and Nex rolled to their feet with sub-machine guns levelled. Carter whirled low and the silenced Browning was spitting in his fist as he dived for the benching. Two Nex took bullets in their faces, blood spraying in bright arcs and were flipped into untidy dead heaps against the wooden floor.

Carter reached for another magazine—

As a gun barrel touched his head.

'Getting slow,' said the Nex, voice soft, asexual, a gentle croon. It had come in through one of the windows behind Carter as he fought.

Carter grinned. 'Yeah, I'm too fucking old for this game.'

The other three Nex approached, forced Carter to stand, and took his Browning and M24 carbine. They bound his hands tightly behind his back with wire and one of the Nex – seemingly the leader, although they wore no insignia or marks of rank – turned and stared at the two Nex dead on the floor.

He spun back, copper eyes burning, and moved close to Carter.

'You have been a thorn in our side for a long time.'

'Good.'

Carter's own Browning smashed against his head and blackness whirled in patterns against a sea of red, floating with bright brittle stars. He was dragged to his knees and blinked, working his jaw, and spat a little blood onto the boards.

'Can we kill him?'

'Not yet. They're bringing the others.'

Carter cursed inwardly and, licking his lips, scanned the room. He tried to loosen his bonds and caught another blow from his own weapon that sent him crashing to the wooden boards with a heavy thump. He lay stunned for a few moments, pain pounding him. The Nex dragged him to his knees again and he started to laugh, a long low evil sound.

'What's so funny?'

'The detonation.'

'What detonation?'

'Better get looking, little worms. Not long now before

314

this whole fucking LVA plant blows sky-high . . . after all, you dumb motherfuckers, I *am* in a Demolition Squad . . .'

The Nex exchanged glances, and two whirled, leaving the Op HQ at speed.

'*Down to two,*' whispered Kade.

Carter did not look, but was aware of his ECube nestling against the digital map's terminal. He calmed his breathing, head throbbing with pain, and turned a little to reposition his body, relaxing his muscles, waiting . . .

The door swung open.

First came Mongrel, badly beaten and bleeding from mouth, nose and forehead; he was bound tightly and he was – understandably – scowling fiercely. Two Nex held him. Then came Mila, also bound, staggering weakly and moaning in Slovene; again, two Nex followed and Carter cursed as they piled into the room . . .

'*This should be more fun,*' said Kade.

'What the fuck does that mean?'

'*More bodies for me to burn,*' he said darkly.

And then—

Then came Durell and another figure: a tall man, with a grey-flecked beard and neatly trimmed greying hair. He was large, a powerful man, and his gaze fixed directly on Carter as he entered the room. The pair halted, leaving the door wide and a cool breeze flowing in from the night.

Silence fell. Then—

'Mr Carter,' said Durell softly, throwing back his hood to reveal the monstrosity that was his face. His narrow slitted copper-eyed stare burned into Carter. 'How nice to see you again. This is such a pleasant surprise.'

'I thought you fucking killed him!' murmured Mongrel.

Carter nodded. 'I'll make sure I shoot him in the

315

damned face next time, mate – although since he looks so fucking hideous I think somebody already tried.'

Durell chuckled, drool pooling from his twisted jaws.

'I commend you for your tenacity, Mr Carter. It has been a long time since we had an enemy so worthy of us.'

'Too bad he has to die,' said Gol, eyes still fixed on Carter.

'So you the real Gol, or what?' snapped Carter, turning his attention from Durell to his old friend and ally. 'I saw you fall from a mountain, and then I gave you an HPG to eat – both times I saw you fucking die. It would appear that you have a little bit of immortality flowing in your blood.'

'The first time I did not die,' rumbled Gol. 'The first time I was saved . . . by Durell. And the second time you met a—' He smiled softly. 'Shall we say a changer . . . a form of Nex we worked on a long time ago.'

'And now you show your true colours?'

'True colours?' Gol frowned. 'This is no betrayal, Carter. Spiral has had its day. Spiral is weak. It has had its time and now it needs – shall we say – a little gentle persuasion to move over.'

Carter said nothing.

His gaze moved to Mongrel and the two Spiral agents exchanged a silent communication.

'This LVA all your idea, Durell?' growled Mongrel.

'Who is this puppy who yaps at my feet?' snarled Durell – and whirled, a true blur of movement, an incredible display of speed as claws emerged from the depths of his dark robes and hammered into Mongrel's head. The big man was picked up and tossed across the Op HQ to clatter against the wall, falling heavily to the ground, blood spilling from his mouth. He groaned, looked up, then slumped back down and lay still.

'What do you want with us?' said Carter coldly, amazed at this show of speed from the twisted husk.

'No,' said Durell, slitted eyes burning with anger. 'What is it that *you* want with *us*? Are you here to destroy the pumps? Or to look for . . . enemies?'

Carter stared into Durell's eyes, breathing deeply and calming himself. 'We have come to find Jam. We tracked him here; this whole discovery of your LVA set-up is incidental and, to be honest, I do not give a fuck about your aspirations for world fucking domination – I just want to find Jam.'

'*Strange.*'

Durell paced up and down as the cool breeze brought in night scents. He moved towards Mila and one claw cupped her chin, lifting her face so that she had to stare at his deformities. Her eyes were wide in terror, her mouth agape.

'Tell me, Carter – your needs would seem unbalanced.'

'My woman, Natasha, is dying. Jam can help her. Is he here? Or is he dead?'

'Ahh, the sweet Natasha. I remember her well. She had a hand in the fall of Spiral_mobile . . . well, Carter, my oldest and bravest adversary—' Durell seemed to smile. Releasing his grip on Mila's chin he turned and moved, making crackling sounds, to stand in front of Carter where he lowered his head until his broad twisted face was only a few inches from Carter's own. 'It would seem that you are in my control once more. So, unfortunately, things will not be going to plan for you and your little band. Yes, in answer to your first question, Jam is here. And no, he is far, far from dead . . .'

Durell backed away.

Carter could smell the strange Nex stink that had haunted his darkest nightmares. He shuddered. Blood rolled down his wrists as the wire continued to cut into his flesh.

Something moved in the doorway, and a massive shape filled the frame, stooping to enter. It unfurled, its triangular head coming up with tiny copper eyes fixed directly on—

Carter.

It moved forward, its heavy armoured feet booming on the wooden floor, and halted, swaying a little, its eyes blinking in the bright light.

'It is too warm here,' said Jam.

'I agree,' replied Durell softly. He glanced at Carter. 'Welcome our new ScorpNex. It has taken a long time to achieve such a fine specimen, but shall we say that this time we had a rewarding subject on which to build; from which to *blend*.'

Carter frowned.

He stared at the huge ScorpNex in front of him – and then the lines of the deformed face clicked into place. Carter blinked, and felt his knees go weak. He staggered against the two Nex who held him tightly and shook his head wildly in disbelief . . .

'It . . . it can't be . . .'

Jam, the ScorpNex, smiled. Drool pooled from his twisted jaws, stretching to the floor in viscous strands.

'No, it fucking *cannot* be!'

'Hello, Carter,' said Jam, his voice soft and deformed – but still recognisable. Just.

Carter found tears on his cheeks.

'Jam! What have they fucking done to you . . .'

'Carter –' the ScorpNex spread its arms wide, making tiny crackling sounds as its chitinous armour shifted '— this is good, this is progress, this is *evolution*.'

'*Jam?*'

Jam's head moved, dipped, turned to stare at Mongrel who had crawled to his knees in the corner, blood coating his face, eyes wide in horror.

'Welcome to my home, Mongrel,' Jam growled softly.

Durell chuckled. 'Such a beautiful moment. Oh, my heart bleeds . . . but now, now to business. Jam?' Jam turned his gaze on Durell.

'Yes?'

Already the Nex were backing away, dragging Mila towards the door. The two Nex holding Carter suddenly dropped his arms and stepped away, leaving Carter and Jam in the centre of the room and Mongrel on his knees in the corner.

They left the building with Gol. Durell remained . . . watching from the doorway. 'They wanted you, Jam. Now they've found you. Kill them both.'

Jam's huge head wavered, shifted, and his stare fixed on Carter who stood, head down, eyes dark and brooding, his hands bound behind his back.

Jam seemed to grin, light reflecting from the tips of his long twisted teeth.

And in a blur of movement, he attacked . . .

CHAPTER 12

WARHOST

The Priest's eyes narrowed.

Something clicked against the hard floor.

Then there was a long, low and terrible hiss . . .

He whirled in the gloom that was speckled with light from far above, as a huge bulk rushed towards him. He reached for his Glock but too late – he was thrown across the chamber, grunting with pain, hammering into the wall and crumpling into a heap. Wheezing, The Priest struggled to his feet and peered through the darkness, his sandals scrabbling against the loose sand scattered over the fused glass floor of Spiral_Q.

It moved slowly towards him.

The Priest's eyes went wide.

'What in God's name are you?'

It moved on all fours, like a huge cat; its head was triangular, armoured and tufted with thick strands of fur, and its eyes were a deep and iridescent copper.

Its head dropped low, almost touching the ground, eyes looking up at The Priest with a kind of primal curiosity. Then its lips curled back to reveal long fangs and it snarled and claws clacked against the floor and thick heavy corded muscles bunched—

'I know you,' said The Priest, placing his hand against the Bible within his robes. 'You are a Sleeper and I remember you.' He smiled gently, nodding, his face lit with a serene light as he was listening to some distant voice.

The creature snarled and The Priest saw it ready for the kill: each fraction of a second filled with a rippling of muscle, a vibration of sinews, a focus of intent . . .

He sighed, hand moving from his Bible, brushing past his wooden beads as his sandals fought for purchase on the uneven sandy floor and dipping beneath his robes to reveal—

A big, broad-bladed, serrated knife.

'You are an abomination under God's Law,' he said, his voice now strong, booming almost, and eyes glittering in the gloom. 'And as such you must – die . . .'

The Sleeper attacked, bounding across the chamber towards The Priest who leapt forward to meet it, his huge frame silhouetted against the gloom as they smashed together. The huge jagged knife slashed up, and then out, slicing fur and bone and sending a dark spray of blood up over The Priest's face, splashing against the wall and floor.

He gasped in shock at the icy coldness of the blood as the Sleeper hissed in pain, rolling to one side. It skidded across the ground and The Priest ducked, whirling in a circle. Then it uncurled and stared first at the deep bubbling wound in its armoured flank, then back at the Priest.

He smiled, arms spreading wide, blood dripping from the tip of the glinting blade.

'Come, my friend. God has a very important lesson that he would wish me to teach you.'

The Sleeper rolled to its feet and edged forward, with infinitely more care this time, clawed pads clattering against the ground in a slow, hypnotic rhythm. The Priest moved away from the wall, face settling into a calm mask of understanding. The knife weaved in front of him, the steel blade his only defence . . .

The Sleeper charged.

The Priest rolled with awesome speed as a claw flashed past his face and the bulk of the creature smashed against him. The knife struck out, but the creature had spun to one side and whirled, huge heavy head swinging from side to side like a pendulum, to return and glare at The Priest – who ran at it, sandals flapping against the sandy glass floor as the Sleeper leapt again at the huge man. There came a sudden flurry of blows, and The Priest's powerful arms encircled the blood-dripping Sleeper. The large-bladed knife clattered across the floor and they hit the ground hard, rolling to a halt against the wall in a tangle of violence—

The Sleeper snarled.

The Priest head-butted its lower jaws, three, four, five times—

The Sleeper suddenly scrabbled against the huge man like a cat trapped in a cage, claws shredding his robes and the flesh beneath in a spraying shower of crimson. The Priest's face compressed in a titanic strain of effort, going through shades of red and purple as muscles writhed like eels along his arms and chest and his eyes searched desperately for the fallen blade—

A claw shot up, slicing through the already tattered grey robes. The Priest felt a warm sluicing of blood as the claw continued, and there came the wooden clatter of rosary beads against the glass floor.

The Priest's eyes went wide.

'My beads!' he hissed.

He slammed his right fist into the Sleeper's triangular head again and again and then kicked himself backwards, scooping up the blade and leaping at the stunned creature. The knife slashed down five times, and blood splashed across the floor and over his grey robes in pumping arcs. The Sleeper seemed to deflate and lay still, wheezing in the throes of death. Its huge head turned and the copper eyes bored into the blood-soaked Priest, hands slippery with gore and beard spattered with tiny pieces of armoured shell, which had been pulverised by the pounding blows of the broad serrated blade.

The Priest was panting, his eyes wild.

Staring down, he said in a deep and solemn voice, '*My brethren, be strong in the Lord and in the power of his might. Put on the whole armour of God, that ye may be able to stand against the wiles of the devil. For we wrestle not against flesh and blood, but against the darkness of the world!*'

He took a menacing step forward.

The Sleeper snarled, its blood forming huge pools on the ground. It struggled to rise, claws raking the glass, but sank back again as The Priest stooped towards it. Their stares became locked, joined to one another by dark threads of understanding . . .

'. . . *Wherefore take unto you the whole armour of God that ye may be able to withstand the evil day* . . .' The blade rose high above The Sleeper's head, and the beast's copper eyes lifted to follow the eerie glint of steel. '*And having done all, to Stand!*'

The blade plunged down, striking just above one eye.

There came a heavy crunch.

And the Sleeper died.

Panting, The Priest backed away and looked around the chamber, searching for more enemies. He then got down slowly onto his knees to retrieve his rosary beads.

He returned swiftly to his task. He cut through the alloy panel and reached inside, hand curling around a sheaf of metal documents. He stowed them beneath his robes, found his Glock, and with sandals leaving bloody imprints in puddles of death he moved to his Skimmer so that he could ascend from this pit.

Heneghan stared down from behind the facial shield of HIDSS as The Priest toiled across the sand. As he climbed into the Comanche's cockpit she half-turned, glancing at his shredded and bloodstained robes; the dark splatters on his hands and face; the look of thunder in his features.

'You been fighting again, holy man?'

'The bugger tore my beads!'

'I can see how that would be your greatest worry during a bout of violent combat,' the pilot said softly, eyeing the vicious serrated blade, which dripped blood onto the floor of the Comanche's cockpit.

The Priest's gaze met Heneghan's.

He was serious. Deadly serious.

'It was an act of blasphemy!' he growled.

'Was it?'

'The beads were my mum's! Now – take me to Greece.'

Jam's claw lashed out towards Carter's face and the Spiral agent rolled swiftly to one side, rising smoothing to his feet and launching himself into the air. Both his boots connected with Jam's triangular head, knocking the ScorpNex back a step. He gave a grunt and a deep hiss of surprise—

Carter landed and sprinted, arms still wired behind

324

his body. Mongrel had produced a hidden knife from his boot and cut his own bonds . . . now he cut Carter's as Jam charged.

'Don't do this, Jam!'

Claws lashed out and Carter ducked, landing a savage right hook on Jam's armoured head. He punched again and again, then dodged a blow by the ScorpNex and skipped to the left, boot lashing out in a powerful side-kick to connect with Jam's chest. Jam caught Carter's leg and tried to force him down but Carter flipped himself into a roll, boot hammering twice against Jam's face as he kicked himself away and rolled fluidly back upright, despite his previous injuries . . .

'Jam, stop!' he bellowed.

Jam halted, his copper eyes staring at Carter. Mongrel, who was watching almost paralysed, started to sidle towards Carter's Browning and the sub-machine gun on the side benches—

'You the enemy now.'

'We were friends!' snarled Carter. 'Don't fucking do this! I can help you.'

'How?'

'I don't know . . . but I don't want to fight you, I don't want to—'

'Kill me?' Jam chuckled with genuine humour. 'Show me Carter, show me how you will kill me . . .'

Jam leapt and Carter dodged again. Jam came down and spun in a blur, arm lashing out to smash Carter from his feet. Carter hit the ground hard, rolling to a stop and grunting, coughing and holding his chest where pain hammered through him with an intensity he had rarely felt before.

Carter rolled again and Jam's armoured feet landed where his head had been, cracking the thick wooden floorboards which splintered and spat shards of wood into the air.

Carter got to his feet and attacked – launching himself at Jam who plucked him from the air and threw him across the room. He landed heavily, crashing into one of the bunk beds and sending it tipping over – and with sudden panic Carter realised that he was tangled in its strewn wooden slats—

Mongrel grabbed the sub-machine gun.

Growling, Jam charged as Mongrel opened fire. Bullets spat across the Op HQ as Jam swerved to one side, the fusillade tracking him—

And then the whole world seemed to shake with the boom of a devastating explosion. Shrapnel scythed the building and the ground shuddered. Mongrel ceased firing, smoke curling from the gun's barrel—

'Jam!'

Durell was gone from the doorway.

Jam rose smoothly to his armoured feet as Carter clambered from the wreckage of the bed. Their stares met as Mongrel trained the gun on their old friend, snarling.

'Wait,' commanded Carter.

Jam glanced over at Mongrel, then back towards Carter. Another shell howled overhead and the world shook again. The remaining windows in the Op building rattled, and they could hear the roar of distant engines and the sudden clattering of heavy machine-fun fire.

'Tanks!' said Mongrel, eyes gleaming.

Jam stared at Carter. 'Until the next time,' he said, his face twisting into a strange smile.

'No, Jam . . . stay here . . .' Carter was clutching his chest and wheezing from the impact of the recent heavy blow. 'We . . . we need your help. Natasha is dying, Nicky is with her—'

326

Jam's expression changed – from a twisted smile to a snarl. 'Stop, Carter, stop . . .'

'We need the machine, the Avelach . . . you know where it is . . . it was used on you – to *change* you. Listen to me, man, if I don't get the machine then Natasha will *die*—'

Jam whirled, and was gone into the night.

Carter and Mongrel staggered to the doorway to see two of the LVA storage tanks billowing fifty-metre columns of fire into the sky with deafening roars, lighting up the quarry with false daylight. To one side the two armoured tanks sprang into life, engines roaring, tracks rumbling as at the distant head of the valley a group of Spiral SP57 tanks appeared, in desert camouflage – their tracks tearing at the hard-packed ground as they mowed down the perimeter fence and ploughed through barbed wire—

Nex spilled from the barracks.

There came a *whump* and one of the barrack buildings exploded in a titanic ball of fire sending a hundred screaming burning Nex flailing up into the sky where they disintegrated into flurries of charred flesh. The Spiral tanks advanced, churning the earth. The Nex tanks' guns fired and an SP57 was blown into the air and sent crashing into another tank. The two war machines exploded in a massive blossoming purple fireball . . .

'What can we do?' hissed Mongrel, eyes wide.

He turned. But Carter had gone . . .

The quarry was a battlefield.

Nex with sub-machine guns had taken up defensive positions and their JK59s roared. Another barracks was sent flashing into the sky at the same time as a Nex tank. It spun lazily on a rising blanket of fire, its gun blasting a shell up towards the heavens even as it rose and was slowly consumed by purple HighJ fire before arcing gently and toppling back to earth as a burned and blackened steel carcass . . .

Carter sprinted across the quarry, head down, Browning in one hand, face grim . . .

Four small black attack helicopters leapt into the air. The SM7.8VLS Vertical Launching Systems whirled on heavy-duty motors, arming the SM-7 missiles . . . but they did not engage.

They recognised their own.

Carter forgot stealth as bullets and shells screamed all around him. His face was illuminated by the light from the burning LVA tanker stores. Machine-gun fire stitched a line of dust spurts in front of his boots and his Browning smashed a Nex from its feet. He halted, dropping to a crouch beside the Nex warrior which scrabbled at the hot metal in its throat . . .

'Where is Durell?'

But the Nex died before it could say anything.

Behind the tanks came the roar of machine guns as DemolSquads on foot came to their aid. Using the heavy tanks as shields, they advanced across the tracer-lit quarry, an SP57 pushing a burning Nex truck chassis out of the way. Then the tank climbed over it and crushed it under its heavy tracks.

Carter saw the distant small black helicopters. Jam was climbing into one of them. He looked left, towards the nearest sniper tower. His eyes narrowed as he watched its two snipers firing, reloading, firing again and he ran towards the tower, grabbed the slippery alloy ladder and started to climb.

Bullets whistled past him, making him flinch and curse. Carter palmed the Browning and took out three

Nex with three head shots. They hit the ground, rolling, rag-dolls whose brains merged with the hard-packed ground in streamers of gore.

Carter continued to climb.

Below him the quarry spread out, a battlefield populated by a couple of hundred Nex and Spiral DemolSquads. The tanks had centre stage and, off in the distance, Carter saw more Nex tanks rumbling from some distant reserve post—

'The fuckers.'

To his right, the helicopters containing Durell and Jam started to climb into the night air, engines howling, mounted machine guns raining bullets down into the battle raging below. Carter increased his efforts, sweat rolling down his face and body, breath coming in gasps, stare switching between the battlefield and the ascending choppers—

Carter reached the top of the ladder.

The two snipers were busy – busy dealing out precision death.

As Carter's boots touched down on the rough-sawn planks, the Nex whirled round, suddenly looking confused. Carter shot the first one in the face at point-blank range and saw the pale white features disintegrate in an instant as blood sprayed across a wooden beam. The second Nex threw a punch but Carter ducked, came up on its left and powered his right elbow into its face. It took a step back, and Carter smashed a right kick into its chest – it hit the barrier, and was flipped over to topple to the ground far below.

Carter grabbed at his belt, produced a tiny matt-black disc the size of a small coin – a TrackingDisc – and as the helicopters lifted past the tower he pulled back his arm and threw it with all his might. It spun across the void and connected with a click to the tail section of Durell's helicopter – which disappeared up into the blackness.

Panting and shaking, Carter glanced down at the raging battle.

Machine-gun bullets slammed into the beam behind him, spitting splinters of scorched wood into the air.

'Cheers, guys,' he muttered, taking hold of a Nex sniper rifle. He hefted the Barrett SilverScope III thoughtfully, then leant it against the wooden parapet and sighted on the nearest sniper tower directly opposite.

The two snipers there leapt into view as the sight clicked and buzzed. The Nex were busy with their shooting, rifles kicking smoothly and emotionlessly in black-gloved hands.

Carter sighted his weapon and sent a bullet across the gap.

It hit a Nex in the side of the head, the high-calibre round smashing it from the platform with only half of its skull left. The second Nex looked momentarily stunned, then whirled as the bullet hit it high in the chest and it, too, was punched backwards from the tower to flip and fall, legs kicking as it spun towards the ground.

Carter turned his attention to the third tower.

And, smiling coldly, killed the snipers there too.

'*I fucking hate snipers as well,*' snapped Kade. '*Go on . . . give them a taste of their fucking medicine . . . do you know, in the Fourth Gulf War if we caught a sniper we used to—*'

'Kade?'

'*Hmm?*'

'Shut up.'

Carter sighted on the final operational sniper tower. They were raining hot death down on the DemolSquads supporting the SP57 tanks below and Carter sighted on the first Nex – could see the copper eyes leap into view through his scope, could read the focus of intent, and licked his lips, allowing breath to flow easily from his lungs as—

The whole tower top exploded in a sudden bright inflorescence and disintegrated in a bloom of purple.

The Nex snipers were vaporised.

Carter frowned, and followed the line of trajectory. And there, on the top of the cliff, squatting like an angry insect against the hard ground with its matrix-engine hissing was the HTank – the Spiral Edition HoverTank – driven by Simmo.

Carter grinned.

Then saw the gun start to track round—

Towards him.

'You've got to be fucking—' But he was moving, climbing onto the ladder and praying like a lunatic. He clamped his boots to the outside of the ladder and loosened his grip . . .

The ladder thrummed under his gloves.

The ground rushed towards his boots – as his eyes saw the kick of fire from the HTank's massive barrel and the tower above him exploded in a shattering blast. The shock waves sent him crashing from the ladder, chunks of hot wood raining down on him, to land in a bush.

All the air was kicked from his lungs.

Carter lay there, dazed. He watched the HTank engage and with a cold matrix-engine hiss flip over the lip of the canyon and speed to the wide floor of the quarry down the rugged near-vertical slope – and behind the positions of the fighting Nex.

Three shells sent bodies sailing, burning, through the air.

Another shell destroyed the final Nex tank.

Carter looked up, looked around.

Mongrel was grinning. 'Carter, what the fuck are you doing in that bush?'

Carter realised that he was on fire, and hurriedly patted at his flaming clothing. 'Trying not to get shelled,' he muttered, as Mongrel helped him from the spiky branches with small curses and yelps.

'They got away,' said Mongrel, as Simmo's HTank roared up behind the Spiral agent and Mongrel looked calmly over his shoulder. The hatch opened with a clang and Simmo's huge shaved head appeared, throat-tattoos glistening under a layer of sweat.

'The Sarge think that fine sport!' he yelled.

'Not done yet,' said Carter, pointing.

One final small black attack helicopter was trying to take off. It rose into the air, then fell back again, its engines screaming. Then it leapt once more—

'Simmo take care of this.' He disappeared.

Carter and Mongrel exchanged glances.

The HTank, so close that Carter could have reached out and touched it, elevated its bulk on a cold-cushion of hissing vapour and the gun fired a shell that caught the helicopter's tail section, ripping it free and sending the machine into a spinning nosedive. It crunched against the concrete landing pad and fire erupted along one flank from severed fuel pipes . . .

Simmo leapt down from the HTank and strode towards the chopper.

'What you doing?' yelled Mongrel over the sounds of distant gunshots.

Simmo just shrugged, reached the burning copter, and pulled free a lithe but muscular man with a heavily scarred face and red eyes. He was unconscious from the impact, bleeding, and Simmo calmly dragged him away as the black chopper flared bright and exploded, sending a thick plume of black smoke up into the moonlit night.

'There are more tanks coming,' said Carter. 'From down the valley. I saw them from the tower.'

Simmo nodded, dumping Kattenheim to the ground. Mongrel rolled him onto his belly and bound his wrists and feet with wire. Simmo spoke quietly into his ECube and a group of waiting SP57 tanks turned, tracks grinding against the hard earth and turrets rotating smoothly to face this new threat.

'We get call,' said Simmo proudly. 'We come! Heli-lift tanks in from local depot in Italy and many of TankSquad men fast-jet here from London . . . including me! Well done, Mongrel! Your message tie in with The Priest's and suddenly it make sense!'

Carter lit a cigarette.

'And I see you brought the HTank there, Sarge.'

'My HTank. Italian prototype. Ducati engines.'

Carter frowned, smiling softly. 'You mean *Spiral*'s HTank, surely?'

'Is mine.'

Carter breathed deeply, then nudged Mongrel as Simmo climbed back into the HTank and revved the cold matrix-engine. 'Me go kill more Nex!' he shouted down. 'The Sarge not seen battle for too long! The Sarge soon run out of tattoo space!' He steered the thundering HTank across the quarry, scattering DemolSquad teams who were clearing the area of any remaining Nex . . . and disappeared from view.

'We need to get the bikes and get back to the Comanche.'

'You got a plan?'

'I tagged Durell's helicopter.'

'So we know where they're going? Smart move.'

Carter took Mongrel's ECube and punched in a code.

It hummed as it tracked trajectories and gave a list of possible destinations. 'Yeah, looks like we're going to . . .' He groaned.

'Where?'

'Of all the fucking places!'

'Where is it, Carter?'

Carter grimaced. 'Looks like we could be going to Egypt.'

'I thought you were a wanted man in Egypt?'

'I am. Everybody wants me *very* dead.'

'Why?'

'It's a long story, my friend.'

Mongrel kicked the trussed-up body of Kattenheim. 'What we going to do with this piece of shit? You think he might have some answers?'

'I'm pretty sure he does. If we ask the right questions.'

'I bet,' said Mongrel, sharing Carter's cigarette as machine guns blasted to one side and five DemolSquad operatives found the last remaining Nex and drilled it full of holes. 'I bet he's one of those tough bastards who just doesn't want to talk.'

'Simple solution,' said Carter, eyes glittering.

'What's that?'

'We'll let Sergeant Simmo question him.'

Mongrel nodded, enjoying the smoke and gazing around at the fire, the bodies, the devastation. He laughed out loud then, and shook his head, eyes haunted.

'You thinking of Jam?'

'Yes,' muttered Mongrel. 'Come on. I want to get out of this place.'

'Let's tool up and move out,' said Carter. 'Simmo can give us information while we're on the move.'

'Can I come with you?'

Carter turned, and saw Mila. She was watching him

with a strange look on her face. Blood had dried on her skin and he smiled kindly, wearily.

'No.'

'We might need a sniper,' said Mongrel.

'No.'

'Listen, you can't leave me *here*,' Mila said, gazing round in horror at the battlefield and the corpses. 'This is my fight as well – these Nex, they are my enemies. I have helped you get this far – without me you would not be on the trail of that . . . *creature* you need to hunt.'

Carter glanced – murderously – at Mongrel. What else have you blabbed? he thought.

'It will be dangerous,' said Carter softly. He placed a hand against her shoulder, gently, feeling a little guilty for having placed a bullet in her flesh.

'I can look after myself,' Mila said.

'So be it,' nodded Carter.

'*Pussy*,' whispered Kade, a dark sneer in his tone.

CHAPTER 13

RENDEZVOUS

The lights were dim inside the barracks.

Simmo stood at the centre of the room, wearing nothing but combats and boots. His chest, heavily scarred and heavily tattooed, rippled with muscle. The huge soldier carried not one ounce of excess fat.

Around the outskirts of the room designed to house a hundred Nex warriors stood several grim-faced DemolSquad troopers. Haggis and Mo stood side by side, huge squat bullet-headed men, one British and one Pakistani: both awesome fighters. Lurking in the shadows, weapons held loosely in their hands, cigarettes trailing smoke to the ceiling stood the TankSquads – Fegs, Kavanagh, Oz, Remic, Root Beer, Rogowski, Falconer, Sagar, Graham and Holtzhausen. Kinnane and Samasuwo both held brews in their big scarred fists, and Bob Bob was looking forlorn, still with custard – his favourite food – staining his combats. All of them watched with barely suppressed hatred as Simmo reached down, dragged Kattenheim onto the chair at the centre of the room, and slowly tied him tightly to the thick wooden frame.

Simmo stooped a little, looking into the red eyes.

'I know you're a tough lad,' he rumbled, 'and The Sarge be honest – he not really like doing this sort of thing. Well, not much. Well, not unless he in bad mood. But you know answers to our questions and we want answers.'

'Fuck you,' said Kattenheim softly, and stared straight ahead.

Simmo shrugged, flexed his shoulders, and delivered a crashing left hook. They all heard the crack of bone before the chair hit the ground and Kattenheim lay, stunned and bleeding and staring at the wooden boards.

'Simmo?' said Fegs, holding a cigarette casually between his tattooed fingers.

'Yeah?'

'Aren't you supposed to ask him a question?'

'Hm. Yes.' The Sarge nodded, then dragged Kattenheim upright once more.

'Nothing like a fair trial,' said Kattenheim smoothly; his face was swollen around his cheek and his gaze lifted to meet Simmo's. 'Once, when I was on para-ops in Colombia, I was captured by the enemy. The drug-purifiers tortured me for five days with alkaline chemical agents – and you see the results of their handiwork. And do you know something, Sergeant Simmo? I spoke not one word. Not one fucking word until my team mates found me and burned the enemy – alive – in large pits. I have a pact with pain, Mr Simmo. Me and pain, well, we just agree to disagree.'

Simmo nodded, then delivered a right that smashed Kattenheim's nose and sent the chair crashing backwards, thumping against the boards. A splash of blood stained the timber. Simmo moved forward and stood over Kattenheim, staring down, his face twisting as he felt his massive temper rising. Simmo felt the other TankSquad men retreating further into the shadows. When Simmo exploded, nobody wanted to be close.

'The Sergeant very sorry you suffer at the hands of your enema.' He chuckled nastily. 'But I have watched one thousand, five hundred and sixty-three men – and, ah, Nex – die. One could say Sarge is professional. One could say Sarge have no soul. One could say Sarge have pact with the Devil. Whatever, you need answer questions or your pain will be incredible.'

'Pain is something I can live with,' said Kattenheim softly as the chair was righted and somebody handed Simmo a long, heavy, rusting iron bar. Simmo weighed it thoughtfully.

'You have made your peace. That good, Sarge thinks. Now, I need know links between Durell and the LVA fuel. I need know why Nex are guarding LVA pumping rig. And I need know where Durell has gone with little cronies.'

Kattenheim stared straight ahead, mouth a grim line.

Most of the TankSquads looked away as Simmo swung the heavy bar.

And they knew that the night was going to be a long one.

The Comanche's twin LHTec engines were humming softly as they cleared the south-west coast of Slovenia and headed out over the Adriatic Sea. The sun was rising in the east, casting tendrils of soft orange light over the silver waves, and the huge expanse of water stretched out ahead of them.

Carter, still weary and exhausted, checked the blip from the TrackingDisc and smiled to himself. He thought of Natasha lying in the hospital bed and the smile changed immediately to a grim scowl.

His mind spun with confusion.

And hatred.

And . . . exhaustion.

How much longer can I go on? he asked himself.

How much longer can I fight? Kill?

'For ever and ever. Amen,' said Kade.

'Who dragged you kicking and screaming back into this universe?

'I was just thinking.'

'About?'

'About Jam. I know his weakness.'

'Which is?'

'Ahh, now that would be telling. Let's just say that when we meet the fucker again, let me have a stab at him. We'll see who's the fucking daddy then.'

'The only stab you'll ever get is a nine-inch blade in the back.'

'Your humour is what keeps me alive, O Master,' chuckled Kade.

The Comanche flashed low over the sea, heading south-east a couple of miles off the coast of Croatia and then Albania. As they headed over the Ionian Sea to the west of the Greek mainland Carter's ECube buzzed softly.

'Yeah?'

'Carter, this is The Priest.'

'Long time no see, you religious maniac. What do you want?'

'We need to meet.'

'I'm a little busy.'

'Make time.'

'You're not listening, Priest. I'm a little fucking busy to be arranging social events with Bible-wielding lunatics – even if they are in charge of the Spiral secret police.'

'Carter, this is important. It involves Spiral, it involves Jam, and it involves Natasha.'

Carter was silent behind the insect-visor of the HIDSS helmet.

'What do you suggest?' he said, finally, quietly.

'You are heading for Egypt. The Spiral mainframes have you plotted. Touch down in Crete, coordinates 224.361.762. I will meet you as soon as I am able.'

'How long?'

'I cannot say. We have just discovered Durell's game. I will bring you up to speed when we meet.'

'This better be important, Priest.'

'It's important, Carter. Trust me and trust God.'

'God? I'm pretty sure that fucker has abandoned me.'

The ECube cut out and Carter was left staring at the silver sea below his humming war machine. He thought back to everything that they had been through; thought back to Feuchter and Durell and the QIII processor and The Priest's involvement in the events that had almost toppled the world.

'*You think he could be a traitor as well?*' asked Kade.

'No . . . I don't know. I find it hard to trust people in, shall we say, the current world climate.'

'*Let me kill the fucker,*' said Kade.

'Jesus, don't you have another fucking tune to play?'

'*The day that I die will be the day I stop killing,*' said Kade. '*And you are the same, my boy, my brother. You are the same. We are as one; peas in the same pod.*'

In silence they cruised towards the distant shimmering island of Crete.

Freddy killed the engine and sat in silence, in the absence of the Honda's 8600cc rumble. He nodded to himself.

Hmm, he thought, this LVA seems to be running a treat! Maybe Charlotte had been right after all?

He climbed from the cabin and stood in the darkness, hands on hips, and then lit a cigarette. He noticed that his hand was shaking – just a little bit. As the weed touched his lips he could just distinguish badly scrubbed bloodstains on his fingers.

The ground trembled beneath his boots.

A gentle caressing.

A tender warning . . .

The quake singing a soothing grinding lullaby.

Freddy stood on the moors, filling his lungs with nicotine. He moved around to the boot of the Honda and popped the catch. It slid smoothly upwards to reveal a dark interior.

And there lay the bin-bag-confined body parts of Charlotte.

Freddy sighed.

Why couldn't you have been normal? he thought.

He reached in and pulled out a long parcel. It was wrapped very neatly and Freddy prided himself on the tight binding of the silver duct-tape around the seams that made sure that no blood could possibly escape.

He chuckled to himself as he stepped onto the heather and headed away from the Honda. The heather was wet, springy, sinking a little beneath his footsteps. He carried Charlotte's leg under one arm and a spade in his free hand.

It wouldn't have to be a deep hole.

Just a shallow grave.

He found a suitable spot.

Rain started to drizzle down. As he dropped the parcelled leg on the heather, it made a wet thump. He slammed the spade into the earth, cutting neatly through heather with the sharp edge of the blade. The blade struck four times, creating a square of sliced vegetation and soil – and then Freddy levered the mound free and threw it to one side.

Slowly, Freddy began to excavate.

After twenty minutes he was panting hard and his breath was steaming in the light rain. The hole was quite big – almost big enough for the body of his ex-lover, at any rate.

Freddy felt a twinge of guilt then.

He acknowledged that Charlotte probably hadn't deserved what she had got. He acknowledged that death and dismemberment were gifts that one shouldn't really bestow upon one's girlfriend. And he acknowledged that burial on the moors was perhaps rather savage a punishment for perpetual moaning, whining, bickering and emotional blackmail.

Freddy smiled.

His eyes glinted – a little insanely.

But then . . . but but but fucking *but*!

He shovelled another spade of earth onto the pile of waterlogged soil. It smelled creamy, rich, musty – like a proper grave on the moors should.

Something glinted through the rain, distantly, across the heather.

Voices drifted; the sounds of ghosts.

'Pedal, fat man, pedal!'

'Is this insanity – or fitness training?'

'It must be insanity. We never see any other fucker out in the rain, ice and snow!'

'Fucking warm-weather riders. Bunch of pussies to a man.'

'Yeah, bit of frost and they fanny out! The little girls.'

Freddy's head whipped left. His eyes narrowed. Water dripped from the tip of his nose.

Lights glittered dazzlingly through the rain.

'What the hell is *that*?' he muttered.

Two sets of twin halogen lamps sparkled. Freddy could hear puffing and panting – laughter. Through the increasing downpour came two mountain bikers, their silver titanium full-suss machines sloshing easily through the mud, lamps glittering. The riders were wearing full army combats, wet-proofs, and floppy desert army hats. They splashed to a stop a few feet away, halogens cutting a bright slice from the night and illuminating Freddy, his spade, his hole, and a bin-bag-wrapped leg.

The two bearded men stared hard at Freddy.

Then they looked at one another.

'What the fuck is *he* doing, Ravioli?'

'Fucked if I know, Worzel.'

They both stared back at Freddy, eyes narrowing to glares as they stepped from the saddles of their mountain bikes and allowed the machines to fall in the mud. They took a step closer, then another. Freddy took a step back.

'What you doing?' said Ravioli, goatee beard making his tapered face look quite evil in the gloom.

Freddy shrugged a little, spade loose in one hand.

'Is that a fucking *grave*?' spat Worzel, round face, bushy eyebrows and thick black beard glistening in the murk.

'I've got a bad feeling about this – worse than the time you swallowed that mescal worm and I had to take you to the hospital when the alcohol-infused grub burnt away part of your lip! Hey, and what's that parcel wrapped up there?'

They moved forward, curious.

Again, Freddy backed away – and in a fit of sudden panic, dropped his spade and ran for it. He sprinted across the moors, stumbling across the heather in the darkness, heavy rain obscuring his vision, blind panic filling his soul with a need to get away. He ran and ran, pushing himself to levels of exertion that he had never realised he could reach. Then, suddenly, he splashed to a halt, panting, eyes scanning nervously as he spun around – twice – in circles.

Where am I?

Shit.

Where's the car?

Bitch!

He calmed his breathing, and listened to see if the two men were pursuing him. He whirled in the gloom, twitchy, nervous, mind filled with leaping shadows.

And he could sense—

Sense something there.

Freddy stared as hard as he could into the darkness. He knew that the night could play tricks on you, and places like the moors were renowned for being spooky in the dark. He had been in the habit of coming up here with Charlotte a few years earlier, before they had their own place – the moors had been a good place for covert sex. But many times, even during their soaring passion and Charlotte's moans for a new toaster, vacuum cleaner or tropical holiday, the light could move in such a way, or the wind moan through the oppressive darkness and you could believe that a knife-wielding maniac was only a few feet away.

How fucking ironic, he mused bitterly . . . as something large and black and moving faster than thought slammed into him. He caught a glimpse of bright gleaming copper and then the pain screamed through him. He gagged and choked on his own blood as a fist like a sword tore open his chest. The dark heather was so cool on his face – it smelled fresh, like that summer's day when he had first brought Charlotte up to this romantic desolate haven . . .

Worzel knelt by the package and prodded it gingerly. He glanced up at Ravioli who was staring – a bit aghast, mouth open and nose wrinkled in distaste.

'Open it,' growled Ravioli.

Worzel scowled. 'I ain't fucking opening it. It might be a body or something.'

'What, the body of a midge?'

'You mean midget.'

'Whatever. Go on, it won't bite you. If it *is* a body then it's obviously dead. But it'll just be a porn stash or something.

'There's nothing wrong with porn!'

'I never said there was.'

There was a pause for thought. 'So why *bury* it?'

'I don't fucking know. Are you going to open it or what? Or are you just going to start crying about being the most unpopular man at the party again – just because you have to drink a half-pint of tequila? Like a big pussy?'

'At least I haven't got a ginger fucking afro!'

'Hey, I had that shaved off a long time ago, so—'

Something clicked.

From the gloom, past the dazzling halogen headlights shining across the rainswept moorland and tufts of heather nestling at ground level, came the sound of padding armoured claws.

A bulky shape stopped in the gloom, tantalisingly hidden by the edges of shadows cast by the bright bike lights.

Ravioli and Worzel ceased their petty argument.

A large dark rain-slick triangular head swept towards

them. There came a gleam of copper eyes. The ground trembled softly underfoot, and Ravioli and Worzel took a step away from the hole, the spade, and the severed leg. They licked dry lips and swallowed, their throats coarse. They glanced nervously at each other – as if to confirm that this was not a bad moorland night-mirage.

'Nice doggy,' said Worzel.

'That ain't a doggy.'

'You think I don't know that? You think I think it's a fucking donkey or something?'

'I think we should run.'

'Run or fight?'

'Or . . . the third option?'

Ravioli produced a Mars bar. He took off the wrapper and broke off a chunk of chocolate, stretching strings of soft toffee. Worzel stared hard at his friend.

'What the *fuck* are you doing?'

'I was going to entice it away with chocolate.' Ravioli looked suddenly a little uncertain.

The creature . . . growled.

Ravioli and Worzel turned to run – and felt something crash into them with the force of a train smashing into a wall. Claws rent flesh in the darkness, slashing left and right with economical movements. A spray of gore and blood filled the temporary shallow grave. Two bodies rolled away in several separate pieces, skin, bone, intestines and muscle flapping loosely – and blank dead eyes stared up at the heavy downpour.

The Sleeper turned, its own eyes glowing for an instant like miniature twin suns caught in the beams of the halogen bike-lamps – and from behind the bikes came more shapes, moving through the rain: two, three, five, ten . . . twenty . . . dark bodies glistening with chitinous exoskeletons. They moved on armoured claws, warily, heavy muscles bunched as the world trembled in the fist of the impending and building quake. Their eyes turned towards the distant lights of the city and the scent of the humans beyond.

They sprinted into the night.

And were gone.

Ivers stared with incredible boredom at the titanium-carbide VII drill bit rotating at high speed within its protective Plas-7 sheath. The platform was solid beneath his feet, his lust for Michelle even stronger as the minutes until their next amorous meeting ticked by . . . but something else had wormed its way into his brain—

A needle.

A needle of . . . curiosity.

'Hey, Oldroyd?'

'Yeah?'

Oldroyd was in his late thirties, and although only small in stature he made up for his lack of height with his character. He was chirpy, cheerful – bouncing, some would say. He always had a clever quip, a witty put-down, a humorous piece of pornographic verse: many underestimated Oldroyd, but always to their own cost. With a smile he could destroy a room full of cocktail party guests. With a quip he could decimate a legion of underrated comedians. With a baring of his arse on live TV, he could offend a nation. Which he had done on four occasions in life, thus far.

'You know when that inspectorate team came here, with the guy in the robes?'

'Durell.'

Ivers met Oldroyd's look but for once the small man's humour had evaporated. Ivers waited for the punch line – none came. I suppose there are some things in life which are just not funny, he mused.

'I think they went down the tubes under the Sub-3KM control quarters.'

'Why do you think that?' Oldroyd's normally cheeky expression was deadly serious.

'I don't know . . . the equipment looked like it might have been moved.' Ivers shrugged. 'Forget it, forget I said anything about it. I'm just fucking imagining things.'

Oldroyd tutted. 'Aye lad, you should get yourself a girlfriend.' He smiled roguishly. 'That usually cures supernatural imaginings for me.'

Ivers chuckled, and went back to checking the titanium-carbide VII drill bit. Fantasies played through his head – fantasies of small cars with large engines, his ambition to rebuild and customise a Helix Coupe 6.0 litre, replacing the motor with a 1250 bhp 24-cylinder monster . . . and his inherent need to lavish love, care and attention on his most favourite of favourite hobbies: bike racing – preferably on 1296cc Ducatis.

Kenny's voice came from the ComChamber, whining a little. 'Something's going on. Upstairs.' 'Upstairs' was their nickname for above ground. Away from the drilling sites.

Ivers frowned. 'Like what?'

'The order's come down to shut down the drill bit.'

'What, slow it down?'

'No, *shut* it down.'

Ivers shook his head, but Kenny was already punching in the digits. The huge bit slowed to a crawl and, hissing loudly, rolled to a halt. A strange silence seemed to pervade the underground site.

Ivers glanced upwards, almost nervously.

He could feel the weight of the world – and it weighed heavy.

'Come on.' The others were ascending the pressure lifts and Ivers followed, watching his fellow LVA-ENG team members disappear up the tubes. He stumbled just before the tube engaged, fell to one knee on the hardwood deck – and then glanced up.

Buzzers were sounding across the console.

Ivers turned and moved swiftly to the hatchway leading to the tube which in turn led under their control deck; it was intended for service personnel and led down towards the bottom of the shafts to allow deeper servicing of the titanium-carbide VII. He popped the hatch and stared down into the gloom.

He licked his lips.

Going down there is a sackable offence, mused his inner voice.

But he knew. Knew that something was *wrong*.

Taking a deep breath, Ivers climbed into the tube and hit the SEND button; he felt his whole body *compress* and then he stepped out in the tiny alloy work bay.

It was very dark. But something was glowing – displaying soft blue digits.

Frowning, Ivers moved forward and stooped, finally dropping to his knees to get a closer look. There was a long thin grey box, with a small alloy cube attached. Digits flickered across the cube, and it was these that glowed.

'What is it?' he muttered.

And then he heard a noise – a scuff behind him.

He whirled – to see the barrel of a gun pointing straight at his face. He blinked, swallowed, and tried to step back. But the alloy wall was there – and he had nowhere to go. No escape. No path to freedom and life.

The figure was slim, athletic, wearing a body-hugging grey jumpsuit and a balaclava. The eyes glowed like molten copper and burned into Ivers with their fearsome fixed intensity.

Ivers lifted his hands in front of his face, as if they could halt the bullet.

'No . . .' he whispered.

The Nex moved forward, gun nudging past Ivers's defensive fingers until the barrel touched against his forehead, sliding a little against the sudden sweat there. Ivers closed his eyes. He prayed, images flickering like movie scenes through his scattered thoughts . . .

Tears rolled down his cheeks.

The Nex's finger tightened imperceptibly on the trigger.

'No . . .' whispered Ivers.

And then – the unimaginable. The pressure of the gun was released, and Ivers opened his tear-filled eyes. The Nex had tilted its head, its copper-eyed stare still fixed unblinkingly on his face.

It gestured with the gun.

'Huh?'

'It's your lucky day. Go on. Fuck off.'

'Th— tha—'

'Just go. But first, a word of advice.' Ivers halted, reluctant to turn his back on the entity with the gun. Those copper eyes made him want to pee his pants – but stinking of urine was not something that filled him with enthusiasm so he contained himself. 'There are some things that you are destined never to see in life,' the Nex said softly, its voice asexual. 'This is one of them. I suggest that you keep your mouth shut. Or I will have to shut it for you.'

Ivers scuttled away.

Calmly, the Nex folded its arms and retreated into the shadows.

*

The Comanche spun low over the Mediterranean Sea, rotor blades flashing in the sunlight as the LHTec engines whined.

The war machine came in wide across the lapping silver waters, crossing the coastline of Crete midway between Keratókambos and Ierapetra on the large island's southern shores. Carter touched down on a section of rough ground that Spiral used for such covert operations – miles from civilisation – and he and Mongrel quickly unloaded the KTM LC7 motorbikes and cammed up the chopper using netting woven with fake foliage.

They fired the bikes into life and Mila scrambled on behind Carter. They headed a short distance cross-country until they reached the narrow winding coastal road. Here Carter halted the KTM and, its engine rumbling between his legs, he peered out over the sparkling waters as the autumn sun rose above, high into the sky.

He breathed deeply, feeling simultaneously free and enslaved – jerked back on his leash by The Priest and his request for a meeting. Carter knew it would be important – and The Priest had specifically mentioned Natasha.

'Ah, fuck it.'

He twisted the throttle hard and the rear tyre spun, kicking out sand across the wind-scarred dusty tarmac. Then he virtually fired the bike down the road on an insanely accelerating surge of power.

Mila clung tightly to the back, her hair whipping in the mad breeze – and wondered at their wisdom in wearing no helmets—

Carter, eyes streaming, relaxed into the bike's rhythm and allowed his mind to merge with the machine. He could feel the thump of the tyres over the rough terrain, the violent vibrations from the broken ground through

351

the handlebars – and he grinned without humour into the wind as a sharp corner reared ahead. He leaned deep into the bend, feeling Mila squirming behind him – fighting the kick of physics – as tyres slid and barely managed to keep their grip on the dusty trail.

Behind them sand clouds bloomed.

Mongrel coughed in the dust-trail and cursed Carter with all his might.

Ten miles saw them reaching the outskirts of Ierapetra on a high coastal cliff which looked down over the distant narrow streets of Kato Mera, the old town of Ierapetra and the Kales medieval fortress which had once housed Saracen pirates.

Carter stopped the bike again and they stared down at the traditional white-walled buildings. Mongrel finally caught up, coughing on dust and glaring at Carter.

'You fucking maniac on that thing!'

'I try my best,' Carter drawled through gritted teeth. 'We going up to the Serakina?'

'That's where the co-ords specified.'

Carter wheelied the bike up the beginning of the rise, feeling Mila's hands digging like claws into his hips, and as the front wheel touched down they hit the *really* rough trail, bouncing and bumping their way along.

The Serakina was a small white building, a single-storey hotel and bar overlooking the Mediterranean. The road to it led between two mounded hills, effectively giving a single entrance into and out of the compound. Tables and chairs had been set out on a wide lawn that ended with a fence and a steep drop down a cliff onto rocks and crashing waves far below. A couple of cars were parked next to the building, beside a large 5.0-litre BMW X550 off-road vehicle with tinted windows and heavy knobbled tyres.

'I see George is home,' muttered Mongrel as they kicked the bikes on to their stands in the shade beside the white wall of the Serakina, and stretched their aching backs. Shouldering their kit, they moved to the front door which was open, allowing access to the cool interior within.

'George?' bellowed Mongrel.

A large black man appeared, his biceps thicker than a normal man's thigh, his face stern and scarred. But the scowl broke into a beaming smile when he caught sight of Mongrel. The two embraced like old friends, laughing.

'The Dog is back.'

'Nothing but a half-breed,' agreed Mongrel. 'You remember Carter?'

'I remember Carter,' said the heavily muscled man, transferring his focused round-eyed gaze and fixing Carter with a dangerous glare. 'You not bring trouble to my house this time.'

'That's a promise I cannot keep,' said Carter softly.

George stared for a while, then transferred his gaze to Mila. 'My, what a pretty creature. What is your name?'

'I am Mila.'

'She's travelling with us,' added Mongrel helpfully.

George nodded. 'Why don't you go sit in the sun-shine – I bring you out drinks. You look worn out.'

'Is there somewhere I can have a bath?' asked Mila.

'I will see to you in a moment, my sweetness,' crooned George and Mongrel flashed him a wicked smile.

'She could do with some fresh clothes. And chuck her a sterile pad while you're at it. I know you're a dab hand at dressing injuries and you not turn down the opportunity to maul her flesh.'

Carter and Mongrel walked across the grass towards the cliff edge and the timber tables. At that time of year

353

the tourist trade had quietened – trailing off after the heat of high summer – and with the recent earthquakes and their unpredictable effects and locations many people worldwide had chosen not to fly. The tourist trade had been seriously damaged by the quakes, but this suited the Spiral agents.

Mongrel slapped Carter on the back. 'How you feeling?'

Carter sighed, glancing at Mongrel 'Sore. I thought that fall from the sniper tower was going to break every fucking bone in my body. And it didn't help with Jam trying to cave in my head . . .'

'*Da*, you've been through the wars, mate.'

'I've felt worse.'

Carter went quiet suddenly and glanced out over the sparkling sea. They could just hear the crash of the waves on the rocks down below. In the distance the town of Ierapetra glittered like some ancient story of Arabian deserts and miracles.

The sound of an engine reached them, a large engine working hard up the incline towards the cliffs. Carter automatically found his hand on the Browning. Both he and Mongrel stared at the single entrance leading to the land in front of the Serakina.

A black Toyota Land Cruiser 70 4X4 rumbled into view and parked. The door opened and a lithe athletic woman stepped down. She glanced across at the two men, almost nonchalantly . . . and then froze. Her gaze met Carter's.

'Isn't that . . .' stuttered Mongrel.

Carter nodded, swallowing hard.

She was tall and slim, pale-skinned and dressed in black trousers and a short-sleeved black blouse. Her face was oval and had a light sprinkling of freckles below piercing green eyes. Her hair was long, straight and dark

354

brown, fanning behind her shoulders. And she wore a red hat, a striking contrast against the black of her clothing.

'Didn't you two . . .'

Carter nodded again, slowly, watching as the woman tilted her head – almost in confusion, almost acknowledgement – and then turned and disappeared into the cool interior of the building.

'*What's that bitch doing here?*' snapped Kade.

Carter did not reply.

Carter couldn't reply.

It had been a long time since he had seen Roxi.

A long time since he had tried to *murder* Roxi.

And the feeling tasted bad in his soul.

George arrived, bearing a tray with four bottles of beer and a plate of food. Mongrel stared at it suspiciously.

George grinned. 'Don't look like that, bad dog. That is *vrasti gida*, and that is *kolokithocorfades*. You will enjoy, this George promise you!'

'It looks minging,' growled Mongrel.

'Minging?' George frowned and boomed laughter. 'Now, you eat your breakfast and drink your beer. The sun is shining and there is lovely lady who need bath and expert medical help from ol' George.'

'You be good to her.'

'I always am.'

'Different cultures, different customs,' said Carter softly. 'Don't be such an English egg-and-chip heathen!'

George ambled across the grass in his flip-flops, his huge size making him look out of place. His shoulders squeezed together to allow him to fit through the doorway. Mongrel grasped his beer and took a long, refreshing pull. He slapped his mouth and patted his lips in appreciation. 'I fucking needed that. Didn't think I was ever

355

going drink beer again, not when that Nex put gun to my head and beat me and threw me in the truck. Carter, we up against some bad enemies this time.'

'The fuckers just won't lie down and die,' agreed Carter, taking the beer and staring at the brown bottle. He placed the chilled glass against his lips and heard a sharp intake of breath in his mind – Kade's hiss . . .

Carter paused, then closed his eyes and took a long cool drink.

It tasted good.

'What the problem between you and George?' asked Mongrel, poking suspiciously at the *kolokithocorfades*. He could have sworn the dish was staring back at him.

Carter shrugged. 'I shot some of his customers once.'

'Bad men?'

'I always shoot bad men,' said Carter sombrely. Standing suddenly, he said, 'You wait here. I'm going to call Nicky.'

Mongrel's battered face paled. 'Are you . . . you . . . ?'

'Am I going to tell her about Jam? You've got to be fucking joking! What would you say? Oh yeah, we found Jam but he's not dead, and the enemy seem to have deformed him into some kind of super-breed of Nex and he's grown body armour and tried to kill me. Should go down real well.'

'Somebody has to tell her.'

Carter rubbed at his weary eyes. 'I – just can't do it. I'm running out of energy, Mongrel. Yeah? I'm running out of the fucking will to live. This world has just got so fucking crazy.'

Mongrel nodded, and watched Carter move towards the cliff edge. He watched Carter lean over the low fence and for a moment – a split second, a fleeting slice of infinity – he thought that Carter was going to jump. Carter fished out his ECube and punched digits into the tiny alloy device.

I'm running out of the fucking will to live.

Mongrel shivered.

If someone like Carter is nearly ready to give up, then what hope is there for the rest of us? he thought viciously.

'Nicky?'

'Carter. Any news?'

'We're on the trail.'

'Have you . . . seen him?'

'No.' The lie felt bad. 'But he's – not dead.'

'Thank God!'

Carter felt a spear of ice pierce his heart. He could picture Nicky's face. Read her eyes. Understand her tears . . .

'*Tell her*,' said Kade softly at the back of his mind.

'No.'

'*Fucking tell her. She's a big girl, she can cope with it. Go on, make her fucking* century.'

Carter gritted his teeth. 'How is Natasha?'

'Stable. After you left she went into decline, but the doctors worked hard; they saved her life, Carter. But you will have to hurry – they can't say how long she can hold on.'

Carter gazed down at the cliffs and the crashing sea. The gentle blue rolled away for eternity, and the sea breeze filled him with a sense of vastness and life. He took a deep, deep breath. The air felt good in his lungs.

'Don't let her die on me,' said Carter softly.

'I'm doing my fucking best,' said Nicky. Carter could hear the strain in her voice. And he did not know why he said the next sentence; could not explain to himself the lie . . .

'I will find Jam. I will bring him back.'

They cut the connection and Carter stayed leaning over the fence, allowing the sea breeze to ruffle his hair and soothe the bruises on his battered face.

'Fuck.'

The frustration tasted bad.

Suddenly, Mongrel was there. His hand rested on Carter's shoulder and for once Carter was glad of the contact, glad of the company. He turned red-rimmed eyes on Mongrel and felt his anger melt away like heated butter.

'I'm scared, Mongrel.'

'Don't be.'

'I'm scared she's going to fucking die on me.'

Mongrel clumsily embraced Carter, hugging him hard. 'You fucking listen to me, Carter – I never seen you like this before, but you just remember I here by your side and I give my life for you, I give my life for Natasha. We find this machine, and if we have to kill Jam in process then he is casualty of war. We not make these fucking rules – and we not have to play by them. Now, you come and sit down and damn well drink this beer, or Mongrel drip-feed it to you and make sure you be drunk when The Priest arrive!'

'The Priest.' Carter laughed, rubbing at his eyes. 'Mongrel – cheers, mate. Thanks. You might be a dog and a cunt – and I know I toyed with the notion of shoot-ing you in the face back at the hospital . . . but – just thanks.'

'You not mention it, bruv.'

The sky was heavy with purple contusions of cloud. Huge swirling banks filled the night sky, blocking out the moon-light. Occasionally, a beam of white would delicately find its way free and creep tentatively across the sea, across the black oil of churning waters. Tendrils would dance across the waves, taste the crests of foam, caress the rough cliff face leading up to a low rough fence, against which a figure leant, dressed completely in black. The figure stood nonchalantly, at ease, a sea breeze ruffling his short hair. From between thin, tight lips hung a home-rolled cigarette, staining the darkness with a silver plume of smoke. The figure coughed on the harsh Greek tobacco, gazed up at the shafts of moonlight shining down from the dark broiling heavens – then lifted a bottle to his lips.

He took a drink.

A long drink.

'Fuck it,' he said. 'I can't wait any longer.'

'*You have to,*' whispered Kade.

'Why do I have to?' The snarl was filled with whisky-fuelled violence. 'What the fuck do *you* know about it?'

'*The Priest is coming. He has information. But he may betray us – and I will kill him. I will savour the death.*'

'Kade . . . I truly am fucking sick of you. I'm sick of the metallic stink in my brain. I'm sick of your bad fucking advice . . . What are you? What do you want with me? Why won't you just *leave*?'

Silence.

Carter lifted the bottle of cheap Greek whisky. He took another long pull. A little spilled down his black jacket and whisky spittle gleamed wetly on his lips, which he licked, leaving a nasty gleam.

'*You know she is going to die.*'

'Fuck you.'

'*Don't hide from the truth, Carter. Don't hide behind your stupidity!*'

'Like you give a shit.'

'*I . . . I would like to help you.*'

359

'The only person you help is yourself.'

'*Not true, Carter. Not true at all – what about in Egypt, all those Arabs with machine guns? Or in Poland? That fucker with the garrotte? And then in Belfast . . . don't get me started on Belfast . . . You should leave this place, Carter. Leave now. Get back to the Comanche, fuck Mongrel and that sniper bitch into the night and it will be like old times, just the two of us . . .*'

'I will wait for The Priest.'

'*You won't like what he has to say.*'

'And what would that be?'

'*Trust me,*' said Kade smugly.

'Get out of my head.'

'*The Priest will be here in a few hours – at dawn. You need to make your decision and make it now . . . if you meet with him you won't like what he has to say. It will be a threat to Natasha's life . . . and fuck only knows you've moaned about that dying bitch for long enough . . .*'

Carter frowned. He drank the cheap whisky, which burned his throat and his belly with its unrefined harshness. 'How could you possibly know that? How could you know such things?'

'*Trust me. I know.*'

Kade's sinister voice faded, and Carter listened to the sea crashing against the rocks in the moonlight. He frowned to himself, remembering random events from his life all leading to the insane moment where Natasha had gone down with the building under the crashing fury of the quake . . .

He remembered leaping, and being engulfed by concrete.

He remembered their last kiss. A long and lingering sweet-tainted caressing of lips.

And he remembered Kade . . . haunting whisky dreams with his vitriol . . .

360

Kade.

Kade . . .

Something pressed against Carter's back – a hand, its outline and the familiar pressure. It was Roxi, behind him, looking out over the dark sea. For a long time he said nothing, just allowed his mind to calm. Then, finally, he turned and looked into her emerald green eyes. Her hand slipped down and rested on his hip like an intruder.

Carter shivered.

'You like a whisky?'

'I thought you'd stopped drinking that.'

Carter grinned wryly. 'You never did like my Lagavulin addiction, did you?'

Roxi smiled then, and her oval face beamed like the birth of a new sun. Carter took a drink from the bottle and then reached out, touching her cheek.

'I just want to say—'

'Shh.' Her finger touched his lips and she shook her head. 'You don't need to say it. I understand.'

'You *understand*?'

'Yes.'

'About him?'

She nodded, then stepped to his side and leaned on the fence. The breeze from the sea whipped her straight brown hair out behind her and she closed her eyes, revelling in the coolness.

Carter blinked.

And remembered:

The bedroom. Her high pert breasts, the sheen of fear on her brow, the trembling of her fingers, the enticing pulse beating rapidly in her throat.

'*You're fucking insane!*' she had shouted, eyes on the gun in his fist and her tongue darting out, moistening her fear. And Kade had been like a worm in the back of his mind, whispering, hissing, filling his brain with confusion . . .

'*Kill her. She will betray you – betray us. And we shall be nothing. We shall be ashes and dust. Do it . . . or, if you're such a fucking coward, let me do it . . .*'

Carter had walked past her, thrown the gun into the lake and Roxi had left him, hurriedly pulling on her clothes, their manic animal sex of the previous night forgotten in her need to get away from him . . . From the shores of the lake he had watched her leave.

Returned, lain on the bed where he could still smell her sex and the lingering bright dregs of her perfume . . .

And cried . . .

'I believe you have a problem.'

Carter snapped back to reality. He glanced sideways at her. He found it strange – almost surreal – to be talking to somebody he had assumed he would never see again. It had been years – four or five at least, he could no longer remember, since she had walked out of that cabin room. She had not reported him – his threats, his apparent insanity. He had contacted her ten, maybe twenty times but she had ignored his calls and he could not blame her.

Their missions for Spiral had never crossed from that moment forward. They had never met.

Not until now.

'We all have problems,' said Carter coolly.

'With Natasha? The ECubes are alive with news of the quakes ripping across the world and the resurgence of the Nex soldiers. I saw Natasha's name mentioned . . . she was injured . . . *is* injured. I'm sorry.'

Carter nodded, watching the sea.

'You here on Spiral business?' he said, finally.

'Yes.' Roxi produced a cigarette, lit it, then passed it to Carter and lit another for herself. He could taste her subtle lipstick on the weed and long distant memories came flooding back—

Her naked, arching back—

Her soft skin, the welcoming velvet between her legs . . .

'No,' he hissed to himself, exhaling smoke. He met her strong gaze and she smiled, hand reaching out, stroking his stubbled cheek, thumb rubbing at a mark on the end of his chin with obvious affection.

'I've missed you.' Her words crashed like sweet thunder in his brain.

'I missed you,' he found himself saying.

She reached forward to kiss him, but he halted her, smoke stinging his eyes and carried away on the breeze. 'No, Roxi. Not now, not like this. I loved you once . . . still love you. But my mind is fucked up – I haven't the time for complications.'

'All life is a complication,' she said, moving closer, her voice husky. He looked deep into those green eyes and her beauty was astonishing to him. He could feel her body pressed against his and he was waiting for Kade to jump in, but the dark side of his soul had apparently vanished . . .

Carter pulled away, and took a long drink of the whisky.

'I cannot. *Will* not.'

Roxi smiled. 'I hated you. For a long time.'

'I understand.'

'Do you? You kept me in the dark. *He* forced us apart, wanted me dead. But what hurt me the most was that you did not tell me. You couldn't trust me, and that hurt more than a bullet in the face.'

'I was . . . scared. Scared I would lose you.'

'Like you're scared you're going to lose Natasha?'

363

'No, that's different.' Carter sighed, and took another long drink. He turned his back on Roxi and it took all his strength, all his will-power not to look round.

'Maybe in another life,' he said softly.

She came up behind him. Kissed his ear. 'I still love you. I always will . . .' She laughed. 'Maybe in another life-time, as you say, my love.' And then she was gone, gliding into the darkness.

Carter shivered, retaining her scent.

He remembered it well.

It reminded him of . . . sex. And more.

It reminded him of love . . .

Carter retired bitterly to his room to finish the bottle.

Carter was spinning, spinning down into dark dreams and the sand was hot under his bare feet, ragged trousers flapping around his ankles as the Arabs marched him out into the desert and the sun scorched his back.

Shit. Cairo7.

The Battle for the City.

Occasionally, the whip would crack against the bare raw pink skin of Carter's sunburned shoulders and through sweat and blood he glanced left at Slater – who grinned a savage grin through his own individual pain – and Carter ground his teeth as the leather bit deep. The Arab screamed at him and he whirled in the sand with eyes narrowing and lips mouthing motherfucker—

'*Let me,*' Kade had whispered.

Like silk.

Smothering his fevered brain in an ice-cool shroud.

'No.'

They heard the scream of the fighters. They thundered overhead, long and dark and gleaming, engines glowing and their noise a sonic boom that filled the heavens. Cairo

364

stood, a massive swathe of buildings and here, from the distant desert, the pyramids squatted in front of the group – the glowing scene a vast expanse of beauty, almost a perfect postcard, with the city ranged behind the pyramids. Then the bombs began to fall—

The pyramids were shattered. Smashed into rubble. Cairo was crushed by HighJ and spinning silver steel.

Carter and the other captured Spiral agents watched with mingled horror, fascination, fear and awe as buildings were swept away in a tide of fire and billowing bright gas. An armoured Egyptian column caught beside the pyramids was lifted on a wall of flame and sent spinning and howling up into the fire-filled sky.

Machine guns rattled.

Men screamed . . .

Carter watched solemnly as the distant soldiers fought. More fighters howled. More buildings were destroyed and, slowly, the Cairo skyline began to change, to warp, to disintegrate . . .

'That way!'

The whip cracked and sub-machine guns poked into backs.

Carter and the ten others were herded further into the desert, away from the savage destruction behind them. They stumbled on through the sand.

On they ploughed.

'Where are you taking us?' snarled Slater – and caught the butt of a sub-machine gun in the jaw for his persistence.

The Arabs, all brutal and battle-hardened soldiers, herded the prisoners through the fast-falling darkness. The men stumbled clumsily across the sand, hands bound tight and bodies covered with the marks of heavy beating.

The group halted, and were all given sips of water.

Carter felt himself growing weary, and for once he welcomed the return of Kade.

'*They're taking you to be executed.*'

'No, we are political prisoners. There will be an exchange. Maybe a ransom.'

'*No. They know you are Spiral. They will execute you in cold blood.*'

'Why don't they kill us here, then? Why not now?'

'*They need fucking permission from their leader, a man called A'shiek Elmora. You should keep more up to date with your fucking reading, Carter.*'

One of the captors, a short squat powerful man dressed in a grey shawl and wearing sandals, slowly approached. He offered Carter water, but as Carter reached for the cup he poured it at Carter's feet. His eyes glistened with challenge.

'You the Spiral men!' he snarled, dark eyes filled with hatred. 'You have killed many of our people . . .'

'No,' said Carter, shaking his head.

The man pulled free a long curved knife, the blade black and heavily chipped from battle use. Carter stared up at the Arab, could see the twenty other shamag-cowled men surrounding him. Camels were grunting wearily in the heat and the drone of a distant Land Rover sounded in the desert air.

'*Let me,*' crooned Kade.

'*Let me fuck them . . .*

'*Let me eat their souls.*'

Carter had smiled at the man then, staring at the scars across his cheeks with hate-filled eyes and said out loud, dry voice a croaking command to slaughter:

'Fuck them, Kade.'

And slitted feline eyes opened on a desert scene carved in black and white.

★

Kade calmed his breathing. The scene was bleached – shades of desert grey that suited Kade just fine as he tested the strength of his bound wrists and glanced down. Rope? *'Fucking amateurs,'* he snarled and—

Kade leapt towards the Egyptian, and the knife came up in a clumsy movement so sudden was Kade's attack. He twisted, and the blade sliced neatly through the rope, freeing Kade's hands. His boot came up, connecting with the Arab's chest as he whirled and took the curved blade from the man who grunted in pain and surprise, stumbling back under the force of the heavy blow to teeter and fall –

Everything seemed to move so slowly.

Kade grinned.

Kade leapt again, the blade hacking into the Arab even as the surprised man fell – and as he hit the sand the man's blood gushed out in a pulsing arc. Kade stabbed him in the face and left him gurgling as the rest of the twenty men turned their attention towards this *blur* of an escaped prisoner—

Shouts split the cool desert night – tinged with panic. Sub-machine guns were cocked in twitching hands.

Kade surged forward with a savage snarl. The blade slashed left, then right, leaving scarlet globules hanging suspended for microseconds as throats gaped wide and blood flooded from the wounds . . . Kade spun low and rammed the curved knife into another Arab's groin, wrenching it to the side as the man screamed, hands clutching at the warm flow of blood. Kade smoothly took his sub-machine gun . . . instantly bullets blasted from the muzzle – heads and chests caved in under the heavy impact of flying metal as Kade strode forward, deep into the group, with the gun hammering away in his powerful death-dealing hands—

Bodies flipped to the sand, torn wide open. Heads popped. Jaws were smashed from faces. Bullets chewed flesh and Kade swept his dark gaze without emotion across the men who died screaming and scrabbling at his feet . . .

The noise slowly died down.

Camels were barking with nostrils flared at the scent of blood and at the noise of the guns. They stamped on the sand, tethered and nervous.

Two men were groaning, lying prostrate on the desert floor.

Not a single Arab had fired a shot.

'Carter!'

Kade's head snapped left. The other Spiral men were bound, and Kade grinned at them savagely and said, 'Just give me a moment to provide an encore, gentlemen.'

Kade picked up another sub-machine gun and moved to the two groaning men. He knelt beside the first, looked into the dark cruel eyes, then smashed the butt of the gun against his forehead several times, cracking open the skull.

'Carter, man, what the fuck are you doing?'

Kade lifted the gun and pointed it at the group of captured Spiral agents.

'You got a fucking problem?' he screamed, insanity dancing in his eyes, across his twisted face. 'I'll fucking kill you all, I'll fucking smear your blood on my face and—'

He glanced down.

Shot the last Egyptian in the face. Emptied the magazine until there was nothing left of the man's head, just a dark purple pulp with shards of bone splintered obscenely on top of a bullet-torn neck stump strung with skeins of twitching muscle and ligament.

The body jerked spasmodically, a last pulsing of its blood staining the sand.

Kade climbed to his feet, staring around at the twenty dead bodies. He realised that he was breathing hard and he dropped the gun to the ground and started to laugh. 'Welcome to Egypt,' he screamed as the other Spiral operatives looked on in horror. 'Yeah, welcome to fucking Cairo as well!'

And instead of this being the end of the horror, it was, in fact, just the beginning.

Carter awoke, shivering. The whisky bottle was by his side, drained, and his head was pounding. Weak light crept from behind the shutters. A diseased rat had crawled into his mouth and died.

Cairo7.

He shivered again, horrified at the dream – at the reliving of Kade's first bout of true insanity, on show for others to appreciate.

Before Cairo7 Carter had always retained some semblance of control. But in the desert that night, Kade had pushed Carter into a deep mental recess and locked the door. Kade had mocked him. Kade had punished him. Kade had fucked him very severely.

Carter still remembered, as they made a cross-desert dash for friendly lines, the fear emanating from his own men, the other Spiral agents whom Kade had reluctantly released. They sat near him only so not to antagonise him further. They shared their water only so that he would not shoot them in the face.

Not Slater.

Slater had watched him with a dark intelligence.

Slater had shown no fear.

It was as if Slater had understood.

Carter heard their comments as they made camp without fire in wadis, hunkering under outcroppings of rock or in shallow caves. They had whispered among themselves.

'Did you see him move?'

'He was so fucking fast . . .'

'Like a fucking demon . . .'

'He killed twenty armed men single-handed—'

'They couldn't even fucking touch him!'

'And what about when he unloaded a full clip into that poor bastard's face?'

'He was fucking insane . . . did you see it? In his eyes? He was possessed *. . .'*

Carter rolled from the bed and stood, naked, scratching his belly. He moved to the sink and poured himself a glass of water, downing it in one. His door burst open and Mongrel stood there, fully kitted and ready to move.

'Carter?'

'Hmm?'

'The Priest is a couple of miles away. The ECube comm says he'll be fifteen minutes. Get your shit together.'

Carter smiled at Mongrel. 'I told you not to let me drink the whole fucking bottle.'

'Hey.' Mongrel spread his hands, gaze fixed on Carter's face. 'You looked like you needed it, mate. I'll meet you out front in five.' He stared, frowning, at Carter's dangling penis, his nakedness, realising Carter would need time to dress. 'Better make that ten. And don't forget to put your fucking pants on!'

Then he was gone, leaving the door wide open and a cool breeze invading Carter's privacy.

'You're an animal,' muttered Carter, searching, eyes bloodshot, for his clothes.

★

Carter and Mongrel sat in the dawn sunshine, looking down over the steep winding trail and waiting for The Priest.

Carter sipped at his steaming coffee.

'You feeling bad?' muttered Mongrel with a smirk.

'I've felt better.'

'Did you speak with Roxi last night?'

'Yes.'

'Did you fuck her?'

'Mongrel! Natasha is dying and my only thought is of saving her life . . . do you really rank me so low in the scheme of things? Lower than a fucking reptile?'

'*I* would have.'

'She's pretty,' acknowledged Carter, 'but I think my energies are best put to other uses. And my bastard ribs are cracked, I swear it. That bastard Jam didn't half give me a kicking . . .'

'Have you thought any more about him? And that ex-Spiral fucker Gol?'

Carter downed his coffee and refilled his mug from the jug, tipping in plenty of sugar and milk. He sighed, shaking his head. 'Hey, Mongrel, as far as I'm concerned the whole world has gone mad. We've got earthquakes ripping up various countries, Jam transformed into God only knows what sort of experimental entity by Durell, Gol back from the dead, and now I've got Roxi drifting into my life from a past I had practically forgotten – a past where I tried to murder her. I can't really say that anything else could possibly surprise me.'

'Well, let's see what The Priest has to say.'

'It better be pretty fucking damn important,' growled Carter, 'because he's wasting my time right now.'

'You soon ask him,' rumbled Mongrel, gesturing at the trail.

371

The Priest laboured up the path.

His grey robes flapped around his titanic frame, his bushy beard swayed in out-of-synch rhythm with his rosary beads, and his sandals trod the rocky sand trail with an awkward step. He carried his Bible in both outstretched hands, like a magic talisman, a totem of power.

Carter and Mongrel watched the barrel-chested man's long haul up the mountain.

It gave them some small pleasure to see him sweat like a pig.

The Priest finally arrived on the plateau and smiled down from his great height, sweat streaming from his forehead and great patches of it staining the cloth under his arms. 'Behold, my children!'

'At last, the prodigal returns,' said Carter through a veil of smoke. 'Coffee?'

'Yes. Six sugars.'

'*Six?*'

'A growing lad like me needs to keep up his strength. Now, down to business.' From within his robes he brought out two ECubes and passed one to Carter, one to Mongrel.

'Updated?' asked Carter.

'More than an update, my son,' said The Priest. 'These are new revisions, running V5.0 ICARUS op systems, now up to 18GHz dual-RISC processors and 1024 gig of Optical-RAM. The whole network has been revised after many recent breaches by the Nex – the whole encryption stage has been revamped, and if you key in your DSquad code then you can see the schematics and check out all the new functions. There are a few new little tricks. The Lord would be proud of such innovation.'

Carter and Mongrel handed over their old units. The Priest took his coffee and sat cross-legged on the grass.

The sea crashed distantly, and a cool breeze ruffled his beard and cooled the sweat on his brow.

'I have answers,' he said, simply.

'What is going on?'

'Since we sunk the Spiral_mobile battleship just over a year ago, we have become complacent. We thought the Nex were on the decline. The SAD teams were doing their job, exterminating what Nex filth they could ferret out in small pitched battles. But we have all been wrong. The Nex soldiers that the SAD teams were taking out were *rejects* – the weak and the lame. Apparently, when a Nex is created there can be many problems with the DNA coding and restructuring – the blending, as Durell would call it. For the past year we have been fed these mewling weaklings as decoys while Durell built an army.'

'An army?' rumbled Mongrel. 'You mean . . .'

'We estimate that Durell has a quarter of a million Nex soldiers, although he could have more. He has also enlisted many thousands of mercenaries to do his bidding. It would seem that his company – Leviathan Fuels – has provided him with the funding he needs.'

'LVA?' said Carter. 'So Durell owns the fuel company?'

'More than that,' said Durell softly. 'I have encoded documents – the code took us many hours to crack and I risked my own life and limb to retrieve the items concerned. They show a machine – a machine, built to a very specific and strange design, that can control *earthquakes*. Now, there seem to be strategic points around the globe where Durell drops a shaft, mainly under the pretence of mining LVA, when really the LVA is a *catalyst*. In every shaft he plants a machine – which he calls a QuakeEngine, or Foundation Stone – and when networked through a "QuakeHub", a central unit devised to focus all this power and allow networked command

373

globally, our enemies can force earthquakes at quite specific locations.'

'Why would he want to do this?' rumbled Mongrel.

Carter sighed. 'Durell believes that Spiral has grown weak and fat on the spoils of war. He believes that he and his happy band of Nex can do a fucking superior job. But first he has to persuade everybody that he's the boss. If he can target cities, even whole countries with earthquakes – fuck, combined with quarter of million Nex soldiers in support he can hold the world to ransom. What he failed to bring about with the QIII processor, it would seem he now seeks to achieve with brute force.'

'His Achilles heel is that the network is not fully functional,' said The Priest. 'For whatever reason, events are accelerating beyond his control and his QuakeHub network is not quite fully operational. Governments have received encrypted messages outlining how the quakes that recently ripped through London, LA, Moscow, Paris . . . they are just warning shots. Jabs to the nose. Tasters. But when the network is complete then he can truly play God. His sacrilege will be complete and he will be ready to administer a smiting from Heaven.

'You did an excellent job in Slovenia. Spiral have instructed Simmo and the TankSquads to hunt out the LVA pumps and destroy them – if we move quickly then Durell will not be able to get his QuakeHub network fully functional, and even though he can control the quakes it will be as nothing to the power he could unleash if all the sites are linked and uploaded. Spiral is working with world governments even as we speak, and if we move with enough speed we can destroy his sites quicker than he can build them . . . we can halt Durell and his army before they begin to march. All it needs is the cooperation of the international powers.'

'You could have told us all this via ECube,' growled Mongrel. 'Why you drag us from our mission? Why waste our time sitting here on dumb arses getting fat and frustrated?'

'The whole network is compromised,' said The Priest sombrely. 'Hence the new ECube machines . . .' He glanced then at Carter, and the Spiral operative felt suddenly, deeply uneasy.

Cold.

Kade's words came back to haunt him.

'The Priest will be here in a few hours – at dawn. You need to make your decision and make it now . . . if you meet with him you won't like what he has to say. It will be a threat to Natasha's life . . . and fuck only knows you've moaned about that dying bitch for long enough . . .'

Carter fixed his stare on The Priest. Smoothly, under the table and out of view from the cross-legged Spiral man, he eased free his Browning and it rested bulky in his palm like an old friend. Something was not right, Carter realised. This whole meeting was *wrong*.

'What is on your mind?' said Carter softly.

The Priest bowed his head for a moment. One hand touched his rosary beads, as if for reassurance. Then he met Carter's glare with his piercing gold-flecked eyes and there was strength there, an inhuman strength that could only belong to the head of the Spiral secret police.

'You must abandon your mission,' said The Priest.

'What mission?' said Carter easily. He flicked free the safety catch.

'You seek the machine that creates the Nex. You seek to use the machine for its original purposes – that of healing. You wish to bring Natasha and your unborn child back from the brink of death. All these things I know to be true. All these things I understand.' The Priest was

375

calm, and perfectly collected. He did not blink. 'But you must still abandon this mission.'

'Why?'

'The answer to this question is a complicated one.'

'Fucking try me,' snapped Carter. Mongrel placed his hand on Carter's arm, and Carter could sense his friend's sudden fear. 'You ask me to abandon my fucking woman. You ask me to let her fucking die and you will not give me an answer? Fuck you.'

'I do not ask,' said The Priest softly. 'I tell.'

'Tell?'

Carter laughed harshly and The Priest found himself staring down the Browning's dark muzzle. 'I think you need to give me some fucking answers, Holy Man – before I send you to meet the God that you claim created you.'

'So be it,' said The Priest softly, his eyes glittering. He sipped at his coffee, his huge frame relaxed in his seated position on the grass. Then he smiled, as if amused by some internal dialogue.

'Carter, put the gun away.'

Carter ignored Mongrel.

'Durell has machines that were built before our civilisation arose. One is the machine used to create the Nex, the Avelach. Another is the QuakeEngine – which is based on the design of the original machine found by the Nazis in 1940 and unlocked decades later by Spiral research teams led by Feuchter, Gol and Durell. These machines are thousands and thousands of years old and use archaic electronics similar to those of the machines we currently field, but they operate using different materials and superior processes. In truth, they are much more advanced than our own technological developments.'

'Get to the fucking point.'

The Priest sipped at his sweet coffee once more, unperturbed by the Browning and the thirteen rounds in its magazine. 'You seek the machine that will heal Natasha. Durell holds this machine – as he holds the QuakeHub. And yet he is in delicate negotiations with major world governments right now . . . If you stumble in, firing off a thousand rounds of ammunition, and take this machine from Durell – or piss him off in some other unexpected way – you could accelerate proceedings. You could destroy the bridges that the politicians have worked so hard to build.'

'You think I would start a war?' said Carter incredulously.

'Maybe unwillingly. We cannot antagonise Durell directly. You must put off this mission – at least for a couple of days. When the politicians – the governments of the world unite against this gigantic threat, and when the TankSquads start hitting the LVA mines, then events will escalate at a catastrophic rate . . . But we cannot move until we are ready . . . We are buying time, Carter, buying military muscle, and the last thing Spiral needs are loose cannons. I fear Durell has become too powerful even as we speak. We *need* this time . . .'

'In a few days Natasha may be dead.'

'Then Natasha will be dead. She will be a casualty of war. Her fate is in the hands of God.'

'Not my fucking God,' said Carter brusquely. 'There is something you're not telling me, Priest. You're holding out on me . . . come on, who are the other players in this game?' He waved the Browning towards The Priest's face.

'There are some factors of which I cannot speak. I can only repeat the direct order – which has come right from the top. Spiral is ordering you to abandon this mission – to *postpone* it, if you will – until you have the all-clear. If you choose to ignore this direct order then I have instructions to kill you.' He glanced at Mongrel coolly. 'And any who stand with you.'

Carter lifted his coffee and drained it.

'I think that you should leave.'

The Priest climbed ponderously to his feet and stared at Carter. Hard. 'I know it is a bitter pill to swallow, but trust me, Carter. There are things at work here that you could never understand. The doctors give favourable reports about Natasha's progress – you may yet have the time to save her. But the world does not. It is a sacrifice that we must all make – it is what she would expect. What we would *all* expect. The sacrifice of one to save many . . . Natasha is not divine, Carter. She cannot live for ever.'

'You have no idea what you ask,' whispered Carter.

'I do,' said The Priest gently, his gaze softening. 'Don't make me come looking for you, Carter. Don't make me hunt you down – it would be a waste of a good man. One of the best we have.'

The Priest turned and lumbered towards the trail. There he met Roxi, and they exchanged quiet words. The Priest disappeared behind the house and they heard an engine fire up.

Roxi approached.

'Will you do as he says?'

Carter frowned. 'You are working with The Priest?'

'Yes. This was our meeting point.' She reached out to stroke Carter's cheek but he pulled away. 'Until the next time, lover.'

'There will never be a next time.'

Roxi smiled, a dazzling smile, bright green eyes glinting. 'Oh, but there will.'

'Do you want me to burn her?'

Roxi moved away and climbed into the Toyota Land

Cruiser. Wheels spun and the big vehicle disappeared in a roar of black fumes. Carter sat down again, toying with his Browning idly, his face an unreadable mask.

'More coffee?'

'No, we're moving out.'

Mongrel frowned at Carter. 'Where to?'

'After the machine. Fuck The Priest, this isn't his woman dying on a doctor's slab. I don't trust him – I think he is spinning us a whole crock of shit. If we find Durell, then we find the machine to heal Natasha *and* the QuakeHub – we can take out his control of the earthquakes. And a bullet in his brain will end his thoughts of world domination once and for all.'

'They will have people on that,' said Mongrel softly. 'Specialists.'

Carter laughed hollowly. 'And what the fuck are we? No, there is some other game being played here and I will not follow their rules. I refuse.'

'You heard The Priest. He said this was an order. Straight from the top.'

'I don't care,' said Carter. He glanced at Mongrel. 'It's up to you, Mongrel. You can either come with me, or you can stay here. Either way I am going after Jam, I'm going after Durell – and I will find that fucking machine or die in the process.'

'I don't know . . .'

'Make your mind up. But do it fast.'

Suddenly, George came pounding out of the house carrying three Heckler & Koch MP5 A3 9mm submachine guns. He tossed one to Carter and one to Mongrel. Mila appeared in the doorway, face ashen, the sniper rifle gripped in her shaking hands.

'What is it?' growled Mongrel.

'I've just had a call. There's been trouble. Down in the

town, a shoot-out with local police. Eighteen dead local policemen – murdered by masked killers. They are in three trucks and are heading this way.'

'You sure?' snapped Carter.

George nodded, heavy brows creased.

'Nex,' said Mongrel.

'Has to be. Quick, get your shit together . . .'

George pointed. 'Too late, my friends.' He cocked the weapon in his huge hands and Mila sprinted over to the small group. Coming up the distant trail, engines screaming and dust pluming around their wheels, came three squat black trucks, sunlight glinting menacingly from their darkened windows.

'Fuck. Mongrel, go grab the packs. We'll cover the road.' Carter's eyes scanned the trail, which led up through sparse woodland and mounds of rough grass and coarse sand, then checked the two natural hills – low humps of grass-covered rock that formed a natural funnelling point ideal for defence, before the road opened out once more onto the plateau on which the Serakina was built overlooking the sea. 'Mila, you get up there with your sniper rifle. Start shooting as soon as you can. George, you get on the other side.'

'And where are you going?' rumbled the huge black man.

Carter grinned wolfishly. 'I have a fucking surprise for our little masked gatecrashers.'

The three black trucks lurched up the rough trail, tyres bouncing in ruts and suspension smashing into over-stressed chassis. Carter calmly checked the magazine of his Browning, holstered the weapon and weighed the Heckler and Koch MP5 thoughtfully in his grip. The trucks were coming closer quickly and he could spy the distant glinting Mercedes logos splashed proudly across matt black grilles. With howls of metal agony, the trucks were being hammered by their Nex drivers . . .

Mila started to fire . . .

Heavy-calibre sniper rounds flew through the early-morning sunlight. The lead Merc's windscreen took two hits, then the front tyre exploded in a shower of mashed rubber and the truck veered to one side, listing dangerously before rolling onto its side and sliding across the rough ground towards the edge of the cliff . . .

'Keep shooting!' yelled Carter, sprinting up the incline behind Mila to gaze down at the stricken truck. Carter pulled free the tiny black alloy cube and slotted it neatly onto the Browning. There came a deep hum as Carter aimed at the vehicle with the NeedleClip-modded Browning. There was a click and the tiny missile flashed from the gun's barrel. The doors of the Mercedes were opening as the projectile hit the underside of the chassis. Metal exploded and the van was picked up and tossed over the cliff in a fist of curled flames. Trailing thick black smoke, it disappeared into the sea far below—

Mongrel appeared as Carter sprinted back down the incline. George opened fire on the two remaining trucks from the opposite hill; bullets slapped along their flanks as Mila continued to fire shots from her sniper's weapon. Mongrel tossed Carter his carbine, and with their sub-machine guns they opened fire from the centre of the trail . . .

Bullets ate the grilles of one truck and Carter and Mongrel split, sprinting in opposite directions as the vehicles broke through onto the plateau and skidded in wide arcs. One Mercedes crashed through the wooden tables and scythed in a circle, tail end smashing through the fence overlooking the sea—

Doors slammed open and bullets tore the turf at Carter's feet. He dropped to one knee, and his return fire picked up a masked Nex and spun the rag-doll figure over the fence and down towards the crashing waves. One truck's rear doors opened and everything became an insanity of bullets and crackling gunfire. Mongrel crouched by the edge of the Serakina's white building and drilled the trucks with bullets. Hot metal tore a line of holes up the wall by his face and he retreated, changing mags, concrete dust stinging in his eyes.

Three Nex charged at Carter.

He shot two of them in the face as their bullets zipped past his shoulder and throat. Then a heavy-calibre round cracked from behind him, exploding the third Nex's face in a bloom of blood. The body fell into the grass, tumbling up to Carter in a tangle of limbs, and Carter whirled low, hearing another exchange—

'Carter!' shouted Mongrel. 'The back of the trucks are empty!'

Carter cursed. Of course – the rest of the Nex would be coming in on foot from different directions. The trucks were a decoy . . . He glanced up to George – who was shooting at figures unseen. *Something* chilled Carter's soul.

He sprinted across the ground, yelling, 'Mongrel, start your fucking bike! And take Mila with you!' George was changing mags as Carter reached his side, and Carter gazed down on the rough hillside to the east of the track. Across the rough ground raced thirty Nex from different positions, firing as they came, using the trees for cover. Carter ducked back, but George took three rounds high in the chest. His blood splashed sickeningly across Carter's face and he was tossed limply down the slope and rolled to a halt at the base, his huge limbs quivering.

Carter scrambled down to George's side as Mongrel's bike started. With an abused-engine howl, the KTM rocketed up the hill and Mila climbed onto the back. The bike churned rough ground, skidding in an arc towards Carter who pointed down the road.

'Get the fuck out of here!'

Mongrel's anger-filled gaze surveyed George's blood-speckled face.

Then, without a word, he screwed the throttle hard around, the back wheel spat sand and grass, gripped and then propelled them down the road and away from the Serakina. Carter heard Mongrel's sub-machine gun fire from the road . . .

He stared at George.

The large black man smiled, blood staining his teeth.

'I thought you said you not bring trouble to my house?'

'I'm sorry, my friend.'

George grasped Carter's hand with an iron grip. 'Shoot a few in the fucking face for me, Carter? You manage that?'

Carter nodded. 'I'll see what I can do . . .'

But George was already dead.

Carter dropped the MP5. Swinging his M24 carbine across his back, he sprinted to the KTM LC7. He fired the engine, locked the front brake, spun the bike around in a circular skid then released the brake. The front wheel lifted and Carter dipped his head low, chest touching the tank as he howled the bike towards the road leading from the plateau mountain top.

The bike raced from between the small hills, through the natural gateway and onto the dusty trail. The Nex were closer now, coming in from different areas of cover. Bullets whined past him as Carter palmed his Browning and glanced left. He launched ten NeedleRounds into the charging ranks of the Nex.

383

The explosions stuttered like fireworks, fire leaping into the air with charred bodies spinning in its midst. Nex were slammed into one another, into the air, into the ground, into the trees and rocks with their flesh pulped, their weapons mangled. The explosions blasted, and flames curled and ate flesh.

The Nex were consumed . . .

The KTM powered down the track.

Bullets chased Carter, and he held the throttle full open as the first bend – and temporary safety from bullets – loomed ahead.

Something slammed into his back.

The KTM faltered . . .

Carter leaned into the corner, pain pulsing through him, and increased the speed of the bike. He hammered along a dusty road, the dirt trails dropping away under his wheels from the immediate danger behind.

Carter coughed, his tongue thick in his mouth.

The road seemed to shimmer ahead of him.

Suddenly, agony took Carter in its fist and crushed him. The bike's front wheel slammed against a rock with a crunch of steel and Carter, weight pitched forward from the blow against his back, felt the front suspension sag on heavy oil. The handlebars slammed to the left with a snap of metal against metal. Nausea flooded him with horror as he was flung from the KTM at eighty miles an hour and the world rushed around him in a confused blur as he tried to curl into a ball and behind him the bike screamed a high-pitched metal scream grating along the trail pissing its death sparks across the gravel . . .

The ground slammed up to meet Carter.

He hit hard, all air kicked from his body, and slid along the rough trail for what felt like a lifetime. The bike spun off to one side, twisting and groaning in metal defiance.

Still sliding, gravel biting through his clothing, Carter wanted to scream, to reach out and halt himself, to tell himself this was just a bad dream. But a bend in the trail loomed and Carter struck a low ridge of rough sand and grass. He was catapulted up, flung tumbling into a sparse copse and rolled to a final crunching halt on dead wood, old leaves and discarded pine needles.

Carter lay stunned, just trying to breathe.

For a lifetime.

Pain hammered through him.

In the gloom under the canopy of trees the world had suddenly gone very dark. Carter, finally managing to breathe in heavy gasping gulps, saw that most of the skin had been scraped from his right arm. He groaned and tried to sit up but rocked back as pain punched him down.

And then he was suddenly looking into copper eyes.

The Nex stood, sub-machine gun loose in its gloved hands.

Part of its mask was scorched and torn, the skin on half of its face beneath the eye a mess of molten flesh. It was watching Carter as it breathed smoothly, apparently undisturbed by its half-melted visage.

With hands that – Carter noticed – did not shake, it ejected a spent magazine, which tumbled lazily to the ground. Slowly, it retrieved a fresh one and slotted it home. There was a click that seemed to last for ever.

Carter tried to reach his Browning.

Then realised the weapon had gone.

'Mr Carter.'

He glanced at the Nex. 'Yeah, fucker?'

'It's been a pleasure.'

The Nex lifted its gun and pulled the trigger.

CHAPTER 14

BRAWL

The WIC – or World Investigation Committee – had a central headquarters in Washington DC. The building was massive, an incredible modern structure of glass, steel, alloy and stone glinting menacingly in the strong sunlight. It sat in grounds patrolled by soldiers armed with seriously heavy weaponry. Sniper towers and advanced air defences squatted at every corner. At any one time the WIC HQ was manned by elite soldiers from no less than fifteen different countries.

At the HQ's heart lay the Central Chambers, attended either in person or by digital personifications of world leaders. One such meeting was in progress, chaired by General Tetalyahevsky of Russia, Patron San Lee of China and Lady Emma C. Dickinson from the United Kingdom. Nearly five hundred officials from around the globe were present, and a general murmur was echoing softly around the huge vaulted stone ceilings of the Chambers. The noise died to a hush as the images of earthquakes and global chaos faded from the huge fifty-foot optical-plasma screen against one wall to be replaced by a dark, hooded figure who lifted one finger and held it up as if waiting for something of importance . . .

The murmurs increased in volume and Durell looked out from the digital screen at this gathering of the world's most important and influential people, who had their fingers on the red buttons of nuclear doom.

Durell smiled within the folds of his hood.

And when he spoke, everybody present was totally focused on his soft, gentle voice.

He had gained their attention. 'You have seen before you the power of the quake. And you have been shown the proof that I have complete control, and can command the earth's plates to move at will.'

There came a hiss of alarmed voices.

'Now, ladies and gentlemen, I have a most serious proposal for you.'

The sky was a massive expanse of blue, a huge vault soaring over the gentle curve of the world. It was scattered with trailing wisps of bedraggled cotton-wool cloud and brightness glinted off a small black alloy object that spun – and hammered past at an incredible velocity.

A rolling sonic boom followed it and the tiny single-seat aircraft, nicknamed a *Manta*, banked gently, sunlight glittering along its pulled-back black alloy wings. The twin tail jets glowed white with cold matrix fire as the machine hit 1,900 k.p.h.

'PDSK57 calling in, over.'

'We have you, PDSK57. Over.'

'I've found a Charlie. Sending coordinates now.'

'Thank you for that, PDSK57. Out.'

Haggis looked over at Mo and gave a thumbs-up. Mo nodded, and slowly – inching forward – the two men moved through the rainforest on their stomachs, crawling through the thick dense foliage and evergreen *Chinchona*, noses twitching at the heavy fragrance of the flowers.

Twenty miles behind them sat ten TankSquads, awaiting their report and an update from the Spiral mainframes. They knew there was an LVA site there – south of San José del Guaviare, Colombia – but had been put on hold just as they thought they were about to see action. A wave of disappointment had swept through the ranks and Haggis and Mo had scouted ahead to gather any possible further intel.

The two men slowly emerged on a clifftop, a jagged ridge tumbling away to a basin of dense jungle foliage. The sun beat down and the men – both of them large – were sweating heavily, their clothing sporting huge stinking stains.

Mo ran a hand across his shaved bullet head, wiping off a sheen of sweat, and turned his obsidian-eyed gaze on his partner, who passed him a canteen.

Haggis, who chain-smoked a hundred and forty a day, was quivering from nicotine withdrawal. He nodded down into the basin to where a huge section of hardwoods – mahogany, oak and lignum vitae – had been cleared and bundled with wrist-thick strands of heavily woven rope. The mammoth logs formed an outer perimeter wall. The LVA pump was working hard, and the drone of distant engines could be heard over the rich and exuberant sounds of the jungle.

'I fucking hate jungle missions, said Mo, dribbling water down his triangular black beard. 'It's just so bloody hot! I was not built for this kind of climate . . .'

'Yeah, you're a bit of a fat walrus, mate.' Haggis grinned. 'I've relayed the coordinates. Better get back or that lunatic Simmo will go bananas! Come on.'

The two men turned, and eased themselves back into the jungle.

From the cloaking darkness of the thick vegetation, Nex soldiers watched them leave, their copper eyes bright and emotionless.

The wastelands of the Arctic spread out in front of Jader as he dropped the jet's speed and heard the decelerating whine of the engines. He spun the *Manta* low over the broad undulating plains of ice and could see an awesome, colossal arc of white. Ice crackled from the *Manta*'s wings and Jader dropped the SK even lower, skimming the snowy expanse. Below him he could glimpse the mad rush of wind-sculpted ice-towers, the diamond sparkle of stalactite-crusted chasms and a territory that was wild, vast and untameable.

Jader grinned.

He loved the magic of the Arctic.

Lifting the *Manta* he soared up into the cloudless freezing skies. Engines howled with cold matrix pulses and he levelled the Spiral jet, which seemed to float for a while. His scanners scrolled fat green readings of data over the jet's monitors. Jader watched them with one eye, again slowing the *Manta*'s speed and peering out.

'There,' he muttered.

Hidden among a small range of ice hills, and surrounded by walls of banked white ice sat an LVA pump. It had been painted, obviously to camouflage it against this Arctic landscape, but Jader's sharp eyes had picked it out.

He blipped the coordinates.

'Well done, Jader. Over.'

'How many we got, Control? Over.'

'That's eighty-six Charlies. You coming home? Over.'

'Be home soon, Mother. You make sure my tea is ready.' Jader grinned within his HIDSS. 'Out.'

As he killed the ECube-linked comm, red warnings suddenly scrolled and flashed over his monitor. 'Shite.' Jader jinked the controls and the engines screamed as the jet leapt forward. Something glinted beneath it, a sudden snapping flash of silver. The jet banked and Jader's eyes went wide as a sliver of alloy spun in a wide glittering arc ahead of him and then—

Hung. Suspended.

Jader smashed the *Manta* down towards the ground and the glinting missile dived, following closely, locked on. Jader banked right and severe-turn and proximity warnings lit up on the console as he felt his guts wrenching within his suddenly fragile human shell. The missile powered past over one wing and Jader steadied the jet – then spun it in a tight curve and began to climb.

The missile followed.

Heading away from the LVA site, Jader licked his suddenly parched lips and the HIDSS flickered through different types of offensive weaponry, attempting a match. It could not target the missile, could not recognise the weapon – and so could not suggest the best evasive action.

Jader urged the jet until it was clipping 2,100 k.p.h., a tiny black blur flashing low over the landscape. The missile paced it, just behind and slightly to one side. Jader felt himself go cold and dead inside. This was like no missile he had ever before encountered – or seen – even in the high-tech development cells below several Spiral HQs.

'PDSK57 to Mother, I have been compromised, I repeat, I have been compromised. Sending images now . . .' The HIDSS whirred around him and relayed data on the missile. Jader dropped the jet towards the ground, eyes frantically searching—

The ice blow him rose and fell.

And then he spotted it, a wide crevasse glittering blue and as inviting as death . . . He spun the *Manta* in a tight circle and then down into the crevasse, reducing his speed slightly as the walls leapt up above him and he was suddenly plunged into a world of cold ice and shimmering frozen slick walls.

The jet flew through the deep blue silent gloom.

Engines whined, noises reverberating from the ice walls.

Still, neither the HIDSS nor the on-board computers linked to the Spiral mainframes showed an enemy: no missile in hot pursuit, nothing. The *Manta* jet flittered through and beneath the ice, which flashed past at a terrifying rate to either side. Data crackled across Jader's scanners. And then—

The crevasse plunged under snow. An ice ceiling appeared above the jet and Jader felt himself slowing it even more, his eyes searching for the missile. Rear scanners displayed nothing – it was no longer tracking him but something told him not to believe that he had evaded his pursuer.

It had been too—

Too . . .

He groped for a word. And settled for 'sentient'.

Now, encased in ice, Jader spun through the Spiral mainframes' inventories.

'Jader? Over.'

'Yeah, Mother. You find anything?'

'Sorry, Jader. Unidentifiable. You're on your own, buddy. I'll keep you online, see if anything materialises while you—'

'Fuck!'

The jet was smashed down, wings flashing into the

vertical as a fall of ice and rock invaded the space within the crevasse. Then the world opened up above. Sunlight glinted through snow and ice and Jader tentatively brought the jet to ground level and shot like a bullet from an ice gun up into the waiting infinite sky—

The missile was hovering.

Patient.

It accelerated at an awesome rate and ploughed into the underbelly of the *Manta* like a needle piercing flesh. There was a sudden, silent microsecond of impact – of suspension—

And then a purple explosion. Gases bloomed and curled, like flames around the edges of paper. They sucked in on themselves until they glowed, an intense inferno of melting alloy and steel merging with dripping white-hot flesh and liquid bone.

Jader and the *Manta* became, for a nightmarish instant, as one.

And then scattered in glowing arcs across the ice in a scree of twisted detritus.

The explosion echoed across the snowy wilderness.

Simmo sat on the HTank, elbow on his knee and chin on his fist. His expression was thunderous. His eyebrows were dark-bushed storm-clouds. His lips were razors of ruby lightning. His eyes were pools of comet-fallen mercury. And his clenched fists were the threatening knots of tropical hardwoods battered by the eternal elements.

'Are you . . . OK?'

'Of course I'm not fucking OK!' screamed the Sergeant, gazing down at Oz and Rogowski. The two men took a step back at Simmo's wrath, Oz spilling his tea from his plastic pint mug, huge crooked nose wavering a little. 'We're here, in the fucking Colombian jungle, fucking sweating like fucking pussies, we've found the enemy and what do Spiral HQ fucking say? The fucking politicians are fucking working on a fucking solution and so we can't bomb the fuck out of the bastards.

'Of *course* I'm not fucking OK! In fact, I'm ready to . . . *kill*.'

His dark gaze swivelled around to where Kattenheim was seated on a felled hardwood tree – his face and upper torso a mass of battered, bruised and *sliced* flesh.

Kattenheim was staring at Simmo. And then he smiled.

Simmo felt his temper exploding, but calmed himself.

'You want a cigarette?' said Oz uncertainly.

'The Sarge not smoke cigarettes.'

'A drop of whisky?' suggested Rogowski.

'You boys should know by now! Sarge not drink on ops.'

'Yeah, I know, but I just thought . . .'

'Yes?'

For such a simple word, it carried a wealth of threat. Like a barbed wire maggot in an apple. Rogowski, a soldier who had been shot in the head once and in the body fourteen times, was oblivious to such verbal niceties.

'. . . I just thought you might savour a nip, you know, after Kattenheim there wouldn't speak despite your best efforts with the iron bar – God, I thought you were going to kill him! And then we get lifted all the way out here, spend ten hours piloting fucking tanks through jungle lanes just to find . . . to find . . . that we . . . we are . . . we are not allowed . . .'

He finally faltered.

Simmo's scowl could not get any blacker. He glanced again at Kattenheim, seated calmly on the log with his hands tied tightly behind his back with wire. His ankles and knees were also bound tight. Spiral were taking no chances with the Nex warrior.

Simmo drank from his canteen, then hopped off the HTank and moved forward past the stationary bulks of other tanks to where Kattenheim sat. Simmo glanced down at him and the Nex looked up, scarred red eyes defiant, gleaming.

'You want a drink, fucker?'

'That would be pleasant.' Kattenheim's words were a little distorted by his broken jaw and cheekbone. Simmo stood, drinking, water dribbling down his chin.

'Well, fuck you. Talk to us and I might allow you to drink. And eat. And maybe even sleep a little.'

Kattenheim merely smiled, a smile that disheartened Simmo. Deep down he wanted to kill the Nex – but Spiral had instructed him to bring him back alive for trial.

He moved back to the HTank, frustration gnawing him.

There came a call from the jungle, and some of the TankSquad men lowered their weapons as Mo and Haggis moved into view, M24 carbines held pointing towards the ground in case of NDs.

Mo made his report to Simmo, who nodded, face blank. Then they sent the report to Spiral and awaited further orders. Simmo sent some more scouts out, securing a wider perimeter around the tanks. As night started to fall the men began slinging hammocks between the tanks and some surrounding mahogany trunks. Simmo had only once – obstinately – slept on the floor in the jungle. He'd suffered 239 ant bites, huge swellings that had left him in blood-red throbbing agony and in no fit state to piss, never mind fight in a covert jungle operation. Simmo was a big man, who hated hammocks – but in this contest with the vicious and uncompromising rainforest he had backed down after the first jab, never mind waiting for the end of the first round.

Darkness was falling quickly.

They kept a cold camp, no fires, and the jungle seemed to creep in on the TankSquads. The huge black outlines of the silent weapons of war became shadow-haunted structures around which the enemy could creep and hide. Trees reared all around, sometimes erupting with bursts of monkey chatter or the hiss and click of large invisible insects. Other jungle night sounds warbled around the sixty or so men, some of whom stood guard, eyes alert, and some of whom relaxed within the barricade of heavy steel and mammoth metal tracks.

Simmo squatted next to Rogowski, Mo and Holtzhausen. They were boiling a pan of water for tea over two chemical kem-blocks, which glowed softly in a tiny ring of stones.

'You want some tea?' drawled Holtzhausen in his German burr.

Simmo nodded, dropping a bag and spooning sugar into his mug. He held out the plastic vessel and Holtzhausen poured the boiling water in. Simmo inhaled the steam hungrily. Simmo was the sort of man whose appetite was eternal. And if you fell asleep, he wouldn't just eat the last slice of pizza, he'd steal the entire contents of your fridge.

'You like your sugar,' said Mo, grinning. He too held a large plastic mug, larger than everybody else's – from which he drank a whole litre of tea. His mug looked more like a paint pot.

Simmo nodded. 'The Sarge surprised you not piss all night, drinking so much tea.'

'Hey, Sarge, what did you do with that fuck Kattenheim?' Holtzhausen spat on the ground and continued to sharpen a sliver of wood with his broad-bladed combat knife.

Simmo frowned. 'What you mean? He over there.' Simmo turned, peering through the darkness. Their little camp was lit by nothing more than kem-blocks, the occasional dull luminescence of a NightCube, and the glowing tips of a few cigarettes. Simmo squinted.

'*Where?*' asked Mo. 'I can't see him.'

Simmo cursed, spilling his tea over his combats as he lurched to his feet and sprinted forward, tea sloshing over his huge fist. A sound alerted him even as he reached for his holstered SigP7 9mm pistol strapped to the small of his back and he turned – into a heavy uppercut punch that rocked him back on his heels and sent stars spinning through his head . . .

Simmo staggered, dropping his tea.

To see Kattenheim, fists raised, grinning at him with a mouth full of broken teeth. The huge German ex-para came forward slowly and there was a chorus of clicks as several of the TankSquad men cocked their weapons.

Simmo grinned nastily, holding up his hand. 'No, lads. The Sarge handle this.' His fingers were covered with blood from his split lip. 'You do well slipping the wire, Nex.'

'Lots of practice,' said Kattenheim, rolling his shoulders and then settling into a boxer's stance. 'You gonna fight me fairly this time, you ugly hunk of army meat?' Sweat was rolling down his heavily scarred head and in the weak red light of the NightCubes he looked totally demonic. His red burned eyes seemed to glow – and within their depths shone the copper heart of the Nex warrior.

Simmo cracked his knuckles by clenching his fists, then strode forward.

'Lads – if he kills me, then you can fucking shoot him. But as long as I still live you will be disobeying direct order and The Sarge have you up on a charge!' He squared up and looked down at the smaller man. Nex, he thought. It is not a man, it is a concoction. Either way, I pulp fucking face.

Kattenheim attacked, a fast fluid combination of punches – straight right, right hook, left hook, left upper-cut, right straight. Simmo found himself backing away under the flurry of heavy precise blows which he man-aged – just – to block with his forearms. Simmo returned with a thundering right straight but Kattenheim rolled smoothly to Simmo's left under the punch and came up, hammering a right hook that caught Simmo on the side of his head and staggered him with the colossal impact. Another right straight shook Simmo's head again, and then a front kick to the face sent the huge man stumbling down on his knees.

Kattenheim stepped back, folded his arms, and waited.

Slowly, Simmo climbed to his feet.

He is too fast, realised the huge soldier. Just too fuck-ing fast.

Simmo approached warily, and Kattenheim still had his arms folded across his chest, a look of arrogance on his face. Simmo spat on the ground and around him he could feel the pressure of the TankSquad soldiers, of the Spiral agents who were watching and understanding and he knew that he had to kill this fucker with his bare hands – and rip out its spleen.

The Sarge was a legend.

To lose a fist fight?

With a fucking *Nex*?

'Better off dead! Sarge not let that happen!' he said, unintentionally out loud, and then threw himself at

Kattenheim. They exchanged a series of heavy blows at great speed, and Kattenheim tried another kick, but Simmo punched down on his opponent's kneecap. The onlookers all heard the splintering of bone.

The two fighters drew apart.

'You move well, for such a big man,' said Kattenheim. He displayed no obvious pain but had altered his stance, favouring his left leg instead of the right and moving so that the damaged limb was partially shielded by the one that was still sound.

'And Sarge *kill* well for such big man – as you find out.'

Simmo charged again, teeth glinting in the red light.

They exchanged punches, and Kattenheim landed another right hook that shook Simmo. Growling, The Sarge launched himself on top of the smaller Nex warrior and gripped him in a tight bear-hug, lifting him from the ground and exerting a massive pressure on the Nex's spine. Kattenheim growled, and slammed his head into Simmo's face – but after the second blow Simmo twisted and shook the Nex like a rag doll . . .

Kattenheim continued to head-butt Simmo – in the neck, in the face – as tendons popped along his spine. Somehow he managed to free an arm and started raining down blow after heavy cracking blow until Simmo was forced to drop him. Kattenheim leapt high into the air and came down with the butt of his elbow on the crown of Simmo's head. Simmo hit the jungle ground hard, stunned. Blood seeped in pulses from the wound and Kattenheim stood over Simmo, who was rocking and groaning, down and temporarily blinded and out of the fucking game . . .

Kattenheim glanced around, to see what stood between himself and freedom.

And only then, in the dull jungle glow, did the TankSquad Spiral operatives suddenly realise that the Nex held Simmo's matt black SigP7 gun.

The pistol lifted and, as shots that sent bright muzzle-flashes piercing the gloom rang out, the men split up. They leapt for safety, their own weapons coming up but unable to fire because immediately in front of Kattenheim was Sergeant Simmo . . .

Simmo felt as if his skull had been cracked open. Pain pounded through the centre of his brain and pulsed like hammer beats as blood soaked his shaved scalp. A rage like nothing he had felt for years arose – a red tide engulfing him. He could not speak, scream, shout nor curse because this intense, and insane tidal wave of hatred consumed him and carried him to—

Consciousness.

His eyes flickered open.

Kattenheim was firing *his* pistol at *his* men.

'Cheeky motherfucker,' Simmo snarled. He lifted back his boot and from his position on the ground kicked as heavily as he could at Kattenheim's injured knee. This time a real crack echoed through the jungle as the knee folded in on itself and the leg collapsed, pitching the man to the ground as he howled through blood-speckled lips and clenched teeth. Simmo grabbed the wrist holding the gun and they both lay, locked for a moment, staring into one another's eyes.

Simmo slammed his head into Kattenheim's nose. Then he released the hand that wasn't gripping the gun and, reaching down, punched at the twisted broken knee – five times, six, seven, eight. Then he took the gun like a man taking an ice cream from a child, and climbed ponderously to his feet.

Simmo levelled the SigP7 at Kattenheim's face.

'Say your prayers.'

Kattenheim said nothing, merely glaring at Simmo with hatred.

As something leapt from the darkness of the jungle, something huge, armoured and with a triangular head.

Simmo's gun came up as he spun round. A bullet smashed in the ScorpNex, which scooped Kattenheim from the ground and disappeared into the blackness. Sub-machine gun rounds ripped after the Nex, slicing through leaves, tree trunks and ferns and spitting soil from the ground. Ricochets whined all around as bullets bounced off hardwoods.

'Cease fire!' screamed Simmo.

The gunfire stopped.

The TankSquad men turned towards Simmo. Both Mo and Haggis had taken rounds from Kattenheim's crazy erratic firing and Haggis was seated, nursing his stomach. Simmo glared around angrily. This wasn't supposed to be how the game went.

'Fuck. Get your shit together – we as compromised as a man fucking his brother's wife in his brother's bed as his brother walks in. In other words, we fucked from both sides – by exposure of our location and by Spiral.'

'We going in, Sarge?'

'Yeah, we're fucking going in.'

'I thought the order was to wait.'

'They're the enemy, aren't they?' snarled Simmo. 'Hundreds of them tried to take us out back in Slovenia – tried to turn us into mincemeat. And now we supposed to sit by as fat-arsed politicians argue over who gets the rights to the LVA fields when all this over? Fuck 'em. We do this Simmo way! That LVA installation guarded by Nex. Nex are outlawed. We have licence to kill.'

The Sergeant's eyes gleamed.

All eyes were on his blood-encrusted shaved head, which was still pumping thick crimson that glistened in the red gloom.

'So let's kill,' he growled huskily.

Jam sat in the dark frost-filled cold, breathing slowly. He watched the clouds of vapour exhaling from his twisted jaws and something pricked his memory; something was different. And then he realised, with a growing sense of horror, that his eyes had physically shifted. They were in a different place; his head had broadened, flattened, and his eyes had moved further apart, thus expanding his field of view – his *predator*'s vision.

He considered Carter – and their exchange.

He knew that he could kill Carter.

Ultimately, he knew that he *would* kill the man . . .

But Carter's words had disturbed him – somewhere deep down in his twisted soul. Jam had sensed the reluctance to fight. Carter had some long perverse connection with the past, some distant impulse of honour and friendship that Jam could understand in a cool and detached way. And Jam had been happy to slice the fucker in two, smash his bones into splinters and then piss on his grave. But the words . . . the distant words from a warm and welcome deathbed . . .

'*No, Jam . . . stay here . . . we need your help. Natasha is dying. Nicky is with her. We need the machine. The Avelach . . . you know where it is . . . it was used on you, Natasha will* die—'

Jam pictured Natasha's face; her short dark spiked hair, her deep brown eyes and slim, athletic figure. Jam's head tilted softly. He could see – see Carter and Natasha together, laughing, holding hands as they walked along the pier, kissing in the rain—

The images flickered.

And Nicky was there, her sweet oval face, piercing bright eyes filled with tears. Was she unhappy? he wondered. And if so, for what reason?

Words drifted to him—

Words from a million years ago—

'It's a war – Durell, and Feuchter – they brought us a war. They tried to wipe us out; now it's time to give them a bullet up the arse.'

And Nicky; smiling weakly, standing there on the . . . on the Kamus, the disused Spiral base in the Austrian alps. 'Yeah. But . . . not everybody is going to make it back.' Reaching up, suddenly, she kissed him – and their lips lingered, tongues darting.

Jam stared into her beautiful eyes.

'I need some company tonight,' she said, voice husky, and she led him by the hand inside the cold confines of the dark and dank mountain base . . .

Jam lowered his huge triangular armoured head.

He stared at the floor, remembering their lovemaking.

Something is wrong with me, he realised.

I loved this woman. Loved her.

And yet – yet now I feel . . . *nothing?*

He spat, and lifted his head once more, breathing deeply, making strange rasping sounds. But a connection – from the man he wanted, *needed* to kill, this Carter and the two women who touched him in some strange way in his dreams, in his memories – something hard to grasp, something esoteric twisted inside his head. He could hear the whisper of deep voices he could not understand.

And Durell?

And *Feuchter?*

Jam lowered his head again, and the deep coldness

402

seeped into his limbs and into his brain. It soothed him. The cold calmed him, relaxed his mind. His worries bled away and his anxieties melted away and he rocked, on armoured heels that bit deep grooves in the stone cell floor.

With tiny clicks his eyes closed.

The World Investigation Committee central headquarters in Washington DC was in a turmoil. Voices rang around the huge vaulted ceiling of the chambers in a myriad different babbling languages. Human and electronic interpreters babbled, adding to the confusion; and Runners sped between benches and tables, in and out of doorways.

Voices could be heard above the hubbub, rising shrill, borne on currents of anger, disbelief, outrage, frustration, incredulity—

'I think he's fucking insane . . .'

'But he's got us by the balls . . .'

'Who is this man? I think it is one huge bluff!'

'But haven't you seen what he can do? The reports are flooding in from a thousand different media agencies – this is no insane dictator whom we can ignore . . .'

'The countries of the world should stand together, unite. We can mobilise millions of men and this Durell could not stand against such a tide of world strength—'

'But who would lead the armies?'

'Why, the USA, of course . . .'

'Why not the UN?'

'I think China is the obvious choice . . .'

'We can crush this worm before he moves—'

'Assassination would be more direct – a fucking sniper bullet in the back of the skull.'

'Yeah, when we find him – but if he *is* controlling the

earthquakes, then he can hit any central government, any capital city, any military installation in the world.'

'It is a preposterous claim, impossible!'

'Who is backing this lunatic? Which fucking countries? There must be some here who know of him. This is an outrage! It would spark a—'

'World war.'

The words hung like a storm cloud on a static-charged summer evening: heavy, ominous – and threatening.

The wide oak doors at the head of the chamber slammed open, smashing against the walls with twin crashes. Slowly, the noise subsided as faces turned to peer at the man who stood in front of them, the man who – with his stern silence and bushy-eyed frown – commanded their attention.

He was a huge barrel-chested man.

He wore v-neck grey robes, with dangling rosary beads which bounced against his curly-haired chest as he walked.

His sandals slapped against the floor as he moved to stand on the Central Podium. All attention focused on him. Many of the world leaders knew the face but could not name its owner.

The Priest seemed to be angry.

Furious.

His face was red, lips curled back, beard damp with sweat. His intense gaze swept the gathered men and women in front of him, and he pointed, eyes bright and holding a glimmer of insanity. Then he pointed again, his mouth working spasmodically, and again and again and again until total silence descended on the chamber—

'You *argue!*' boomed The Priest at last. 'You stand here, with the power of the world at your fingertips, and you – you bloody *squabble* like monkeys over a dead maggot. You whine at one another like spotty children in a playground arguing over a lollipop. You must *decide* . . .'

People began to shuffle their feet.

Nobody spoke.

The Priest began to rant, spittle flying from his lips and drenching his beard, '*Woe unto you, scribes and Pharisees, hypocrites! For ye are like unto whited sepulchres, which indeed appear beautiful outward, but are within full of dead men's bones, and all manner of uncleanness . . .*'

His stare roved.

'I say,' began one of the English delegates, 'that seems a tad harsh, old chap . . .'

'Shut up!' screamed The Priest with the fury of God flashing like lightning in his eyes.

All eyes were on him now.

And he felt—

Filled. With the Power. With the Glory. With Divine Insight.

'*And almost all things are by the law purged with blood; and without shedding of blood there is no remission!*'

Faces were turned towards The Priest; no one spoke. Despite their power, despite their learning and wisdom, in this moment of greatest confusion the leaders of the world truly did not know what to do . . .

'*And I saw as it were a sea of glass mingled with fire: and them that had gotten the victory over the beast, and over his image, and over his mark, and over the number of his name, stand on the sea of glass, having the harps of God . . .*'

'We should fight.'

'No, he could destroy us. He has the power of the earthquakes at his fingertips . . .'

'How many infantry can you field? 80,000? 100,000?'

'Yes, but mobilisation takes time, and if he sees the armies of the world mobilising then he may attack first . . .'

405

'May attack, will attack,' boomed The Priest. 'You have heard his demands, and you must here – and now – decide among yourselves whether this Durell is a threat to world peace. If you bow to his demands then decide here and now – with a single voice before God! But if you choose to fight – and a hard fight it will be – then decide it *now*. You do not have the luxury of time. *We* do not have the luxury of time. Things move apace, my brothers and sisters, and I beg you, before the Holy Father—'

Voices rose.

Squabbles broke out.

And The Priest looked down in despair at these, the most powerful people in the world, unable to decide upon the best course of action for the future of the whole planet.

Politicians, he thought sourly.

And slumped to the ground, listening to a hundred languages and a thousand dialects washing over him. People swarmed about him now, but The Priest ignored them. They shouted questions at him but he merely shook his head, clutching his Bible.

And by the end of the day they had made a decision.

The world leaders had finally made a decision.

They had *finally* decided to meet again in three days' time after lengthy discussions – to make the ultimate and *final* decision.

Some countries wanted to fight.

Some pressed for peace.

Some would mobilise armies.

Some would prepare talks.

The unanimous agreement was disagreement.

The undisputed choice was a non-choice.

The definite decision was no true decision at all.

'Chaos is finally here,' muttered The Priest.

SIU Transcript

Section WORLD SCALE MOBILISATION INFORMATION/
Spiral Information Transcript

Selection: Units 12-18, from total info
units 2844

US Army Pacific:

Hawaii – 35,300 troops mobilised from 2nd, 4th,
6th and 9th Battalions and comprising 20th to
43rd Infantry Regiments; 400 soldiers from 30th
through to 78th Aviation Battalions with UH-78
Black Hawk support; Paratroopers from 1-501st
Parachute Infantry Regiment deployed; 3rd, 8th
and 10th Battalion Field Artillery Regiments
deployed. 16,000 troops from the 9th Theatre
Support Command scrambled and put on High
Alert, including USARJ at Camp Zama.

German Federal Armed Forces:

16,000 Mechanisierte Division troops
mobilised, made up from Femmelde and
Aufklarungs Batallions, Mechanisierte
Brigades; also 3800 men from the Division
Spezielle Operationen, Division Luftbewegliche
Operationen and Heerestruppen-kommando units

made up of Artillerie-brigade, Pionier-brigade, Heeresflugab-wehrbrigade, ABC-Abwehr-brigade and Logistik-brigade.

2400 jets have been scrambled across Europe and are currently on a state of High Alert, both Luftwaffenführungskommando and Luftwaffenamt.

600 naval units have altered their patrol courses, both Flottenkommando – Flotille der Marineflieger and Zerstörerflotille, and Marineamt Kommando Marine-Führungssysteme, Schulen der Marine and Marinestützpunkte.

Australian Army

A total of 52,000 personnel deployed from:

1 Armd Regiment; 1 Fd Regiment; 1 JSU; 1/19 RNSWR; 10/27 RSAR; 12/16 HRL; 12/40 RTR; 13 Fd Sqn 13 CER; 11 CSR (141 Sig Sqn); 16 RWAR; 2 Cav Regiment; 2 HSB; 2 RAR; 2/14 LHR (QMI); 2/17 RNSWR; 51 FNQR; 6 RAR; 7 Fd Bty 3 Fd Regiment; 7 Fd Regiment; 8 CSSB; 8 CER; 9 CSSB

The Chinese People's Liberation Army Navy have mobilised over 2200 naval units including:

Destroyers
Type 956 Sovremenny
Type 054 Luhai
Type 07 Anshan

Guided Missile Boats
Type 520T Houjian
Type 343M Houxin
Type 021 Huangfeng

Amphibious Warfare
Type 074 Yuting
Type 072 Yukan
Type 073 Yudao

Frigates
Type 059 Jiangwei III
Type 057 Jiangwei II
Type 053K Jiangdong
Type 065 Jiangnan

Submarines
Type 094 NEWCON SSBN
Type 092 Xia SSBN
Type 093 NEWCON SSN
Type 091 Han SSN
Type 039 Song

The Chinese reserve militia currently numbers
sixteen million personnel and mobilisation (of
unknown scales) is in progress.

** We are on the brink of war.
** The verge of chaos.
** The edge of destruction.

more intel to follow>>>>>>>>>>

CHAPTER 15

EGYPT

Carter stared up at the Nex – watched the bright light in its copper eyes and thought:

What are you?

What do you want?

What does Durell *really* want?

'*We'll never fucking know . . .*' came the bitter, acid response from Kade as—

The Nex pulled the trigger.

There came a click – not the dead-man's click of an empty magazine, but the heart-pounding click of a stoppage. A bullet that the hammer had failed to kick into life and out of the barrel because the previous bullet casing had not been smoothly ejected . . .

The Nex glanced down and shook the sub-machine gun—

As Carter growled and his boot lashed out and up, slamming into the Nex's groin as the Spiral man rolled, whirled low and came up with his battered and bruised body screaming at him from a thousand different places. Carter felt a warm flush down his back and realised . . . he had been shot. Staggering back, the Nex dropped its gun and charged at Carter, who sidestepped and rammed a right hook against the masked face, knocking the Nex to the ground. The Nex rolled and came up smoothly, its stare fixed on Carter. They circled like caged tigers, awaiting the opportunity to pounce.

Carter's arm was throbbing; he could feel the skin hanging loose and weeping crimson tears. His lower spine was aching, as was his right shoulder and neck from the impact when he'd fallen from the KTM LC7 motorcycle. And the bullet wound . . . blood was pooling down and soaking into the waistband of his trousers, and he could feel something pressing hard against the back of his ribs, grating against the clicking bone within . . .

Carter spat.

Mainly to see if there was blood mixed in with his sputum and so find out whether the bullet had damaged his lungs. He was relieved to see no traces of blood but the pain was still excruciating and the waves of agony rolled over him and he felt himself sway—

Darkness started to spiral in front of his eyes, like the thick black corpse-smoke from piles of burning bodies just before the GreyDeath TankerRuns – before the governments finally realised that burning the disease-riddled human corpses merely spread the terrible designer disease and did not exterminate it . . .

'*My turn*,' said Kade.

'Kill it . . .' said Carter despondently as he felt pain overwhelming him. The trees swayed nauseatingly around him, whirling in some sickly sweet hallucinogenic vision of crystal insanity . . .

Kade opened his eyes.

He saw the copse in black and white, gloomy and filled

411

with hollows and shades of grey. Kade savagely pushed the pain aside and quickly analysed his wounds as the Nex circled in apparent slow motion. Kade smiled fiendishly and launched Carter's tortured body forward at an incredible speed—

Kade delivered ten blows in rapid succession and the Nex blocked them all, responding with a low sweep over which Kade leapt. Kade's boot came up, a high kick that caught the Nex under the jaw and lifted it from its feet to summersault backwards, landing lightly and smiling back at Kade.

'You are too slow.'

'Come and taste my pain,' snarled Kade, blood staining his teeth.

They danced through the black and white shadows of the trees. The Nex punched Kade, connecting twice, but he rolled easily and grabbed the Nex by the throat, dragging it to the ground and pounding his fist repeatedly against the mask. Something rammed between Kade's legs, and the Nex's fingers found the bullet wound in Kade's back, dug gloved fingers in with all its strength and wrenched sideways—

Kade's scream was filled with a dying animal's urgency.

He rolled through the leaves, mind overcome for a moment.

Red flashed over the scene in grey—

And for the first time Kade knew colour.

He growled, pushed himself to his knees in the tangle of vegetation and looked up—

Into the barrel of the Nex's gun.

'Let's fucking try again,' snarled the Nex. Its composure had gone and Kade realised, grinning savagely through his pain, that he had hurt it. He lifted his middle finger, face in a broad smile . . .

'Any time, cunt.'

The Nex's trigger finger tightened—

And its head exploded as a heavy-calibre round struck the side of its skull. There was a moment of compression as the cranium caved inwards, its shape becoming deformed . . . and then a rapidly expanding cone of flesh and bone and brain was forced inwards, creating a funnelled intensity of pressure that smashed free from the opposite side of the Nex's skull in a bright red, white and grey spray that pattered down onto the ground. Kade met the copper stare. The Nex looked momentarily stunned. Its gun tilted, barrel down, and fell from twitching gloved fingers. Then its knees buckled and it toppled sideways, rolling slightly downhill with leaves and twigs sticking to its gore-encrusted clothing.

Kade rose to his knees. Glanced right—

To where Mongrel and Mila were making their way cautiously forward through the trees. Kade spat on the ground, pain ripping him. He slumped into a seated position and tracked his two companions as they approached. Mila held the sniper rifle, Mongrel his M24 carbine.

'We wondered what was keeping you.' Mongrel grinned.

'You took your fucking time,' snapped Kade.

Mongrel frowned. 'But she a good shot, yes? She prove herself to you?'

Kade nodded, chewing his lip in thought. 'You brought your pack? I've got a fucking bullet in my back and you're just standing there like a dumb fuck, letting me bleed to death.'

'I see your manners have not improved,' said Mongrel coldly, and dropped to his knees, opening the pack. 'I'll have to work quickly – there are fucking Nex everywhere. This might hurt a little.'

413

'Just do it,' said Kade, turning away from Mongrel. His face contorted and he forced himself into a kind of calm. Kade hated Mongrel. In fact, Kade just hated people in general. *All people*. . .

Mongrel cut away Carter's jumper with a broad-bladed knife and inspected the wound. Bits of cloth had been dragged into the wound and, unwrapping a sterile pack, Mongrel slid a hypodermic needle into the crust-circled edge of the bullet hole and injected antibiotics and a chemical agent devised by Spiral for emergency field surgery. Kade gasped a little at the coldness of the injection . . .

'*Let me back*,' hissed Carter.

'I want some fun,' said Kade.

'*Fucking let me back!*'

'Wait . . . there's something wrong . . . trust me Carter, just for a dumb-fuck moment in your life, *trust me* . . .' Kade surveyed the scene again, in black and white, his stare examining the forest scene. He knew, he could *feel* that something wasn't right.

Mongrel placed an SSG – Spiral StapleGun – against Kade's back, which was also Carter's hot flesh, and there was a *kerchunk*. Kade ground his teeth as white-hot agony flooded his body. Mongrel pressed a second time, then a third before removing the device and reaching for another hypodermic needle.

'Last one.'

Kade threw himself backwards with all his might and sent both himself and Mongrel toppling over to roll a few feet down the slope – as a shot hammered the silence and a heavy-calibre sniper round tore into the soft earth. Kade reached out, picked up the syringe, spun and hurled it with every ounce of strength that he possessed—

Mila, standing with her rifle aimed, took the

hypodermic in her left eye. The needle struck deep, splitting her eyeball and sending blood pumping down her face. She did not scream, so sudden was the movement and the blow . . . she merely gasped, dropping to one knee as Kade climbed to his feet and Mongrel looked around, stunned.

'She would have shot me!'

'Us,' corrected Kade, retrieving Carter's Browning and checking the magazine with care. He turned to confront Mila. 'You fucking led us, didn't you? To that quarry? The Nex knew we were coming. You fucking set us up, you little bitch.'

Mila said nothing. She had tried to take hold of the needle but had just screamed: it was too painful to touch. Blood was flowing freely and she glanced up at Kade, her other eye wide. Her blood-splattered hand reached out to him pleading, her sobs echoing through the copse.

'Please,' she said.

Kade lifted the Browning.

The muzzle stared, small and round and black and unwavering.

'You betrayed us,' said Kade softly.

He fired.

The bullet took Mila in the throat, pitching her backwards. Kade walked over, staring down at her pretty face. 'I fucking hate pretty little blonde bitches . . .' he snarled and lifted the gun as rage swamped his brain. He wanted to destroy that face.

Carter at last wrenched Kade from his body and dropped to his knees, the Browning hanging in his limp grip. He breathed deeply, pain rocking him, and stared down at Mila's face – still pretty but undeniably dead.

'Why?' said Carter softly, almost despondently. 'Why did you do that?'

Mongrel placed his hand on Carter's shoulder. 'You did what you had to do. She would have killed us both – tried to on several occasions, in fact. I was a fucking blind man.'

'We were both blind,' said Carter softly, looking up at his friend. Carter stood, swaying, resting against Mongrel's broad powerful shoulder. 'God, I fucking hate killing women.'

'If it left to me, we would now be dead,' said Mongrel softly.

'Yeah, me too,' whispered Carter, reliving the scene – the mad scene with the syringe thrown like a knife and then the fatal bullet to the woman's throat.

They left the small copse behind, left behind the heavy scent of pine and the last warm dregs of the Greek autumn, left behind the body of a Nex and the bloody corpse of a woman whom they had trusted and who had betrayed them.

Just two more deaths.

Just two more corpses . . .

'Sometimes I think this madness will never end,' said Carter as wretchedness filled him.

'You OK?'

The Priest glanced sideways at Roxi and shook his head, lips pursed tightly, eyes glancing back down at the ground. 'We are ruled by morons,' he whispered. Frustration ate him from the inside out. It made him want to weep – to stand there and weep huge tears and beat his hands against the Comanche's war-spattered fuselage.

He sent the message to Spiral.

Kicked it through a thousand miles of space.

His ECube rattled, and he squeezed it softly, expecting a reply from the WIC to his update. Instead, the blue letters glowed and The Priest read them with a further sinking in his heart. He climbed up and belted himself in behind Heneghan, the pilot. Roxi leapt in and took her position beside The Priest in a supple, easy movement; she was all glistening leather and bristling guns.

'Now you look even worse,' she said, large oval eyes watching him with concern.

The Priest sighed, hands in his lap, folded protectively over his Bible. Without looking at Roxi, he said softly, 'These fools cannot decide whether to run, stand or fight. They cannot make a single decision and with each passing moment Durell grows stronger. He needs to be stopped – for his power has become great, so great that I fear he could overthrow many, if not all, of the world's governments. And that would give him a firm handhold on the face of the earth – and from thence he would move forward in great strides, for he is ruthless indeed. By far the greater and more noble decision is to fight. But we must stagnate for three days, awaiting the decision of the men in power. Who knows what might happen during that time to give Durell the opportunity to deliver the first blow?'

'What did the ECube say?'

The Priest sighed again, meeting Roxi's beautiful gaze. 'It is Carter. He has not heeded my warnings – nor Spiral's orders. He is disobeying direct instructions from the very top. He is going to Egypt. Our intelligence shows that Durell is currently in Egypt. Carter could jeopardise everything.'

'And?'

'I have been ordered to intercept him. To stop him. At any cost.'

'To *kill* him?'

The Priest nodded, his eyes hard. 'Yes, to kill Carter. If that is what it takes.'

'That *is* what it will take,' said Roxi, squeezing The Priest's hand.

'I know. The Lord will guide me,' he whispered, and closed his eyes.

The Sikorsky Comanche cruised into Egypt from the north-west, coming in over the Mediterranean Sea just west of Alexandria on the coast. Carter fancied he could almost feel the heat shimmering up from the long-baked sands as he slowed the chopper and its twin LHTecs whined down to spit their fumes into the arid Egyptian night.

As the darkened coastline gave way to a mixture of ancient and modern hotels scything along the coast in a glittering string of false emerald and ruby lights, Carter banked the Comanche over the half-lit suburbs around the heavily built-up centre of this, the second largest of Egypt's cities. The machine cruised calmly through near-total darkness.

'How are you feeling?'

Carter glanced back at Mongrel, thoughts racing through his mind. He shrugged, turning to gaze out over the poorly lit shanty towns, suburban sprawls where *fella-heen* subsistence workers lived in densely overpopulated crushes of seething humanity. The buildings were crazily crowded masses of mud-brick, breeze-block and red-brick dwellings, built in and around and often on top of other buildings. Between houses stood pens, some with corrugated roofs erected for animals. Some of the narrow streets sported small iron braziers that glowed like tiny fireflies as Carter eased the Comanche in stealth mode over their owners' unsuspecting heads.

'About what, in particular?'

'I don't know,' rumbled the large man, rubbing at his

eyes. The Spiral agent looked suddenly tired in the weak cockpit glow, huge rings circling his eyes and his face taking on a slightly haunted look. 'It worry me, that thing what happen with Mila.'

'You mean killing her?'

'Yes, and her betrayal of us. It sit bad with me.' He shook his head, sadly. 'I know you had to do it, I know you in pain about – Jesus, Carter, a syringe in the eye?'

'It was the nearest weapon,' said Carter slowly, carefully. He could remember the pure adrenlin-high ecstasy of Kade's exultant glee, his joy at seeing the woman fall with blood pouring from her eyeball – and he shivered.

Passing over the last straggling streets they headed south above dark undulating sands, pacing themselves and flying parallel with the Nile. Carter checked his ECube constantly as well as the tag – the TrackingDisc – that Carter had risked his life to attach to Durell's helicopter as the leader of the Nex made his escape.

The darkness flowed over and around them. For a while Carter remembered his good times in Egypt – the *best* times – and then, making him shudder, Kade's memories came back to haunt him and he remembered the *bad* times: the killing of his Arab captors in the desert, which was just the beginning of Kade's all-powerful consuming insanity—

And then the horrors that had come later.

The murders . . .

The events that had made Carter a hated, wanted and *feared* man across the whole of Egypt. A man wanted dead not just by the military, but by the civilian population as well . . .

And I can't say I blame them, he thought.

If I was them, *I*'d want me dead.

I'd want me crucified on a cross of crumbling bones.

'What happened down there?' asked Mongrel suddenly, intuitively, his face lit by an eerie soft blue glow, his eyes focused as if reading Carter's mind.

'I'm sure you read the reports.'

Mongrel nodded. 'Yeah, I read them. I know about the murders in the desert, the killing of twenty Arab captors and how you single-handedly rescue all the Spiral men – but that only tip of iceberg, I thinking.'

'What do you mean?' Carter felt a craving for a cigarette. He wanted to feel the nicotine buzz in his veins to help ease the pain from his bandaged arm, his battered bruised body, the stapled bullet wound. He was still carrying the flattened slice of metal in his back and he could feel it pressing against the slope of his ribs. The powerful painkillers seemed to be ignoring his agony.

'I run several missions in Egypt, in Cairo, Alexandria, Beni Suef, Sohag, Luxor, even over in Port Said at the Suez Canal and as far west as Al-Tor at foot of Mount Sinai. I speak good Arabic, make good Spiral agent in these parts and look damn fine in *galabiyyas* robes and, hell, even enjoy smog that pass for air in Cairo. I can dance with *tahtib*, even do a bit of Sufi dancing and only thing I not like here is damn food, just not never as good as egg and chips back in Yorkshire, bloody funny bits of meat in rolls with God only know what stinking fiddly herbs all black and shrivelled. I know rules of Islam so not make fool of self, and can blend in on streets and can pass as construction worker or *bawwab* without problem. In all this time, for the years I work here and after you finish your run of three missions, they put up wanted posters – *everywhere*. And not just outside police stations, but lining roads, up on big mad billboards usually used to advertise movies. They wanted you dead, Carter. Very dead.'

'I don't want to talk about it.'

'Well, I reckon it must be bad.'

'It *was* bad,' said Carter softly, remembering Kade with the long blackened knife and the soft flesh that had parted with such ease . . .

'Well, I know they had your face plastered on billboards for what seem fucking *years*. And you look no different – just little bit older and more careworn. I think lot of people remember you. We definitely have to stay covert when we go down there on streets and in desert.'

'Yes.'

Mongrel stared over Carter's shoulder, at the ECube. 'Where it taking us?'

'We'll cut across Cairo, then head south and east down over the Eastern Desert. Looks to me like we're heading just west of Hurghada, near the Red Sea Mountains.'

'Hmm. I've not been there.'

'Well, you can add it to your list of interesting places visited in the name of demolition, can't you?'

'I thinking Carter not in good mood.'

'Well, you be fucking right. I've been shot, come off my bike at eighty per and played "Grate my fucking skin with a gravel road" – a wonderfully fun little game. I've been pounded to fuck by God only knows how many Nex and by Jam, my oldest and best friend who just so happens to have become a mutated monstrosity. And then I had to shoot a woman in the throat, which isn't exactly something that makes me sleep easily at night. You could say I'm a bit fucking *tetchy*.'

'Mongrel take your point.'

Engines humming, they reached the outskirts of Cairo and within minutes had passed the shanty towns and city buildings – indicated by a proliferation of lights. The Nile snaked through the centre of downtown Cairo; they passed the glittering mosaic that was Tahrir Square and the bright pointing finger of Cairo Tower and flew on past the lights of the Arab League Building, the Cairo Opera House and Gazira Island where Cairo's money people resided. The Nile was split by lights cutting over the Sixth of October Bridge, and Carter reined in the Comanche. They hovered near Tahrir Square, gazing out over the visual confusion of advertisements for Coca-Cola, Sushi Burgers and AOL that adorned most buildings higher than a single storey and sent a million wavering colours cascading across the night-ebony waters of the Nile.

'Bad memories?'

Carter nodded. 'It was being bombed last time I was here. They have rebuilt well.'

'The Egyptians are a resilient people.'

'You have to be these days. Jesus, I could do with a cigarette.'

'Let's go there and get this done, then,' growled Mongrel, and Carter eased the Comanche forward. They spun darkly over the bustle of lights and the bumper-to-bumper traffic that filled the roads, pumping out yet more black pollution into the already toxic air. Even from their height they could hear shouts and the general rumble of the traffic, the sounds of a city crammed with people to the point of meltdown.

Carter gradually increased their speed, and the Comanche lifted gently, banked and left Cairo behind. They followed the winding course of the Nile for a while and then cut out over the desert towards Gebel al-Galala al-Qibliya.

'Long time since I been on the plateau,' Mongrel muttered.

Carter said nothing; his eyes were dark, haunted with memories . . .

Memories of Kade.

The Eastern Desert was far from being a flat and feature-less plain. As dawn broke, its pale tendrils spearing the horizon with a gentle glow and a promise of intense baking oven-heat to come, Mongrel yawned, rubbing at his eyes.

The desert world was a nightmare of sand-baked val-leys, hills, mountains, troughs and massive boulders. Huge sheer scree slopes battled with high walls of moun-tainous rock and gentle undulations of rock and sand.

'Beautiful,' said Mongrel.

'Not when you're being marched out to be shot.'

'It's better to die in beautiful surroundings,' chided Mongrel, smiling. 'Better than dying in a sewer in Soho with all the other fucking rats.'

'Better not to die at all.'

Carter kept the Comanche low and as the sun crept up the sky they cruised across the gradually rising plateau, which sloped upwards from the Nile towards the distant jagged volcanic mountains lining the Red Sea. As they approached, Carter spun the Comanche around and they settled easily into a small basin lying deep with windswept sand. The rock bowl lay scattered with massive oval boulders, each larger than a house and seemingly tossed casually across the basin floor. A few sprinkled date palms, acacias and jacarandas sat half within the shade of several boulders, indicating a water source of some kind.

Carter brought the Comanche down beside a sprawl-ing jacaranda that was not yet in flower, its branches spider-webbing out to the green baked leaves at their tips. The rotors buffeted the tree, and as Carter shut down the engines, so the swirls of rotor-swept sand slowly died with them, settling. Carter leapt out under the baking sun and looked up at the clear deep blue of the sky.

'Fuck, it's hot,' breathed Mongrel, jumping down beside him. 'How far we got to walk?'

'Two or three klicks. Maybe a little more, depending on the terrain. I didn't want to get too close – we don't know what sort of air support they have. Back in Slovenia they had some serious weaponry but it was all linked close to the quarry. It seems they could have a similar set-up here.'

Mongrel leant his back against the trunk of the tree, and took a long swig from his canteen. 'You think Jam will still be here? After all, we've had to detour and delay thanks to The Priest, that moaning bastard . . .'

'The TrackingDisc led us here, and the bugged helicopter hasn't moved. There's always the possibility they've travelled onwards, using a different vehicle –' Carter smiled grimly '– and if that's the case, then we're probably fucked.'

'Let's get moving then,' grunted the large squaddie, pushing himself away from the tree. 'Longer we stand talking, more chance they have of escape.'

The two men quickly sorted their equipment, travelling with light rucksacks, black shamags wound around their heads to protect them against the relentless sun.

Walking across the basin floor, they climbed the gentle rocky slope leading up and out to the rising plateau of rock and sand, and then started the short trek in silence, eyes alert and M24 carbines slung across their backs.

It was only when he started walking that Carter realised how weary he was; exhausted, in fact. And now they were heading into the lion's den – heading towards the enemy with no back-up and no prospect of calling any. Spiral had forbidden Carter to travel to Egypt but though it hurt him deeply to do it, if this was what it took to save Natasha's life the insubordination came easily.

I wonder if this was how Durell felt?

How Feuchter felt?

To bite the hand that feeds . . .

The sun pushed slowly on up the sky.

Carter and Mongrel moved steadily on, using the new ECubes to navigate and hoping that this new model was as secure against Nex digital infiltration as The Priest had promised. Wading through hot sand that came up to their ankles, they climbed ever upwards, tabbing between walls and gulleys of red rock, sometimes dropping into a narrow wadi and negotiating their way forward towards—

The rock basin, and the town that lay within.

Carter and Mongrel knelt beside a large jagged outcropping of rock, which overhung the steep drop ahead of them.

The basin spread out and was filled wall to wall with a town built from stone and mud bricks. Carter rested back on his haunches and Mongrel dropped to his belly as they sweated heavily under the burning sun, gazing down on the activity below.

The basin was perhaps a kilometre and a half square, three sides bordered with steep jagged volcanic walls rising to a high peak over to the north-east. At the head of the basin there was a temple of some kind, a large imposing building built from the red rock of the mountains and faced with marble, the upper layers of which had been stripped off. Ancient carvings, wind-worn and smooth, sat along a balcony above thick circular pillars, and sand swirled around the steps that led down to a main street, which in turn sliced through the heart of the town.

'Looks like the town built up around the temple,' said

Carter, soothing his parched throat with a gulp of water.

'Yeah. And look.' Mongrel pointed. Beside the temple, in a narrow fenced-in and sand-swept yard sat five black helicopters, squat and gleaming and shaded by the high rock walls.

'Nex,' said Carter softly, indicating with his canteen.

They moved in patrols through the main street and the narrow side-streets of the town. They moved in twos and threes, dressed in black, heads shrouded in black shamags and carrying machine rifles of various types. They moved easily among the populace of the town who seemed to ignore the Nex, almost accepting them as their own.

'What is this place?' asked Mongrel.

'Durell's secret hideaway? Who fucking knows? But our tagged helicopter is in that compound and I would bet that Jam and Durell are inside that temple: with the machine.'

'What's your plan?'

Carter rubbed at his stubble. 'I'll be honest, Mongrel – I'm tired of fighting, and I'm in no fit state to be taking on people like Jam. All I want to do is get the fucking machine and get back to Natasha . . .'

'What about if we disable Jam? Knock him unconscious and take him with us?'

Carter looked into Mongrel's eyes and saw the pain there. He wanted to say, *Don't be insane – Jam has been changed into a Nex, he's fucking dead . . . he's the enemy . . . he will try his utmost to kill us, to burn us.*

But he could not bring himself to speak the words.

'What we need to do,' said Carter carefully, 'is move in – covert infiltration: steal the Avelach and then get the fuck out, using one of their helicopters. If an opportunity arises then we can take Jam with us.'

426

Mongrel shook his head. 'No, that not good enough. And we also have problem with Durell and the earth-quakes. He ripping the world apart, Carter. We got to stop him.'

Carter pursed his lips.

'*You shot that fucker once, through the heart,*' said Kade softly. His voice whispered through Carter and he felt himself shiver despite the heat of the desert.

'I thought you'd disappeared – gone off somewhere to shoot more women in the face, you fucking coward.'

'*Tut tut, Carter. You can't use me to do your dirty work and then criticise me when it's over. That just isn't* sportsmanlike. *She would have shot Mongrel in the back of the head – you know it, he knows it, and I fucking know it. And anyway, Carter – shooting pretty blonde bitches is as easy as shooting fish in a barrel.*'

'What do you want now?'

'*I want nothing more than to offer good advice.*'

'Such as?'

'*Kill Durell. Then kill Jam. Then kill all the Nex in the whole town.*'

'Wonderful,' muttered Carter sourly. Then he realised that Mongrel was looking at him, head tilted to one side, face a frown within the folds of the black shamag.

'You OK, Carter?'

'Yeah, yeah. What do you have in mind?'

'Well, when we find Avelach I'm thinking we find Durell. Let's take fucker out, *then* steal machine and drag Jam out to helicopter. I'm sure two men like us can pull quite simple suicide mission.'

Carter shook his head. 'We do this one step at a time. Carefully. No fucking mad dashes, nothing without us agreeing. Yeah? Or we'll both end up as minced dog meat.'

Mongrel stared down at the town. Watched the patrols of Nex, amidst the barking of the occasionally excited dogs that ran through the streets. He knew from experience that dogs made covert travel at night quite impossible.

'I think first we got to get to temple.'

Carter grinned. 'I've got an idea about that.'

With sunset came a respite from the heat. Carter and Mongrel watched the glowing orb sinking slowly over the shimmering horizon, over the distant desert plateau which dropped off in kilometre-long strides towards the far distant Nile.

Carter focused his actions to stop himself fidgeting with frustration. All he could think about was more waiting, more hanging around while Natasha lay dying on a cold hospital slab. He cleaned and oiled both his Browning HiPower and his M24 carbine, checking and reloading their magazines, oiling the moving parts of the weapons. Back in Crete when the Nex killer had been about to shoot him in the face and its gun had suffered a stoppage, he had been made aware once again just how vulnerable life could be – hanging by a thread, awaiting a cruel twist of fate that would swing the pendulum of favour from one combatant to another. The Nex was dead, slowly decomposing next to the body of Mila the sniper. And why? Because his submachine gun had been dirty, or lacked oil, or the bullet had been poorly manufactured.

Mongrel, after quenching his thirst and chewing on dried beef to satisfy his huge deep-bellied hunger, finally followed Carter's lead and oiled his own weapons. As the sun set and the blue faded from the sky, allowing darkness to cast a veil over the town, the two men found that they were finally ready.

Carter watched a small sand-coloured scorpion scuttle in front of him and pause, seeming to turn and look at him. He aimed his Browning casually – and watched the scorpion scuttle away, its sting held high and proud.

'You little fucker. No compassion in your insect brain, is there?'

Dogs barked in the distance, and Carter and Mongrel shouldered their packs. Clutching their guns in their hands, they moved off slowly against the now dark sky-line.

Their boots trod softly against the rock and sand, along the ridge that dropped towards the main gap leading to the village. Halting some distance away, they saw several Nex standing idly by the roadside. The two Spiral men crept down through the steep rocks until they reached, panting and with sweat-stinging eyes, a narrow back street. It was unlit and had an unpleasant aroma of something rotting.

'What now?'

Carter gestured, and they moved forward. For six hours he had been watching the Nex patrols and planning a way across the town towards the temple. He had the route imprinted on his cortex.

They halted, carbines at the ready.

As they waited, three Nex drifted past, boots silent on the sand-scattered street, heads scanning left and right. Deep in the shadows Carter and Mongrel held their breath – and once the Nex had passed they moved from one backstreet to the next, hugging the shadows and treading carefully, their eyes alert.

A dog barked, the noise echoing across the town. Another mutt took up the call, and for a few minutes about twenty of the beasts decided to make a nuisance of themselves, their echoing barks reverberating through the town and out into the desert.

'I understand why they fucking eat 'em now,' muttered Mongrel, who had made no pretence of liking Egyptian food, and referred to most foreign dishes placed in front of him as a mishmash of either shredded dog, donkey or camel.

They crept along through the shadows, halting often, listening to the local denizens chattering in Arabic. Small groups of men wearing *galabiyyas* robes in varying colours and styles sat outside some of the houses at small wooden tables, sometimes smoking strong Egyptian tobacco through bubbling hookahs and drinking tiny cups of thick black treacle-like coffee. They kept their voices low. There seemed to be an undercurrent of fear pervading the air.

Finally, Carter called a halt and dropped his pack to the ground. He handed his M24 carbine to Mongrel and rolled his neck as if readying for action.

'What are you doing?'

'Wait here.'

'You said no single-handed heroics! We need know what both up to!'

'I'm buying us our passage into the temple – unseen.'

Mongrel frowned, then watched Carter draw a long black steel blade from a boot-sheath. Mongrel licked his lips, tasting dried sweat-salt caught in the stubble around his mouth, and watched Carter move towards the end of the narrow darkened backstreet.

Carter crouched between an overflowing bin stinking of old vegetables and a square cardboard box reeking of rancid, pungent dog piss. He waited, eyes almost closed, counting . . . and then sensed rather than heard the foot-steps of the two Nex guards . . .

He uncoiled from his hiding place like a striking cobra,

430

leaping forward without a sound to plunge the long dagger through the eye and into the brain of the lead Nex. Blood gushed, drenching his fist, as his left boot kicked up and out, cannoning into the second Nex's throat. Carter whirled, pulling out the knife in the same movement and, spinning low, brought the blade up, ramming it into the second Nex's heart. It fell forward against him, and Carter withdrew the blade, supporting the Nex as blood poured out onto the sand and their stares met for a long horrible moment. Carter waited impatiently until it died in his arms.

Dragging the body back down the alley, Carter dumped it behind the bin, then sheathing his dagger he ran and dragged the first Nex corpse back, depositing it next to its companion.

'Strip them.'

'You want us to look like the Nex?'

'Can you think of any better way of sneaking in?'

'I bloody hope Simmo not arrive.'

'Yeah.' Carter grimaced, remembering the incident on the sniper tower. 'So do I.'

They stripped the Nex bodies of their clothing and pulled themselves into the outfits, finally rolling the thin balaclavas over their faces and turning to check one another.

'It stinks,' complained Mongrel.

'Don't you ever stop moaning?'

'And we haven't got copper eyes! They spot us for sure!'

'Jesus, Mongrel, we're not supposed to satisfy intense scrutiny in this Nex gear, just casual glances. We're going over the fucking roofs until we reach the street – it's just for the last few feet.'

Moving back out into the alley, Carter swept sand over

the blood as best he could. They took the Nex's weapons, slinging their own carbines over their backs. Then Carter led the way down several more alleys until they came to a low building and Carter leapt up onto a bin, then jumped, hauling himself to the low roof. Mongrel followed, muttering morosely to himself as he heaved his bulk up and scratched his dragging belly against the roof's rough edges. Then they crouched for a few moments in the darkness, getting their bearings.

Moving along behind the parapet, they climbed to the next building, finding easy handholds in the badly constructed mud-brick breeze-block wall, and then looked out over the main thoroughfare.

Fires flickered, casting long golden shadows.

Occasionally Nex patrols would pass. Carter focused his gaze on the opening to the temple – six steep steps, blown with sand, leading to a dark interior with a ramp. Were there any guards inside?

He took his ECube and stared at the tiny alloy device for a few moments. Digits glittered. Carter bit his lip, frustrated and mistrustful. Could he risk it? Was the new version of the ECube truly undetectable?

Could he trust it?

Carter stowed the tiny device away once more and calmed his breathing, peering into the temple. He took a SniperScope from his pack and lifted it to his eye, flicking it to night-vision mode. The world sprang to life in green and purple. Carter zoomed in on the temple but could see only the ramp rising out of view. He watched for a while but saw no movement.

They moved from roof to roof, slowly, carefully, making sure that they made no noise. They could not afford the hiss of cloth scraping against stone, or the negligent kick of a pebble that would rattle against mud brick.

Any such mistake could not only cost them their lives, but the lives of others who relied on them . . .

Finally, after further climbing and more of Mongrel's silent curses – which he threw with mental vitriol at Carter's back – and sweating like pigs, they reached the edge of the street overlooking the temple.

It reared ahead of them, supported at the base by heavy carved rounded pillars and rising to a single sculpted spire about a metre in diameter whose top rose just above the high cliff wall behind. Carter glanced down at the small black helicopters, and then up and down the street.

They waited, watching the occasional Nex patrol.

'They seem quite relaxed,' said Mongrel.

'Good.'

'Maybe it a bluff?'

'Maybe.'

'What happen then?'

'Then we're dead.'

'Oh.'

A pause. Silence. The stone around them, after baking all day in the sun, was now releasing the naturally stored heat. Both men were sweating heavily, and the Nex-scented balaclavas did nothing to relieve their sombre mood.

'You see anything?'

'No,' said Carter softly.

'When we going in?'

'When you learn to shut the fuck up.'

'I need to be moving. I'm overheating.'

'Your body or your brain?'

Mongrel frowned. 'You not take piss when I on bad mission with you. You listen hard, Carter boy, I not take this sort of—'

433

'Shh.'

Mongrel lapsed into silence.

'Come on.'

They climbed onto the parapet, jumped onto a low ledge, then lowered themselves to the ground. Nothing stirred, no breeze to cool the air, no wind to blow the sand on the street around. Carter and Mongrel strode towards the entrance to the temple with heads held high, weapons in hands and hearts in mouths . . . waiting for the shout to halt . . . waiting for the blast of bullets that would eat the backs of their skulls . . . Their breath coming in short gasps, they jogged up the sand-blown steps and disappeared into the temple's gaping black maw.

The room had a red sandstone floor, gently grooved from a thousand years of use. The lower sections of the walls were lined with panels of marble and obsidian. Light came from globes in the high vaulted stone roof, and benches on which rested the most advanced computing equipment in the world stood against the walls.

Durell stood by a rectangular black screen. The surface of the screen seemed to ripple as he touched it. Then it sprang into liquid fire and lights glittered around his twisted black clawed hand.

He smiled within the folds of his dark hood.

And his copper slitted eyes glittered.

'Are we ready?' came Gol's voice from close behind in a hushed whisper.

'Yes,' said Durell, and touched the screen. 'We are finally ready.'

Carter and Mongrel crouched in the gloom, weapons primed. They were allowing their eyes to adjust to the

434

weak light cast from well-spaced flickering torches whose amber flames danced in iron brackets along the smooth red walls.

From where they waited, senses alert, one long wide corridor stretched off, filled with nothing but shadows.

'It's like being back in the annals of history,' said Mongrel, shivering.

'Yeah, I always had a thing for Ancient Egypt.' Carter smiled and slowly unfolded from his defensive stance. He glanced around, moved forward cautiously a couple of steps, then halted once more. His head cocked and Mongrel came up beside him, sub-machine gun gripped in unsteady fingers.

'I do not like this,' said Mongrel softly.

'Where are the guards?' asked Carter.

'They would not leave this unguarded,' said Mongrel. 'Something very wrong.'

Carter nodded. He activated his ECube and scanned on different frequencies. 'Over there – a wall of blue k-laser. Invisible to the naked eye.'

'A fucking digital tripwire that cut you in half with delayed action!' muttered Mongrel. 'Very nasty. You any idea how we get past?'

'Yeah.' Carter stared at Mongrel hard. 'And so should you. Where were you during the seminars?'

Mongrel shrugged awkwardly. 'I had this bird, down in the town. She had great pair of breasts that wobble all over place . . .' He petered off when he saw the look on Carter's battered face. 'I sorry,' he finished. 'I really am. But you should see tits! They mark a step in man's way forward through life . . .' Mongrel trailed off feebly.

Carter moved carefully on while Mongrel covered their backs. Stopping within the stone-floored corridor, Carter

435

lifted the ECube and digits flickered, tracing patterns across its alloy face. Nothing seemed to happen – visually – but physically they had become surrounded by an invisible globe of blue k-laser.

'Come on.'

They walked slowly forwards, with Carter's gaze never leaving the flickering read-outs on the ECube. As they moved through the invisible wall – the digital tripwire capable of cutting the two men into cubes of flesh – the ECube absorbed the sentry laser into its own field and allowed the signals to flow uninterrupted by the physical intrusion of the two men. They slid silently free on the other side and stood, Mongrel panting softly, looking around in the flickering light of the corridor.

'We through?'

'Yeah.' Carter checked the mag on his sub-machine gun. 'I kind of expected spikes, or something.'

'This not Indiana Jones!'

Crouched in the shadows once more, the two men waited patiently. Carter allowed the ECube to perform a full scan – realising that it could save them many hours. Anyway, if the new version of the ECube had been breached by the Nex then they had already been discovered.

A drift of fine sand blew across the floor, and a cold breeze wafted from the temple's depths.

'What you doing?'

'Shh.' Carter held up a finger, then turned the ECube to Mongrel. Mongrel nodded, eyes wide. 'This is some fucking huge temple. Look, it goes back into the mountain rock for nearly two kilometres.'

'We never find Jam in here,' said Mongrel.

'I have an idea.'

Carter played with the ECube for a few minutes.

436

Whilst not an expert on the machine like Natasha or The Priest, he could navigate his way successfully through the myriad coded terminals and keys and rhythms. Finally he smiled. 'Yes, it's here.'

'What you doing? This place giving me the willies.'

'The *willies*?'

'I been watching some *old* vid recently.'

'The fucking *willies*?' Carter laughed then, a brittle sound in the cool dry interior.

Mongrel touched his arm. 'It good to hear you laugh. I know you not got much to laugh about. It good to see you keeping it together.'

'Hey, insanity is my middle name. Now, when the Spiral mainframes picked up a stray signal from Jam's ThumbNail_Map it held a pattern. A grid of the location that Jam was trying to traverse . . . If I can match that grid to a pattern of corridors here, then we have a link, yes?'

Mongrel looked sideways at Carter. 'You crafty fucker.'

'So you agree? That's a possibility?'

'Aye,' nodded Mongrel. 'Sound feasible to ol' Mongrel.'

Carter played with the ECube for a few more moments. Then he smiled. 'Game on,' he said.

They moved through the shadows of the stone corridor, most of it just bare sandstone-block walls, scuffing through the fine sheen of sand that scattered beneath their boots. Three times Carter had pulled them into smaller corridors that led off as teams of Nex moved slowly past, JK49s held with barrels pointing at the ground.

Three times they waited, risking discovery and a sudden blazing firefight that would end their quest . . .

Three times the Nex moved on silently, their black boots leaving nothing but imprints on the sandy floor.

From the wide central corridor at the entrance to the temple, they moved steadily downhill towards a hub – from which radiated another ten stone walkways, some leading up, some down, and some spanning away on the same level. All these corridors were extremely narrow and had no distinctive features to differentiate one from the other.

Using the ECube, Carter navigated them through the *labyrinth*.

For the next twenty minutes they moved slowly, gently pressing their hands against worn stone-block walls. Mostly, ceilings were high and obscured by distance and darkness. At irregular intervals iron brackets held flaming brands, some guttering low and leaving the two men practically without light. They had the back-up of NVGs but night-vision aids gave off a subtle whine that was easy for the Nex's superior senses to pick up.

'What is this place? I never heard of it before?'

'I don't think it appears on any tourist maps,' said Carter, leading them down a steeply sloping stone ramp. He halted at the bottom, holding his hand up. Mongrel glanced nervously behind, the muzzle of his gun wavering.

'What?'

'Listen.'

They could hear a noise, like a gentle rasping. Leather against glass. Or—

'What the fuck is that?'

They crept forward and suddenly the walls ended and the ceiling soared high above them, disappearing into blackness. The floor fell away into a dark wide pit with gently sloping sides. The flat expanse of floor was spanned by an ornately carved stone bridge which arced gently over the depression, which in turn was filled with—

'What the fuck are *they*?'

Carter and Mongrel stared. In the darkness, apparently sleeping, were a hundred or so *creatures*. They each had four limbs ending in savage black claws, and their bodies were tightly and hugely muscled, armoured with contoured interleaving plates. They were big – bigger than any wild feline – and their heads were triangular and tufted with thick strands of fur.

The large group were all breathing softly, intertwined in sleep.

'You get the feeling we truly fucked if they wake up?'

Carter scowled at Mongrel, and prodded him in the chest. Then he moved forward, slowly, placing each footfall with care. He checked with the ECube and found another blue k-laser digital tripwire near the centre of the bridge.

'*A beautiful trap, don't you think?*' said Kade.

'Shut up.'

'*Lure you to the centre of the bridge and – bam! – a hundred fucking Sleepers descend on you and rip out your belly with their teeth. Fucking primeval!*'

'What did you call them? Sleepers? How do you know that?'

Kade remained silent, watching, dark and brooding at the back of Carter's mind.

Carter stepped onto the bridge.

He began to walk forwards. Below him, the creatures continued to breathe deeply, their eyes closed and Carter felt the tension rising in his chest. He licked at dry lips.

Out of the darkness rose columns, six-sided and carved from red and yellow stone. On the summit of each squatted a finely carved and crafted figure like nothing Carter had ever seen. These carvings were strange, alien almost.

Halting, Carter activated the ECube and the two men

slipped neatly through the digital trap, then padded down the other side of the bridge and into the relative safety of another narrow stone corridor. Mongrel wiped sweat from his brow and then rolled his Nex balaclava back into place.

'You OK?' said Carter.

'I've felt better,' muttered Mongrel harshly.

They disappeared like ghosts into the dimly lit corridor. Behind, in the pit, there came a glimmer of movement as one of the Sleepers opened its eyes.

Copper slits glinted.

And slowly, gracefully, it began to uncoil . . .

The tunnel led down.

It was horribly claustrophobic, with a low rough ceiling which made both Carter and Mongrel stoop to avoid banging their heads. The narrow walls of the tunnel were mostly rough-faced, with some crumbling edges worn by time, but they would sometimes blaze with panels of ancient Egyptian hieroglyphs. The walkway was rough, and grooved down either side. Carter pointed, frowning, and Mongrel merely shook his head.

They moved even more slowly now, even more warily. Ahead, a strange noise sounded: a high-pitched keening wail, not altogether human. It rose in pitch, then faded away until it was nothing more than a distant dream of aural melancholy. Then it would wind up once more, into a terrible thrumming whine that hurt the men's ears. Carter scanned with the ECube – but there was nothing.

'I got bad feeling about this.'

'Yeah, me too,' said Carter. He checked his Browning and continued forward. He pulled off his Nex balaclava with a cursed, 'Fuck it,' and rubbed at his face. 'I don't think we'll need these disguises now.'

'But what if—'

'Then we shoot the fuckers in the face.'

The corridor continued to lead down. Sand swept around their feet, pushed by a cool breeze that moaned softly. Carter's nostrils wrinkled as a coppery and unpleasant odour drifted past them.

They passed the holding cell which they assumed was where Jam had been imprisoned. It was empty, with a few shards of twisted copper on the ground accompanied by a few dried bloodstains. With no other option, they continued to follow the passageway . . .

Which led further down.

'I do not like this. It feel like the Kamus.'

'And that place was haunted,' said Carter softly.

The whining sound lifted and fell, a ululating call of stressed metal. Occasionally there came the sound of a heavy impact like stone crushing stone. Both men felt their hackles rising as the tunnel came to an abrupt end. They crouched by the edge, looking out into a mammoth cavern.

It was almost circular. A million strange patterns were carved across the floor, walls and high distant ceiling, and the floor was littered with huge engraved blocks of stone, marble and granite. The floor was divided down the centre by a crevasse of black – which not only cut across the floor but up the walls as well, almost giving the impression that the huge hall *floated*. It was very dark, and a bad smell was carried by the cold – by a now chilling – breeze.

Carter gazed at the crevasse, the sheer drop that they would have to cross. It measured perhaps ten metres and was too wide to leap over. His gaze scanned from side to side, following the gap upwards and noting that it also crossed the ceiling. He also saw a bank of carved rock on the floor, a bridge across the actual ceiling that spanned the black crevasse, and a strangely angled doorway at the distant opposite side of the hall.

The wail returned, moaning softly from the depths of the gash in the rock.

'Shall I check it out?'

'Wait,' said Carter softly.

They waited, watching, sweat beading on their brows despite the chill. This is some puzzle, decided Carter.

He scanned with the ECube, but it revealed nothing.

His stare raked the ceiling, the walls, searching for spikes, or holes, or tips of barbed spears.

'*An active imagination you have,*' sneered Kade.

'What do you want?'

'*To help, of course.*'

'Yeah, to help yourself.'

'*Let me have control and I will get you past the traps.*'

'Fuck off. What do you know of this place?'

'*I have my contacts.*'

'Yeah, and I have mine.' Carter pointed and lifted his M24 carbine as a tall, broad figure stepped out from the crooked stone doorway opposite. The man held his large hands wide in an act of supplication, and his face was at peace, filled with serenity. His grey-flecked beard was just how Carter remembered it and the brown eyes were the brown eyes of the killer, the Spiral killer – the Spiral *traitor . . .*

Carter stepped down—

And almost fell.

The rocky floor seemed to sway, to shimmer. He felt it move like ball bearings beneath his boots and his M24 slammed up. His eyes narrowed and fixed on Gol as he strode across the subtly moving stone floor towards the segment of falling space.

The stench grew worse.

'Welcome to our laboratory,' came the deeply melodic voice of Gol. The man had halted beside a group of red stone cubes stacked beside the crevasse.

Carter moved closer, warily, glancing all around. He could sense Mongrel behind him, frantically searching for a source of danger. Carter glanced at the ten-metre-wide drop that separated the two men.

'How are you, Gol?'

'In truth,' said the huge man, letting his hands fall to his sides, 'I have felt better. I find it sad when those who show themselves to be enemies by their actions but not by their morals must die.'

'Meaning?'

'Meaning that I no longer have a choice.'

'You always have a choice,' said Carter softly. His senses were screaming at him, and Kade – the blood-scream demon in his brain – was howling like a pig stuck on a spear.

'You have come for the Avelach? To save Natasha?'

'Yes,' said Carter, staring hard into Gol's unreadable eyes. The big killer had always unnerved Carter. Natasha had once claimed that he and Gol were the same – men, yes, but murderers too, fashioned from the same mould. Carter had reluctantly acknowledged then that she was correct. But now, staring into Gol's eyes, he was not so sure. 'How the fuck did you survive?'

'They turned me into a Nex,' said Gol softly. 'They saved me, using the machine that you seek. The Avelach. But they deviated from the normal formula.'

'You do not have copper eyes?'

'What makes you think all Nex appear the same? It is down to the different chemicals in the inhibitors.' Gol's voice was deeply melancholy, an actor's voice, a voice belonging on the stage, not in an ancient temple.

443

'You have a question for me?' said Carter.

Gol smiled then, seeming to relax a little. But Carter did not; the M24 remained trained on Gol and he felt the Browning creep into his left hand. He could almost hear the frantic searching of Mongrel behind and he allowed himself to flow with the situation, to calm his heart and brain and notice everything . . .

The floor rolled gently – nauseatingly – beneath him.

The distant wailing and stench poured from the crevasse. Moving towards the edge and glancing down, Carter saw it disappear into an apparent infinity.

Beneath his boots, the carved stone shuddered softly, then started to move. There came a deep and thudding crunch of rock against rock and, glancing up, he saw the ornately carved bridge creep across the circular ceiling and towards the side of the circular cavern. Spanning the ten-metre gap that separated the two men, it would soon provide a means of linking them . . .

Carter smiled, suddenly understanding.

'How do you know that I have a question?' asked Gol.

Carter tilted his head, eyes fixed. 'We are talking, not fighting.'

'The fighting will come later. You remember the QIII? The cubic processor developed by Quantell . . . Spiral_Q? By Feuchter and Durell? You remember it? The processor that you blasted into oblivion with your bullets and hatred?'

'How could I ever forget?'

'It could not see you,' said Gol. 'How was that so?'

'I do not know. Where is the Avelach, Gol? Where is Jam?'

'We both want something,' said Gol, spreading his hands again. 'We need to know why the processor could not see you. Could not predict you.'

'I do not know.'

'Who is Kade?'

Carter froze, his stare fixed on Gol. His mouth was suddenly dry. His eyes drilled like diamond bits into Gol's face.

'I don't know what you mean.'

'Kade, the demon in your soul. Who is he, Carter?'

'I think – think you are mistaken.'

Gol smiled then, and Carter's attention shifted back to the distant doorway. Durell stood there, and now Jam heaved his bulk forward, swaying softly as his claws struck tiny sparks from the stone. Jam started to move forward, swaying as the uneven floor rolled beneath him. Carter's gaze returned to Gol who now held a pistol, a heavy Sig P5, black and evil in his huge hand.

The floor continued to move, pushing Carter off balance. Kade was screaming in his head but still he did not open fire; there was something strange about Gol. The big man's mouth opened and Carter shifted his aim to where Jam strode purposefully forward, heavy triangular head swaying gently from side to side—

'Kill him,' Jam snarled.

Gol's stare met Carter's.

'You seek to save Natasha,' Gol said softly. 'When you find the Avelach, the codes and the secret to its control are inscribed on the silver box that protects it. They must never be separated.'

Gol smiled, then turned and opened fire on Jam with a sudden booming burst of bullets. Jam moved with incredible speed, taking one round in the torso as he bounded forward. He gave a deep gurgling growl and flipped suddenly to one side . . . Gol was moving, sprinting forward, still firing as he leapt to meet the larger Nex—

The gun was smashed from Gol's fist as a huge

whirling blow sent the big man spinning from his feet. Jam reached down *into* himself, his claws coming up with dark blood. He glanced over at Carter, then reached towards Gol who kicked out, hatred in his eyes . . .

Jam grasped Gol, lifting the grey-bearded man by his groin and throat. Gol's boots lashed into Jam's head, powerful blows that rocked the Nex, but Jam pulled Gol into a bear-hug. Their stares met, their faces almost touched and it was as if Carter was witnessing some bizarre act of love. Jam's claws came around and slammed into Gol's back. There was a tearing of cloth and flesh, followed swiftly by a heavy pattering of blood droplets.

Gol's body kicked. Spasmed. Went limp . . .

Then spewed blood across Jam's armoured torso.

And Jam allowed the dead rag-doll body to fall, to lie limp and broken and torn apart on the stone in a crumpled heap. Jam's head came up, glistening, and he stared across at Carter—

Who opened fire, M24 bullets shrieking across the crevasse as the bridge rolled around the walls towards the two combatants. Jam leapt back behind the bank of red stones; more noises of stone on stone were heard, and the bridge slid into itself until there was nothing but an incredible fall into the black pit keeping the two enemies apart.

Carter ceased firing, smoke rising to sting his nostrils.

Jam turned and sprinted for the opening in the following wall. Carter sent more bullets blasting after the fleeing Nex – but failed to hit him.

'Carter, we're trapped.'

Carter glanced around at Mongrel. 'What do you mean, trapped?'

'I leap out to give supporting fire, and this stone door slab thing come down behind me. It block us in.'

'Shit.'

Carter moved forward and stared down into the crevasse. The floor was still moving beneath him and he could see Gol's mangled corpse on the opposite side of the hall.

What's fucking going on here?' he thought.

He glanced up to where the ceiling was revolving and he suddenly realised that it was getting harder to stand. Glancing back, he saw the far end of the chamber slowly lifting, so that he stood on a slope leading down towards the spinning abyss—

'Carter, you stop this thing . . .'

'The whole fucking chamber is suspended, it's going to tip us into the pit . . .'

The angle of elevation gradually increased.

Gol's corpse started to slide away, rasping against the stone, back towards the far distant end of the chamber, leaving a long smear of blood in its wake.

'There no way out, Carter!' Mongrel's voice was filled with panic.

Carter's boots started to scrabble against the rock as it tipped him towards the crevasse. The whining of distant machinery increased, and again crashes of stone on stone reverberated around the huge cavern.

'Bloody Egyptians!' howled Mongrel.

Carter felt himself slipping.

Ahead of him the looming chasm seemed to spin crazily closer, and he felt suddenly sick, filled with an insane nausea and vertigo.

How ironic!

How sweetly fucking ironic.

Not for Carter hot scything steel in his brain, nor a snapped and twisted spine from a crazed motorcycle crash, nor machine-gunned in half on some distant future battlefield. No, this was death by stone—

The old-fashioned way.
The abyss loomed closer—
Death grinned with a mask of dark, aged bone.
And Carter could do nothing to stop them falling . . .

CHAPTER 16

SYSTEM SHOCK

The stone chamber spun, elevated on the scream of ancient gears and tried to spit Carter and Mongrel to their deaths. Boots scrabbling, guns clashing against the stone floor that lifted in front of him, out of the corner of one eye Carter saw something incredible—

Gol was moving. His head came up, beard stained with blood, and his stare fixed on Carter. He heaved himself along the floor, grunting with pain, hauling his torn and shattered body across the incline towards the precipice that threatened to swallow both Carter and Mongrel . . .

Carter fought to stay on his feet. He felt himself slipping towards the revolving crevasse and glanced over at Gol, who was leaving a trail of blood against the intricately carved floor.

Gol had halted, ten feet from the cubes of red stone.

He was panting. Blood was dribbling thickly down his chin.

'What that fucker doing?'

Carter smiled crazily, the whining noise filling his head

and making his ears want to bleed. 'I think he's trying to save us.'

'Why he do that?'

'Mongrel, *stop asking fucking questions*!'

Both Carter and Mongrel could not help themselves; they slid closer and closer towards the edge of the abyss. Gol fought his way upwards until he disappeared behind the red stones – and suddenly the noise died. A terrible eerie silence now filled the massive, tilted, disjointed chamber.

The world halted.

Carter glanced at Mongrel.

'I think he stop it,' said Mongrel.

'I hope so.'

'I hope so too. Not good way to die.'

'What isn't?'

'Falling into a stinking pit. It remind old Mongrel of a story . . .'

'Not . . . fucking . . . *now*.'

Sounds of machinery wailed up from the crevasse once more and for a terrible heart-wrenching moment it seemed that the two men were going to be pitched to their deaths after all. Instead, the whole chamber started to right itself. Carter and Mongrel slumped backwards to the ground, and sat staring at the stones that hid the mangled body of Gol.

Finally, levelling out, the bridge slid out into an arc of interleaving stone panels over the ten-metre gap. Carter climbed to his feet, pulled a grumbling Mongrel up behind him and together they padded over and placed their booted feet warily on the bridge.

'This not another trap?' asked Mongrel.

'Only one way to find out.'

Carter marched across the bridge and stared down at

450

Gol. He lay on his back, staring up at Carter. His eyes were wide and bright.

'Why are you still here?' growled Gol, spitting through blood and froth. 'They've gone to Austria. Every second you stand here you are letting them get away!'

'Why did you do this for us?' asked Carter softly, kneeling and taking Gol's huge hand in his.

Gol met Carter's gaze. 'Maybe I'm just going fucking soft,' he spat through blood-froth.

'I thought you were the enemy?'

'I have been blind, blinded by that fucking machine. But Carter, the Nex . . . they are not just life unworthy of life . . . they feel, they have emotions . . . they can be *changed*.'

'I think you are different to the others,' said Carter.

'Find the Avelach. Use it to heal Natasha. Then you will see, then you will understand . . . but first, up ahead, you will find Durell's control centre for this place, his laboratory . . . there are digital maps, explanations of the Foundation Stones and how LVA is used to control the earthquakes – but you must move quickly . . .'

Carter stood. He exchanged glances with Mongrel as Gol started to cough, his whole body convulsing, blood pouring out of his mouth and nose. Carter lifted his Browning, and sighted it on Gol's forehead. He met the man's gaze.

'Do it,' gurgled Gol.

Carter . . . froze.

'Don't fucking leave me for the *Nex*.'

Carter closed his eyes, and a single echoing shot rang out across the carved stone chamber – ending Gol's life.

The black helicopter lifted from the ground, rotors swirling wide arcs of sand and blasting the other choppers, the

451

wire-mesh fence and the temple walls. Engines howling, the small aircraft lifted off vertically – high into the black Egyptian night – spun in a tight circle and headed off into the darkness towards Cairo.

Lights glittered in Durell's eyes.

'Do you think they are dead?'

Durell glanced at Jam, at the twisted jaws that had straightened a little since he had last examined his subject, allowing Jam's speech more of a human quality. 'Nobody has ever survived that chamber.'

The helicopter spun through the darkness, following the plateau as it fell away from the Red Sea Mountains. Away from the town the pilot dropped them closer towards the rock and sand, and without lights they spun like a black bullet through the night.

'When will we begin the Domination?' asked Jam quietly. The Nex's huge triangular head tilted to look at Durell and Durell found himself shivering at the look in the slitted eyes of the creature he had . . . created.

'Mace tells me that all Foundation Stones are in place. He tells me that the World Investigation Committee is playing games with us, stalling for time and I believe they will never give in . . . I believe they will not relinquish control. I thought some of the weaker states might have folded without a real fight – but I feel our demonstrations are still being viewed as natural events. I will give them something more to play with. I will smash their armies, I will crush their navies and air forces. I will bring down every fucking government building in every fucking city of the world. And only then will I seek to negotiate. Only then will I seek to talk about peace. Once again I find myself surrounded by weakness and indecision, the very factors that will topple Spiral and world governments from their heights of abused power!'

'And we will orchestrate this from Austria?' asked Jam softly.

'It can be the only place.' Durell smiled from the darkness of his robes.

The Priest climbed up into the helicopter, and Heneghan turned, meeting his gaze from behind the HIDSS.

'Code Black?' she whispered, her eyes haunted by the touch of fear.

'Code Black,' rumbled The Priest with a great melancholy in his voice.

The Comanche's twin LHTecs howled as Heneghan hurled the machine into the night sky, cutting through the rain and sleet that pounded against the fuselage of the war machine.

The Priest settled back, lips pursed together, gold-flecked brown eyes narrowing as he considered the mission to come.

It was very simple.

To the point:

Hunt down Carter and stop him. By any means necessary.

'Why did you do this to me, you foolish old bugger?' rumbled The Priest to himself. 'Why did you force me into this path of unrighteousness? I do not want this . . . I do not want to see you die.'

Because he knew.

Knew in his heart and in his soul.

Carter would not cease with his mission to save Natasha . . .

He would never stop.

And he would condemn them all—

The only way to 'stop' Carter would be to kill him.

'Damn you,' muttered The Priest darkly, hand on his

small Bible, which was of little true comfort now as they howled through the dark night's rain and sleet.

Mongrel followed Carter into the chamber, stooping a little beneath the rough red sandstone archway. The lower section of the walls were lined with panels of dark marble containing veins of some mineral that glittered softly. All around the room were benches on which sophisticated computing equipment lay. Carter's head swung back and forth, his eyes narrowed, his M24 clasped tight.

'This place is *old*,' said Mongrel. 'I do not like it here.'

'Is there anywhere you *do* like?'

Mongrel thought deeply, nodding to himself. 'Brothels,' he announced after a few moments.

Carter moved forward, to a large rectangular black screen. The surface of the screen seemed to ripple as Carter reached out and touched it. Lights danced gently around his fingertips and it made a soft lulling sound.

'Kebab shops.'

Carter moved his hand, and with a shock realised that the screen obeyed the same movements as an ECube. Of course – Durell was ex-Spiral. The betrayer. His technology was based on Spiral technology. His computing equipment was a bastardised deviant version of all that Spiral used . . . only warped, twisted and perverted.

'Porn museums.'

'Mongrel, *shut up.*'

Carter traced patterns with his hand and the screen sprang into life. He scrolled through intricate interwoven data, strands coiled with DNA. His eyes searched and he became lost in the digital world. *The chamber no longer existed, this temple in Egypt no longer existed . . . Mongrel pacing the room, keeping a lookout – none of it seemed real as he sunk into the data and felt himself* absorbed . . .

After a few moments, Carter disengaged.

'You find anything?'

'Oh,' said Carter softly.

Mongrel stared at Carter's face. It was ashen.

'Now I understand,' he whispered.

'Is it bad?'

Carter nodded. 'It's fucking bad, all right. We have to tell Spiral. We have to stop Durell.'

'Is it the earthquakes?'

'It is worse than earthquakes,' whispered Carter, turning away and grasping his machine carbine tightly. 'If Durell makes a wrong move in this game he's playing, he could destroy the world.'

'You mean take over the world, right?' growled Mongrel.

'No.' Carter shook his head. 'If Durell fucks up, he'll take us all out with him. Every single living creature on the planet. Have you got that ECube booted up yet?'

'It's flickering between states of stupidity and unreliability. I think the Nex may have compromised the network.'

'Give it to me. We have to tell Spiral – and tell them *now*.'

Simmo halted the HTank and breathed deeply, staring down at the tiny DigitalMap on the tank's ECube-linked scanners. Crushed under the wide heavy tracks, trees and other jungle vegetation creaked softly and Simmo could feel sweat running down his head, stinging the cuts to both the crown of his skull and lesser wounds on his face from the pounding he'd had from Kattenheim. Beneath him cold matrix engines hissed.

They know, said a small voice in his head.

They know you are coming.

Kattenheim has warned them . . .

The LVA depot deep in the Colombian jungle was a large one; it was perhaps five times the size of the one back in Slovenia and one of the largest finds reported by Spiral men across the globe. Hence, logically to Simmo, it had to be the one he personally came to investigate – and destroy. Twenty-four huge tankers containing fuel squatted in the darkness and Simmo's scouts had reported back that there were at least fifty enemy tanks, greytracked Nex TK79s supported by another twenty or so six-wheeled Can-trucks.

Simmo's TankSquad itself sported only thirty Spiral SP57s armed with twin 135mm M512 smoothbore cannons, firing HEAT-X2 combat rounds, and triple heavy-calibre machine guns. They would need the element of surprise to win this one . . . and in Simmo's mind they had been guaranteed that simple necessity before Kattenheim's escape.

Now they would have to make the best of a shit situation.

'I should have let the guys shoot him,' Simmo muttered.

'You OK, boss?' rumbled Oz, his mission co-op.

'Hmm. I is thinking the plateau is nice and wide, hard to protect at front – this why they have so many tanks and trucks. We need to hit them – fast and *now*.'

'Frontal assault?'

'Poor tactic but we have little option. I will take HTank in from behind, down the gulleys and through perimeter fence when you engage. Send message to Rogowski – synchronise for five minutes.'

'Will do,' growled Oz.

Simmo lifted the hatch and poked his head up into the night. A deep dense blackness surrounded him and he felt sweat dribbling under his shirt and down inside the legs of his urban combats.

Parrots shrieked somewhere in the jungle, followed by the chatter of squabbling monkeys. Insects buzzed. Simmo squinted, staring off into the darkness. On the scanners below, he could see the SP57 tanks moving smoothing into position, their twin cannons looking ominous in the gloom.

'You think they know we're here?'

'Maybe,' said Simmo. 'They not move on scanners. ECube reports no engines starting, no activity whatsoever.'

'If this attack is not a surprise, we're fucked, Sarge.'

'You think Sarge not know that?'

'Sorry, Sarge.'

'Is all right, lad.'

The valley was a wide scoop from the Colombian jungle, with steep walls climbing from the basin's base in an insane flurry of tangled trees, flailing creepers, nature-ravaged trunks, ferns and climbers, all competing for life and light. Trees tumbled across trees in great cataracts of spewing vegetation. Ferns mated with creepers, snaking over and around and through huge hardwood mahoganies and oaks. The whole basin was an insanity of jungle through which a wide road had been scythed, leading to the Colombian LVA depot at its heart, and bordered by a natural rough-sawn mahogany barricade at the rear – a huge impassable arc of titanic trunks.

Rain started to fall from heavy clouds swirling in dark skies. It increased quickly to a tropical downpour and Simmo lifted his face, revelling in the large warm droplets which filled him with a sudden vigour – a feeling of youth and indestructibility.

He glanced down at the scanners and watched his

TankSquads moving into place through the rain and wet vegetation. Once a time had been agreed the men kept radio comm and ECube silence.

'Still nothing,' came the voice of Oz. 'Looks like you were wrong about Kattenheim.'

'Don't be too sure.'

Simmo clambered back down and took the controls; he liked being at the controls, he liked to be *in* control. He revved the HTank quietly, engines hissing and cold matrix fumes blowing from exhaust ports in the darkness, then activated the CamCloak. There was a tiny hum. He grinned through his own personal pain.

Easing the HTank forward, he drove it carefully through the thick jungle. Tracks crushed trees and vegetation – and with each sound Simmo winced, hoping to God that his intel was correct and there were no scouts or enemy lookouts nearby.

The huge HTank slowed as it reached the precipice of the valley wall in front of him. Trees scattered off into a treacherously steep black abyss – and distantly he could see bright halogen-II lights through the torrential downpour, illuminating the hive of activity that was the massive LVA depot. He peered at the vid. The tangle of fallen, twisted trees were like dark black emaciated limbs and the strings of creepers were like shrivelled muscles stretched across black pitted bone.

Simmo shivered.

The tracks crunched to a halt, matrix engines hissing.

'Here we go, then,' he whispered.

In an inverted V formation, the SP57 tanks crept forward, two at the point of the advance, then a considerable distance break with most of the remaining tanks following. Tracks crunched and crushed their way noisily through the foliage. The two lead SP57s halted, engines rumbling, and their turrets began a smooth traverse as the tanks readied for a sudden high-speed assault—

From nowhere, the darkness to either side of the lead Spiral tanks suddenly became alive with unexpected explosions and flashes of tank cannon fire. Twin combat rounds flew from the darkness and struck with precision timing, crushing the two lead Spiral tanks from either side and lifting them, suddenly blazing with HighJ purple fire, spinning high into the air where metal disintegrated and dripped flowing in a liquid stream to the forest floor far below.

Rogowski, in the second row of tanks behind this sudden onslaught, froze for a moment as realisation struck him like a brick. There were TK79s camouflaged in the jungle to either side of the trail . . . the Spiral TankSquad had rumbled into an ambush.

Simmo had been right . . .

They had been compromised.

And, thankfully, they had sent the two lead tanks in on REMOTE – as bait, for the enemy to make the first strike and expose their positions. This would give Simmo justi-fication for attacking without specific orders.

It would have been a trap—

Without Simmo's simple but effective battle strategy.

Suddenly, the night lit up like day as tanks camou-flaged with jungle vegetation surged forward and pounded shells into the formation of Spiral tanks, which returned heavy-metal fire as the battle exploded in an onslaught of violence. Engines screamed and tracks ploughed towards the centre of the LVA camp as the Spiral heavy armour roared ahead in a sudden planned attack—

Spiral tank turrets whirled.

Shells spat at savagely close quarters.

Tanks, both Spiral and Nex, caught fire and burned with hellish flames.

Noise ruled.

Noise and fire and destruction . . .

A TK79 was hit, skidding along under the impact, tilting and then collapsing onto one side as it slid through the mud, bulky chassis and heavy tracks crushing five workers to the accompaniment of screams and the snaps of broken bodies. It struck a huge spherical storage tank of LVA fuel. A million gallons of LVA washed out over the trail—

From his vantage point, Simmo stared down in grim silence, watching the raging battle.

The timing has to be right, he thought.

Growling, he dropped the HTank into the darkness . . .

Shells were booming through the halogen-illuminated rain, which swept down in great dark sheets. Fire belched from huge gun barrels as they thudded back in recoil. More tanks were pulverised, sent hurtling skywards in unfolding veils of purple and violet. Exploding gases and billowing bursts of fire seemed to envelop the whole world . . .

'There.'

The HTank fired. The shell hit the TK79 target, spun it round and sent it tumbling through the LVA camp. Machine-gun fire rattled, ricocheting by chance from the HTank's camouflaged armour.

The TK79s were converging now, pursuing the Spiral tanks to the centre of the site. There were more Nex tanks than the Spiral men had at first thought, perhaps seventy or eighty, and they seemed to be unstoppable.

Simmo's HTank squatted at the base of the steep rocky tree-clad slope. He watched as the outgunned and outnumbered Spiral SP57s turned, engines screaming, and started a hasty retreat through the mud and crushed trees.

The TK79s pursued them.

Simmo watched impassively from the safety of his camouflage as he realigned the HTank's superior gun and waited for the right moment . . .

Another LVA tank had been smashed by a well-placed shell. LVA soaked into the glistening mud. The SP57s retreated, crushing a barracks as they apparently fled the enemy in a sudden panic – and the Nex tanks formed into a fighting unit with their guns facing forward. They slowed to manoeuvre through the bottleneck leading from the LVA depot—

Simmo smiled, sighted, and hit the launch key.

Six programmed K-TF8 guided missiles were loosed from the HTank's camouflaged and electronically invisible hull. Rockets trailing blue jets of fire sped out, seeking the massive containers of LVA premium-grade fuel . . .

Simmo and Oz hunkered down inside the HTank and prayed.

Engines howling, the SP57s fled from the LVA-depot basin, the site of their supposed ambush . . .

Missile warheads detonated.

LVA ignited.

And the night was suddenly lit with an unfurling of gas and fire which seemed at first to creep into the sky, consuming vegetation as it went, tracers spinning around the ever-expanding cloud of destruction—

Then came a roar of infinite devastation.

Followed by the sounds of nearly a hundred TK79s being smashed together, superheated and fused into a single solid lump of steel and alloy. Melted Nex briefly ran like candle-wax fat and were then vaporised in the sudden apocalypse. Barracks were kicked into oblivion, the LVA containers disintegrated into shards of twisted steel which then melted and rained fiery droplets from the now-contracting fireball—

A deep rumbling followed.

The very earth shook.

Simmo, panting, waited for the noise to subside. He checked his scanners – and learned that the SP57s had followed their orders precisely, forming a huge wall in their apparently chaotic but well-timed 'flight' and flinging up combined protective shields against the fury they knew was about to engulf the camp.

Simmo flung open the hatch, which clanged against the HTank's hull as he climbed up into the rain. All was darkness and shadows, lit by a million scattered small fires at the edges of the blast zone – the perimeter of the titanic combined missile and LVA explosion. Simmo could smell gas and the stench of burning vegetation. The whole LVA depot had been disintegrated, vaporised – destroyed.

Simmo jumped down onto the hard-baked mud. He strode forward with his Sig in his fist towards the twisted, fused block of steel and iron, its shape almost organic in its sculpted curves and waves.

Oz joined him.

Rain poured down on them.

'Good plan, Sarge,' Oz said. 'We sure nuked the fuck out of those bastards. Good job the lead tanks had no crew, eh? Did *we* lose many in the rest of the battle?'

'We always lose too many,' growled Sergeant Simmo. 'But no – we lose only four men this time. Four good men. But at major loss to enemy! Go get me a sitrep from the rest of the TankSquad. And get some scouts out, do some ECube scans, see if there are any other fuckers waiting for us . . . and get the fucking shields recharged.'

'Aye aye, cap'n' said Oz, grinning.

'And Oz?'

'Hm?'

'You *ever* speak to me like a Trekkie again, and I will shoot you in throat without trial.'

Oz gulped. 'OK, Sarge.'

Simmo sat on the HTank's hull, watching the fires that still lit the jungle through the rain. ECube scans had revealed no organic traces of Kattenheim in the massive tank wreckage, nor organic slivers in the rubble of the barracks and the surrounding destroyed LVA storage tanks. What remained of the derrick and pump were nothing more than tiny blackened stumps, broken fingers poking forlornly into the tropical downpour.

Rogowski approached with Mo, who was carrying his usual huge mug of tea. Simmo watched the curls of steam from the Pakistani's massive container of sweet brew for a moment, then transferred his gaze to the two men's worried faces.

'Anything?'

Rogowski made his report. 'Another squad of Nex tanks has been alerted. They're at some sort of refinery twenty klicks down the river. We reckon about sixty machines in all, TK79s again with a few TK82s thrown in for good measure and bang-per-buck firepower. There's still no sign of Kattenheim, although that doesn't mean he escaped.'

'You sure are a mean motherfucker, Sarge,' said Mo, dark brown eyes gleaming. He sipped from his huge mug of tea, grimacing as he burnt his tongue. 'That was a very clever manoeuvre, getting them to chase us and line up with the LVA tankers . . . *nasty*. I wouldn't like to be on the opposite side to *you* in a war.'

Simmo scratched at the weeping red line on his skull,

where his head had been stapled back together again after Kattenheim's heavy blow. He smiled a dangerous smile as he surveyed the fused work of art. 'Better fucking believe it,' he growled, and lit a cigar. Puffing out huge grey clouds of tobacco smoke, he muttered, 'A refinery, you say? It not appear on our Spiral scout maps?'

'They must have missed it. Or it was too well camouflaged to be spotted from the air,' said Mo, glancing around nervously at the flickering shadows. Raindrops sent concentric ripples across his lake of tea and the huge Pakistani soldier tried to shelter his precious brew.

'You gonna send an ECube blip? Let Spiral know what went down here?'

'Yes.' Simmo nodded. 'But only after we pay this LVA refinery a visit. Don't want to spoil our fun, do we?'

'So we're a private army now, are we?' said Oz softly, meeting Simmo's gaze.

'No – we just carrying out orders *before* they been issued. You trust The Sarge on this. The Sarge never been wrong in battle. *Never.* We just taken on and destroyed a force more than double our own . . . and you still here sipping your tea. Now we go visit refinery and see how this new Nex tank threat measure up. You with me, lads?'

'We're with you, all right,' said Oz, eyes glinting in the light of the fires of the burning LVA site.

'Sure, we'd follow you to Hell and back,' said Rogowski.

'Not wise offer to make,' said Simmo, drawing heavily on his cigar and still constantly scanning the periphery of the destroyed LVA refinery. 'Because before this thing over, Sarge think you may have to do just that.'

Carter paused on the steps, his body screaming in raw agony, and glanced further down the stone spiral to where

Mongrel stood, legs braced, chest heaving and a look of pain and nausea on his broad face.

'Come *on*!'

'I'm shagged. You go on without me!'

'I'll put a fucking bullet in your head if you don't shift your arse.'

'Suddenly, Carter's Browning lifted and there was a deafening series of shots as five bullets spat from the barrel, skimmed Mongrel's shoulder and took a pursuing Nex in the face. Its body flipped backwards and toppled down the narrow stairwell.

'Looks like the rest have realised that we're here.'

Mongrel grunted something incomprehensible, and started to sprint up the steep stairs after Carter. The two men ran, their bodies throbbing with pain, sweat coursing down their faces.

A cold breeze blew from above and they suddenly emerged—

Into the Egyptian night. A short walkway led around the side of the temple from the small hole – Durell's escape tunnel – where the two Spiral operatives had appeared; it was paved with black marble and led to the—

'Helicopters.'

'They're on the move,' muttered Carter. 'Come on.'

'Should we not go back for Comanche?'

'*Why?*'

'It ours. It Spiral's. It fucking expensive. I don't want *that* deducted from monthly salary payment, that for sure. I want to retire as fat old man, happy with pension, not paying for damn stupid mistake in desert with billion-dollar combat helicopter.'

'God,' said Carter, 'it's like being on a fucking mission with my wife. Stop fucking nagging.'

They crept around the outskirts of the temple and

465

could see further squads of Nex in the street outside. But none inside the compound. Quickly but cautiously they edged towards the four remaining black helicopters—

As machine-gun hell broke loose from behind them . . .

Bullets, some of them tracer, flew all around. Carter sprinted for the nearest chopper as Mongrel shoved his shoulder against the temple wall and opened fire. Carter dropped to one knee beside the machine and opened fire, allowing Mongrel time to retreat to his side and change mags. Then Carter leapt into the cockpit as a line of bullets slammed into the alloy beside his head. He flicked the controls, set the rotors spinning and palmed his Browning, holding it double-handed and taking careful aim—

Tracer lit the sky.

Carter shot the Nex in the face.

Silence reigned for a few moments. Then engines whined, the rotors started to spin and Mongrel clambered up beside Carter.

No alarm sounded, and there were no shouts of distress or warning. But suddenly a huge swarm of Nex came out of the darkness. Carter hurled the small black helicopter up into the night with Mongrel shooting furiously from the doorway, his face lit by muzzle flash, his few remaining teeth clenched in concentration and grim determination.

The temple and small town fell away. A few rounds of tracer spun past them up into the darkness and were lost as Carter armed the chopper's machine guns.

'What you doing?'

'Hold on.'

The helicopter, engines screaming, suddenly levelled and then dropped nose first from the heavens, plummeting towards the temple, the valley and the three remaining helicopters. Bullets blasted from the on-board heavy machine guns, cutting lines of sparks across the three remaining choppers.

There was an explosion and Carter lifted the helicopter higher on a cloud of flames that reached out with a yellow fist to smash the Nex into oblivion. Fire raged across the helicopter landing yard, scorching the ancient walls of the temple, followed by the clatter of falling metal panels, twisted and blackened.

Carter and Mongrel cruised through the darkness.

The blue glow from the ECube lit their faces.

'Where they going?' Mongrel was breathless, sweat staining his brow.

Carter frowned. 'It looks like Cairo.'

'I thought Gol said they go to Austria?'

'Who fucking knows? But they have the Avelach and the QuakeHub, and we must stop them.'

'I just think it strange they off course.'

'Maybe they're avoiding SAM sites we know nothing about.'

Mongrel shrugged.

Carter pushed the helicopter hard, crossing the desert over Gebel al-Galala al-Qibliya, heading towards Cairo. Engines howling, it took them a little over two hours and as the dawn light started to creep over the horizon so the scatter of buildings below began to increase in number as they approached the Nile.

'We're gaining on it,' said Mongrel.

'Good,' snapped Carter, eyes weary, hands gripped tight on the helicopter's controls.

'No – wait.'

'What?'

'It's stopped.'

'*What?*'

'No . . . no, I've lost it.'

Carter glanced at Mongrel. 'How can you fucking *lose* it? The ECube is never wrong.'

'I fucking tell you Carter, I lost damn thing! It not on ECube scanners, and it . . . oh.'

'What now?'

Mongrel shook the ECube, and Carter met his gaze, scowling. Digits flickered, then died. Mongrel's expression grew puzzled and he placed his finger against his lips.

'I'm thinking . . .'

'Don't just fucking think,' snapped Carter, peering through the helicopter's cockpit at the dawn-bathed city below them. 'Sort it!' He cruised closer, reducing his speed as the towers, apartment blocks, statues and minarets came gradually into view. They passed the Nile, and the Tahrir Bridge. Even at this early dawn hour the city of Cairo was heaving, a bustling hive of activity. Faces turned up towards them as they buzzed overhead.

Machine-gun fire erupted and Carter slammed the controls to the right. The helicopter flipped to one side, diving towards the city below with a wail of engines as Durell's machine closed on them at high speed, gun barrels blazing fire and rounds slamming into the hijacked chopper.

Carter spun the machine, flipping it down almost to street level and then slamming along, people cowering beneath him as he wrestled with the controls. Durell's machine followed closely, machine guns blazing as bullets chewed up the street and sent civilians to their deaths in showers of fine blood mist. Carter dragged the chopper back up into the sky, narrowly missing a shabby tower block.

Mongrel glanced out of the cockpit.

'They close, Carter.'

Carter growled something obscene and the helicopter dipped again, thrumming low towards street level and the closely packed structures. Durell's machine followed as Carter tried to shake them, weaving between buildings, spinning through the narrow streets, thousands of faces staring skywards in wonder and fear as machine guns fired once more and a bullet ricocheted from the stolen 'copter's rotors—

'Carter!' yelled Mongrel.

Carter slammed the helicopter to the right, whirling tightly around a minaret and heading for a densely packed group of crumbling suburban apartment blocks sporting neon roof signs for Coke and SmashVID. Dipping lower, the helicopter raced through the streets, buildings tightly packed to either side, Durell's howling machine close behind.

More machine-gun fire followed.

'This is getting tiresome,' growled Carter, spinning the helicopter in a tight bank down a side street. Engines screamed, the whole helicopter vibrated and the landing struts scraped a shower of concrete dust from an already tottering wall.

Durell's machine pursued.

Carter slammed the helicopter left, then right. They powered away from the cluster of apartment blocks as the following heavy machine-gun fire chased them relentlessly.

The sun was rising higher in the sky.

Light bathed Carter's face, blinding him for a split second.

Guns blasted.

Machine-gun fire over Egypt,' sighed Kade. *'Now that* is *a beautiful sight. A Wonder of the World, no less.'*

469

Carter found his way back into the maze of three- and four-storey apartments. Activity seemed almost to have ceased on the ground below as people abandoned their cars and took shelter wherever they could.

More bullets slammed into the back of the stolen helicopter and Carter cursed, Kade screaming inside his head, unable to shake the pilot of Durell's helicopter. Panic washed over him in a wave but he forced his body to relax and grow calm – and tried to think.

He slammed the machine to the left, dipping low, landing struts almost clipping the roofs of the cars lining the street bumper to bumper. Men and women ran for cover, hands raised futilely for protection. Some cowered in doorways as the screaming engines smashed over their heads.

Bullets chewed a wall to Carter's right.

He started to lift the helicopter, but realised that something was wrong as Mongrel shouted, 'We've got a fucking fire.'

'Jump!' Carter yelled.

The helicopter started to wobble furiously in its trajectory and Carter realised with horror that he could no longer control the wounded beast. Below, people were running, screaming and sprinting for cover. Mongrel's stare met Carter's and Mongrel stepped to the doorway as a building loomed close. Powered by instinct and without a second to think, he leapt.

Mongrel fell through the air, arms flailing wildly, and hit a concrete roof hard. It slammed into his face and body and he rolled madly for what seemed an age, his gun cutting into his ribs, until he slammed to a halt against a yellow-painted parapet, crushing a plant pot between himself and the wall. Shards of pottery speared his flesh like terracotta knives.

Mongrel tried to breathe—

But could not.

He levered himself up and saw the helicopter connect with an apartment block. It seemed to fold in upon itself, rotors bending at right angles as the machine compacted with a shriek of tortured metal and then—

Then it exploded.

A huge wave of fire erupted upwards and outwards, and Mongrel blinked at the sudden gaping hole in the apartment block. Black smoke rolled up. The flaming helicopter carcass shifted and then dropped from the hole that it had smashed for itself in the concrete wall and hit the ground, crushing eight people.

Hearing their screams as they burned, Mongrel staggered to his feet and scanned the sudden chaos below. People were swarming everywhere. Car horns were honking, men were shouting, women crying, and Mongrel searched in vain for Carter as pain stabbed him from a thousand sources and he tried hard just to breathe . . .

Where are you, Carter?

But he could not see his friend.

'Fuck.'

Suddenly, horrified at his vulnerability, Mongrel ducked and glanced up at the sky. But Durell's helicopter had gone. He glanced back down at the chaos and saw a few snarling men pointing his way.

Mongrel frowned.

Bullets ate a line along the parapet.

'What?' he wailed down at the gun-wielding Egyptians. 'It was a fucking accident!'

More bullets nearly took his head off.

'You fuckers.' He returned fire, then ran for it, head low, towards an adjoining roof. He leapt, missed the parapet, and fell a single storey, landing heavily on a folding

471

table stacked with bottles of beer. Glass smashed all around him.

People started shouting, their voices harsh.

Bullets crackled from various handguns.

Stinking of cheap Egyptian beer, Mongrel put his tufted head down and ran for his life.

CHAPTER 17

QUAKE

Carter was being attacked from all sides. Sandstone blocks came out of the darkness and hammered him against the desert. People were screaming – and he realised that it wasn't people but an engine, howling through the centre of his brain. He felt himself falling, wind rushing through his hair as a blood-red insanity screamed through him. He gasped and the heat rushed up. Pain smashed through his body and he lay, panting, listening to the sounds of his own ragged breathing. He felt the horrifying warmth of blood running slowly over his flesh. And then screams, and chanting, words recited over and over again in an Arab dialect that he thought he understood, in words that he should have known. But his understanding fled him. The chanting reverberated around his skull. And then he felt boots and sandals kicking him and he curled into a ball in the sand. Single gunshots rang out, then the rattle of automatic gunfire – and the physical blows suddenly stopped.

Carter opened his eyes warily.

He could see a sandstone wall, smeared with beautiful

curving red swirls of Arabic graffiti. And he could see sand and feel the heat. And smell the camels.

More voices shouted.

In the distance, there came the roar of an explosion. People screamed. Carter could smell burning flesh. He sank into a state of unconsciousness and he thankfully allowed the blackness to take him. He remembered no more.

We need to tell Spiral. About the Foundation Stones – and about the LVA and how it all links in with Durell and his fucking QuakeHub . . .

Well – you're no fucking good like this.

What has happened? Where am I?

Open your fucking eyes and you'll find out.

I don't want to open my eyes. I am afraid of what I might see.

Your worst fucking nightmare, my friend. You remember them kicking you? The mob kicking you? They remember you, Carter, remember your face . . . from before. They know who you are, they know the things you did, the children you slaughtered . . .

Children? Where am I Kade?

You are in Egypt, Carter. And you are a prisoner.

Oh my God . . .

Yes, Carter, your worst nightmare . . . you remember? Me and Egypt – well, I will teach that fucker a lesson it shall never, ever forget . . .

Oh no, Kade, I remember the last time I let you loose in Egypt—

So do I, gloated Kade.

Carter fought.

He fought for a long time. But too much had happened – he

had lost a lot of blood, taken too many beatings at the hands of men and Nex intent on his murder. His fears and frustrations over Natasha had put him in a prison of his own horror and weakness.

Carter folded.

Folded like damp newspaper.

And Kade took control.

Kade opened his eyes.

The scene, as ever, glistened in glorious black and white. Kade tilted his head, felt the smash of pain hammer through his body and with a silent snarl of contempt hurled it away. The bruises and bumps, the cuts and grazes, the cracked ribs, the fractured knuckle, the stapled gunshot wound in his back, the loss of skin and the impacts from the KTM crash, the battering from the helicopter crash – were as nothing, merely ant stings to an elephant. Kade surveyed his grey-spectrum surroundings.

He was in a cell made of light grey sandstone. Bars ran from floor to ceiling, and without moving his head Kade could see a broad rough-timber desk on which a fan whirred softly, stirring a sheaf of papers held down at one corner by a makeshift paperweight. A gun.

Kade's stare fastened on the weapon.

It was Carter's Browning. And he could see that the magazine was still in place, the safety catch off. Kade smiled, a flickering of his lips – a dark expression, something that should never be seen on the face of a mortal.

Kade watched a man moving around what he assumed was an office. He shifted his head slightly, took in the row of perhaps fifteen cells, some occupied, most empty. The other cell occupants – separated from Kade by floor-to-ceiling barriers of bars – looked bedraggled, worn, poor and ill. Kade wrinkled his nose in distaste.

Fucking criminal scum, he thought.

Kade watched the policeman shuffling papers, then turning in response to a call and shouting a reply in Arabic. Kade shifted gear in his brain and tuned in.

Shut up, or you'll get another beating, the Egyptian policeman had said.

Kade pushed himself up on one elbow, hearing a broken rib click. Despite his stealth, the policeman heard him and turned, smiling humourlessly. He had very black hair, quite shaggy, and bushy eyebrows. He also had a moustache that drooped over his top lip and down to the line of his jaw. His eyes were dark and Kade noted how lithely he moved. Like an athlete. A *warrior*.

'Ah, the bad man awakes.'

Kade said nothing.

'Oh, it was such joy when you were delivered to us. God punished you, my friend. He brought you back to us for repayment.'

The Egyptian moved closer to the bars and Kade stood smoothly, stretching with an almost feline grace, arching his back. Kade leant his head left, then right.

The Egyptian placed his hands on his hips and grinned at Kade. It was a savage grin. 'Do you remember? Do you remember the things you did here, English man?'

'You have the wrong guy,' said Kade smoothly. 'I am a citizen of the United Kingdom and I demand to see a representative of my country immediately.'

'Well, I am Abdul Hassaq, and I *know* you, I *know* the things you did here. I was a member of one of the many teams who helped to clear away the bodies. I was involved in the search for you after the burned children were scraped from the streets. I do not forget. I am not stupid. And you will *die*. Now, I suggest that you sit down and make your peace with God, if that is possible. He will

476

judge you for your crimes, and deny you your rights – by all that is holy.'

'No, no, my good man, you really have made a most grievous mistake. A case of mistaken identity, in fact. I am a journalist here to investigate the recent earthquakes and seismic activity in different parts of the globe. Jonathan Swift is my name, a graduate of Oxford, ha ha . . .'

Kade clasped the bars. His knuckles were white. He smiled and his eyes held pure dark evil. His gaze danced from the Egyptian policeman's face to his clothing to his belt, and then to the gleaming smooth leather holster that held his *gun*.

Kade slipped free the MercG from his pocket and spun the mercury garrotte to activate it. The liquid metal thread flashed in two powerful horizontal swipes and Kade stepped back, watching as four thick metal bars tumbled and clanged to the stone floor. The Egyptian's expression turned from righteous contemplation to sudden and acute horror.

The policeman froze for an instant, and Kade leapt through the neatly sliced hole in the bars as the man grabbed at the holstered pistol at his hip and aimed it. Kade lashed the MercG like a whip – which sliced vertically down the weapon's barrel, continuing on to cut the policeman's hand in two as far as the wrist. There was a clatter as the two parts of the weapon hit the ground in a shower of bubbling crimson. The Egyptian was staring in disbelief at his pumping appendage even as Kade whirled and, in a continuation of the same movement, placed the MercG through the Egyptian's neck with the precision of a Samurai swordsman.

Kade lifted himself from his crouch and deactivated the MercG, coiling the thin wire into the pocket of his badly torn and bloodstained trousers. He tilted his head, considering coolly the shocked gaze of the Egyptian policeman – and the narrow line of red across his throat. Then one of his knees buckled, blood flooded down his chin, turning the tips of his moustache into a dark glossy beard, and his head slid free and slopped onto the floor. Kade saw the yellow glimmer of severed spine within fat-pulp and flesh.

He gave a mock shiver.

'Ooh, I am *dangerous*,' he crooned softly and lifted the Browning from the table, settling the stocky grip in his battered hand.

One of the other prisoners, the nearest one, started to get a bit twitchy. He was peering through the bars of his cell and could make out the severed head of the police-man lying limp and bloody on its side, spilling a little yellow neck-fat to the stone floor. He opened his mouth and started to shout something . . .

Kade hissed, in Arabic, 'Shut the fuck up or I'll cut off your balls.' The man took one look at the levelled Browning and retired to the corner of his cell, curling into a ball and closing his eyes to blank out the demon gaze of Kade's insanity.

Kade took a large bunch of keys, including digital PlasSticks, from the policeman's pockets, and found a small bag of chewy sweets. Popping one into his mouth, he started to hum as he moved to the barred windows and stared out into the street. Across it, on the other corner, a group of people had gathered – and Kade could see by the looks in their eyes that they were a lynch mob. Obviously they did not believe that the police would conduct a fair trial with him, and believed that their own meat cleavers could deliver a finer slice of retribution to the evil man in the cell.

'Dum de dum de dum.' Kade chewed his sweet and

strolled – almost happily, certainly calmly – to the front door of the police station, locking it and sliding three thick bars into place. Then he heard a voice shouting from the station's interior and he moved smoothly to the doorway, standing discreetly to one side.

Another policeman appeared, carrying a yellow folder. He stopped. His gaze dropped and he gasped. Kade blew his head open. Still chewing, Kade stooped and pulled the policeman's gun free, checking the magazine.

'Yum yum, cherry flavour,' said Kade, helping himself to another sweet. More shouting erupted from the interior of the police station and Kade sighed, almost resignedly, hoisting both weapons in his blood-slick grasp.

He tilted his head, smiling at a cowering prisoner and shaking his head almost in sadness.

'Time to go to work,' he sighed.

It had been a hard climb, but at least the two pilots on the roof of the *Egyptian Times* news building had not been armed. Two punches and two broken cheekbones later, Mongrel had dragged them away from the civilian helicopter and stared in horror at the white flanks of the RT10 with their bright red and yellow stripes. Mongrel glanced around, realised he had been caught on some form of CCTV, and decided that standing next to two unconscious men while armed with a sub-machine gun was not going to endear him to the journalistic staff of the building below – nor to the inevitable security and police forces who would follow.

Mongrel stared at the name etched on the machine's flanks.

An RT10 Dandelion.

'An RT10 fucking *Dandelion*,' he muttered.

Mongrel fired up the helicopter, and listened in agony

as the rotors began their snail-speed acceleration. There came a curious metallic squeaking sound that made Mongrel shudder.

From a nearby building Mongrel had watched Carter being beaten up by a mob, and had been just about to open fire with his M24 when five policemen had waded in, driving back the crowd who were armed with sticks, bottles and rifles, and dragging a bloodied Carter into their battered old Land Rover. Thinking that he and Carter needed transport fast, Mongrel had decided to secure the helicopter from the nearest logical source – the news building. But, just after punching the two pilots into oblivion, he had heard the familiar distant report of Carter's Browning from the police station below – and decided that his best option was to take to the air and monitor events from there . . .

Carter was obviously looking after himself.

The 'copter spun into action and Mongrel climbed on board. He hated flying – and admitted to everybody including himself that he was, basically, an awful pilot.

The RT10 Dandelion helicopter waggled into the air, a dangerous combination of underpowered civilian engines, a worn rudder and a lack of engine oil. Mongrel's lack of experience and confidence didn't help. Mongrel watched as men ran onto the roof of the *Egyptian Times* news building, waving their arms at him. He swooped high over their heads with the metallic noise singing a discordant song in his ears, and headed off to the west in what he considered to be a decoy manoeuvre in case these men wanted to chase him.

Mongrel came around in a wide arc, noting that crowds seemed to be gathering in the streets below. Many seemed to be armed, and were waving and chanting.

'Not look good,' mused Mongrel.

And something else gnawed at him. He tried to place his finger on it. It was something to do with the guards on the rooftop.

What had it been?

The helicopter thrummed around again and Mongrel was searching now. Where would Carter emerge from? It would not be the front door – there was a crowd there already, hammering against the old worn wood. The roof, then? It had to be his only way of escape.

Mongrel prayed that Carter had seen him . . .

He swooped, the engines whining in a strange way that he had never heard before inside a chopper. And then he saw it: on the roof of the police station a door flew open and Carter came into view, firing a gun in each hand. Blood pooled across the floor at his feet and he slammed shut the door, reaching and grasping a bar and sliding it into place through rope hooks.

Mongrel dropped the helicopter.

It still nagged at him: what had been wrong with the men on the roof of the newspaper building?

The helicopter touched down on the police station roof.

Carter leapt in, and his dark-eyed stare moved over Mongrel arrogantly. Carter was soaked in blood, and for a moment Mongrel thought he was wounded . . .

'You OK?'

'You took your fucking time,' snapped Kade. 'I'm fucking covered in blood, had to kill sixteen fucking policemen in there – not that that's a bad thing.' He flashed a shark smile. 'All fucking police deserve to die, whatever their nationality.'

'Carter?'

'Hmm?'

'You're not hurt?'

481

'Nah, never felt better.'

A figure appeared on a neighbouring rooftop and opened fire with a sub-machine gun. Bullets kicked up tiny showers of dust and Kade stepped calmly away from the civilian chopper as the rounds ate their way towards his legs. He aimed the Browning and the gun bucked in his fist, firing three bullets that smacked into the Egyptian soldier's head and dropped him in an instant.

'Now the military is involved. What a bummer! I was enjoying shooting the pigs,' he chuckled darkly.

Mongrel lifted the chopper into the sky. He was frowning . . . and knew that something was badly wrong with Carter. It did nothing to relieve his misgivings about their situation.

And now the Egyptian military as well?

Shit . . .

Kade popped another sweet into his mouth. He held out the bag to Mongrel as the chopper wobbled over Cairo, rotors whining above them as crowds of civilians, police and military swarmed through the streets below in an attempt at pursuit.

'You want a sweet?'

'A fucking *sweet*?' bellowed Mongrel. 'We've got the fucking Egyptian army fucking after us now, and you ask if I want a fucking *sweet*? There'll be fucking military 'copters here in a few minutes, with fucking heavy machine guns.'

'Yeah? So? It's only a fucking sweet!' snapped Kade, frowning. 'And anyway, what's wrong with this pile of shit? Couldn't you find something a little more –' he searched for a word, licking at his cherry-tinted lips – '*exciting*?'

The rotors whined again, and now there was a grinding note in the sound.

And then Mongrel realised what had been wrong with

the guards on the rooftop. They had been waving their arms to him – and yet they'd carried sub-machine guns slung over their shoulders. Their intention hadn't been to stop him . . . but to *warn* him.

Why?

Another grinding sound came.

'I think you've picked a dud fucking chopper, my fat friend.' Kade fired a few bullets into the swarming crowd below, laughing as bodies rolled in the dust.

'What are you doing?' hissed Mongrel.

Kade ignored him – then suddenly whirled, pointing down. 'Over there. Towards the south. There's a military airfield. Take us there *now*!'

Mongrel flew in silence, jaws clamped tightly closed, his mind whirling. He glanced across at Carter – and saw an expression on the man's face that he had never seen before. Mongrel looked at Carter: the battered and torn clothing, the cuts and bruises, the drying blood, the pieces of brain tissue and fragments of bone in his hair. He was a demon figure, a nightmare horror-show walking the earth, dealing out hot gunfire from his bruised and sliced hands . . .

He feels no pain, Mongrel realised.

And no remorse . . .

The chopper banked, leaving the surging crowds in the streets behind. It swept down low over buildings, mostly built from sandstone and a few from breeze-block and rusting corrugated metal sheeting. Dogs barked, and women shouted.

The rotors continued to scream above the two men—

And then the control-panel dials started to flicker madly as certain pressures dropped.

Kade caught Mongrel's stare. 'You fucking looking at something?'

483

'Yeah, something bad,' snapped Mongrel.

'There.' Kade pointed. 'The El Kashem airfield. I don't think this bag of shit is going to get us anywhere. You see that grey plane over there?'

'You mean the MiG?'

'Aye.' Kade nodded, smiling slyly, and popped another sweet into his mouth. 'Land next to it.'

'And what about those guards with those big fucking dogs?'

Kade slammed a fresh magazine into his Browning. 'You leave them to me,' he growled, sucking hard.

Carter tumbled through darkness, falling for ever. He spun, curled in a ball, round and round and round, wind lashing through his hair. His eyes were clenched shut and he contained the *pain*. It was an animal raging within him and he cursed Kade; Kade had trapped him, ensnared him within a cage of agony and in fury Carter punched out at the dark invisible veil all around him—

He heard the gunshots. The yelps of the dogs.

Carter's jaw tightened grimly.

The pain beat in huge tidal waves against the shore of his brain.

Pulsed, like an evil cancer.

Smashed him with the eternity of death . . .

Light flooded in, as if somebody had torn a hole in the canvas of darkness surrounding him. Carter pushed away the pain, felt it slide between him and Kade as Kade fought him with claws of steel. He dropped to his knees, spittle drooling from his mouth and the desert sun scorching his eyes, lancing directly into his tortured cerebellum . . .

Carter coughed.

The Browning felt solid in his throbbing fist.

He glanced up – at the airfield, at the sand under him, at the corpses of Egyptian soldiers – and four dead Alsatian dogs, their heads twisted back, long canine tongues protruding and their blood staining the desert.

Carter breathed deeply, cursing, as Kade's laughter drifted into a haunting nothingness. He glanced back at Mongrel, who was staring at him with disgust.

Carter climbed to his feet.

'I'm back,' he said softly.

'What's that fucking supposed to mean?' snarled Mongrel.

Carter approached the large man, weariness suddenly hitting him with an incredible intensity, sucking away his will to go on. He reached out and placed his blood-caked hand against Mongrel's tattered Nex clothing.

'I am sorry, Mongrel. That was not me.'

Mongrel's eyes glittered. 'What you mean, Carter? I don't like what I fucking see here.'

Sirens wailed from the distance. Carter stared down at the eight dead Egyptian soldiers, their faces and bodies blown apart by the wrath of the Browning. He felt something go cold inside and he made a promise to himself – when this was all over he would find a way to kill Kade. He would burn that fucker in the furnace of his mind.

'Those men did not deserve this,' said Carter softly.

'What?' snapped Mongrel. 'I seen bad things in my time, and you one of them, Carter.' And Carter caught it, the big man was afraid.

And Carter felt shame.

A deep shame that burned him.

The sirens were getting louder. Across the airfield jeeps sped into view, displaying the red flashing lights of military police. Carter stooped under the grey belly of the big Russian MiG 8-40 MFI – *Mnogofunktsionalny Frontovoi*

Istrebitel – and kicked out the wooden block from behind the front wheel. He moved under the wings, kicking out the rear blocks as Mongrel heaved himself up the narrow ladder to the cockpit and climbed into the co-pilot's seat.

Carter followed him up. He stopped for a moment, glancing over at Cairo. The sights and scents of the city had filled him with an awe that he would never forget. But he knew that he was cursed in this place, hated and reviled, condemned to die. He could never again witness its wonders without risking a bullet in the back.

Carter breathed deeply, dropped into the cockpit and pushed the ladder into its housing. He stared at the controls in front of him, reached out, and flicked on the power. Powering-up whines came from the aircraft's batteries and Carter touched the control screen, which sprang to life with a display of Russian and subtitled Arabic.

'Hmm.'

'You know how to fly this, Carter?'

'Aye.'

The sirens were getting uncomfortably close. Carter started the engines, which roared into life with the awesome, deafening thunder of quad Saturn/Lyulka A184-F turbofans and the reined-in energies of 200,000 pounds of thrust. Grasping the controls, Carter eased the MiG 8-40 around in a circle to face the long expanse of sand-blown tarmac. The runway stretched into the distance, meeting the horizon through a shimmer of desert heat.

Excitement welled in Carter's breast – excitement at such awesome and mind-blowing power, mixed with his fear of flying and falling and heights. He also had the terrible certainty that if he fucked up then he would be dog meat, pulped in a battered can, within about thirty seconds flat . . .

Machine guns rattled from the jeeps.

Bullets zipped over the wings . . .

Carter hit the burners. The MiG 8-40 MFI's engine note rose to a scream and the fighter juddered around the two men. It screeched down the runway, leaving trails of rubber on the dusty tarmac, lifted its nose towards the sky and the orange sun – and soared smoothly up into the heavens . . .

Sunlight gleamed along the fighter's grey flanks.

The wheels lifted neatly into the machine's underbelly with tiny and precise clicks.

And the MiG 8-40 banked, wings gleaming, and headed towards the south and west.

'We're going in the wrong direction.'

'No, we're going to pick up the Comanche.'

'Why?'

'All our equipment is there. And our explosives. Everything we could need.'

Mongrel frowned. 'How long will it take?'

'In this?' said Carter, gazing out over the rapidly undulating desert. 'Well, we're currently cruising at 2,000 kilometres an hour – so a little over ten minutes. Now *that*'s pretty fucking fast.'

The MiG 8-40 MFI was a multi-functional front-line fighter. It was built primarily for air-to-air combat but it also carried payloads both in its belly and on pylons beneath its wings for tactical air-to-air surface strikes. Built by MiG – the Mikoyan & Gurevich aviation, scientific and production complex of the MAPO military-industrial corporation of the Northern Russian Confederacy – the war machine had quad Saturn/Lyulka A184-F engines with turbofans and Needle_injectors capable of upwards of 200,000 pounds of thrust when using afterburners. It had

System5 thrust vectoring channels to allow the fighter to make extremely sharp turns. The jet could supercruise at an awesome 2,600 km/h, had a top thrust speed of 3,245 km/h and a flight ceiling of a little over 27,500 metres. The plane was a cranked delta-wing, with triple tail fins, and it had intakes under the nose. It measured twenty-two metres in length and had a wingspan of sixteen metres. It sported Phazotron Plasma TW-35 phased-array fire-control radar, rearward-facing N-018 radar and Global PK18 TSAM control radar. It also carried the latest generation of plasma-cloud stealth systems – known as PCSS-5s – for the simple beauty of undetected infiltration.

After scanning the machine's systems and struggling through the Russian and Arabic instructions, Carter could see that this machine packed quad 30mm canons, and carried eight R-80 AA-e Aphid air-to-air missiles, and twelve KH-68 AS-13 Kilter tactical air-to-surface missiles, each 4.98 metres long.

Carter grinned to himself sombrely.

Fucker must be worth a few million, he mused.

One could say that airfield security had been lax.

And somebody was going to lose his job, and then his balls.

There was silence for a while, interrupted only by the noise of the engines as they cruised at low altitude. Carter knew that he wasn't a fighter pilot and despite arming the PCSS-5s he still felt nervous. He didn't want to engage in air-to-air combat with pilots sporting thousands of hours of training.

'Mongrel, we need to talk.'

'So talk.'

'That wasn't me back there.'

'Who was it, the fucking Queen? I didn't realise she was so fond of shooting dogs with a Browning.'

'Mongrel, listen to me. There is a demon inside my head. Sometimes I go a little – *insane*. I try to control it, really I do. But sometimes, when I am weak, or I've been beaten up or shot – sometimes the demon takes control.'

Mongrel was silent. The engines hissed behind the two men. Below, the desert flowed like golden mercury. Rocks flowed past and the distant landscape lay cratered like the moon.

'I find that hard to accept.'

Carter took a deep breath. 'You have heard Natasha – and I – mention the name of Kade? I know you have. It is the name of the demon in my soul, the dark brother I have to carry like a seed. And yes, he is evil, and yes, I wish him dead. But I cannot banish him, Mongrel, I cannot get rid of him without terminating my own fucking existence. And I want to, believe me, I want him to die . . . but he lives, inside me, in my brain, and sometimes he breaks free . . .'

For decades Carter had carried this secret.

And he realised that he was talking as much to himself as to Mongrel. And now he was exorcising his secret, the words flowed with ease, like fine sand in an hourglass.

Carter realised that there were tears staining his cheeks.

'Sometimes I do really bad things,' he whispered. 'But it is not always me in control. Sometimes I have no say in my actions. Sometimes Kade holds me in his fist – trapped behind the bars of his strength – and there is nothing I can do.'

Mongrel leaned forward and tapped Carter on the shoulder. Carter turned, savagely wiping away his tears. Mongrel smiled at him, his dark eyes glistening.

'I accept this for now, but later we must talk. When this – this *Kade* is out, he have real attitude problem. I considered putting bullet in him with M24. He real fuck-wit.'

'Yeah.' Carter laughed. 'Fucking tell me about it. I have to listen to his voice 24/7. It drives a man a little mad.'

'So what the plan now?'

'I'll drop you by the Comanche . . . shit, you *can* fly it, can't you?'

'Ha, I'll fly anything! Not very well, but I fly it.'

'Then we'll rendezvous in Austria. I'll scout ahead. The fucking speed of this thing, I'll probably get there before Durell and Jam!'

'I doubt that. We spend too much time fucking about here.'

'I knew coming to Egypt was a bad idea. Have you checked the ECube?'

Mongrel fished out the machine. It glowed blue.

'It's working. But I fear Nex still have control of systems, despite this new revision of our magical little alloy friend – real piece of shit The Priest gave us here, I am thinking.'

'Send an ECube blip on the WarChannel. When the shit hits the fan, my disobedience will be as nothing – and the world is at stake here, our whole civilisation at risk. We need Spiral back-up; I doubt we'll come out of this alive without *some* aid . . .'

'But you are disobeying Spiral's orders!'

Carter nodded. 'I will save Natasha – and I will destroy Durell. But I cannot fight a war alone. Let Spiral do what they will do – if they cannot see I fight for the greater good, then fuck them to the darkest reaches of Hell. But I won't turn down a bit of heavy artillery help, that's for sure . . .'

Mongrel nodded, and started to spin the ECube in his

fingers. 'If Durell *does* have control of channels, when I send this he might know we're still alive. He might know we're coming . . .'

'Fuck him,' said Carter. 'Send him one as well. And tell him I look forward to our next joyful meeting, because there will be only one fucker leaving the room – and it won't be him.'

The MiG cruised on, sunlight glimmering along its dull grey hull. The Russian tri-colour was the only bit of colour on its otherwise blank alloy fuselage. Soon the machine dropped, howling from the deep blue skies, and skimmed low across the desert rocks of Gebel al-Galala al-Qibliya – and then on towards the Red Sea Mountains, searching for a place to land . . .

```
■
■■
■■
>>>>>
>
■quakehub@IV initiated
waiting
waiting
waiting
  proc zgrade
matter (q) clocks initiated
zones (q-z): checking ...
■
OPEN 6364786398-QIV{
  isort(A, Ø); check(A, Ø)
  genid(A, 1); isort(A, 1); check(A, 1)
  genrand(A, n); isort(A, n); check(A, n)
  gensort(A, n); isort(A, n); check(A, n)
  genrev(A, n); isort(A, n); check(A, n)
```

```
identical integers //q12
  genid(A, n); isort(A, n); check(A, n)
qq)

function isort(A, n,     i,j,t) {
  for (i = 2; i < = n; i++)
  for (j = i; j > 1 && A[j-1] > A[j];
j--) {
  # swap A[j-1] = A[j]
  t = A[j-1]; A[j-1] = A[j]; A[j] = t \\\}

zones cleared;
  call fzone sort; 7y879ehwi
  x897xx89x897x90
  x5x675x45x5657b
  x876x79-x076x9x7
  x6xx454x76x765x
  call 76538973454784
  call 43876438973492
  call 23765723862348
■
quakehub systems online
quakehub foundations linked
quakehub systems operational
01010111ok
10101010ok
11101010ok
10010101ok
10000010ok
00000000ok.
```

492

```
qengines complete
please specify targets . . .

OPEN tactical :GUI

done.
■■■■
```

New York, the United States of America

Darkness flowed majestically over the sleeping city. Lights glittered from a billion different coordinates, a swathe of electronic eyes focusing and keeping the world alive. Cars moved in tracer streamers along the twisting concrete highways, headlights slicing the dark and adding to the great sweep of phosphorescence flowing up and out towards heaven.

The night was peaceful.

Sleeping.

The rumble seemed to shake the whole world. Buildings started to tremble, softly at first, jiggling against their foundations as windows clattered in frames. Several shattered, glass shards and slivers tumbling in long glittering falls to the sidewalks far below. From Queens to Staten Island, from Brooklyn to Manhattan, the Big Apple felt the clenched and threatened fury of the quake's titanic fist-fuck.

Cars started to rattle against road surfaces, bouncing on protesting suspensions.

Shop windows cascaded onto sidewalks in huge sheets of diced glass.

Alarms started to squeal from a million different tenement blocks and wounded vehicles.

The George Washington Bridge began to shudder, swaying violently.

On the subway, trains ground to a halt as rails were distorted, twisted, wrenched from concrete blocks, their tortured bolts torn.

And then the quake seemed to grow, to expand, to rise swiftly into a sudden fury – as it washed across the whole city in a titanic crush and devastating smash of unleashed energy worse than any single warhead that had ever been directed at the United States . . .

Buildings toppled.

Houses disintegrated.

Cars were crushed.

And all to the accompaniment of a constant wail, a high-pitched eternal cacophony, a moaning writhing bleeding symphony-scream of apocalyptic human suffering.

Shanghai, China

In Shanghai Harbour at the head of the Yangtze River, the water trembled gently. Small boats started to bob, the rhythm gentle at first but growing more violent until they jiggled as though they were on wires. Moored ferries started to rock, crunching against wharfs and one another, and on the mainland the streets started to move, some actually erupting as tarmac buckled and thrust upwards in grey-black showers. The new T12 HyperTubeway ground to a halt, and screams echoed as the waters from the Yangtze poured in, picking up trams and spinning them violently down the wide bright underground tunnels, washing people like sticks of debris from the platforms, drowning those who were already trapped and struggling.

The Huxinting tea house, built in 1784 and nestling like a proud jewel, a national symbol of heritage at the centre of Nanshi's ornamental lake, shifted as dust drifted down from its ancient supports, peppering the still lake waters with tiny flakes of debris. There was a beautifully constructed zigzag bridge, linking to Yu Yuan, that was said to keep evil spirits away . . . As it tumbled into the still waters a roar so loud, so devastating that it could dwarf the sound of a nuclear explosion, scythed across Shanghai. The whole area moved and tipped and a devastation, an abomination like nothing the city had ever seen smashed down without mercy through the darkness . . .

To leave a mass of pulped flesh in its wake.

Delhi, India

The Red Fort of Delhi, quarried and built in 1648 from the local deep red sandstone and once serving as the imperial palace of the Mughal Emperors, started to shake. The Lahore Gate and the Delhi Gate started to rattle against their ancient iron hinges, and stonework began to crumble around sand-blasted fixings. The two-and-a-half-kilometre defensive wall began to buckle, writhing like a huge red snake in its death throes, and all around people stared up in wonder – and horror – as the ground trembled beneath their feet.

The huge and beautiful Great Mosque – the *Jama Masjid* – was shuddering as if some great hand had taken the tapering minarets and rounded bulbous domes and was shaking them. Several minarets toppled to the ground far below, scattering debris like a child's abused building blocks under the fists of a tantrum-screaming toddler . . .

The River Yamuna shook as if in the grip of a fit; it sloshed up its banks, smashing boats and overturning several small ferries. A huge wave washed up, over, dragging people and barking dogs from the banks and away in a sudden deep swell of flood waters . . . In the suburbs surrounding the city people came outside to stand in the street, staring up into the sky or over towards the crumbling Red Fort, which dominated the skyline and seemed to *shimmer*.

And twelve million people watched in muted terror as the quake made its presence felt, smashing, stomping and branding its presence into the brain of every screaming human who endured its buckling stampeding smashing *torturing* onslaught . . .

'Is it done?' asked Jam through twisted jaws.

Durell shook his head. 'No, my boy, it is not yet done.' His eyes stared down at the screen, at the swirl of colours, at the scattered flickering images of destruction being relayed back to him via thousands of satellite eyes around and above the globe.

He reached down beside the screen where a small black box sat, its lights flickering softly. He glanced down, a curious smile etching his face within the folds of the dark hood. Frost coated the box – the QuakeHub – and with blackened claws Durell flicked open the lid to reveal a dark cube squatting at the heart of this terrible weapon that was wreaking such havoc across the world.

Jam peered closer.

'What exactly is it?'

'The heart of the QuakeHub. It is a processor, Jam. The most advanced military processor ever designed. It is controlling the earthquakes, and it is controlling the world . . . watch closely, for no more will we offer ultimatums, no more will we bow under the onslaught of world powers and world armies and the slime that is Spiral . . . we will control *everything* because, my friend, as you can quite clearly see, the QIV processor, the QIV military-organic-cubic processor is now fully operational and permanently on-line.'

The Nex poured out in their thousands from hidden bunkers – cold-storage facilities, secret subterranean chambers – across the globe.

As satellites became blind and governments and army leaders panicked, appalled at their sudden terrifying loss of control, the Nex attacked targets that had no idea of what was coming.

In Germany, armies clashed in the streets as civilians fled, screaming, to be machine-gunned in the back. In Sweden, the Nex landed in swarms of black helicopters, storming airfields and army and naval bases, taking them in minutes. With stumbling leaders blind, oblivious to the fact that they were even under attack, nuclear power stations were overrun and complete control was taken of poorly defended nuclear missile silos – from Russia to America to China.

The Nex – thanks to the QIV military processor – had control of digital locks, satellite navigation, world finances. In certain high-tech army barracks hundreds of thousands of men were simply locked in. No need for bloody warfare in such cases, no need for hand-to-hand combat in the streets – the Nex could prevail with far inferior numbers due to technological and digital superiority.

The power base across the surface of the globe began to shift.

Durell stood over the QIV processor, revelling in his supremacy, revelling in his power, his apotheosis – and he turned, throwing back his hood as his glittering eyes surveyed Jam. He placed a claw on Jam's shoulder and smiled. There was a taste on his lips like . . . *revenge*.

'Carter is coming,' said Jam softly.

'I care not.'

'And Spiral, with their TankSquads.'

'I care not.'

'We should leave this place.'

'No, Jam. This Carter, he must die. By coming to us he simply makes this game easier . . . he cannot stand against you, and he cannot stand against *us*. It is too late, the game is in play, the world is toppling even as we speak, we blink, we breathe. The time for running is over.'

'Is the QIV processor blind to Carter? Like the QIII before it?'

'It is.'

'Why?' asked Jam. 'Why can it not see him?'

'Carter is an anomaly in the system. A bug in the software. A virus in the code. He needs to be ironed out; he needs to be quarantined; he needs to be *eliminated*.'

'I will do this,' said Jam softly.

'Good,' whispered Durell, nodding with satisfaction, and he turned back to the screen which rippled like mercury. His hands moved deftly over the controls as thousands of images flickered across it, showing scenes of battle and death.

And all the while they could hear the deep and distant rumbling of the quake.

The huge hospital car park on the outskirts of London was dark and rainswept, filled with shadows. Sections of it were packed with cars gleaming glossy under the downpour; several spaces provided nothing more than raindrops dancing on tarmac. A soft noise echoed through the darkness at the perimeter fence – where a single Sleeper Nex stood, water gleaming on its shell. It turned copper eyes within its triangular head, left, then right, and dropped to all fours like a huge cat. Muscles bunched and its whole body quivered. It seemed to scent the air – then, eyes glinting eerily, it turned its nose towards the Accident & Emergency neon sign and the bright glare of strip lights inside. An ambulance had just pulled up, blue lights flickering.

The entity sniffed again and, head dropping, its claws raked the tarmac as it headed towards the bright entrance and the heavy stifling stink of the people within.

Earthquakes had ravaged London. Most wounded had been airlifted away because the capital was said to be still unstable, at best – with the threat of more quakes to come. People were leaving the capital in their thousands – or, rather, sitting on motorways, crawling along bumper to bumper.

It had been suggested by the hospital authorities that Natasha should be removed along with other patients, airlifted to a quieter hospital by military Chinook, to a city that had not been savaged by the fury of the earthquake, such as nearby Oxford or Coventry. Nicky had made it plain to the doctors that Natasha would be going nowhere and had sat at her friend's bedside for long hours, holding the cool flesh of Natasha's hand.

Nicky came awake with a start.

The steady beep-beep-beep of the monitors soothed her suddenly racing heart and adrenlin kicked her system into wakefulness. She glanced at Natasha.

What woke me? she thought.

She tilted her head, listening.

Something felt wrong. Out of place.

She tied back her hair, pulled tight the laces of her boots and lifted free her Smith & Wesson 11mm pistol, checking the 24-round 'compact-shell' magazine and flicking free the safety.

Tiny hairs prickled across the nape of her neck.

A distant shout echoed from the depths of the hospital. Nicky glanced at Natasha's recumbent form, and moved quietly to the door.

Somewhere, distantly, a woman gave a muffled scream.

There came a crack.

What's going on? she thought, blood nightmares raging in her skull.

Nex?

Mercs, even?

The return of the quake?

She tugged free her ECube and paused for a moment – Spiral were already stretched to full capacity . . . and beyond. The last thing they needed was some jumpy bitch sending in an Urgent Request for Heavy Back-up – just because a locally anaesthetised patient on a cold operating slab was being sliced open by a careless doctor.

She toyed with the tiny black alloy cube for a moment.

Then pocketed it.

Pull yourself together, girl, she thought with a long blink and a deep breath.

Clutching the S&W pistol tightly, she moved down the corridor and then stopped, listening, head tilted slightly, eyes narrowed in concentration.

Nothing.

'See? Panic for nothing . . .' she muttered to the stagnant air.

She moved towards the double swing door, boots

squeaking a little on the sterile tiles of the hospital corridor. A man screamed – a long low animal sound, full of pain and horror and ending with a savage nasty gurgle.

Nicky paused then—

A real pause.

As a fist of fear punched her in the brain.

She started to reach for her ECube, thinking *Fuck it, they can send me some of the boys* – when something rounded the corner at the end of the corridor, about twenty metres directly ahead of her. Something big and black, heavily armoured and moving stealthily like a large cat. Thick armoured legs supported a wide stocky chest and a triangular head, with tiny copper eyes. Claws raked the ground and the head snapped up, around, a blur of movement. She saw blood dripping from twisted jaws.

Twin copper eyes focused on Nicky.

There was recognition there, in that bright copper-eyed gaze. It *knew* her. Dropping its head it started to pound towards her, leaving trails of blood from its claws against the white tiles . . . she could see strips of flesh flapping from its twisted maw . . .

And she realised—

For whatever reason, it had come for Natasha . . .

Come to murder Natasha . . .

And any one else from Spiral who got in its way.

Gritting her teeth, Nicky fired off five deafening shots, then heeled back through the double doors and began to sprint towards Natasha's room. In her pocket, she stabbed a PB on the ECube and let out a little gasp of fear, glancing over her shoulder as the huge black gleaming monstrosity hammered through the doors, wrenching them from their hinges.

Nicky slammed through into Natasha's private room, kicked shut the door and slid the bolts into place – gun up and pressing against her cheek as the pounding claws suddenly halted and silence flooded the corridor.

Nicky backed away from the door.

Fear beat a tattoo within her chest.

And she watched in horror as the triangular head, twisted jaws drooling and trailing strings of human meat, lifted – slowly, purposefully – and those tiny copper eyes tilted and stared in at her through the rectangular frame of wire-mesh glass.

Nicky lifted her gun and took slow and careful aim.

CHAPTER 18

AUSTRIA

After a hurried desert landing to allow Mongrel to hop from the MiG 8-40, Carter gave a small salute with blood-encrusted fingers and urged the jet over the hard-packed desert rock, aviation-shocks pissing oil from their abused suspension. Leaving a huge dust trail in its wake, the tortured war machine climbed from the ground and powered hungrily into the vast blue bowl of the sky.

Carter flew the fighter north – skirting Cairo in a wide arc and heading out over the Mediterranean Sea.

The sun was high, and climbing to an altitude of 23,000 feet Carter breathed the crisp oxygen-recyc of the cabin and stared out over a cloud-carpeted world. Below, Durell had somehow managed to gain control of the Earth, and the savage fury of its earthquakes. Both Carter's and Mongrel's ECubes had been screaming – reports, intelligence, damage information, casualty figures, panic calls, mission briefings – the tiny alloy devices had never been so much in need.

Carter hit the wide expanse of the shimmering sea and found himself focusing, calming his heart and mind.

Kade squatted, silent and dark and sullen in the back of his brain, refusing to speak and refusing to share his pain. This suited Carter just fine.

The MiG banked as he headed north and west. Behind him, quad engines thundered and Carter took the time to familiarise himself with the weapons systems. He watched in horror as Russian script flowed across the control monitor. Carter used his limited knowledge of languages to translate some of the instructions from Russian, some from Arabic and fill in the rest through context. Still, he wasn't happy.

After a half-hour, alarms sprang to life.

'What now?' he muttered.

'*You have company,*' said Kade.

'And how the fuck would you know?'

'*I just do. I read Arabic better than you, I think. The MiG has identified the aircraft – Lockheed choppers and five British-made Sea Harriers. They have Sea Cat missiles, and they're piloted by Nex.*'

'You sure?'

25mm cannons roared, and shells screamed past the fighter, several thumping home as Carter banked the fighter sharply, cursing. Engines howled, the System5 thrust vectoring channels kicking in, and Carter lifted the machine, nose up, peering intently at his scanners as the sky spun.

'They're not on the scanners – nor the ECube,' he cursed.

'*Durell must have some way of shielding them.*'

He banked the machine once more, dropping in a tight arc, and saw the enemy: five Harriers SK15s – hovering and turning – with perhaps fifteen choppers accompanying them. Carter's jaw set grimly and he wondered if they had been on their way to intercept him. In Cairo? Maybe at the Red Sea Mountains? But they had been too slow to the call, and he armed the MiG's weapons systems almost without thinking, Russian flowing through his mind as he settled into the mindset of combat and sped below the Harriers – which accelerated after him in deadly pursuit.

Engines howling, Carter saw the Harriers spread out behind him, losing the entourage of helicopters which were far too slow for this kind of aerial battle. Carter raced across the skies, climbing, and sensed rather than saw the AAMs detach and accelerate away from his pursuers. Carter banked again, more tightly this time, and the Sea Harriers couldn't match his manoeuvre. The MiG flashed up through cloud as the six missiles forged ahead and he wheeled, rolling, and then dropped from the skies and powered with only inches to spare between the clustered group of searching black helicopters—

Six missiles met six targets.

Thunder rolled across the sky as the choppers exploded in gaseous balls of flame. Another two choppers caught fire from being too close to the explosions and were sent spinning, rotors screaming, into the Mediterranean where they plummeted beneath the waves, leaving wide circles of churning foam.

'*Neat*,' said Kade. He sounded a little sulky.

Carter lifted the machine, vibrating under his battered hands, and armed his own missiles. His Global PK18 TSAM control radars started to buzz but he couldn't understand the flashing Russian commands. Carter looped, coming up behind the Sea Harriers, which had temporarily lost sight of him – and sighted, smiling savagely as he accelerated towards the five glinting machines—

Wing pylons retracted. Four of his eight R-80 AA-e Aphids released as he was almost upon the Harriers and he flashed overhead, climbing steeply. The missiles ate into the Sea Harriers like hot knives into soft fresh butter. There came the sounds of four impacts, like rapid detonation charges exploding in quick succession. Flames roared into the sky, purple and orange globes of fire spinning off hints of green and blue from superheated burning slivers of steel and alloy. Nex pilots melted into their seats, faces ridged in screams, and were then vaporised, spat up and out and finally down into the all-encompassing waves.

There seemed to be a moment of silence.

A long, long silence . . .

'*One left,*' said Kade smugly—

As Carter dropped the MiG and opened fire with the quad 30mm cannons. Huge heavy-calibre rounds roared across the bright blue sky, slamming into the Harrier and taking out its fuel tanks. There came a blossom of purple fire and the jet nosedived into the sea where it sank in an upsurge of foaming bubbles. Huge white rings spread out from the point of impact, and Carter watched for a moment as they dispersed.

'*You remind me more of me every day,*' said Kade.

'Fuck off.'

'*Tch. Tetchy again, Carter. Hey, where you going? You've left some choppers behind . . . hey, Carter, you're leaving some of them alive! You fucking pussy! Where are you going?*'

'I've seen enough of death to last me a million lifetimes. They'll never catch us.'

'*Carter! Breaking your own fucking rules, my man. Never leave an enemy behind, that's what you always told me. Come on, brother, let's see some more of those diseased fuckers burn . . .*'

Carter ignored Kade, and with his tight-lipped mouth a grim line as he wiped sweat from his hands, he

506

thundered through the skies towards the coast of Greece, Albania, Yugoslavia and then onwards and up into Austria . . .

'*You butcher,*' muttered Kade, before disappearing from Carter's sombre thoughts.

The engines were whining softly.

'You make sure you come back to me, you reckless fucker . . . You make sure you come back to *us* . . .'

Natasha's face came into his mind, her twinkling eyes, her short spiked hair. He sighed, wondering if he would ever see her again.

He remembered those words, just before the dam detonation at the Tennagore Valley in Chile, South America – where everything had gone horribly wrong and he'd gone speeding down the face, screeching motorcycle bucking out of control beneath him, the near-vertical concrete surface flexing beneath him like the wildest of roller-coaster rides . . . and as the dam exploded and the waters picked him and the bike up, threw them down the valley on the surging crest of foam he had truly believed that he would die . . .

'*You make sure you come back to me, you reckless fucker . . . You make sure you come back to* us . . .'

Much later, Natasha's tears had awoken him. Spiral had picked him up, unconscious, half-drowned, in a Chinook chopper. Her tears had dripped into his face and Carter had hugged her, wincing from the pain in his broken bones.

'I love you, Nats. You knew I was coming back.'

'You nearly died out there, you fucker. And you *promised* . . .'

And now? The sweet irony! A reversal . . . a need not to kill, but to *save* and every bastard who got in his way was

507

paying the ultimate *ultimate* price – but Carter felt like he was on a wild pillion ride straight into the heart of Hell, and the only way he could surface to heaven and reality was to cling on and ride the throbbing screeching insanity engine all the way – down the deep dips and through a world of madness and death, hopefully re-surfacing on the other side clutching the Avelach and with the ability to bring Natasha back from the brink of death . . .

'*No fucking chance,*' mocked Kade.

'Shut your face.'

'*You know my philosophy Carter, there are more fresh bitches in the sea. All you have to do is prime your maggot and do a little fishing. It's really not that fucking* hard *to understand.*'

'Shut up!' he screamed, slamming one fist against the inside of the MiG's cockpit. He coughed then, and a pain smashed into his head and it reminded him, back when he had been in Africa with Natasha and the pain had crippled him, dropped him like a bullet and the pain washed over him in great pulsing waves and he was almost blind, crippled, flooded with an intense pulsating vision and for a long time he drifted on the verge of consciousness and allowed the auto-pilot to correct the navigation of the MiG fighter's journey—

Engines hissed.

Sunlight sparkled, then dropped behind towering clouds which rolled billowing shadows over the sea far below. And Carter fell into a world of wonder and better times, when Natasha had been well and their lives had seemed so simple, so pure, so *complete*.

Before his world and sanity had seemed to finally end.

Simmo's HTank roared towards the unsuspecting Nex tanks guarding the refinery. Shells screamed overhead and this time they *did* catch the enemy by surprise. Guns thundered, smoke billowed in clouds and the Nex hardly knew what hit them. Tracks ground heavily across damp ground and when the battle was over Simmo leapt free, sinking up to his ankles in mud and gazing around, a beam on his broad flat face. He lit another cigar, and coughed a little on the blue smoke before letting it drift lazily from his nostrils.

'We do well, lads!' he roared, and the TankSquads cheered, standing on the hulls of the battle-scarred SP57s and throwing their helmets and water canteens into the air. Several Nex had been herded together and bound with wire, and Mo, Haggis and Rogowski were scoping out the smoking remains of the actual refinery, which, by some miracle, still stood amidst the twisted tank carnage and smoking devastation.

The TankComm rattled. Simmo picked it up, eyeing the TankSquad squaddies who fidgeted nearby. Simmo's face fell from elation to horror as he realised that he was speaking with Field Marshal Jacobs, Acting Commander of the Spiral TankSquads.

'Yes – Simmo, isn't it?'

'Yes, sir.'

'OK, lad, clearance has come through for you to take out that Nex-held LVA position in Columbia. Do you foresee any problems?'

'Um, no, sir.'

'Good, good.'

'Um, sir?'

'Yes, what is it, Simmo?'

'We also spot a refinery a few klicks away and it not on Spiral scout map. You want us investigate and take out if necessary?' Simmo eyed the smoking ruins in front of him, his shoulders hunched, teeth bared in a grimace.

'Yes, you go and investigate. If there are hostiles, by all means destroy them.'

'Yes, sir.'

'And Simmo?'

'Sir?'

'We have a Code Black across all bands. You will shortly be forwarded scrambling points. It would seem there is a madman on the loose with the ability to control earthquakes.'

'Ah. OK, sir. Thank you. Out.'

Simmo stared at the TankComm with obvious relief. Then he grinned. 'It turning into a good day,' he muttered.

Mo and Rogowski appeared, shaking their heads.

'We get an airlift outta here?' asked Kipper, sidling over to Simmo and staring hungrily at the The Sarge's cigar.

Simmo glared at him. 'Fuck off with that hungry look, Kipper. You proper fish-kipper, me thinking, when you go and leave all your own stash at home.'

'Aww, come on Sarge, you know I'd buy one off you but I've run out of money.'

'Yar, you lose it to me playing poker. Dumb ass. Find your own cigars.'

'Maybe I'll steal some from you when you're asleep!' laughed Kipper. Then he saw the look on Simmo's face. Stealing The Sergeant's cigars was not an option.

The TankComm rattled again. Simmo accessed it and strode away from the tank, trailing the bobbing curly umbilical cable behind him. Puffing on his cigar, he barked, 'Yeah? Simmo here.'

'Mongrel.'

'The Sarge was just thinking of you, lad.'

'Me? Why?'

'I was shelling a bunch of Nex, watching them burn in their tanks.'

'That supposed to be symbolic or something?'

'No, just little Sarge's death wish. What I do you for, Mongrel?'

'You heard about the sitrep on Durell, the fucker who almost brought the world to its knees with the QIII?'

'No. Fill me in.'

'We need help, Sarge. We need tanks – lots of your lovely tanks. Carter has gone ahead alone, to bring down this Durell, the Spiral betrayer. That mad Nex fucker is playing at being God again . . . he can control earthquakes all over the world and this is where the very big shit pie is going to hit the razor-fucking-bladed fan. You want to be at the heart of the battle? The big one? Then this is where it's going to be.'

'Simmo interested. Give me your coordinates.'

'Austria, target 226.443.223.457.'

'I've got a few hours to fill,' growled Simmo, realising that he had to be seen to be doing *something*, or Spiral might notice the fact that he had attacked two installations without actual permission. 'You leave it with The Sarge, lad. He see what he can do.'

The MiG 8-40 barrelled through the skies. It sped up past Slovenia's west coast, tipping slightly inland and cruising above the Austrian City of Klagenfurt, in Kärnten. Carter glanced down and saw weak autumn sunshine sparkling on the Glan river. Peering up ahead, he could make out the dark towering peaks of the Karawanken Mountains.

Carter started to decelerate, flashing over countryside, rivers, scatterings of trees. Checking his ECube, he began to visualise the coordinates against the landscape and plan his descent.

Where to land? he mused.

Passing over the stunning Niedere Tauern Alps, huge jagged teeth rising sheer and vast from the maw of the ground, he banked the MiG and realised that the place he wanted, the direct coordinates being fed through his tracking system, was an actual castle near to the village of Sankt Nikolai im Sölktal, high up in the Alps. Not the easiest of places to reach by fighter jet. Or by any other mode of transport . . .

Oak, hornbeam and pine lay scattered below Carter and he felt a strange calmness descend on him once more. The pain in his skull receded – as if it had simply been his brain's own warning jab. He licked his lips and composed himself.

Below, a narrow river snaked past a wide stretch of field carved unevenly from the mountainside. Along the opposite edge of the field meandered a long dirt track. Bracing himself, Carter turned the MiG and released the undercarriage; engines whining with deceleration, he lined up with the distant dirt track and watched his half-reflection glinting back at him from the cockpit interior.

'This is gonna be *real* fun,' he muttered.

The MiG came in, nose slightly raised. Carter touched down, gritting his teeth as the rear wheels impacted with the trail and the jolt almost threw him through the cockpit canopy. The whole fighter juddered with awesome violence, then its engines howled as they powered the plane into a frantic deceleration. Thundering down the rough trail, Carter's hands shook wildly on the controls and his teeth rattled in his pounding head. He could hear the shrieking stresses of tortured metal and the thuds of thumping wheels and battered suspension.

Carter watched a wall of trees rushing towards him and the hackles rose on the back of his neck.

Whining in protest, the throttled-back engines kicked

the fighter's speed down by degrees. Carter's sweat dripped into his eyes as the trail narrowed. He fought the weaving plane and watched the trees, a swathe of wide-boled oaks, growing ever closer.

The MiG slammed to a halt scant metres from the trees and there came a soft whine of exhaust. Carter lifted the cockpit canopy, worked his way down the first few rungs of the alloy ladder recessed in the fuselage and then leapt the final twelve feet to the ground.

He stared up at the dull grey flanks, sucking in the cold Austrian air. His breath emerged as smoke and he grinned, ears hammering, head pounding, eyes watering, and rolled his neck to ease the tension. Thought I was going through the mincer, he mused, and took a few steps back, his field of view widening . . .

Austria opened up before him.

Beautiful and serene.

A wide valley lay scattered with evergreens, undulating away and then sloping violently upwards towards and into the Niedere Tauern Alps. The mountains created a huge tunnel in front of Carter's awe-struck gaze, a giant's tunnel. The walls were sheer, unforgiving, blue-grey and wholly dominant, oak and pine scattered the lower slopes and Carter could make out a few distant streams and wider waterways. A couple of narrow roads and trails zig-zagged off to Carter's left, and he moved quickly beneath the wall of trees as he checked his ECube.

Blue digits glowed softly.

Carter matched the coordinates and realised that he was four kilometres from the bug planted in Durell's helicopter. He relayed the coordinates back to Mongrel and then, as an afterthought, to Spiral, with a short encoded digital transcript:

> Have found Durell vb447. Will attempt to
> halt his insanity.
> By whatever means. Coordinates to
> follow.
> Request immediate back-up.

Carter attached his vb codes and the coordinates, and sent the blip on the WarChannel. He had no idea if the channels and the ECubes had been compromised by the Nex – they had done it successfully once before. Carter had to assume the worst: a total digital breakdown.

Carter had to assume he was on his own.

He took a deep cold breath, checked his weapons, and looked up through the trees. How many Nex between me and Jam? he thought. How many Nex between gaining the Avelach and finding Durell? And getting the fuck out alive?

Carter checked his pack, freshly stocked with ammo, grenades and HighJ explosive from when he had hastily dropped Mongrel at the Comanche. Then Carter checked himself, prodding warily at various bruised and battered parts of his flesh. Pulling free a PlasGrip™ bandage, he wound it tightly around one wrist and felt it pull tight, electronically adjusting to offer maximum support to injured limbs. He could still feel the staples pulling tight in his back where the bullet had entered, and before that where glass had sliced his flesh back in Switzerland. Reaching into the pack he popped five K5 combo painkillers and antibiotics, then pulled free a tiny vial. Taking the yellow safety tag from the needle, he injected his arm, needle slipping easily into the barely visible vein – felt the kick as the small slow-release capsule entered his circulatory system, being carried to lodge in his spinal column where it would effect a slow and steady release of

514

chemicals. He would pay a high physiological price later . . .

But that was later.

Carter sighed, gazing around at the cold woodland. A fresh breeze made the trees hiss and sigh, and chilled the skin of his face. It was pleasant after the dry heat of Egypt, and he ran a blood-encrusted hand through his short hair, wondering how bad he looked: like a man who had been through the wars, probably.

Carter climbed wearily to his feet.

Nearly there, he thought.

One more burst, and then it will be over . . .

One way or another.

Carter moved up through the woods, slowly at first but speeding up as the chemicals kicked in. When he reached the edge of the trees he monitored for Nex activity.

Nothing local, but hostiles swarmed over the coordinate target on his ECube.

Settling his back against a tree, and pulling the straps tight, Carter secured his Browning and M24. He began a slow, loping jog.

He followed the rough stony trail for a while, then cut across fields scattered generously with hornbeam, their leaves rustling. Carter paused beneath one, breathing heavy now, and rested his hand against the smooth grey bark. He could see something ahead, the top of a grey – almost black – crenellated tower peering over the nearest hill.

Carter continued, reaching the crest of the slope and dropping to one knee beside the bole of another tree, eyes scanning. The castle came into view, built into the side of the mountain. Jagged uneven ground, rocky and scattered with a few pines led steeply up to the vertical grey walls of the castle. A slightly offset central tower rose from within, capped with dark red tiles. Another narrower tower rose from this central edifice. To the right the structure was more square in shape, like a vast cube of black, whilst to the left, leading away from the mountain, it fell in a series of small circular towers, each rising to a black or red spire. The building looked ancient, and very, very strong. Built to resist an attacking force. Built to rain down fire on the enemy. Built to resist an invasion . . .

A single wide dirt track swept up from the valley below, far to Carter's left, zigzagging through heavy woodland which thinned as it reached the castle's huge twin iron gates.

Carter could see a swarm of Nex activity by the gates, and up over the lower battlements he could make out more distant movement. His eyes narrowed, lips pursing in thought.

The whole castle was a massively imposing edifice, dominating the landscape below while in turn being over-shadowed by the magnificence of the vast mountains behind it.

Carter checked his ECube.

Durell's helicopter was there, somewhere in the castle.

Which meant that, logically, this was Durell's centre of operations – the heart from which he was controlling the earthquakes.

And this was where Durell had the Avelach. Guarded by Jam, Carter's oldest friend . . .

'*Let's do it,*' said Kade.

Carter said nothing.

He moved slowly, warily now that his target and desti-nation was in sight. The temperature was dropping as he moved higher from the valleys and up the vast steep slopes before him. His calves burned and offered him yet more

pain. Despite the drugs, Carter felt far from OK. He felt
a million fucking miles from fit, healthy, and ready to take
on the greatest of his enemies . . .

'The Avelach.'

The word sounded strange, spoken out loud. And it
felt bad on his tongue, like Carter was pinning his tentative hopes for Natasha's life on a machine that he did not
understand, had never seen work, and that was the core of
Durell's Nex creation.

It sat badly with him.

Carter moved forward, slowly, carefully, continually
scanning for the enemy. If they know I'm coming, he
thought, I don't want it to be because of carelessness. A
disturbed bird, the crack of falling rock upon rock. Carter
wandering aimlessly out into the open or silhouetting
himself against a skyline like a shooting-range target . . .

Carter took his time. Used his eyes, and occasionally
his Sniper Scope, which clicked and whined softly as a
magnified and digitally enhanced landscape, castle and
Nex came into Carter's field of vision. He noted the
enemy's pattern of movement, and watched as a patrol of
four tanks and two trucks growled through the gates,
heavy steel tracks grinding the stone trail to dust.

Carter worked slowly, coming in from the south with
the mountains to his right and hugging them, their sheer
vast walls, almost as if for protection. The landscape was
slowly changing as he gained height, long grasses scattered with more and more huge rocks which gave him
plenty of cover.

'*They know you are coming,*' said Kade smugly.

'I don't care.'

'*You'll care when Jam shoots you in the face.*'

The sun was toiling across the sky, plunging behind
towering clouds that sent vast rolling shadows tumbling

517

across the valleys. The cold wind blew stronger, ruffling Carter's hair and chilling his fingers, nose and ears.

Reaching the base of the huge mound of rock on which the castle had been built, and with a sheer blue granite wall to his right, Carter started to clamber up the steep incline whose gradient steepened the further he went. Using his hands to help pull him forward, he found himself quickly sweating – sweat that was instantly chilled by the cold wind to leave him shivering almost uncontrollably.

A beautiful place, he thought.

But also a barren, deadly place.

A desolation.

After a half-hour of climbing, he reached the base of the castle wall. He crouched for a long time, searching for Nex, or cameras, or any other type of high-tech scanning devices. He could see nothing, and his ECube could see nothing . . . but Carter found it hard to believe.

Still, he couldn't exactly walk through the front gates.

He gazed up at the vast vertical expanse of stone ahead of him.

There were no windows, and no handholds that he could see.

Just stone . . . stretching high above his tilted head like some vast plain of rock, a towering wall of smooth sheer impossibility.

Breath coming in plumes, Carter pulled free his Sp_drag, his Skimmer, and reaching up he allowed the tiny alloy jaws to chew into the stone. With the aid of this digital crampon, Carter began the long long climb up the vast grey-black bulwark.

The climb was protracted, incredibly treacherous and an act of insanity. Wind smashed against Carter as he climbed; slowly, deliberately he moved upwards, and within minutes his hands were numb with cold and pain. Sweat ran and then chilled him, and he pressed himself tight against the flat wall, a limpet against a stone with the waves of cold air washing in violent crests up and over him.

Carter felt awesomely vulnerable. Perhaps more vulnerable than at any moment during his life. All it would take was a helicopter to spot him, or a sniper to sight him . . . and *bam*. Fish food. Dead meat.

Carter smiled grimly, and continued to climb.

Up, endlessly up, he travelled.

Carter did not look up. To do so might destroy his resolve, and so instead he focused on the grey wall to which he clung. The stone was rough, cold under his numb fingers. Pins and needles raced along his hands and arms, and cramps spiked his thighs and calves. The staples holding the bullet wound tight in his back moved and stretched his flesh, and he felt a little blood weep out, soaking into his torn battered dead Nex clothing.

Up, he climbed.

Eternally upwards.

Reaching for Heaven?

Or climbing to Hell in an ironic reversal?

Carter licked his lips, pausing, panting, and gazed out over the valley. He could hear distant noises, crashes and booms, the whines of engines and suddenly he brightened – when he realised that it sounded – *incredibly* – like Spiral TankSquad tanks being airlifted and fast-jetted to this location . . . backup?

I fucking hope so, he thought.

Squinting through the cold light, Carter could see nothing through the swathes of lowland forest. Then he heard a distant rattling and watched forty Nex tanks trundle onto the trails sweeping down from the castle and speed off, engines roaring. Something big was going down.

Something heavy—

But Carter had his own problems.

He continued to climb, and at one point broke his own rule and glanced up. The summit was tantalisingly close and the Sp_drag continued to eat stone, tiny spiral trails of grey stone dust whirling away down the face of the sheer castle wall and then, when he thought his endurance had finally reached its pain-filled limits, thought he could go on no longer, his aggrieved and screaming hands grasped the edge of the parapet and he hauled himself up onto a low crenellation, squatted, eyes quickly skimming the area before him as he drew his Browning with stumps of numbness and clumsily flicked free the safety.

The wind howled, a soft moaning, blowing eerily through the castle.

Below him spread a broad platform of uneven and time-worn stone flags. It measured perhaps forty or fifty metres square, was bordered on the left by a high stone wall leading to a tower and whose only feature was a narrow arched doorway. Ahead squatted another battlement that dropped away to what Carter assumed was the castle's central courtyard. To the right stood a high stone wall with three ancient doorways, all shrouded in gloom.

The sun disappeared behind towering black clouds. Carter glanced back at the dizzying fall, at the sheer wall he had ascended and the vast slopes beyond, dropping through to distant valleys. It was a fucking awesome drop.

Carter hopped down to the rough-worn stone flags and something moved in the shadows of the narrow doorway leading to the tower. Dropping to a crouch Carter sighted along the Browning's barrel, finger tightening on the trigger and eyes narrowing as Jam stepped into view.

Jam had changed since his last encounter with Carter.

He seemed less . . . deformed.

Jam moved forward, triangular head swaying, and stopped a short distance away. He carried no weapons, only a silver box in black claws that had once been hands.

'Hello, Carter,' he rumbled softly.

Carter stared into those slitted copper eyes and his words caught in his throat. This was his oldest and greatest friend, and they had fucked with him, turned him into a Nex and now Carter would have to . . .

'*Kill him*,' supplied Kade.

Carter uncoiled slowly, lowered the Browning and slid his pack from his back, allowing it to drop to the stone flags. Clouds whirled across the bleak grey sky and the wind stung his face with its cold sharp needles.

'You knew I was coming?'

Jam nodded and stooped, placing the small silver box on the ground at the base of the tower. Then he smiled, his once twisted jaws now aligned and straight, his stance more powerful, more erect. The copper eyes looked at Carter coldly: calculating and appraising.

'Of course,' said Jam. 'You told me yourself that you wanted the Avelach. To save Natasha . . . and here it is. The prize you seek. The gift you would wish to steal. Our power, and our source for the creation of the Nex . . . it is in the silver box which protects it, encodes it, and yet haunts it.'

Carter licked his lips, glancing down at the box.

'You have changed,' said Carter.

'Yes. You misunderstand the process of creating a Nex. When I was created, at first I was horribly disfigured, deformed if you will. The ScorpNex always are – it is the price of the more complex blending, the more complex and savage inhibitors used. But then the subject refines itself, heals itself, becomes more stable, more *beautiful*. To become a ScorpNex, Carter – it is a symmetry . . . it is celestial. It is an act of perfection, of healing, of evolution. You would not believe the way I feel; it is sublime. You could never understand unless you yourself became Nex.'

'And why the fuck would I want to do that?' snarled Carter.

'Because it is your future,' said Jam softly. He took several steps forward, and Carter found himself backing away involuntarily. Jam's movements were precise, controlled, and awesomely powerful. Carter felt a deep fear gnaw at him from the depths of his belly . . .

'I don't fucking think so,' said Carter. 'You have betrayed your race, Jam. Betrayed mankind . . . You have become something you are not – yeah, you never volunteered for it, but now you are part of Durell's fucking insanity.' Carter's eyes stared fiercely into Jam's copper slits. 'What do you want from me?' he said, his voice a hoarse whisper.

'Durell wants to turn you into a Nex – like me. A ScorpNex – the ruling elite. The all-powerful. As close to God as God.' Jam chuckled, a deep-throated rumble. 'He says you would make the perfect ScorpNex . . . and if you do this, then we will let you take the Avelach, we will let you heal Natasha. Everything you desire will be yours. Your life will be complete.'

'Fuck you.'

'Come on, Carter.' Jam moved forward again, armoured claws scraping the stone as his huge muscles coiled under black chitinous armour. Jam stared at the man in front of him. 'You can save Natasha's life – and we can be friends again, comrades – you can join our army, you can rule the world with us, Carter, with Durell and I, you can be a part of this first great step to power and glory – when we overthrow Spiral, smash and control the world governments . . .'

'You want to rule the fucking world?' snarled Carter. 'Have you fucking heard yourself? It's like a dictator's wet fucking dream . . .'

'You do not understand, truly you do not.' Jam halted. Behind him, Carter could see the glitter of the silver box – a tease, he realised. Clouds broiled overhead, carried on the fury of the gathering storm. 'And if you do not wish to save Natasha, if you do not want to join us, then there is only one thing I require from you.' His head tilted. Slitted copper eyes surveyed Carter coolly.

'My telephone number?' Carter smiled as his whole body tensed for the battle and he slowly brought the Browning up.

'I want your *death*.'

Jam leapt forward and Carter started firing, the Browning slamming in his fist. One bullet took Jam in the leg, one grazed his armour, another passed over his shoulder, a fourth sliced a line across his throat and then—

The claw lashed out.

Carter's Browning skidded across the stone and he stumbled back.

Kade rattled against the bars of his mind but Carter ignored him. He would not allow him life.

Jam lashed out again. Carter ducked, smashed a right hook against Jam's triangular head and heard one of his own knuckles crack under the impact. Jam's armoured elbow crashed into Carter's sternum, slamming him back, and Jam's leg powered out, armoured foot catching Carter under the jaw and lifting the Spiral agent from his feet. He flailed backwards to roll against the battlements.

Carter slumped against the stone.

Stars danced in his head and he breathed in deeply. Rolling swiftly to his feet, he spat out blood and worked his jaw – but felt no pain.

Fuck pain, he thought.

I am beyond pain.

'Is that all you have to offer? Your future fucking wife could do better.'

Jam's copper-eyed stare fixed on Carter, who charged – and Jam leapt to meet him. Carter spun and whirled, dancing under Jam's heavy blows and then jumped, boots striking Jam's chest. Jam took a step back. Carter delivered a kick to Jam's throat, then another to his groin. Leaping up, Carter came down with his elbow smashing into Jam's broad head. Carter dodged a swipe from the glistening black claw and another kick to Jam's throat sent the huge ScorpNex stumbling towards the battlement wall above the cold square expanse of black cobbled courtyard below . . .

Snow started to fall, gentle swirls of flakes that danced on flurries of cold bitter wind from the mountains and landed, making the battlements slick and slippery. *Deadly.*

'*Go on, one more,*' hissed Kade.

Carter braced himself. He had hurt Jam, amazingly; could see it in the ScorpNex's face – in his eyes. His blows, although devastating to his own frame, had smashed through Jam's armour—

Carter sprinted and leapt, his boots aiming for Jam's head and a deep long tumbling fall for the ScorpNex into oblivion . . . and beyond.

Jam twisted with a blur of speed, caught Carter and smashed a heavy punch to the Spiral agent's forehead. Then another to Carter's nose, then a third to his jaw. He dropped Carter on the flags with a dull slapping sound and as Carter looked up Jam kicked him savagely in the face, snarling with contempt.

Jam paced around Carter in a wide circle.

He seemed agitated.

Filled with unease.

Carter rolled in a world of agony, his nose broken, pain screaming through his face. Through scattered flickerings of bright light he gazed up through the soft falling snow. It settled gently over him, a veil of pity.

Distantly, he heard the smash and crump of tank shells. Screams of metal filtered through the swirling snow to his ears. And with a deep dark thankfulness he realised that a battle – *the* battle? – had at last begun . . .

'Come back to us, Jam,' said Carter hoarsely, forcing himself into a sitting position and trying to stem the flow of blood from his nose. 'Come back to the real fucking world.'

'I *am* in the real fucking world,' hissed Jam. 'To be Nex, it is awesome, it is perfect, it is immortality.'

'You are living a lie,' croaked Carter. 'What about your friends back at Spiral? What about your comrades, men you fought with, men who fucking died for you? What about Nicky? Remember her, fucker? You would deny yourself this? You would cast your life away? Piss away your fucking *humanity*?'

'Fuck them all,' growled Jam. 'I do not need them. I am whole like this; I am perfect; I am *evolved*.'

'You are a fucking genetic mess.' Carter laughed weakly, through strings of blood and saliva. He dragged himself to his feet and despite the powerful drugs pain was screaming through him. 'Well then, fucker, come on, come and finish it. You're such a supreme fucking being, you think you are so fucking hard . . .'

'*Let me*,' whispered Kade.

The sounds of the tank battle were coming closer.

Below in the courtyard Carter heard the bustle of activity: the stomp of boots, the rattle of weapons.

Here comes the war, he thought, and watched idly as Jam leapt towards him, as if in slow motion, claws held wide and face an insanity of anger. Jam was finally ready, accepting the inevitability of Carter's death.

Casting off his inhibitions.

At last the ScorpNex was ready to murder those he had loved.

Simmo stared around at the tanks surrounding him on the Austrian valley floor. The last few to be airlifted were being freed of their chains, and the Chinooks were taking off, veering away to the south.

'Things are getting mad,' observed Rogowski.

'They always do,' growled Simmo.

Readying their vehicles, engines revving and tracks straining against the crushed-stone trails, Simmo was just about to close the HTank's hold when the scream of engines swept down to him from the mountains.

Five or six tanks swivelled their turrets, guns elevating towards this new threat, but Simmo shouted for the TankSquads to hold their fire. A battered Comanche leapt into view, slewing sideways and touching down on bobbing suspension beside Simmo's HTank.

The rotors were still whirling as Mongrel jumped free and moved towards the huge sergeant. Their gazes met, and over the noise of the machines Mongrel shouted, 'Carter's up there.'

Simmo shrugged. 'Do you know what's happening? With the LVA?'

'Have you been briefed?'

'We only know that Durell is commanding the earthquakes. What you tell us.'

'Yeah.' Mongrel nodded. 'He's doing it through the LVA. The Nex drop shafts to mine LVA, and while they are down there they plant Foundation Stones – control devices. Under the ground there is a whole massive worldwide fucking network of LVA running in underground streams, rivers, lakes . . . the fucking shite is a conductor of some kind – I know this sound crazy but it true – and through this natural grid network of LVA Durell control the quakes. He using a machine called a QuakeHub. If we can destroy it and Durell, we can stop the Earth being torn apart . . .'

'Let's just shell the fucking place,' growled Simmo.

Mongrel shook his head. 'Not so simple, Sarge. This LVA grid, this liquid network under the earth – Durell is playing game with what he shouldn't. If he fuck with it too bad, too *wrong*, then whole fucking world go up! God only know what will happen . . . maybe quakes across the whole globe. Maybe this underground sea of fuel ignite. Spiral not know and this simple squaddie not know, but Spiral say we not just blow everything up, we need to take control . . .'

Simmo rubbed at his chin.

'Easier said than done, Sarge thinking.'

'Sarge, they've spotted us.'

'Shit.'

Up the valley, the gates to the castle had opened. Dark grey Nex tanks poured out, tracks grinding, dust pluming behind them.

'At least in this battle we keep the shells away from castle,' said Mongrel, a weak smile crossing his grey drained features. 'Now you understand me, don't you, Sarge? No fucking bombing the castle . . . Spiral say we not risk it yet, they don't know what happen . . . we got a whole shitload of back-up on its way . . .'

'Yes, yes, I understand. You going to give us some air support?'

Mongrel glanced back at the Comanche, which he had nearly crashed three times on his journey to this rendezvous. He shuddered. 'I do my best. I hope they not got helicopters . . .'

Simmo pointed to where a swarm of ten machines had taken to the air from further down the valley. Mongrel cursed again, and Simmo laughed, slapping him on the back. The Sergeant's eyes were wild, and the stump of a cigar squatted between his teeth.

'You not worry, Mongrel, you give us support from air, and *we* give you support from ground.'

'*Cheers,*' snapped Mongrel as the heavy steel hatch of Simmo's HTank slammed shut and Mongrel ran back towards the Comanche. He could hear the roar of tank engines now, and the thumping of distant rotors slamming down the valley.

Above, heavy clouds rolled, and darkness and gloom tumbled across the land.

It's going to snow, he thought as he climbed into the Comanche and stared in horror at the controls. Tentatively, Mongrel squeezed the HIDSS back onto his head.

- Battle data initiated, came a soft smooth female voice in his skull.

- All weapon systems primed.

- Targeting sequences aligned.

- Your Comanche is ready for battle. Please insert the correct Battle Disk labelled BattleDisk 2.

Disk? What fucking disk?

Mongrel cast about frantically as a tiny drawer in the console slid out, awaiting its battle data.

'You got be fucking kidding!' he howled.

And then he spotted the rack, located the disk and slammed it into the console.

```
- Thank you.
- Your Comanche Battle 'Copter is now
fully on-line.
```

Mongrel stared up at the rolling clouds. He took a deep breath, watching as Simmo's tanks spread out into formation and two groups turned, disappearing through the trees to either side of the trail with their stealth motors engaged.

'Here we go.'

He eased the Comanche into the air, wobbling slightly, and watched in horror as the rotors cut the top neatly from a pine tree, sending ragged torn branches and a flurry of mashed pine needles mushrooming into the cold wind.

'I wish I never born!' he wailed.

The columns of tanks joined battle in a deafening metal thunder. Shells exploded in close-quarter heavy-tracked combat, and on both sides the rear tanks spat fire into the sky. Turrets whirred, and Simmo's HTank wreaked havoc among the Nex, its camouflage cloak making it an almost invisible target and its superior engines and turning capabilities giving it an all-important edge . . .

Spiral men and women burned in their metal coffins.

Nex screamed, melting in theirs . . .

'No way to die,' thought Simmo grimly, sweat stinging his eyes as his HTank powered up a slope impossible for a normal tank to climb and appeared behind the enemy. His turret whirled and its gun fired. For just a second his HTank was visible, and an enemy TK79 was kicked flaming from the trail and into a small valley beside the road. Flames billowed, the hatch opened and two Nex clambered out, their clothing burning, their mouths eerily silent . . . Rogowski used the HTank's 28mm machine gun to cut them mercilessly in half.

'We're winning,' said Rogowski, a humourless grin twisting his lips.

Something glinted on the scanner, then was gone.

Simmo threw open the HTank's hatch. Snow was falling, and the HTank's armour was slick beneath him as it became totally visible when the CamCloak powered down. He watched the remaining tanks fight it out on the trail and in the woods, where his TankSquad had come from three sides, crushing the advancing Nex column in a surprise encirclement.

Something caught his eye again, through the ever-thickening fall of snow.

Simmo whirled.

'What fuck is that?'

And then they materialised. They were HTanks, but not like any HTank Simmo had ever seen. They were a dull grey, and quite obviously belonged to the enemy. They squatted side by side on the trail, engines idling, matrix fission hissing cold chemical fumes. Simmo's eyes went wide in disbelief.

'You see them, Sarge?'

'Is fucking *impossible*! Spiral hold blueprints!'

'Sarge? I think we'd better fucking move . . .'

The five HTanks were huddled in a close formation on the trail – as if taunting Simmo with their very existence. Simmo's face darkened, blacker than the broiling clouds cloaking the summits of mountains above him. His fists clenched as a hatch opened in the hull of one of the enemy HTanks. A man climbed up, eyes blood-red and scarred, hiding their copper Nex origins. His head was heavily scarred from his run-in with drug purifiers many years earlier, and he smiled savagely at Sergeant Simmo as their gazes met.

'You!' exclaimed Simmo, pointing.

Kattenheim nodded, then without a word dropped into the tank's interior. The grey Nex HTanks instantly cloaked and all five dropped off the edges of the trail to disappear in the sloped ditches bordering the road . . .

Simmo dropped inside his own tank as Rogowski screwed the engines and the beast, now invisible, powered down the steep pine-strewn trail after the Nex tanks. Behind them, the rest of the Spiral SP57s gathered into a tight unit and started to advance—

'That *fucker*,' growled Simmo, scowling.

Behind him, behind his HTank, one of the SP57s was suddenly kicked into the air by a shell arrowing through the falling snow. Fire erupted and the metal carcass was catapulted into the air, trailing black smoke. The tank sailed in an arc to vanish flaming into a copse of pine trees, setting them on fire with its hellish descent.

'We have to do something *fast* . . .' snapped Rogowski.

Simmo nodded, his mind whirling.

Five HTanks!

Five fucking HTanks!

Five fucking HTanks *just like his*!

'Those bastards!'

Growling, Simmo spread his hands over the panel controls and his shaggy eyebrows met in a furrow of concentration as tracks pounded the ground. The HTank whirled around.

'Fuck you, Kattenheim,' he muttered. 'Why you not die?'

Carter watched the sparkling snowflakes, cascading and dancing around him on their wind-blown descent. Jam leapt towards him but Carter moved easily to one side and slammed the heel of his hand against Jam's neck. As Jam doubled over, Carter brought his left knee up hard into Jam's face and then grasped the ScorpNex's head between both hands. He rammed Jam's face down against his knee once, twice, three times . . . and then again, and again and again. Something snapped and blood poured down over Carter's legs as he kicked Jam away. He crunched back through the snow and watched snarling as Jam stumbled to his armoured knees with blood pooling into his clawed hands—

Reality slammed into focus.

Carter blinked, cold breath smoking, snowflakes settling against his face and hair and shoulders. Jam raised his head up, eyes narrowing, and then he was back up. He attacked in a blur through the snow.

They exchanged blows, backed away, circled.

Engaging again, Jam struck time after time and Carter blocked each punch with his pain-ravaged forearms, returning blows that Jam blocked in his turn. Carter delivered a combination of punches and kicks, but Jam backed away, still blocking, and then, snarling, heaved himself onto Carter, smashing the smaller man to the ground. Jam's claws lashed down, pounding Carter's head. He was left stunned and bleeding heavily onto the snow.

Carter's world spun.

'*Let me*,' came Kade's confident soothing whisper again. '*I can take this fucker – you know I can.*'

Jam hoisted Carter up by the throat, dangling him in powerful muscled arms. Carter's knee slammed up again, but Jam blocked. Their stares met and understanding passed between them. Jam's claw smashed at Carter's head, releasing the man – and Carter reeled in screeching white-hot agony, slipping suddenly on the snow and sliding blindly back to flip neatly over the battlements . . .

For a horrible moment Carter hung suspended. He spun, his hands grasping nothing but air. He fell, twisting, fingers lashing out . . . his left hand grasped the icy lip of the battlements and he whirled round to slam against the stone wall. Below, a hundred Nex looked up with their copper eyes – and lifted their JK49s.

'Fuck.'

Carter scrabbled against the stone.

Time seemed to slow and the cold wind nipped his face. Kade's voice whispered messages in his head and Carter saw a bullet fly towards him, glancing from the stonework by his face. He swung around, boots scrabbling against the icy stone and his free hand reaching up to find a hold. Jam reared above him, leaping up to the crenellation and standing broad and tall and bleeding, staring down with triumph lurking deep within those seemingly emotionless copper slits.

In the valley, tanks blasted one another.

Carter saw a distant tank hull, within a globe of roaring flames, spat up above the tree line to trail dark black smoke into a trench further down the valley.

Carter glanced down, at where the waiting Nex were pointing their guns.

And up at Jam, who had lifted his glistening claws wide as if accepting acclaim from the audience of upturned Nex faces below him. He smiled down at Carter, blood dripping from his fangs onto Carter's face.

'Until the next time, my brother,' Jam breathed and lifted his heavy armoured foot into the air above Carter's face – above Carter's grimace of hatred and anger. And sudden understanding—

Around them, the snow continued to fall gently.

CHAPTER 19

ENDGAME

The cold wind bit into Carter. He watched Jam's armoured foot and knew that there was no mercy there, no forgiveness. They had done Belfast together. Crossed the desert after the Battle of Cairo 7. Suffered the horrors of the TankerRuns after the designer plague GreyDeath had slaughtered fifty-eight million people. And, ultimately, none of it mattered because Jam was a different person . . . Jam was a different *creature* . . . Jam was Nex, no longer human: and for Carter that meant death.

Carter could see Jam's eyes.

Copper slits.

'Wait.'

The words were a low melancholic growl, echoing through the snow. Jam obeyed instantly. He glanced down into Carter's eyes with a look he failed to read, then disappeared from view. Carter flexed his fingers, trying to get a better hold. One hand slipped, and for precious moments he was dangling . . . but he regained his grip and through all his waves of pain and pounding agony he focused his mind: to hold, not to fall; to live, not to die . . .

because to live meant that Natasha still had a chance at life, to live meant that Durell could still be stopped.

Carter glanced down, nervously, at the gathered Nex.

Distantly, more shells were exploding. And then there came silence. The Nex in the courtyard received a sharp barked order, and they filed from the gates in small groups, JK49s held in black-gloved hands, their balaclavas sprinkled with snowflakes. Carter looked back up—

Into the dark slitted gaze of Durell.

His hood was thrown back, his horribly deformed features exposed to the snow and the cold biting wind. He smiled – if his expression *was* a smile – down at Carter.

'Funny how these things turn out,' he said softly. Durell edged closer, boots now so close to Carter's fingers that he could have reached and touched him . . . if he had been able. If he had possessed the strength.

Carter said nothing.

'I hated you, Carter, for a long time I hated you. Yes, I admit I would ultimately like you to join our cause . . . I think you would make the most powerful ScorpNex ever. I think you would be a truly awesome killing machine. After all, look how well you kill with your, shall we say, *pure* blood.' Durell laughed softly, eyes twinkling with some inner humour, some inner irony, as the snow fell thicker now and Carter listened out for more gunfire.

Was Spiral nearly there? At the gates?

Or did they have their own fucking problems?

Kade? He thought. Kade? Where the fuck are you?

But Kade had gone . . .

Carter breathed deeply, fingers cramping. He glanced down. It was a damned long way to fall – and, unlike a Hollywood action film, there was no convenient tent, hay cart or series of balcony awnings to provide a soft landing for the hero. If indeed he *was* the hero. He smiled grimly at that. Have I ever behaved like a hero? he mused idly.

'If you were ScorpNex then I could study you. Examine how and why the military processor, the QIV, the QuakeHub – why it cannot see you and predict your actions. Your future.'

Something went cold and hard in Carter's soul.

'I destroyed the QIII processor,' said Carter softly, staring up.

Durell nodded. 'Yes, you did. But as in most cases of hardware development, as one project is finishing so the next project begins. The QIV was started two years before the completion of the QIII – we had already mapped out the QIII's successor, its superior, the next model. The next generation. And all it took was a further year of development. It was the QIV that decoded the ancient scripts, located the LVA fuel, told us where to mine . . . it was the QIV processor that designed and created the Foundation Stones that we use to control the quakes. But like the chip you destroyed, it is blind to you, Carter. It is as if you do not exist. As if your timeline, your world runs parallel with that of every other living creature on this planet – but they never intertwine.'

Durell was silent then.

Carter squirmed uncomfortably.

Again, his hand slipped. His fingers were too numb to hold on.

'I hope you enjoy your fucking kingship, arsehole,' snapped Carter. 'I hope it burns you into an early grave. Running the world can be so fucking *tiresome* these days, I believe.'

'Kingship? Ruling the world?' Durell laughed with genuine humour. His stare locked to Carter. 'Your schemes are so petty, so small,' he mocked. 'Your vision is so tame – it lacks, shall we say, true imagination, true

536

ambition. Why would I want to rule the fucking world? To rule the world in itself is no great aim, no, no, vision goes much, much further than that – as far as the sun and the stars!' He laughed again, but this time it was a cold laugh. The humour of the dead.

'What do you *want?*' asked Carter, his breath pluming like dragon smoke.

'It is simple. I want everybody to be Nex. We are the Pure, Carter. And if people will not become Nex and experience the purity, the power, the *immortality* that we can offer . . . then those people will die. To be a Nex – you misunderstand the feelings and sensations involved. It is evolution, my friend. The way we are supposed to be. The way we *will* all be. A *controlled* evolution. An *obedient* evolution. A Blending that removes greed, and lust, and hatred . . . it will remove war, and famine, and terrorism.' He laughed. 'If everybody was Nex – evolved to the next stage of humanity . . . then the world would be a much better place. A new Eden.'

Durell sighed.

He glanced back at Jam.

'Now, Jam. Kill him.'

Durell disappeared from view.

'Kade? Where the fuck are you, Kade?' Carter tiptoed along the tightrope of panic.

'*You called, sir?*'

Jam reared into view, slitted copper eyes gazing down at Carter. Beyond the castle more explosions echoed. Carter could feel his grip slipping. Within seconds he wouldn't need Jam's help to find his way to the next life.

Jam lifted Carter's Browning.

You fucker, thought Carter. You'd shoot me with my own fucking gun?

'*Do you require a little assistance, Mr Carter?*'

'You think you're so fucking good, Kade . . . well, *you* fucking kill him!'

Carter felt Kade smile within him.

Felt Kade's *pride* burn him.

Jam's copper eyes narrowed. He aimed the Browning at Carter's face.

'*O sir, your wish is my command,*' said Kade. The world spun around and around and *down* into a flashing glittering knife-edge of razor-sharp shots: all filmed in a glossy and static sequential black and white.

The grey Nex HTank crawled along the gulley and stopped. Its turret rotated slowly, still cloaked and practically invisible to any but the specifically trained and practised eye. Tracks rocked against gravel and above, on the lip of the gulley, a cluster of Spiral SP57 tanks gathered, their engines roaring, their large guns constantly tracking on their hydraulics.

The Nex HTank's gun lifted. The air around it shimmered as it moved.

Time seemed to shift, to displace.

And Simmo's tank appeared with a whine of CamCloak – directly behind the Nex HTank and with its gun pointing straight at the weakest part of the enemy vehicle's structure – the base plate behind the rear tracks. Simmo growled and fired the gun.

There was a concussive *boom* and the gun recoiled. The enemy HTank in front of him was kicked high into the air, one track ripped free with a grinding shriek of steel; purple fire billowed and the tank, trailing smoke and fire, disappeared over the SP57s and the ridge beyond. There came a distant echoing impact.

'Fucked severely up ass,' grinned Simmo, cloaking his tank once more.

'Well done, Sarge,' came the voice of Mo over the comm. 'There's another in the woods to our right – spec co-ords 52.33.53. I got the eyes of an eagle . . .'

'If only you had good looks! I hear you . . . I'm on it,' growled Simmo, lighting another cigar.

The Spiral HTank crawled across the forest floor, tracks grinding through pine needles and patches of snow. Matrix hissed, cold and bright, and the HTank halted in the shadows and uncloaked. Simmo lifted the hatch and poked out his head, breathing deeply the dense damp vegetative stench of the forest and revelling in the rich fragrance.

'They're here,' came Rogowski's growl.

Simmo nodded, and smoked his cigar, eyes scanning the forest. Smoke trailed down past his throat tattoos and up past his shaved head. It curled through the branches above him.

In the distance, another SP57 blew up. Another two Spiral operatives died . . .

Simmo ground his teeth in frustration.

The fuckers were picking off his men . . .

One by painful one . . .

The first of two Nex HTanks came creeping through the forest. Simmo caught the disturbance of branches, the gentle displacement of pine needles and – trained to read the signs of the CamCloak – he smiled to himself and pretended to look in the opposite direction.

'You picked your spot well. The other tank is coming from the other side, directly opposite.'

'The Sarge know good gig when he see one. He know how to play fucking game.'

The two enemy HTanks halted. Now they were totally invisible. Simmo tilted his head and fancied that he could hear the whine of their CamCloaks. Below, Rogowski readied the engines and flicked free the stealth switch. Like all stealth systems, a stealth mode was always a compromise between noise and power. Without the stealth mode activated the awesome matrix engine came truly into its own.

'Here we go . . .' Simmo felt himself tense; he forced himself to take a huge drag on the cigar, pretending to scan the undergrowth away from the enemy HTanks.

The enemy tanks both fired—

But with a burst of exhaust fumes, Simmo's HTank was no longer there. Engines roared, followed by the twin detonations of the enemy tanks. Trees were splattered with hot liquid metal and twin craters, glowing with fire, appeared in the soft forest floor. Simmo's tank skidded around and demolished three trees, its weight snapping thick trunks with ease. Simmo, who had almost been thrown from his perch halfway through the hatch by the sudden insane acceleration, glared down into the darkness at Rogowski.

'Fucking lunatic!'

'That went smoothly, I think,' said Rogowski.

'Yeah, except for mad-arse driving! You need take test again, lad! You need learn three-point turn and how to parallel park fucking big tank!'

'Sorry, Sarge! But we got 'em!'

Simmo suddenly grinned. 'Aye. We got 'em, lad.'

Simmo hammered the cloaked HTank up the trail, tracks crushing rocks as they went. Below, the remaining SP57s were moving up through the woods towards the castle. Groups of Nex soldiers had emerged with machine guns. Gunfire rattled and shells started to explode . . .

Suddenly, the HTank uncloaked—

540

And picked up a lot of speed.

'Nearly there,' grunted Rogowski.

Simmo watched his scanners, eyes fierce, cigar clamped between his teeth. Then, as the HTank roared along the rising trail, it suddenly grated against stone and veered right – ploughing through trees with crunches of tearing wood as it sailed inelegantly through the air and heavily falling snow . . .

Simmo held his breath.

They landed with a mighty jolt and a terrible crunch of battered steel. Simmo's HTank seemed to perch on nothingness, and then slowly it crunched its way down the invisible enemy HTank's hull and onto the trail. Tracks squealed and the HTank whirled. The enemy's CamCloak flickered, stuttering like a faulty strip light, and its engine revved but the tank could not move. Its turret groaned as Simmo slowly lined up the crushed enemy tank in his sights and paused, finger over the trigger panel.

'Poor fuckers,' mouthed Rogowski. Simmo glanced at him. 'Trapped in there, just waiting to die. It is every TankSquad's worst nightmare. Bad bad dreams, Sarge.'

Simmo caressed the trigger.

And, grunting, he fired.

The shell shot from one of the HTank's guns and impacted with a terrifying scream against the wounded enemy HTank. Fire flickered out to engulf and swallow it – and then, as if on the end of a piece of elastic, the tank was jerked from the trail and flung into the sky. It spun slowly, awesomely bright flames melting its hull and leaving a stream of molten metal. The HTank struck the stone wall of the rising trail from which Simmo's tank had just jumped, and left a metal smear like dark silver blood against the rock. Then it veered off onto the slope below, bouncing against several large boulders. It came to a final rest as a smoking wreck. Simmo stared, but the hatch did not open. Flames continued to burn and he could make out the almost perfectly drilled hole where the shell had entered the enemy tank and fucked it severely from within.

Simmo stared down at Rogowski.

'Fuck them,' he said slowly, and placed his cigar back between his teeth.

'Sarge?'

'Hm?'

'Look!'

Simmo turned. In the distance, facing them and with CamCloak deactivated, squatted the last Nex HTank. It looked subtly different to his own machine and Simmo bared his teeth in the parody of a grin.

'Kattenheim,' he said.

The enemy HTank revved its engine and cold fumes coughed from its exhausts. Simmo dropped to his seat and settled himself. He pulled tight his harness, buckling himself in, and stared into Rogowski's eyes.

'No,' said Rogowski.

'Yes,' said Simmo, and nodded, his eyes shining.

'No! You can't be fucking serious!'

'The Sarge always fucking serious.'

He throttled up the engines of the HTank to the max and the two machines lurched towards one another across the stone trail, pulping gravel into dust. Above, Mongrel's Comanche spun gleaming through the snow, its guns eating through three black Nex helicopters which plunged into the forest, setting a stand of trees on fire . . . But all this was as nothing to Simmo as he focused on the HTank roaring towards him from directly ahead—

The distance closed rapidly.

Tracks thundered and smashed at the stone trail.

Engines roared, billowing cold exhaust.

And Simmo's head dropped against his bull neck, shoulders widening out as his teeth gripped his cigar so hard that he bit it in half, and the glowing tip disappeared unnoticed . . .

'Come on, you piece of Nex shit.'

The tanks powered towards one another, pulping the snow.

The battle seemed to have paused to witness this insane predestined collision: two juggernauts heading towards each other for a final apocalyptic impact – a head-on crash between two of the most ferocious machines of war ever created.

Rogowski, covering his head with his arms, screamed like a baby.

But Sergeant Simmo did not falter, did not take his intense fixed stare from the scanners and the suddenly expanding hull of the enemy HTank . . . At the last moment Kattenheim's tank veered suddenly to the right in a last-ditch attempt to avoid collision.

With a growl, Simmo veered his own tank to the left, grinding tracks skidding over loose stones, to make sure that the impact took place.

The noise was indescribable.

The tanks collided, seemed to fold in on themselves and then rose up, whirling tracks crunching against one another and eating through steel. With engines howling and smoke pluming, sparks and shards of metal fired off in all directions like shrapnel as the two HTanks joined like nightmarish glittering steel lovers, *melded* in a dark ironic complimentary parody of the joining of the Nex with insect . . .

Metal-bred thunder rolled out.

And together the two HTanks flipped and rolled off the trail, fire and sparks glowing around their chassis and tracks and bent distorted guns. The conjoined beast rolled and smashed down a steep slope of trees and boulders, demolishing trunks, crushing rocks, and came finally to rest on its merged single side, rocking slowly.

Snow fell, melting against the hot flanks.

Flames flickered along one hull on a stream of arcing matrix fuel.

Silence reigned for perhaps a minute.

Then came a distant hammering. There was a heavy clang as Simmo's boots smashed open the hatch, and a deformed hunk of elliptical metal toppled into the snow. He squeezed his frame out – battered, bruised and bleeding from his reopened head wound and several slashes to his face, but with eyes still intent and focused. His groin smoked softly from the fallen cigar-tip, and he carried something in one fist – a package wrapped tight in blue plastic. Reaching back, he dragged a moaning and grumbling Rogowski from the remains of the Spiral HTank and dumped him unceremoniously in the snow where he nursed a broken shoulder; then calmly patted out his burning genitalia.

Simmo stretched his back and glanced up the slope where the SP57s were battling Nex soldiers on foot. Mongrel's Comanche flashed overhead, MiniGun roaring. Another black Nex helicopter trailing fire disappeared over the mountains and exploded. Simmo nodded in appreciation, then turned his attention to the fused steel mess in front of him.

Rogowski had crawled to his knees and vomited before glancing up. Simmo moved around the twisted steel carcass and started tugging at the Nex HTank's hatchway.

'What are you doing?' Rogowski shrieked.

Simmo ignored him. There was a crunch and something moved.

'It's fucking on *fire*! It's going to fucking *explode*!'

Simmo whirled. 'You fuck off up trail away from blast zone, there's a good lad,' he snarled, his mouth full of spittle mixed with blood. Rogowski paled, and started to drag himself away from the battered tanks.

More shells exploded in the distance.

The fight seemed to be going well.

Simmo yanked on the hatch, which finally came free in his battered bleeding hand. He staggered back, caught off balance for a moment, then dropped it in the snow.

Simmo squinted into the HTank's interior gloom—

Snarling, Kattenheim launched himself from the innards of the HTank and Simmo stumbled back, shocked. But Kattenheim was wedged in the opening, cursing and spitting, fighting to drag his body free—

The opening had been crushed.

It was too narrow for the Nex to squeeze through.

Simmo picked up his blue package. Kattenheim was raging insanely, scarred red eyes wide with anger and hatred. He stopped suddenly, his gaze meeting Simmo's.

Simmo smiled.

'You are a lucky, lucky man,' said Kattenheim softly.

Simmo shrugged, initiating the ignition sequence on the package of HighJ explosive. Red digits started to flicker across the tiny digital display.

Kattenheim watched him impassively.

Simmo tossed the HighJ package to the ground beneath Kattenheim's protruding upper body. Kattenheim glanced down, and gave The Sarge a sickly sweet smile.

When his stare met Simmo's his anger vanished, to be replaced by a kind of deep sadness. A melancholy, or nostalgia; a realisation that his time had come.

'I will save you a place in Hell – at my feet,' he said, a blood-slick grimace twisting his lips.

'The Nex don't earn a place in Hell,' snarled Simmo, and turning, started to sprint up the slope, injured body listing to one side, blood pouring over his face and into his eyes, making him almost blind. He dived behind a low wall of rocks—

And heard the click of detonation . . .

Whirling, falling to lie on his back on the slope, Simmo, half screened, watched a column of flame flare skywards. A deep concussive blast rolled out. Superheated air washed over him and he watched droplets of liquid metal start to rain down, setting fire to the trees around the blast zone.

Flames roared—

And then slowly died.

Wearily, Simmo dragged himself back to his feet and continued up the steep slope under the gaze of Rogowski, who was nursing his shoulder.

Reaching the top, Simmo slumped to the ground and stared back down at the purple fires.

'You OK, Sarge?'

'Aye, lad.'

'That fucker had it coming.'

Simmo cocked his head at Rogowski and saw the look of hatred there. 'Yeah, a fucking Nex, eh, lad? I suppose they all have it coming?' he said sardonically.

'*All* the fuckers should burn.'

Simmo sighed, lying back on the hard trail. Tiny stones pressed into his back, into his hands, into his skull, and he could feel the flow of fresh blood running into his eyes.

And a terrible deep sadness filled him, flowed through his body and ate like acid through his soul.

What a fucking world we live in, he thought sombrely. What a world.

Carter's pain fled. Was forced aside. Kade's hand was hanging limp. It dived into Carter's pocket and pulled free the MercG. In the blink of an eye it activated, humming softly, and Kade whipped it above his head where it sliced cleanly through ten inches of ancient parapet, carving a neat arc of stone that dropped silently away towards the distant courtyard below. The high-tech garrotte swung on into Jam's leg, producing a spray of thick dark blood. A shot from the Browning echoed across the courtyard as Jam stumbled back howling and Kade felt something nick his ear. He frowned. 'Untidy,' he whispered.

Scrabbling against the ice, Kade was forced to drop the MercG. He grunted, cursing as it disappeared into the white expanse below. He dragged himself up onto the parapet and glanced over at Jam, who was lying on his back, a huge slice carved from his leg, the wound pumping blood into the snow. Kade leapt down and moved forward as Jam dragged himself to his feet. With a roar, he charged . . .

Kade moved in a blur and they met, fists crashing against heads, Jam's claws striking against Kade's chest. Then they whirled away from each other in sprays of blood.

They circled, leaving vivid trails through the snow.

'That hurt, did it, fucker?' mocked Kade, grinning.

'Shut up.'

'You'll walk like a fucking donkey tomorrow . . . if you walk at all –' Kade launched himself at Jam and again they crashed into one another, claws and fists beating and pounding. Jam slipped on the ice and fell backwards with Kade diving atop him, fists slamming. Jam's knee came up but Kade twisted, head-butting Jam's face twice before rolling free. Jam rolled, lightning-swift, armoured leg lashing out and knocking Kade's feet from under him . . . and for long moments they scrabbled on the snow until Kade's stare fixed on the Browning.

He leapt for the weapon, fingers curling around the familiar solid stock and as it came around in a blur of dark metal Jam bludgeoned down with all the might of both locked claws—

There was a sickening crack . . .

And Kade's arm hung limp as the Browning skittered through the snow.

Kade danced back, twisting to keep the injured and obviously broken arm away from Jam. He glanced down and saw bone protruding from flesh and cloth. He winced, but channelled away the pain for later use.

Jam nodded.

'You cannot win.'

'Ha!' said Kade. 'I'll fuck you from behind and then piss on your mother!'

Jam launched himself at Kade, who stumbled back, blood pumping from his broken arm. Kade slipped on the ice, went down hard, head smashing against the parapet. Stars flashed bright in his mind and Jam placed his heavy armoured foot against Kade's throat – against *Carter*'s throat . . .

They halted briefly, sprinkled with white, like frozen sculptures in ice. Then Jam pressed down, using his heavy weight and his bulk. Kade choked, and with his good arm beat against Jam's injured blood-pumping leg. But Jam did not flinch and did not cry out in pain. He ignored the beating like a man ignores the ineffectual slap of a child.

'Fuck you, fuck you!' screamed Kade, face red with impotent fury.

Calmly, Carter took control from Kade and colour flooded back into his vision. With it came pain, smashing up from the broken arm and the pressure in his throat and he looked up at Jam, at those evil slitted eyes. Tears streamed down his face.

'You cry?' Jam lessened the pressure a little and stooped, staring hard into Carter's face. 'You've changed, Carter. What happened then? It was as if you were a different person.'

'It wasn't me,' choked Carter. 'It was Kade. The fucker always claims he will get the job done, get the killing done . . . but he fucked up this time, didn't he? He has left us both to die . . .'

'Kade?' whispered Jam, copper eyes hooded.

Carter could hear the distant roar of engines – and something else, a distant growling like that of a—

Quake.

'Jam, you and me – we'll both die,' snarled Carter through blood and saliva, his tears hot against his cheeks. 'Durell is betraying you even as he has you do his dirty work. I didn't realise you had stooped so low, Jam, I didn't realise your past and your friendships meant so little.'

Jam's head tilted. He removed the pressure from Carter's throat and moved across the snow, to where the small silver box nestled against the stone flags.

Carter watched him warily.

Beneath him, the castle began to vibrate.

'*The quake's coming,*' hissed Kade. '*Run!*'

'Fuck off, *pussy*. I don't need *your* advice.'

Jam returned and dropped to a stoop beside Carter.

549

He pushed the box out, held clumsily in his dark claws. His eyes were narrowed copper slits and Carter scowled in confusion.

'What are you doing?'

'Take it. Go. Save Natasha.'

'*What?*'

Jam stood, rearing to his full height. And then he *roared*, a terrifying sound that mingled with the cacophony of the approaching earthquake. It echoed around the bleak walls of the castle, filled with anger, hatred and pure frustration . . .

Carter scrambled to his feet, clutching the ornate box. He flicked it open, and within nestled the dark disc – the Avelach. The healing machine that he could use to bring Natasha back from the brink of death . . .

Jam dropped to a crouch, then stood once more. He was breathing deeply, panting, his stare fixed on Carter as he wrestled with inner demons.

'Why, Jam?'

'A present. From an old friend.'

The castle started to groan, and the walls began to sway. Parts of the battlements suddenly fell away, dropping to the distant courtyard where they impacted and exploded, showering the courtyard with stone shrapnel.

'Go, Carter. Go now.'

'I need to know why.'

Jam smiled then, and for just an instant Carter caught a glimpse of his old friend, a glint of the man who had been Jam – imprisoned within the shell of the ScorpNex.

'We all have our internal battles,' said Jam softly. 'Yours is Kade. Mine is – a different kind.'

Carter started to back away, towards the stairwell. The whole castle was shaking now as the quake took it and the mountains in its fist. Distant avalanches rocked the steep sides of the valleys, millions of tonnes of rock and ice and snow tumbling from high reaches and crushing the world beneath—

'You know what Kade is? You *know* him?' said Carter.

'Yes.'

'Tell me!'

But the world was descending into insanity . . .

'Go!' screamed Jam.

Carter turned to run, pain and panic driving him.

'And Carter?'

'Yeah?'

'Tell Nicky I love her.'

Carter nodded, and disappeared into the darkness of the winding stairwell. Through the falling snow Jam stared long and hard at the spot where Carter had been – and then turned towards the tower, the tower containing Durell and the QuakeHub and the core of all Jam's misery, pain, confusion, frustration and loss.

Evolution, he had said.

An evolution of the body – but a regression of the mind.

With a grim look, Jam stalked across the buckling stone flags of the battlements towards the dark confines of the tower and his mentor within.

The quake was rumbling, smashing across the Austrian landscape, shaking the mountains in the fury of its clenched and threatening fists. On the slope leading to the castle stood Simmo, Mongrel, Rogowski, Mo, Haggis, Remic, Fegs, Oz, Kavanagh, Root Beer and Samasuwo. Bob Bob was rubbing at the custard stains on his combats and muttering about detergents; everybody else was staring at the SP57 tanks, their engines roaring as their guns pounded the occasional shell into the shuddering castle.

The whine of abused engines howled through the sky. The gathered men cocked weapons in weary hands and turned to watch the Comanche settle into the snow-slush on the trail, its suspension bobbing.

The Priest stepped out, sandals slopping in the snow and robes whipping madly in the down draught of the war machine's rotors. He was followed by a woman, tall and slim and pale-skinned, with a long fan of brown hair worn loose across her shoulders and with piercing green eyes set in a pretty oval face. She was dressed all in black and carried a sub-machine gun. The Priest carried nothing except his Bible.

'You here for the party?' asked Mongrel, his face grey with exhaustion.

'Bless you, my son. I am here for Carter . . .'

Mongrel stared darkly into The Priest's eyes. And he remembered The Priest's words back on Crete. *'Don't make me come looking for you, Carter. Don't make me hunt you down – it would be a waste of a good man. One of the best we have.'*

With a sudden snarl Mongrel went for his M24 machine carbine, barrel lifting and finger squeezing the trigger. Simmo grabbed the gun, wrenching it skywards as a spray of bullets lifted on trajectories of fire.

'Whoa, lad,' snapped Simmo, easing the weapon away from Mongrel's paws.

Mongrel scowled at The Priest, who held his hands in the air, apart, a soft smile on his lips.

'You misunderstand my intentions,' said The Priest gently. Behind him, Roxi was pointing her Heckler & Koch MP5 at Mongrel. He glared at her, noting the determination and strength in her piercing green eyes.

'You've come to kill Carter,' snarled Mongrel, spraying spittle. 'Yeah, lads, he's come to kill Carter!'

There was a rumbling of defiance and unrest.

The Priest swallowed. He was facing a potential lynch squad. A mutiny. 'No, no, lads, I am here to find out what the hell is going on! The Lord has guided me, and yes, I do need to find Carter. He has disobeyed orders. He has disobeyed *Spiral*.'

'You try and kill Carter, and we fuck you bad,' said Mongrel angrily.

'Where is he?'

'In there.' Mongrel pointed at the shaking castle. Walls were toppling even as they watched. The rest of the TankSquad operatives were shooting any stray Nex who made a run for it from the gates. 'He beyond your wrath now, Priest. He beyond your fiery revenge . . . you fucking bureaucrats, everything in black and white – there no middle ground, no *compromise*. Carter – he in there, he trying to save Natasha, yeah, but he trying to take down Durell, he trying to smash the QuakeHub. He trying to save the world, Priest . . . with or without Spiral's permission; with or without divine fucking intervention. You, Priest – you need God. But Carter is alone, and he ask favour of no man. You understand?'

The Priest scowled. 'I am not here to murder the man,' he rumbled.

Mongrel grinned a shark-grin. 'Not unless he not follow orders, yeah? Carter has own guidance, own morals. He will do what right. If you not see that, then you just as blind as every other fucking bureaucrat in the universe.'

'He is confronting Durell?'

'Yes.'

The Priest took a deep breath. 'Maybe he needs a helping hand, then? We are standing here talking whilst the whole world is crumbling around our ears! We've got to help him . . . to stop Durell . . . to stop the quakes . . .'

'What about your God sending thunderbolts from the heavens to save us?' interjected Remic, his M24 held loosely in battle-scarred fingers. 'You seem to be an expert in that field, Priest. Maybe you could ask for a bit of celestial help?'

'God helps those who help themselves,' said The Priest primly. 'Now . . . gentlemen? Shall we go to Mr Carter's aid? Or wait for him to be served in slices on a cold meat platter?'

Mongrel grabbed his weapon from Simmo's battered hands and stalked towards his Comanche. 'We'll take my chopper,' he said, squinting at The Priest. 'And you can leave your fucking girlfriend behind.'

'As you wish,' said The Priest, fingering his rosary beads.

'Simmo?'

'Aye, lad?'

'Fancy giving me a bit of a hand?'

Simmo prodded the Sig P7 9mm into the small of The Priest's back. 'Don't mind if I do,' he snarled through a demonic mask of drying blood.

'That will be unnecessary,' soothed The Priest, his dark eyes hard, mouth a grim line. 'My mission is not to kill Carter; my mission is to stop the destruction of the Earth.'

'We'll be the judge of that,' said Simmo sombrely.

The castle was crumbling.

Jam squeezed his bulk through the corridors, up the steep steps and into the tower room where Durell stood, facing the rippling liquid screen. Images flickered through it like gun-bursts, flashes of destruction from across the globe; scenes of his Nex armies warring with soldiers of every nation . . .

'I don't understand,' screamed Durell suddenly, without turning. 'Why has the quake come here? What the fuck did I do wrong? What the fuck is the QIV *thinking* of?'

He reached down, grasped the black cube and yanked it free of its housing. But nothing changed – the castle still rocked, pitching violently . . . and now there came the whistle and crump of shells from Spiral's few remaining tanks. They exploded in the courtyard down below, adding to the cacophony of insane noise and the rocking, heaving insanity that had become the world.

'Maybe the processor is betraying you,' said Jam softly.

Durell whirled. 'Come on, we'll take the helicopter on the roof. It does not matter – the quakes are in progress, the world's armies are weakened, the Nex are strong! We cannot fail now, we must return to Egypt, from there we can—'

'Maybe it is the LVA, returning to haunt you.'

Durell stopped then and fixed his stare on the towering figure of Jam. He licked his lips with a small dark tongue. His eyes narrowed. 'What is wrong with you?'

'By making me Nex you promised me Heaven.'

Durell nodded, smiling, moving as if to push past Jam—

'But you delivered me into a waking Hell.'

Jam's claw lashed out, hammering against Durell and throwing him back across the narrow tower room. He struck the bench on which the dark screen rested and it toppled to the ground, smashing with a flare of obsidian fire. Black fluid poured over the stonework, eating into it like acid and burning with dark flames.

'What the fuck are you doing?' said Durell calmly.

'Give me the processor.'

'Come and take it.' Durell shrugged himself free of his

555

robes and beneath them huge coils of distorted muscle tensed. Between the two men – the two Nex – the dark fire from the smashed screen flared up and danced violently, silently, a barrier forcing them apart, a wall through which neither could pass . . .

They waited patiently, slitted copper eyes staring at one another.

'If we do not leave here, the quake will tear down this castle,' said Durell as the flames started to die down. Holes appeared in the stone flags from the powerful black screen acid, expanding circular portals showing a distant drop to the hall below. 'We will both die.'

'Then we both die. Give me the processor.'

Durell said nothing.

The quake was ripping through the Austrian mountainside. Both Nex stumbled as the tower swayed, and more shells could be heard raining down. Outside the tower they heard the whine of helicopter rotors.

Durell leapt suddenly at Jam and they smashed into one another—

As the quake tore the castle apart.

The tower collapsed and millions of tonnes of ancient stone fell. The castle buckled and heaved, was taken in the mouth of the quake and pulverised by mammoth jaws of rock and iron.

Stone sprayed out from the huge crater into which the castle sank and was swallowed, was consumed – as if in some ritual slaughter, some titanic revenge.

The mountains reclaiming their own.

The Alps taking back what was rightfully theirs: quarried and stripped and hewn and now absorbed – once again – into nature.

The roaring of the quake's gradual settling lasted for hours, slowly rumbling to a halt and returning peace and tranquillity to this quiet corner of Austria. It left behind a heavy cloud of stone dust, as well as torn earth, swallowed rock and a crater of war in the landscape. Gradually, the stone dust settled.

The castle had gone.

Nothing moved in the stillness.

The snow continued to fall . . . and soon covered everything in a blanket of virgin white.

Carter stood next to Mongrel on the mountainside. Below, in the valley, the tanks were retreating.

'They died together,' said Mongrel softly. 'We saw them both go down.'

Carter nodded. 'Swallowed by the quake that they created.'

'Spiral will send PopBots to scan for traces . . . when things finally return to normal.'

'What's happening with the Nex?'

'There's been wholesale slaughter worldwide. Human casualties numbering many hundreds of thousands, maybe even millions, I imagine – both civilian and military. Who can foresee the damage of the quake? Not me! But the soldiers of the world are beating the Nex back . . . and without the QIV's influence world military systems are slowly coming back on-line. According to ECube reports coming in every few seconds from different sources – tanks and fighters, satellite comms and weapons systems – the whole fucking WarGrid is self-repairing. Once everything's up and running we'll wipe those fucking Nex out once and for all.'

Carter nodded, his face grey with exhaustion and pain; haunted.

'I've learned one thing from all this,' Mongrel went on.

'What's that?'

'You do not fuck with Nature.' Mongrel reached over, placed his hand on Carter's shoulder. 'You OK, mate?'

Carter stared at Mongrel with war-torn eyes, filled with the horror of a thousand battles he never wished to relive. He took a deep breath of crisp cold mountain air, and with shaking blood-crusted fingers lit a cigarette thoughtfully provided by Mongrel. His broken arm was in a tight sling, and he clasped the silver box containing the Avelach to his chest as if it might bring *him* strength.

'Yeah, I'll fucking live. But we need to move, and we need to move *now*. Are you on for sharing a flight back to London? To Natasha and Nicky?'

'Be my fucking pleasure, mate,' said Mongrel, nodding.

They climbed into the Comanche and, as the sun was setting behind the mountains and withdrawing its light from a snowy landscape of incredible white clean beauty, the machine leapt into the air. With engines thrumming, it slewed sideways through the valley and was joined by a second Comanche piloted by Heneghan and containing The Priest, Roxi and Simmo. The two machines turned smoothly and suddenly accelerated, rotors thumping over the Austrian snow.

CHAPTER 20

NATASHA

The two Comanche war machines powered across Europe. Carter squatted in the back of one helicopter, face drawn, pain enfolding his awareness as he clutched the silver box to his chest and gazed out over the sprawling chaos below.

Occasionally the world would shake, accompanied by sounds of thunder. Carter stared out with bleak eyes, his soul calm for the moment and at least thankful that Durell had been halted in his quest for control . . . but in the same heartbeat he felt terrified at the state in which he might find Natasha when he finally arrived back in London.

It had been a long, hard flight.

And it was far from over.

As they flew, Mongrel ensconced in the HIDSS helmet and the bullet-riddled Comanche juddering around them, rapid-fire messages and comms flashed through on the ECubes – rattling with intel from the Spiral mainframes at a colossal rate.

According to the messages received, the earthquakes were gradually subsiding. Spiral HQs were collating data from agencies, Spiral operatives and governments on a global scale – sorting information and sending it out to their teams. Somehow, the QIV had infiltrated many of Spiral's comms networks, including many of the ECube's functions – distorting information and corrupting the Spiral databases. Spiral were relaying messages through the temporary AnComm Posts, analogue transmitters and receivers that acted as ECube data bridges and had at least managed to slow the QIV's digital assault.

Carter toyed with his ECube, idly watching flashes of information. The world was in the process of getting its shit together after this act of global terrorism under the stomping boots of the earthquakes – finally. Whole armies were on the move, fighter jets were securing and patrolling airspace, navies were steaming ahead, submarines patrolling cold deep waters.

Carter shook his head in disbelief.

He remembered casting the schematics for the QIII military processor into the dark sea, and being thankful that the processor was better off dead. Instead, unbeknown to him, the QIII's successor had been almost complete, almost operational and destroying the QIII had been merely a stalling tactic on his part.

Carter gazed down at the silver box against his chest, running his battered fingers over the finely carved dull silver surface. His fingers fumbled for a moment, and with a tiny click the box opened. He stared down at the simple black disc. His finger moved forward to touch it . . . and he paused.

Something seemed to whine within him, as if some sixth sense was warning him of the dangers of playing with this awesome and terribly powerful machine. The Avelach. Carter frowned, and placed his finger against the surface—

White light pierced his mind, a fan of sparkling laser fingers that circled, and then disappeared to a needle point. The metal was cold and preternaturally smooth under his touch.

And then—

His pain soothed away. He felt the white light spread through his mind and with a shiver he felt it *examining* him. A tiny itching of flesh came from his bullet wound, and then he felt something moving through him, something hard and metallic gliding between his ribs. He wriggled in discomfort – the metal object moved under and *through* his flesh, and then dropped out onto the fabric of the Comanche's seat. He felt his arm straighten, forcing its way through the bindings that held it strapped tightly in place – there came the tiniest of clicks and he *felt* the bone knit together, the swelling around the damaged bone and flesh reducing in swelling.

Carter shivered again – and realised that his eyes were closed against the white light. He opened them, breathed deeply, and his weariness had gone. Not with any great jolt – but gently, as if drugs had just soothed away his troubles as he reclined in a hot bath.

Carter withdrew his finger from the Avelach and, reaching behind him, lifted the flattened stub of metal that had been resting inside him. He stared at it – the flattened sliver of bullet – in wonder at first, and then with a sudden, growing *hope*.

He flexed his arm, and noticed that the loss of skin from the motorbike crash had gone – to be replaced by a perfect sheen of pale newborn skin. His breathing came in shallow, panting gasps.

'Can this thing go any faster?'

'It's going as fast as it can, Carter.'

'Well, push it *harder*.'

'I *am* fucking pushing, Carter.'

Carter slumped back and slowly, with care and respect, closed the silver box. He stared at the finely carved inscriptions. The whorls were infinitely delicate, and peering close he could see that the work was truly magnificent even to his untrained eye.

Carter licked his lips.

Fear suddenly leapt into his mind . . .

'What if I am too late?' he muttered.

'Eh?'

'Nothing, Mongrel. Just fly.'

'Weather's getting bad.'

'Is The Priest still with us?'

'*Da*, Carter, he is. We keep close eye on him, good buddy, not you worry. Simmo keep Sig in The Priest's back, make sure he not on special mission from Spiral.'

Carter shrugged, grinning sourly, and gazed down over the insanity of a crumbled, *crushed* world.

Night had fallen. And with it had come the rain.

The Comanche helicopters flew in over the English Channel, crossing near Dover with the distant streak of white cliffs shimmering through the gloom. Carter watched them flash by in a blur and turned, gazing back over the rain-hammered expanse of sea.

As they approached the hospital in a whine of deceleration, The Priest's voice rattled over the comm. 'There's something going on down there . . .'

Mongrel squinted. 'What?'

'Shit,' hissed Carter, flicking free the safety on his Browning and gazing down with a look of horror. Shapes were sprinting across the wet tarmac, black shells glistening. Several halted, triangular heads turning to examine the helicopter—

562

'MiniGun?' requested Mongrel, grinning wickedly.

'MiniGun,' agreed Carter as the Comanche's engines howled and the machine veered, nose dipping. There came a heavy whirring as the General Electric MiniGun started to spin, hitting five thousand revs as Mongrel's sights locked on to six of the Nex creatures, one standing atop a roof-dented ambulance, illuminated by the flashing blue lights.

Mongrel pulled the trigger.

The gun fired and thousands of heavy-calibre rounds ploughed through the tarmac of the hospital car park and cut the Sleeper Nex into bloody strips. Bullets punched the ambulance with metal fists and the Sleeper on top of the vehicle, staring with slitted copper eyes, was hurled backwards against the brick wall and smashed into smears of gore. The MiniGun whined down and Mongrel landed the Comanche, its suspension groaning. Rain swirled through the blood and pulped sarcocarp of Nex flesh strewn across the tarmac.

Carter stowed the silver box in his pack, grabbed his M24 and leapt from the war chopper. The violent wind from the rotors smashed against him. Mongrel was right there behind him. They were only half aware of the second Comanche touching down . . . and of Simmo and The Priest leaping into the car park with their own weapons. Roxi followed, smoothly, calmly, her watchful gaze fixed on The Priest's back.

There were more of the strange big catlike creatures, and they had retreated into the hospital under the onslaught of the Comanche's MiniGun. They had disappeared far inside, leaving only blood streaks against sterile white tiles to mark their passage.

Carter sprinted forward.

'A panic burst has just come through on the ECube – request for heavy artillery,' called The Priest. Carter whirled, his stare meeting The Priest's gold-flecked gaze.

'From here?'

The Priest nodded.

'Shit.'

Carter sprinted into the Accident & Emergency foyer of the hospital, then into the triage waiting area. Bodies littered the plastic-themed waiting room; some were lying dead, streams of blood leaking from wide wounds in belly and groin, glassy eyes staring impassively at the strip-light squares above. Some had been tossed like toys over the plastic chairs to lie at irregular twisted angles. Some lay scattered in several separate torn pieces.

Carter stepped over a torn-off arm and heard a growl – his Browning jerked up as the Sleeper Nex attacked from the wide white corridor, claws leaving tracks of blood against the smashed tiles . . . it leapt, and the Browning boomed in Carter's fist. Behind him the other Spiral operatives opened fire.

The Sleeper seemed to dance in mid-air, twitching as if controlled by wires like some demonic marionette. It slammed to the floor and its head lifted, copper eyes staring at Carter. A growl rattled from its punctured lungs . . . then it slumped down, blood flowing in a wide pool. Without a further sound it died.

Carter swallowed hard, replacing the mag in his Browning. He had used all thirteen bullets.

Glancing behind him he saw the others nodding at him to take the lead. Carter sprinted forward through the hospital corridors. Twice more they came across Sleeper Nex – and twice more a hail of bullets felled them as they leapt, punching them to the floor and drilling them into a state of mangled death.

'Where the fuck did these come from?' growled Mongrel, wiping alien blood from his face.

'And more importantly, what *are* they?' said Carter.

'One of Durell's best-kept secrets,' said The Priest softly. The others turned to look at him and he shrugged. 'The Sleepers are part-breeds, not Nex but the original template for the Nex: a genetic master from which the Nex evolved. They are older than any of us can imagine, and far too savage and unpredictable to use as an army – hence Durell developing the Nex who are more, shall we say, *obedient*. Durell has been working on the Nex Project for longer than Spiral even *dares* to dream. The Nex you normally see – they are refined, a distillation of the pure hard-core terror, the pure bestial nature of the Sleepers. The Sleepers are *old*. And the Sleepers are pure evil. One avenue of Spiral scientific exploration even considers the possibility that Durell didn't actually create the Nex. Rather, the Nex discovered him. *He* is *their* tool. A reversal of what we believe to be true. Whatever, the fact remains that the Sleepers are Durell's wolves, his hunters, and if they scent you they will never allow you to escape. They will pursue you to the ends of the earth and eat your soul.'

'I think we need a *long* talk when this shit is over,' growled Carter, frowning.

'If it ever is over,' said The Priest calmly, closing his eyes.

Turning, Carter moved forward, down another wide corridor. They came across a few people who were still alive and had barricaded themselves into rooms: doctors and patients, some armed with fire axes and peering through glass with blood-speckled faces. One group of doctors had cornered a Sleeper Nex and between them had hacked it to bits with a collection of axes and kitchen knives. They came across another group of patients, one of whom had a sawn-off shotgun. Again, between them they had managed to severely wound a Sleeper and it lay in a pool of glistening slick blood while they tried to kick it to death.

Carter moved on, his face grim.

The small Spiral group emerged into a corridor and a Sleeper stood, peering in through the small glass window of a door halfway down the passageway. Even as the group arrived bullets slammed through the glass and the Sleeper flipped to one side to dodge the assault, then whirled low and with incredible agility reared and slammed against the door, which crashed inwards on long shards of splintered timber.

Carter opened fire, sprinting down the corridor with his Browning bucking in his fist. His boots ate the distance, grim stare locked on the Sleeper's head which swung towards him. It suddenly charged, huge muscles writhing as its claws smashed the tiles beneath them into powder. Carter's gun clicked on an empty magazine and he pulled around his M24, firing a hail of bullets from the hammering weapon – and as he and the creature were about to collide he flipped himself right, sliding along the tiles as the Sleeper tried to suddenly twist. The carbine's bullets ate a long line across its underbelly. The Nex grunted and hit the ground in a gush of blood and Carter was past the creature as Simmo's and Mongrel's bullets tore into its thrashing carcass. Carter spun around into the small hospital room, gaze turning first to Nicky and her shocked face, her gun held in loose hands—

His eyes focused swiftly on Natasha's bedside . . .

And the flat lines on the monitor screens.

Nicky turned, confusion twisting across her face.

Carter dropped his gun and dragged his pack from his back. He fell beside Natasha, his hand smoothing back her hair, gazing down into the serenity of her cold still features. He pulled free the silver box, dropping it with a discordant clash on the tiles. The Avelach was cool to his touch—

'Place it against her breast,' came Nicky's voice. Carter turned, stared into her eyes, then turned back to Natasha and carefully placed the disc against her soft skin.

He stood and pushed himself back from the bed, his brow furrowed in panic.

Nothing seemed to happen . . .

He heard a commotion behind him. More distant gunshots, and the heavy blast of a shotgun followed by the splatter of its impacting shells. He did not move. His stare was fixed on Natasha's face—

The constant and eerily steady *beeee . . . eeeeep* of the monitor finally intruded on his senses.

'It's not working,' he whispered.

Nicky moved forward, checked Natasha's pulse – her *lack* of pulse. Lack of life. Natasha's heart was not beating. Nicky looked up into Carter's eyes, bit her lip, but could not bring herself to say the words – the words that she knew to be true. She whirled on a surprised Mongrel and Simmo and the two battle-stained warriors took a step back.

'Get a fucking *doctor*!' she hissed.

Carter placed his hand against Natasha's brow. Nicky placed her hand on his arm then, and he turned slowly and looked down into her eyes. She took a deep breath.

'What is it?'

'She's dead, Carter.'

'But . . . the machine . . . the *Avelach* . . .'

'It *heals*, Carter. It does not bring back the dead.'

The room whirled, smashed into him, slammed his face against a wall of chaos. It invaded him, ripped into his throat and tore out his insides. Carter fell to his knees, his hands sliding across Natasha's dead body to rest by his sides.

Mongrel and Simmo appeared, dragging two doctors with them. The men looked confused, traumatised by their violent encounter with a Sleeper Nex.

They stared from Carter to Nicky and then back.

Nicky said, 'This is my friend, Natasha. She is carrying a child – I think you need to work fast, gentlemen.' They moved forward and Carter scrambled back, was helped to his feet where he stood, swaying numbly, watching but unable to watch. His gaze was fixed on the shining silver instruments as the doctors applied their skills despite the shock of their own harrowing and horrifying experiences . . .

Blood splashed and dripped from the bed.

Stained the tiles.

Natasha's blood.

Mongrel's hand was there, right on Carter's shoulder.

There came a cry, the ragged squawk of a premature newborn. Nicky wrapped the babe in a blanket as the umbilical cord was tied off and cut and Carter looked hard at the doctors who stood confused, instruments dripping blood, returning his stare.

'Save her!' he cried, straining to get forward. Mongrel held him back and Simmo moved forward to help Mongrel to restrain the distraught Spiral man. 'Fucking *do something*!' screamed Carter.

But the men did not move.

They looked towards Nicky, confused . . .

And the blood-filled world spiralled down into an insanity of darkness . . .

Of *greys* . . .

Of *black and white*.

★

It was late.

Smoke hung heavy in the small room of The Gunmaker's Arms public house. Against the bar leant three men, clothes ragged and torn, smeared with dried blood. The locals in the pub on the outskirts of London avoided them – had been doing so all night as the three steadily drank themselves into oblivion.

Glasses lay scattered, stools overturned; the atmosphere was one of despair and fear.

'They tried to bring her back for an hour,' said The Priest, savouring his pint of Guinness and leaving a frothy moustache against his beard. He shook his head sadly. 'They should have left her . . . God had claimed her soul. They could never have brought it back from the other side.'

'Did you see Carter's eyes?' rumbled Simmo.

Mongrel nodded. 'He could not understand why the machine did not work.'

'Like Nicky said, it is a machine to heal. It was never designed to bring back the dead. It was never designed to work *miracles*. It is no God Machine.' The Priest tasted the words with a sour grimace.

'It worked miracles when it created the fucking *Nex*,' said Mongrel, eyeing the large barrel-chested man and resting his back against the bar. The pub had nearly emptied now – business was quiet, due to the earthquakes – and it was far past closing time. But the landlord did not have the heart, nor the courage, to demand that these three men should leave.

'That was different,' said The Priest softly. 'Natasha was badly wounded. In reality, she should never have lasted as long as she did . . . Carter should be thankful that the child survived – it was extremely premature.'

'Well, I let *you* pass on those sentiments when you see him next,' snapped Mongrel.

'How is he?' rumbled Simmo. 'They pump him with enough drugs to halt a rhino!'

Mongrel shrugged. 'I think they keep him sedated for a few days. He had look of insanity about him when they could not revive Natasha – damn near tried to kill those two doctors and eight JT8s who arrived to sort out the Sleeper Nex. Fuck, I've never seen a man fight like that . . .'

They all nodded.

'What was that he said?' asked Simmo. 'About . . . *Kade*?'

'He was delirious,' said Mongrel, nodding into his Green King beer. 'Fucker had just lost his woman. Man's allowed to get a little fucked up in the head when something like that happens.'

'It is a great shame that we petty mortals lead such weak and fragile lives,' said The Priest softly, his voice filled with great melancholy. 'Like glass, we shatter. Like pottery, we break. *Yea, though I walk through the valley of the shadow of death, I will fear no evil: for thou art with me.*' He paused. The Priest had his Bible on the bar, and it had become stained with beer. '*Surely goodness and mercy shall follow me all the days of my life: and I will dwell in the house of the LORD for ever.*' He glanced around, tears in his great brown eyes. 'Sometimes, my friends, I find death a very hard pill to swallow.'

'Well,' whispered Mongrel sombrely, finishing his beer and pulling on his heavy combat jacket. Live rounds rattled in his pockets. 'It's just the fucking law of the jungle, ain't it?' he said bitterly.

SIU Transcript

CLASSIFIED XX16/87676523/SPECIAL INVESTIGATIONS UNIT
ECube transmission excerpt
Date: October 2XXX

Due to a combination of the reduction of earthquakes and return of global military and electronic control by the QIV processor upon its [*suspected*] destruction, world powers were able to quickly organise and disseminate armies, air forces and naval forces in order to push back the Nex infiltrators and retake control.

Several pitched battles were fought, most notably in China, Siberia, the UK, Thailand, Germany, France, Norway, Nigeria, Peru, Iran and the central United States. It is ironic that Durell spread most heavy forces of Nex numbers around the globe at strategic positions needed to pull off his scheme, leaving his own central (if somewhat mobile) headquarters relatively unprotected. He was relying more on secrecy and speed of execution and it is acknowledged that if subject CARTER had not been involved in Durell's pursuit, it is unlikely his HQ in Austria would have been discovered – and destroyed – so easily (although it is currently unexplained why an earthquake struck at that exact location when Durell was supposedly in control).

Currently, world affairs dictate an AMBER state of emergency. The Nex forces are retreating or have been destroyed. The enemy's situation can best be described as *disintegrating*. The World Investigations Committee (WIC) has been commended and applauded on its excellent handling of the situation. General Hiamito Kassambra, spokesperson for the WIC said, 'Yes, our priority was action and speed of reaction – and without our decisiveness and ability to operate immediately and effectively on a true global scale, this state of world emergency would have been much more serious, and the traitor Durell probably successful in his machinations. We are to be congratulated, I think'.

Little is known of the LVA channels used to direct the earthquakes at the control impulses of the QIV processor. If this can be understood correctly, then the LVA channels are a freak geological occurrence that has a future potential to make the actual world plates unstable. Several research centres are being set up – even now before the war is truly over – to investigate this phenomenon.

Little is known of the QIV processor, other than it is based on existing QIII technology – all known examples of which were destroyed just over a year ago, again in events concerning Durell. The QIV's base architecture was put in place by Count Feuchter [*deceased*] and the lead designers on the QIV were Jessica Rade at Spiral_Q, and Tademo Svdenska and Suzy Pagan at Spiral_R in Tibet. This processor and all relative computing developments are now under investigation by Spiral Tac and the Spiral SIU.

To conclude:

Spiral has once again been integral in halting a plot for world domination. Further investigations are needed to determine exactly what Durell's ultimate goals were, and we still need to work hard to discover what actually happened to him - or his corpse. The file is far from closed. The game is far from over.

Search >>

Keywords: LVA, FEUCHTER, DURELL, NEX, DEMOL, QII, QIII, QIV, Spiral_Q, Spiral_R, LVA, WIC

ADVERTISING FEATURE

The TV sparkled into life with a digital buzz of electro-hum, diamond-sharp images spinning and morphing into the jewelled liquid logo of [newly formed x35 scale] ***Firestarter Fuels!***

Do you despair at fuel companies always trying to rip you off? Do you tear out your hair at dictators trying to ram their overrated products down your throat with the Maximum in Hardcore? Do you WEEP when other fuel companies try and kill you with their earthquakes because their technology is so DEVOLVED that they cannot control their own drilling rigs? YOU can stop this . . . YOU can change the world. YOU can make a whole big difference . . .

Scene pans: from the ravaged cities of London, New York and Paris, bodies pulped and smashed and bleeding under devastation, people screaming, pulling their hair, fighting and looting in the streets . . .

Scene morphs: into a crystalline metropolis, glittering skyscrapers, the world being rebuilt by happy smiling workmen in gleaming yellow hardhats, sharing jokes, slapping one another on the back, a mix of races, creeds, colours. The site is powered by ***Firestarter Fuels*** [LARGE x50scale PRODUCT PLACEMENT HERE]

Firestarter Fuels *proudly present Premium Grade good ol' Petrol, Oil and Natural Gas – just the way you know it and love it, and without the hassle of genetically altered warmongering dictators using their terrible power to take over the Globe. Go on, use* ***Firestarter***, *because you know your children deserve a better future . . .*

SCENE DISSOLVES TO ETERNITY

some photographs of a summer's day
a little boy's lifetime away
is all I've left of everything we've done
like a pale moon in a sunny sky
death gazes down as I pass by
to remind me that I'm but my father's son

i offer up to you
this tribute

Tank Park Salute
Billy Bragg

SPIRAL

Andy Remic

In a future where nuclear warheads can be hidden in a briefcase . . . In a world where designer plagues are held suspended in a teardrop . . . Prepare for chaos.

Where conventional armies are powerless to defend against a single assassin, the secret organisation known as *SPIRAL* exists to fight a shadow war against fanatics and rogue states of every faith and political persuasion.

Remorseless, unstoppable, of every country and of none, *SPIRAL*'s agents conduct their covert operations throughout the world in a never-ending battle for civilization's survival.

But now *SPIRAL* itself is under attack, and if *SPIRAL* falls the world falls apart with it.

SHADOW WARRIOR

Chris Bunch

The complete Joshua Wolfe trilogy
in one explosive volume from
the master of military SF.

The Great War is over. The last pockets of
resistance long eliminated. For many, the alien
Al'ar are now little more than a memory. But
there is one man who cannot forget: Joshua
Wolfe. Friend, prisoner, then betrayer and
executioner of the Al'ar. To humans he is a
hero, a legend. To the aliens he is the Shadow
Warrior, master of the arts of killing. And his
story has only just begun.

NYLON ANGEL

A Parrish Plessis Book

Marianne de Pierres

In a future where the rich live behind the safety of a giant fortress-wall and everyone else can go to hell, Parish Plessis has learnt some useful survival tactics. Like don't cross Jamon Mondo – unless you want to be dead by morning.

But what's girl supposed to do when a very real chance of escaping his sordid clutches presents itself? Even if it means cutting a deal with the amoral gang-lord Io Lang, and sheltering two suspects in the murder of media darling Razz Retribution. Lang is renowned for being from way beyond the border of psychoticsville, and the media always get bloody revenge on anyone foolish enough to mess with their own – it's good for ratings. But Parrish is sick of doing what she's told. She's tooled up, jacked full of stim, and tonight she's going to take her chance.

NYLON ANGEL is the first Parrish Plessis novel. She will be back. When you've met her, you'll understand why.

MARTIAN RACE

Gregory Benford

March, 2015, NASA's first manned voyage to Mars is about to launch.

But disaster strikes. The rocket explodes, killing the entire crew, and the US government abandons the project. What they come up with in its place will change the nature of space exploration for ever.

Businessman John Axelrod and his consortium have every intention of winning the $30 billion Mars Prize for the first successful mission to the red planet. He knows that it will involve far higher risks than the one NASA had planned. But he has no choice. He has to win.

The Martian Race has begun.

DANTE'S EQUATION

Jane Jensen

In a dusty school room on the outskirts of Jerusalem an elderly Rabbi unearths an extraordinary, and inexplicable pattern within the hidden codes of the Torah.

In a tiny laboratory in Seattle, a young physicist begins work on a revolutionary wave-pattern theory that could change the face of science forever.

In a lecture hall in Orlando, intelligence operative Calder Farris uncovers a clue to a potentially devastating threat to national security.

Soon their investigations will uncover a common link and, as their paths converge, the future of all mankind will hang in the balance.